Other titles by Helen Bryan

Martha Washington: First Lady of Liberty

War
BRIDES

Published by AmazonEncore
P.O. Box 400818
Las Vegas, NV 89140

ISBN-13: 9781612183329
ISBN-10: 1612183328

War

BRIDES

HELEN BRYAN

amazon encore

*This book is dedicated, as always,
with love to Roger, Cassell, Michelle, and Niels,
and now to darling Bo and Poppy too*

INTRODUCTION

WAR BRIDES probably began to take shape long before I was aware of it. I was one of the postwar baby-boom generation whose early years were touched, though in my case gently, by the war's long shadow. My husband and I both had fathers who served in the US Army, as did all our uncles except for one in the navy and one who became an air force pilot. But women played an active role too. An aunt by marriage was an army nurse, and my own mother was an officer in WAVES, "Women Accepted for Volunteer Emergency Service." As a child, I was fascinated to learn that my respectable mother, housewife and pillar of her church, had once worn a pistol on her hip—one she had been trained to shoot if necessary—as she escorted telegrams and urgent communications across Norfolk Navy Yard. Because my husband's father was posted to Europe shortly before my husband was born, my mother-in-law gave birth in a military base hospital in Alabama, far from anyone she knew, and then made a long, arduous journey home to her family in Wisconsin, struggling with a screaming baby on a series of trains packed with soldiers. Stories of how anxious families at home waited and coped with everyday life, living for letters and working extra hard, were part and parcel of our childhoods as much as the family photographs of relatives in uniform displayed in every sitting room.

As a bride in 1944, my mother had walked down the aisle of her local Episcopal church wearing bedroom slippers beneath her satin bridal dress. Pretty louche behavior by the normal standards of her small Virginia hometown, but shoes were rationed and that was what brides did then. But everyone had enough to eat despite the rationing imposed by the US government, and the European war was far enough away to make a German invasion seem unlikely. It was only later, when I studied history, that I learned more about the war and its horrors, the grim and terrifying realities, hardships, and privations faced by people across Europe and Russia. When I moved to England to live, I began to grasp firsthand the impact of this terrible period, how dark and long a shadow it had left. I had lived in London for years by the time an American acquaintance visited shortly before the fiftieth anniversary of Victory in Europe Day, the same occasion the war brides commemorate in this book. Our acquaintance dutifully visited the Imperial War Museum, Churchill's War Rooms, and Eisenhower's underground headquarters. By the end of the day he was shaken by what he had seen and learned. He emerged into the light of day to say he wanted to shake the hand of every English person he saw over the age of sixty. After researching this book, I know what he meant.

In households I knew as a child, family photographs of uniformed men and women were yellowing and gradually consigned to closets and drawers to make way for wedding pictures, new babies, and family holiday pictures. I began to add to what I already knew about how women had coped in the war, not sure at first what I would do with this information. The preoccupations women of any period share—falling in love, marriage, looking after husbands and families, struggling in many cases with financial pressures to make ends meet or forced by circumstances into spinsterhood—remained the same as the war engulfed everybody. In terrible times, and despite the heavy added burdens of war work, rationing, and the threat of invasion, many women fought a personal battle for some kind of normality, with the kind of determined courage never mentioned in the history books. Elsie, Frances, Alice, Tanni, and Evangeline soon invented themselves out of the information I was amassing. They hung about, waiting for their stories to be written.

But if I could pinpoint a single starting place for the book, it lies in the character of Manfred, who was both real and dangerous, responsible for many deaths. All of the other characters in the book are entirely fictitious, and so far as I could discover, there is no ancient de Balfort family in Sussex. If there are living de Balforts anywhere, I apologize for connecting them, even fictitiously, with Manfred. Characters must be called something. But Manfred was a real individual, though it is unlikely his true identity will ever be known. I learned about him after moving to England after my marriage, from an older family friend who had served in British Intelligence during the war. John did not like talking about his wartime experiences. A deeply civilized, kind, and intelligent man, with a wonderful sense of humor and devoted to his family, he was never the sort to nurse a grudge. Even so, on many occasions he spoke bitterly about a German collaborator in the southeast of

England who, Intelligence knew, was sending vital reports to Germans on the French coast to alert them to forecasts of clear weather over England. In the days before radar, notice of a clear night for flying enabled German bombers to navigate over Britain, to bomb it into submission. That the traitor, spy, or collaborator responsible for helping bring down so much death and destruction was never caught and brought to justice clearly rankled John enough to make me wonder about the war's deep scars and unsettled scores, their long-term effects.

Although the real Manfred is certainly dead, I have dealt with him in this book in a way that seems fitting. I am sorry that John, may he rest in peace, will never read it. In lieu of real justice, I like to think he would have been satisfied that Manfred was exposed and punished at last, if only on the printed page.

PROLOGUE

Spring 1995

*I*n the departure lounge of the Atlanta airport on an early May evening, Alice Osbourne Lightfoot, the trip's organizer, smiled at everybody and said, "Hey! How you doin' this evenin'?" as she ticked their names on her list of their London-bound party. A line from the introduction to the *Canterbury Tales*, memorized in her school days, went round and round in her head, about how in spring "Thanne longen folk to go on pilgrimages." Still do, even if the reasons we make pilgrimages are different now, Alice reflected.

Alice was the last to board the plane. Carefully she stowed a heavy old-fashioned dressing case in the overhead locker and took her seat among a group of elderly ladies at the front of the economy cabin. The women were wives of the remaining members of Joe Lightfoot's Eighth Air Force unit, college friends from the Georgia/Tennessee/Alabama area who had joined up together in 1941 and served in Europe. Those still able-bodied enough were making the trip back to England for the fiftieth anniversary of VE Day and a reunion with other air force units at their old airfield in Norfolk, from which they had flown B-17s and B-24s on dangerous daytime missions over Germany.

Alice had volunteered to organize the trip, and because she was British born, and because she had a natural tendency to take charge, the other ladies looked up to her as their leader.

After takeoff, the ladies slipped off their shoes and got comfortable and soon were doing what southerners call "visiting" over their dinner trays. Mostly they talked about their families, and liver-spotted hands passed pictures of grandchildren back and forth across the aisle. "Bet you're lookin' forward to goin' home, darlin'," they said to Alice, over and over. "Wonder if England's changed much since you left."

"Home! Honey, Alice's *home* is *Atlanta*! She's lived in America for fifty years!" Alice's friend Rose Ann protested from the next seat. "I declare, Alice!"

"Shame you aren't gonna be at the reunion and the wreath-layin' and the dinner with us, 'specially after the hard work you did, organizin' this trip for Joe and the boys, but since y'all are havin' your own service, 'spect your old friends'll be right glad to have you! 'Spect y'all got a lot of catchin' up to do," said a lady from the seat behind her.

"Oh, yes, and I'll be real glad to see them," Alice responded in the North Georgia drawl that had crept into her voice over the years. "Oh, yes," she repeated to herself. A lot of catching up indeed. Alice had never been one to shirk, and after what Elsie had written about Frances, it was her duty to go back.

As the flight wore on, the women ignored the growing racket at the other end of the plane, where their husbands were drinking too much whiskey, telling war stories and dirty jokes, patting the flight attendants' bottoms and calling them "sugar." After dinner some of the ladies, including Alice, took out knitting or crewelwork. Others tried to sleep. At last Alice yawned, wound up her knitting, switched off the overhead light, and pulled on the eyeshade from the airline's toiletries bag.

As Alice's plane boarded, another London-bound flight took off, from Ben Gurion airport. Because it was almost midnight the cabin crew served the meal quickly, then dimmed the lights. Soon Tanni Zayman's teenage grandchildren were dozing in their seats on either side of her. Chaim and Shifra had left Tel Aviv wearing thin T-shirts emblazoned with the names of their favorite bands. Now the plane was chilly. Tanni asked the stewardess for blankets and draped one over Chaim, sprawled with his feet in the aisle and his *kippah* askew, and another over his sister. Tanni thought how sweet they looked asleep, but she was glad of a reprieve from their constant sibling bickering when her own thoughts were in turmoil. The thought of returning to Crowmarsh Priors left her too agitated to sleep.

Down the dark aisle a baby wailed. Tanni shifted in her seat as the sound triggered the old nameless panic. There was no reason it should. She shut her eyes and took deep, calming breaths.

She had opened Elsie's letter sitting by Bruno's hospital bed. As she unfolded it, the invitation and first class plane tickets to England for Tanni and Bruno fluttered to the floor. "No!" Tanni had exclaimed out loud when she saw what they were for. Even after all this time, the very thought of returning to England, let alone the village, even with her husband, Bruno, by her side, made her feel sick. And after his recent heart operation, travel was out of the question for Bruno.

Her exclamation had woken him, so she blurted out what the letter said, then protested shakily that she wouldn't think of going anywhere while he was in hospital. Propped up on pillows, Bruno was pale, on a drip, and should have been resting quietly. Instead he was surrounded by books, papers, and university business smuggled into the hospital past the nurses who had forbidden him to work. Now he gave her one of his penetrating looks over the top of his glasses.

Tanni always found these looks of his—as if he knew something she did not—rather irritating, but the flash of irritation passed as Bruno patted her hand, then held it while he considered the best thing to do.

The doctors had assured Bruno that many women suffered severe postpartum depression, though less had been known about it in the 1940s. Tanni's amnesia about the period after the birth and death of their baby all those years ago in England was nature's way of shielding her. Aside from one interlude, she had had a full and happy life as a wife and mother and now grandmother, and they had a lovely house full of light and books and modern Israeli artefacts near the university, with volunteer work at the hospital, friends, and her garden to keep her busy.

He thought it was safe for her to accept Elsie's invitation now and said, "I know it's hard, but think of the obligation to our friends, however long it's been. And with what Elsie says about Frances, you know you must go. But not alone— why not cash in my ticket, take the two youngest with you? You need a break from worrying about me, and in a few months Chaim will be in the army. Anyway, with so many brothers and sisters there's never been money for him and Shifra to travel. Imagine how they'd love a trip to England. Go! Take the children, see your old friends. Spend a week in London afterward, take the children to the museums and the theater. Let them go to those street markets where the kids 'hang out,' as Shifra informs me is the correct term these days. You could even take them to Oxford, show them my old college. They can punt on the river like I used to. Shop a little, enjoy yourself." Bruno's eyes strayed back to his laptop screen. He was in the middle of writing an academic article. "Besides, in London you can go to Foyle's for me. I have a long list of books I cannot get here, and—"

"But, Bruno, I don't want to go! I can't think of leaving you! It's out of the question!"

"So there aren't enough people to look after me? One goes out of the room, and two come in! Thank God the operation went well, no problems, and I'll be home in a few weeks if the hospital doesn't kill me first. Doctors, students, nurses—who knows who all these people are—they come in at all hours, one minute bringing terrible food I don't want, the next, when I'm finally asleep, waking me to check my blood pressure. The physiotherapist turns up when I want to read, don't ask…don't look like that—I was joking. It's all right, my dear. Go already! I'll ring Elsie myself and tell her you will come." He stroked her cheek, then pushed his glasses back into place and turned back to his article.

So, reluctantly, Tanni agreed and invited her grand-children so that she couldn't back out at the last minute. She wouldn't disappoint them for the world. But now that she was actually en route, awake and alone in the dark, her misgivings returned, heightened by the fretting of the unseen baby somewhere down the aisle.

Just then, fifteen-year-old Shifra opened her brown eyes. She smiled at her grandmother and shifted to put her head on Tanni's shoulder. "I'm so excited about going to London, Bubbie. My best friend Rachel from school went and saw *The Rocky Horror Picture Show*. She says it's brilliant. I told Grandfather about it, and his secretary got us tickets for a surprise from him. I saved up my pocket money so I can go shopping in Camden Lock—Rachel told me where the best stalls are. And I'll get to see where Eema was born! And..." Her eyes closed midsentence, even though the baby was now howling lustily down the aisle.

Shifra's soft, curly hair tickled Tanni's cheek. She was the youngest of her large family, and Tanni still thought of her as "the baby" although in the last year Shifra had grown tall and was losing her childhood chubbiness. Tanni had been little older than Shifra when she had stepped off the train and seen Crowmarsh Priors for the first time, not looking forward to a holiday, but married and a mother. Had she ever been as young and carefree as Shifra, with her rock music and T-shirts and wrists loaded with colorful braided friendship bracelets teenagers gave each other? Bruno was right. She had to make this trip for Frances, who had been her friend. What would she have done without her friends all those years ago?

People around her were yawning now and sitting upright, stretching cramped limbs. The flight attendants were coming down the aisles serving tea and fruit. Shortly afterward the captain announced their descent into Gatwick, and her grandchildren craned their necks for their first sight of England as the plane circled over the early morning traffic on the M23.

The plane's shadow swooped over a big silver Mercedes with a plump, bejeweled little woman at the wheel. The Mercedes was travelling down the motorway toward Sussex at reckless speed, darting between lanes of lorries. Lady Carpenter, the third member of the group, pressed a purple kid pump hard on the accelerator. To the dismay of her family she insisted on driving herself, though at seventy-one her concentration at the wheel wasn't what it had been. But since her husband's death she controlled the family fortune and would do as she pleased...

The fourth member of the clique was already in Crowmarsh Priors. She had been there for so long that only a handful of people remembered where she had originally come from. Some who did were still living in New Orleans, white-haired widows who had been at the French convent with Evangeline Fontaine many years before. Now they passed the afternoons rocking on the porch of an old people's home that had once been the Fontaine mansion, fanning themselves and talking about the same things they had discussed for fifty years, including the night they had attended Evangeline's coming-out ball in this very house, before the Fontaines had fallen on hard times and had to sell the place. "It was a real shame, when it had been in the family for so many years. Something to do with the war, why they lost all their money. That was after Evangeline ran off."

Evangeline Fontaine's elopement had been a scandal at the time and still was.

"That's right, just before the war. I forget the name of the boy she ran off with, nobody knew him from Adam or who his people were. I wonder what became of her," said one. "It was a shocking thing to happen in one of our old families." The others rocked and agreed.

"But the Fontaines hushed it up, and nobody's seen Evangeline since."

"I reckon she's dead by now," one or the other of the old ladies would finally remark.

"I reckon she is," another would say. "Most folks we knew are."

In Crowmarsh Priors, Evangeline Fontaine Fairfax was awakened by a fleet of catering lorries that ground to a halt on the village green. Soon cheerful young Australians were shouting "g'days" and directions at each other. Lorries banged open and marquee poles clanked as they were unloaded. Evangeline pulled back the bedclothes and scrabbled for her slippers with blue-veined feet. She pulled on a frayed satin robe, drew the curtains open, and squinted in the bright morning sunshine toward the channel.

She glanced at Elsie's letter propped on the dresser between a jumble of photographs in tarnished silver frames, one of her late husband in his naval uniform, another of herself holding their son, Andrew, as a baby, then Andrew graduating from university, and with his wife and children at their home in Melbourne.

She picked up an ivory-backed hairbrush engraved with a "P" and poured a tot of sherry from the bedroom decanter into her tooth mug. She took both back to the bed and sat down. "Well hey, Laurent, hey, Richard, hey, Frances, fifty years and they say that sorry old war business is over and done with. Folks who weren't there say that, leastways. Maybe today we finish it. Here's to y'all," she said aloud. The southern accent had thickened now and the once-soft voice was husky. She drank some sherry, then brushed her hair while she planned her outfit for the big day ahead. "Yes indeed, y'all watch."

1.

Crowmarsh Priors, Boxing Day 1937

At twenty-two, Alice Osbourne was the sort of girl people called a "brick," sensible and responsible, though they were inclined to add that she was pretty when she smiled. She was tall like her father, the late vicar of Crowmarsh Priors. Her features, brown hair, and air of bookish distraction were also his. She was nothing like her mother, whose early prettiness had faded after years of "delicate" health and disappointed hopes that her husband would rise higher in the church than an East Sussex country parish.

A serious, stolid only child, Alice had few friends among the village children except Richard Fairfax, who was two years older, also an only child, whose father had been at Cambridge with the vicar. Alice spent long afternoons with Richard and his nanny, playing in the Fairfaxes' garden in good weather and inventing games in the cellars where Richard's father kept his wine when it rained. The Reverend Mr. Osbourne coached Richard in Latin and Greek, and after he was sent away to school, Alice saw him only during the holidays. Each time he came home he seemed handsomer, and by the time they had reached their teens, he had become a god in Alice's adoring eyes.

With Richard away and her mother usually indisposed, Alice's main companion and confidant was her father. She was happiest on Saturdays when they rambled across the Sussex Downs, sometimes as far as the coast, and the vicar, who had a lively imagination, indulged his love of local history. He enthralled Alice with stories of the Roman legions who had fortified the coast, pointing out coves where the Vikings might have landed and where eighteenth-century smugglers had had a network of tunnels and caves to bring in contraband—silks and lace and brandy—from France. On the way home for tea one or the other of them would sing "The Smugglers Song":

If you wake at Midnight, and hear a horse's feet,
Don't go drawing back the blind, or looking in the street,
Them that asks no questions isn't told a lie.
Watch the wall, my darling, while the gentlemen go by!

And they took it in turns to recite verses and then joined in the chorus after each one:

Five and twenty ponies
Trotting through the dark –
Brandy for the Parson.
'Baccy for the Clerk;
Laces for a lady, letters for a spy,
And watch the wall, my darling, while the Gentlemen go by!

Then they would race each other back to the vicarage for tea, and Alice would muffle her laughter in case Mummy was resting.

When Alice was sent to boarding school she missed those outings, and during the holidays these happened less frequently. Gradually it fell to Alice to take over her mother's job of preparing the altar for Sunday service on Saturday afternoons, Mrs. Osbourne's only concession to the duties of a vicar's wife. She still saw Richard when he came home but felt awkward and tongue-tied in his presence, though he never seemed to notice. He and his widowed mother, Penelope, often came to the vicarage for sherry after the service on Sunday morning, when he would chat to Alice and call her "old thing." She felt embarrassed later when her father teased her gently about her "beau."

When Alice came home from school for good, it was clear that the vicar was less well than his chronically ailing wife. Dutifully Alice followed his advice, trained as a teacher in Brighton, then came home to take over the infants' class at the Crowmarsh Priors school and nursed her father through his last illness. Meanwhile Richard went to naval college, and Alice heard eventually that he had been appointed as a naval attaché to someone important in London. Penelope took a keen interest in her son's career and passed any news of him to Alice.

As Richard rose in the navy, Alice's world shrank. The first Christmas after her father died was a sad little observance. "I don't know what your father would have said if we didn't keep *Christmas*," said Mrs. Osbourne mournfully, pouring the last of the vicar's port for them to drink with the lopsided Christmas cake Alice had baked. They drank and ate in silence as the gloomy December evening drew in, the vicar's place at the head of the table painfully empty. Alice went to bed feeling too miserable for words.

Next morning, Boxing Day, dawned clear, crisp, and bright, and Alice, cheered by the weather, got up with a sense of purpose. As soon as the holidays were over she and her mother had to vacate the vicarage for its new occupant. They were moving to a small Edwardian cottage on the edge of the village and there was a great deal to be done. Today Alice planned to pack up her father's study. After breakfast she left her mother drinking her tea by the range, briskly tied an apron round her waist, and was on her knees tossing papers into boxes when she heard the front door knocker. "Bother!" she muttered and struggled to her feet. She wiped her dirty hands on her apron and opened the door to find a tall, blond man on the step.

"Alice!" Richard Fairfax exclaimed and kissed her cheek.

"Richard! Oh! I…um…I thought you were away." The unexpected sight of him, not to mention the kiss, had made her head spin. How mortifying that he should find her wearing her oldest skirt and a moth-eaten cardigan she used for housework!

"Got leave in time for Christmas with Mama. Thought if you were free we might go for a walk, as it's such a lovely day—we'll have lunch at that little pub, you know the one. And there's something I want to…well, do say you'll come, old thing!"

Fancy him asking her to lunch! It was the first time a man had invited Alice to do anything. "Oh! How lovely! I'll just…" Alice untied her apron, glancing with dismay at her clothes.

"Come as you are, old thing." And before she knew it Richard had bundled her into her coat and scarf and they were going down the path.

Now, an hour later, Alice, who would normally have looked subdued and cold and red-nosed in her old tweed coat, was arm in arm with Richard Fairfax, glowing with happiness. The wind had turned her cheeks pink and made her eyes sparkle. Darling Richard! The only man, apart from her father, whom she could ever possibly love. As soon as they had reached the top of the downs he had spoken the words. She'd thought she had imagined it, had stopped and stared up at him blankly.

He had taken her hands in his and blurted out, "Dear Alice, I said, 'Will you marry me?' Rather sudden sort of proposal, I'm sure, but we've known each other since we were children, and all through naval college I've thought of you. I used to look forward so much to coming home, because you would be there. I can't imagine you *not* being there, so I thought that, now I'm in a position to marry, you might say yes. Mama has been hinting how much she'd love you as a daughter-in-law. Dearest Alice, please say you'll marry me!"

"Oh, Richard! Oh, yes! Yes, of course! With all my heart!" she had exclaimed, breathless with disbelief at the turn of events. Even Mummy would be pleased.

"Now, darling," Richard said, untucking her hand from the crook of his arm and reaching into his pocket, "of course you shall have a new engagement ring if you prefer, but Mama wondered if you might consent to wear hers. It is rather special." He held out a velvet jeweler's box.

Tentatively Alice took it, undid the clasp, and opened it. Against a satin lining with the jeweler's name in faded gold script, a magnificent diamond flanked by sapphires in an old-fashioned setting blazed at her. She caught her breath. "Oh!" She had never seen anything so beautiful. Richard's father had been dead for years, but how could Penelope bear to part with it?

Richard was waiting anxiously.

"Oh, Richard! I should *love*...does your mother truly mean me to have it?" she added.

Richard chuckled. "Mama was delighted when I said I intended to ask you to marry me, and I'm to tell you there is other jewelry you shall have too. Apparently I'm supposed to have it all reset for you. And she hopes we will live in the house here, which I thought you would like as it means you'll be near your mother."

Penelope Fairfax had been as effusive as her brusque nature allowed when Richard broached the subject. "My dear boy! It's high time you were married. A naval officer needs a wife, keep the home fires burning, that sort of thing, but the *right sort* of wife is *terribly* important in the navy. I'm happy to say that Alice, unlike most modern girls, has her feet on the ground, not like those foreign hussies in that rackety crowd the de Balforts have taken up with."

"Mama, they're hardly hussies! Hugo made friends travelling after university, and naturally he has them to stay. Probably amuses Leander having some young people about. But you're right, except for the shooting, that crowd does run to foreigners, and some of them are a bit fast for my taste, not my sort any more than they're Alice's. There's something so...so wonderfully English about Alice!"

"Thankfully she doesn't take after that mother of hers. No, Alice is a brick. Of course she will have the Fairfax jewelry, and I shall be happy to give up this house for you both. Alice's mother will be company for her when you're at sea, and I've so much committee work in London that it'll be far more convenient to stay in the Knightsbridge flat. I've been longing to move there for ages, actually."

Penelope held up a hand imperiously as Richard tried to protest. "At my time of life, after a busy day of trying to make cabinet ministers to see sense, I prefer peace and quiet, a nice cocktail, little dinners with friends, perhaps the opera or the theater. I've always found it rather quiet in the country. I need to be *doing*, Richard! Besides, you'll be needing the nursery floor before long, darling. Before you know it there'll be nannies, and prams in the hall, so chaotic, but darling Alice will manage splendidly..."

"Yes, Mama definitely approves." Richard slipped Penelope's ring onto Alice's finger. Alice held out her hand at arm's length, and they both admired it glittering in the sunshine. "Bit large for you, darling, I think. I'll take it to Aspreys at the end of my leave, so they can reset it and adjust it to fit," said Richard. Reluctantly Alice watched him replace the ring in the box. He grinned and gave her a squeeze. "Don't look so glum. I'll make sure they reset it beautifully, I promise. The minute I come back we'll name the day."

Back? "Are you going away again?" asked Alice.

"There'll be rather a lot of back-and-forth, but as the wife of a navy man you'll get used to it, darling. And I'll always come back to you. The thought you will be waiting for me makes me unspeakably happy."

Alice had given a little shiver of pleasure at the word "wife." "I'm going to be *married*!" she thought incredulously. "Where are you going?"

"I've been seconded to a mission to Washington. President Roosevelt, you know. The situation in Germany. Then I'll be travelling round the United States, meeting industrialists with businesses in Europe. We leave next month, probably come back from New Orleans. We needn't have a long engagement, need we?" he asked, drawing her into his arms.

Alice nearly swooned at his kiss. "No," she murmured giddily into his shoulder when he finally stopped kissing her and she could speak again.

They walked on briskly to keep warm until they reached a summit where they could see the coast and the sea sparkling in the distance.

"I love it here," said Alice. "Father and I used to…if only he were alive to marry us. He would have been so happy!" Her voice had wobbled. "We used to come up here," she went on, "and he'd tell me stories about what used to go on round the coast. An old man who was dying once told Father there had been a smugglers' tunnel that opened in a grave in the churchyard."

"Is it true?"

"The old man insisted it was, he'd been down it as a lad. Father had an old book about smugglers in his study, privately printed, I think, he'd found it in an old bookshop in Lewes. It even had a map that showed the tunnels, but it wasn't very clear. But Father tried to use it to work out where the tunnels were and actually thought he'd found one. There were some scary stories about a smuggler called

Black Dickon who had a gang and used them to get their contraband past the excise men. Mummy got quite cross when she overheard him reading to me about the gang. They were betrayed and all hanged, and their ghosts came back to lure the customs men to their deaths on the cliffs. I had nightmares about it for a while."

Richard put an arm around her and they gazed out to sea, at the sun dancing on the waves. "I shan't let you have nightmares, but keep an eye out for that book. I like those old stories about the coast too. We'll tell them to our children, and leave out the frightening bits. Now, old thing, let's go and have lunch. I'm starving, aren't you?"

Holding Richard's hand, Alice tried to remember where she had last seen that book. She vaguely remembered putting it into a box with some of her father's papers. She would find it and give it to Richard as a wedding present. Some of the stories *were* grim. Now she remembered they said Black Dickon had been hanged on the spot where the pub stood now. She shuddered.

As they went in, wood smoke from the pub's fire tickled Alice's nose. She could smell chicken roasting on a spit, and Richard called for champagne. She hadn't known you could get it in a country pub. He must have brought it in specially. The publican beamed and led them to a table with a vase of Christmas roses in the saloon bar. "You arranged this beforehand, didn't you! Oh, Richard, what a wonderful surprise!"

Richard smiled and squeezed her hand under the table. They raised their glasses to each other. "I shall remember this day forever," she thought, sipping her first taste of champagne, giggling as bubbles tickled her nose. With such

happiness before her, she knew nothing bad could ever happen to her again. She and Richard would live happily ever
after. She banished all gloomy thoughts of smugglers and
their tunnels.

2.

New Orleans, March 1938

*I*n the shuttered dining room of her New Orleans mansion, Celeste Fontaine surveyed her luncheon table, beautifully laid for thirty. Her brow creased with irritation and she snatched a place card bearing the name "Maurice Fitzroy" from its silver holder, tore it in two, and slipped a card that said "Lieutenant Richard Fairfax" into its place, beside "Miss Evangeline Fontaine." She was upset to have to rearrange her seating plan at the last minute, but Maurice had telephoned to say he was unavoidably delayed by plantation business and would join them for coffee. So rude of him. Or was there more to it? Maurice was too old-fashioned to be rude. She straightened a lopsided flower arrangement. It was such a strain to entertain during Mardi Gras.

Everything went wrong. The colored servants spent every night in the Quarter, drinking and carousing. Next morning they had headaches and were good for nothing. But Celeste's husband, Charles, had insisted they invite an important English delegation, which had met with the president in Washington, to today's luncheon. The day had begun disastrously: the cook had claimed that her rheumatics made her too sick to get out of bed. Celeste had swallowed her pride and telephoned her mother-in-law in the country to borrow her cook, Inez. Now Inez was in the kitchen, grumbling, clattering pans, and bossing the maids at the top of her voice. Suddenly Celeste smelled food burning, heard a slap, then a shriek and the sound of glass shattering. A maid sobbed loudly in the pantry.

She shut the glass dining room doors firmly behind her, praying the commotion would calm down and hoping there wouldn't be repercussions if one of the Englishmen sat next to her niece. Lieutenant Fairfax was a perfectly pleasant young man, nearly at the end of his weeklong stay in New Orleans. If Maurice was annoyed, Celeste would tell him that she couldn't have left the place next to Evangeline conspicuously empty.

Eighteen-year-old Evangeline, debutante of the year, was the guest of honor at today's luncheon. Her coming-out ball tonight—the last night of Mardi Gras—would close the season. Given that all New Orleans expected that when the ball ended at midnight her father would announce Evangeline's engagement to Maurice, Maurice's absence at lunch was awkward. It didn't take much to start people gossiping in New Orleans, and the last thing Celeste wanted was to provoke comment or speculation about Evangeline. Well brought up girls should never be the subject of gossip, and a few vague but worrying rumors about Evangeline had reached her ears. Celeste hoped fervently they had not reached Maurice's. He would not have been amused.

More than twice Evangeline's age, Maurice was a long-time intimate of Evangeline's father. He was the last of his family, sole heir to its fortune and vast estate; the Fitzroy plantation, Belle Triste, was one of the oldest and handsomest in the state. The family was proud of its ancestry—the Fitzroys claimed to have had royal antecedents—but now Maurice was the last of the family and needed sons to keep the name alive. They said the haughty Fitzroys had thought none of the local girls good enough, and in his younger days Maurice had spend a considerable time in Europe seeking a suitable bride. If so, his search had come to nothing. Then the only daughter of the prominent Fontaine family caught his eye.

Maurice had unbent enough to let Celeste know that he had been captivated by Evangeline when she was still a convent schoolgirl. Romantic, Celeste supposed uneasily. He clearly worshipped the girl now, scarcely taking his eyes off her, hanging on her every word, lighting her cigarettes, holding her chair, and claiming every possible dance at balls, despite the fact that Evangeline did not seem to care for him at all. Thoughtless and giddy, she flirted and danced with her younger beaux and visited risqué establishments in the Treme with her friends, without a serious thought about her future or marriage in her head.

Celeste sighed. It didn't bode well. Marriage was a sacrament and, in her experience, often a crown of thorns. But Evangeline's future was dictated by social custom. Among the first families of New Orleans girls married young, unless they entered a convent, and from then on their happiness depended on the clever management of home and husband. Otherwise...

Halfway through luncheon, Celeste frowned down the long table at Evangeline. The girl was pushing Inez's special étouffée around her plate, eating nothing, pale and listless, half asleep. Modern young people stayed out too late at night. Although she was childless, Celeste had strong views on how girls should be brought up, and she disapproved of the way Evangeline had been raised.

Young girls should be trained from an early age to attend to their duties rather than selfish enjoyment. Unfortunately Evangeline was the youngest child and only girl in a family of five children. She had been spoiled by her parents and doted on by her four older brothers who had let her follow them around and taught her to hunt, fish, swim, climb trees, and who knew what else. It wasn't ladylike, but her parents had just laughed. Eventually her father realized she was growing up into a hoyden and stopped laughing. He told his wife to see Evangeline was taken in hand. They had to think about her position in society and her marriage prospects.

The nuns at the school had done their best to reverse the damage, but since graduating from the convent the previous summer and beginning her season, all of their good work had been undone. As a debutante Evangeline had plunged into frivolity and overindulgence. She thought of nothing but shopping, fittings, parties, and running about to nightclubs where well brought up girls had no business. At tonight's splendid ball she would wear a Paris gown and, Celeste happened to know, a Fitzroy family ring on her right index finger, which had been given with her parents' approval and which her mother insisted she wear lest Maurice take offense. But despite it all, Evangeline looked bored.

Celeste disapproved of debutante seasons. She and Evangeline's mother had been brought up in the old-fashioned way. Between school and marriage, they were kept at home, learning how to run a household and keep a husband happy. They had been taught to supervise servants, arrange flowers, plan menus, even cook. There had been no gadding about.

Celeste shuddered to think how Evangeline would manage when she married. Overnight she would become mistress of two grand houses, the Fitzroy plantation house at Belle Triste and the mansion in New Orleans. Maurice would expect them to run like clockwork, of course, and there would be a baby every year. Well, Celeste had tried her best to fill the gaps in Evangeline's domestic education in the past year, but the girl had taken little notice of her aunt's efforts.

Down the table Evangeline was smoking cigarette after cigarette between sips of wine, not making the slightest effort to talk to the Englishman beside her or to anyone else. To the servants Celeste signaled discretely that they should pour no more wine for Miss Evangeline and to bring in the next course. Then, the perfect wife and hostess, she turned back with a look of rapt attention to what the men were saying. When she heard it was politics, business, and what they were saying in Washington *again*, her expression of interest didn't falter but she groaned inwardly. The European branch of the Fontaine business was in deep trouble, she knew. Yet Evangeline's family was lavishing so much money on tonight's ball. She didn't want to think deeply about that. Let the men deal with business. It was all they were good for.

At the other end of the table, Charles's face was red from too many prelunch cocktails as he engaged in a heated discussion about the American government, the situation in

Germany, and how it was affecting the Fontaines' business in Marseille. To her intense discomfort he was slurring his words...

Evangeline studied the dregs in her wine glass, careful not to look up and catch her aunt's eye. She could feel Aunt Celeste watching her like a hawk. Did she suspect what might be wrong? The anonymous notes had begun coming days ago, leaving a trail of poison in Evangeline's handbag, in a box of flowers—there had even been a note on her breakfast tray this morning, in the folds of the napkin where her maid, Delphy, couldn't have seen it. Just a few crudely written, misspelled words.

"BIN WATCHIN YOU NIGGER'S HORE"

Or: "GITTIN CLOSE"

Someone close to her had been spying. Who? It hardly mattered. In New Orleans the consequences would be swift and terrible. Today's note said:

"YOU AND THE NIGGER CANOT GIT AWAY REKONING IS COMIN"

What could she do! Evangeline cast a sideways look at the Englishman on her left. If she had had less on her mind she would have been flirting with him. He was good looking, in a fair, English way, and tall, with an air of command. She had danced with him a few times in the past week. Soon he had wanted as many dances as she would give him, but she found him serious-minded and hopeless at the kind of silly banter and frivolous compliments New Orleans girls expected from men. He bored her. But at least he wasn't Maurice. Maurice had watched him with narrowed eyes. Maurice. She shivered.

Almost from the moment they had sat down to lunch, her uncle had demanded Richard's attention. Evangeline listened intermittently to their conversation, then concentrated on her own worries. She heard that Richard and his fellow delegates hadn't succeeded in persuading the president to take an interest in developments in Germany and they were going home. Well, Evangeline didn't blame President Roosevelt. Germany was so far away, why should he? Richard was sailing for England early next morning. If only *she* could escape to England. They had been so careful…but someone knew.

Her untouched étouffée was taken and replaced with a salad that glistened with mayonnaise. Ugh! Feeling queasy again, Evangeline cut some lettuce into small pieces and wondered again what on earth she was going to do. For the hundredth time, she calculated how many days, how many weeks, since she last had the curse.

This morning her maid, Delphy, had found her throwing up when she came to draw Evangeline's bath. "Too much champagne last night," Evangeline had said, burying her face in a wet towel. Delphy had raised her eyebrows skeptically. Delphy was in the kitchen now; what was she saying to the other servants? Servants' gossip meant everyone knew everything in New Orleans.

Evangeline's eyelids drooped. At night she lay awake, imagining she heard footsteps creeping up to her bedroom door, or slept and endured a recurring nightmare. In it she was hunting after dark with her brothers on

Granmere's plantation upriver. When she was little the boys had shown her how to shine a flashlight to blind the rabbits: they would be transfixed, ears twitching. Unless they jumped fast and disappeared into the dark, the hunters fired and they dropped. Most weren't fast enough to get away. Killing rabbits this way upset her at first, but the boys told her that was hunting; the rabbits destroyed the vegetable garden and Inez used them for jambalaya, so she'd got used to it, had shot plenty herself. But in her dream it was her and Laurent in the darkness, sensing hunters approaching from somewhere. Then the two of them were trapped in a blinding beam of light. Knowing what would happen next but rooted to the spot, powerless to run as the hunters took aim, she would wake as she heard the click of the trigger...

Evangeline's palms had grown cold and clammy. Her glass was empty—damn! Alcohol was the only thing that steadied her jangled nerves, calmed her uneasy stomach. She had been afraid to tell Laurent about the notes. And she was afraid to tell him about the other thing she hardly dared name. Laurent was smart, he knew many things she did not, things no girl suspected. He had known of secret places where no one could find them, had shown her what to do that first time. He had taught her wonderful, dangerous games for the two of them to play, and even though she knew they were committing a mortal sin, Evangeline now lived for their next intoxicating time together.

Laurent would take care of everything...somehow. Evangeline could think of no way out—unless they ran away. But where to? And how could they run? With so much happening today, she didn't even know how she'd manage to see Laurent. After lunch she would be expected at home, to dress under the eye of her mother and Delphy. Tonight was the big Mardi Gras parade, when she and the other debutantes whose fathers were in the same krewe, one of the Mardi Gras organizations, were expected to play the traditional gracious role of girls from prominent families and perch decoratively on the krewe's float. They would wave and smile and throw doubloons and beads to the crowd. Afterward, at her ball, she would be surrounded by people every minute. But she had to do something. Before her parents found out, before *anyone* else found out. Especially before Maurice found out. Before it was *too late.*

A snippet of conversation startled her. "What did Uncle Charles just say?" she whispered to Richard.

Richard smiled at her. "I gather your family's company is sending a new employee to the Marseille office next week."

"Smart as a whip, that boy, best Jesuit education, no real future in New Orleans," Uncle Charles said, a little too loudly. Everyone looked at their plates.

Richard Fairfax asked why such a smart boy should have no future in New Orleans.

"Ha! He's Creole, that's why, *gens de couleur.* Part colored, Lieutenant Fairfax! But smart like his daddy." Charles Fontaine smirked and Aunt Celeste gasped. Evangeline felt as if someone had emptied a pitcher of ice water over her. France! No! Laurent wasn't supposed to go until he was twenty-one, and that was two years away. And he couldn't leave her alone, not if he knew. Holy Virgin, she had to tell him at once.

"Y'all have the colored problem in England?" Uncle Charles asked.

The servants' black faces were impassive as they removed plates.

Aunt Celeste's glass trembled in her hand.

Evangeline felt faint. If Laurent left she would never see him again. And if Laurent didn't save her from Maurice… who would? She realized with terrible clarity that, for the first time in her life, demanding what she wanted would not be enough. She and Laurent were doomed. Never mind that Uncle Charles had sent Laurent to the Jesuits and Granmere doted on him and the family looked after him. His mother had been a quadroon so he was colored, and no colored boy dared so much as look at a white girl, lest he end up swinging from a tree. He couldn't save her from Maurice or anyone else. He couldn't even save himself if anyone knew. And she knew she had to warn him that someone did…because then the safest thing was for him to leave for France immediately. Maybe she could follow him? How? She couldn't sprout wings and fly. But…Richard was English. England was near France, wasn't it? But where exactly? Evangeline played with the ring Maurice had given her. She didn't like it, but her mother said it would be rude not to wear it. She thought distractedly of Sister Bernadette's geography lessons and tried to conjure up a map.

Everyone welcomed the distraction when the dining room doors swung open, and with great fanfare, the servants brought in the traditional King Cake. Was there no one in New Orleans she could turn to?

Evangeline had heard the colored girls went to an old woman named Mama La Bas who did mojos and spells, black magic, but you had to be careful with what she gave you. Use the spell wrong, they said, and it would turn against you. It was a terrible sin to go to a woman like that. The Church taught that voodoo was an instrument of the devil, and having been brought up in the Church, Evangeline was afraid, but she was now so mired in sinful thoughts and deeds there was nowhere to go but on. For courage she boldly picked up the full wineglass in front of Richard and drained it as conversation resumed. Everyone began to talk at once, but not to Richard.

"Hasn't been in the South long enough," said someone, audibly.

"Doesn't understand the situation here; coloreds were slaves two or three generations ago, they're like animals, got to be firm with them," said someone else.

To Richard's immense relief, Evangeline rescued him from the awkward moment. She laid her hand sporting a priceless antique French rose-diamond ring carved with a crest on his wrist, leaned close, and said, in a conspiratorial murmur, "I want to tell you a secret." But first, had her brothers shown him a good time in New Orleans?

Richard, entranced, felt her breast pressing against his arm and smelled her perfume. Her long eyelashes fluttered on her cheeks. "*Quite* the most splendid time," he enthused.

"I bet Andre and Philippe took you down to the Treme," she went on, gazing up into his eyes. "That's where the speakeasies and good-time houses are," she whispered. She smiled, lowering her eyelashes again. "The nuns at school warned us it was a mortal sin even to imagine what goes on down there. But you must have noticed all the beautiful Creole girls. Well," her head was nearly on his shoulder now, "here's the secret. Uncle Charles kept a girl down there in a little house, but she died. Bet the boys took you to hear her son, Laurent Baptiste. Uncle Charles is Laurent's father. Laurent was smart in school, like Uncle Charles said, but what he really likes is music. He's amazing, plays the piano and the saxophone and, oh, lots of instruments, better than anyone—ragtime and swing and jazz—but the only places he can play are in the Treme."

Richard was mesmerized. She was so close he could feel her breath on his cheek and smell her scent, like gardenias at dusk. "Anyhow, he's the family member Uncle Charles meant. And he wouldn't normally have been rude enough to mention it, but he forgets himself when he, um, talks business." She sat up straight as her aunt shot her a sharp look, but let her fingers slide down to brush his thigh, as if by accident.

"Good lord, Miss Fontaine! I...er...your uncle was talking earlier about—I had no idea the fellow was related to the family. He looks, well, like a white person." Flustered, Richard remembered the handsome young man with copper-colored hair at the piano who had saluted Evangeline's brothers and winked, saying, "Don't let on to Granmere I was in here again. Supposed to be in the office." The sleeves of his immaculate shirt were rolled up and the jacket of a well-cut suit folded neatly beneath an expensive Homburg on the chair beside him.

Evangeline shrugged. "You won't see a white man playing the piano in the Treme. This is New Orleans. Everybody knows the relationship between us and Laurent; it's a common situation really, even in the older families, so nobody ever talks about it, it's just there. Everybody pretends they don't know. In fact, Laurent and my brothers practically grew up together, although officially white people and colored don't mix. When Laurent's mother died our grandmother took a liking to him and raised him at her plantation upriver. Then Uncle Charles sent him to the Jesuit school for Creole boys. We used to spend the school vacations together at the plantation. Granmere thinks the world of him because he's got the family blood, but being colored Laurent learned to know his place, which is why most of the family accepts him. Mama and Aunt Celeste, of course, pretend he doesn't exist. And boys like him, if they don't have big mouths, are taken care of, usually doing some kind of work for the family. I thought you should know so you won't mention what Uncle Charles said when you're talking to Aunt Celeste. She and Uncle Charles never had children, so Laurent and children like him are always a sensitive subject. Now, try some King Cake." A servant was bending over Evangeline with a silver tray and she put a slice on Richard's plate.

"Watch out for the gold baby," Celeste called to him down the length of the table.

"I beg your pardon?" Richard, picking up his fork, was startled.

Before Celeste could tell him Evangeline hurried to explain, "King Cake is a Mardi Gras tradition. There's always a little gold baby inside. It's for the Baby Jesus and brings good luck to whoever gets it. If you find it in your cake you have to give the next party, but since Mardi Gras is almost over," Evangeline wrinkled her nose and made a disappointed face, "and my ball is the last of the season, I guess you won't have time to give a party before you go back to England. But you have to do something!"

She dropped her eyelashes again, thinking. I know what you can do. You can get me away from here. I'll get Mama

La Bas to help with a spell so you'll do it. For a gris-gris to work on someone you needed some hair or something from that person, something they had been in close bodily contact with.

"Early tomorrow morning, Miss Fontaine. Dawn tide. Worst luck." Evangeline Fairfax, with her teasing chatter, soft voice, pretty frocks, flowers, and pearls reminded him of a butterfly. He admitted to himself she was enchanting. He remembered Alice and felt obscurely guilty, but seized the moment anyway. "Your uncle tells me I'm to attend your ball tonight. I say, you will dance with me, won't you? Before I go? I leave shortly after midnight for home." If the predictions were true that war was coming he would never see Evangeline again, so he wasn't betraying Alice by asking an exceptionally pretty girl to dance. If only—he bit on something hard and spat it discretely into his hand and put it on the side of his dessert plate just as Celeste rose and announced they would take coffee on the veranda.

Evangeline groped for her bag and stood up. "Oh look, you got the gold baby!" she exclaimed. "I hope it brings you luck."

Richard pushed back his own chair. "Miss Fontaine, it will only bring me luck if you save me the first dance," he said boldly, remembering the tingle of her touch on his arm, her breath in his ear. He suddenly wanted nothing except for her to touch him again.

"Of course I'll dance with you, Lieutenant," Evangeline said, her hand brushing his, "on condition you give me the gold baby. I've never managed to get one in my own cake." She raised her eyes to his, sweetly, and held out her hand. It had been in his mouth, and there must be some spit on it. Surely that would do for Mama La Bas.

"A fair exchange," said Richard. He picked it up and dropped it into her outstretched palm.

"Oh! Here's Maurice," said Evangeline, suddenly nervous as a tall, middle-aged man with heavy dark brows and a stern expression made his way toward them. Maurice ignored the guests and their greetings and stared coldly at Richard, who was struck by the man's resemblance to a Spanish painting he had seen once, of the Grand Inquisitor. He hoped what they said about Maurice being as good as engaged to Evangeline wasn't true. The man struck him as a brute.

Evangeline snapped her purse shut and excused herself. In the hallway she stopped the butler, who was carrying a tray of liqueurs to the veranda. When he went back to the kitchen could he please tell Delphy she needed her for a minute?

At four o'clock in the afternoon, in a shuttered room off Congo Square, Mama squatted on the earthen floor, sucked her pipe between toothless gums, and waited to hear what her visitor wanted. Her feet were bare, tucked under stained calico petticoats, and each bore a flat white scar where the big toe had been. The air was fetid with tobacco, herbs, chickens, and decay. Candle ends flickered on a makeshift altar covered with small figures made of cloth, human hair, animal bones, beads, feathers, and dried snakeskin. She had been born a slave and had once had another name, but so long ago everybody had forgotten it. Now she was just Mama La Bas. It meant "the devil's wife."

Her rheumy eyes blinked. The high-yellow girl Delphy who worked at the Fontaines' had yet to get to the point. Mama guessed the problem concerned a man and knew that men always meant trouble. "What you got to pay me?" she asked finally. Delphy knelt in front of her, fumbling to untie a knotted handkerchief. Finally she removed something from its folds and placed a ring in Mama's pale palm.

The old woman's sight was blurred, but the spirits had given her eyes inside her head. Her fingers told her the gold was soft, the ring old, the stones precious. She traced a cluster of diamonds, felt the familiar pattern, and a shock went up her arm like a cottonmouth had sunk its fangs in it. "This here ring come from a Fitzroy. Bad, bad thing. Uh hunh. Stones make a pattern, family crest. I born on the Fitzroy place. Ise a chile, me an' my sister polish they damn silver every day. Had the same damn crest on it. Ole Miz Fitzroy whup us with the poker if we din' shine it bright enough." Mama spat. "She whup us anyhow. Hard. Hard as she could. Sometime she git that poker hot first. Oh, I know this crest well's I know the devil hisself. My, my, my. Never 'spected to have this ring in my own hand. Whut you doin' with it? You stole it?"

"No, ma'am. Young lady I work for say to 'change it for gris-gris.'"

"You messin' wid evil here, girl, tradin' this ring what bring bad luck. Ev'n if I didn't know it belong to the Fitzroys, I can still feel the evil inside it. I tried to run away once. Miz Fitzroy made them hold me down, took that knife and cut my toes herself, so's I couldn't run away no more, couldn't hardly walk. I only eight.

"I'se cryin' 'hind the barn, toes bleedin', hurt so bad, still do hurt so bad and they ain't even there. Ole uncle born in Africa come creepin' over when it get dark, give me a poultice for my toes, tell me if go steal him a chicken an' he show me how to make a bad curse, last a long time, case I lookin' to curse somebody. You got a bad whuppin' if you stole a chicken, but I crep' out on my hands an' knees an' took that chicken and then Uncle showed me what to do. I cursed 'em good. Sometime helped the gris-gris along a little. Just one Fitzroy lef' now, son's youngest boy, Maurice. He bad too, rotten bad like the rest of the family, done kilt two niggers workin' for him already, beat 'em to death hisself. They say he get worked up while he beaten 'em, like he really enjoin' hisself. His grandmama like that too, when she beat us, cut my toes. Maurice," she rocked silently for a minute, "ain't gwine have no chillun. He gwine die crazy as his daddy. The family gone die out, I done fixed that already. Not to say I cain't do more. But first…hee hee hee." Mama reached over on the altar for a strange little figure with stitched crosses for eyes, human hair, and a crude knitted penis. It was stuck all over with pins. She twisted another pin through the torso.

"Yes, ma'am, but Miss Evangeline cain't wait. Mr. Fitzroy fixin' to marry her. But she scared of him, tell her mama and daddy she don't want to live way out there by herself with the alligators at Belle Triste. Her mama and daddy shoutin', what a lil' girl fresh out of school know, the Fitzroys old family, the richest folks in town, she gon' marry him or they put her in the Irish convent till she git some sense. They say her daddy gambles, owe the Fitzroys money. They say Mr. Fitzroy give her that ring, tell her it belong to his grandma, so it the most valuable ring he can give her, show her and everybody else she his. Other folks say he like Miss Evangeline 'cause her mama give her daddy four boys before Miss Evangeline born, Miss Evangeline sure to give him some sons. She afraid, want to get some help quick, before he kill her. Cause there's another problem."

"You think I ain't heard? Word all round in the Treme 'bout her and her uncle Charles's boy, that Laurent Baptiste, one his grandma ole Miz Fontaine dote on. Everywhere he go, Miss Evangeline not far behind. Just cousins. He down here in the Treme playin' that music of his, Miss Evangeline an' her friends just happen to walk in, hear her cousin playin'. Ole Miz Fontaine make him a nice *garçonnière*, off by the river so he kin do what boys do, in private with a Creole girl, colored girl, no white girl! He there, here come Miss Evangeline to pay her grandma a visit. Sneakin' down to that *garçonnière* at night. Miss Evangeline," Mama spat again, "a damn fool. Laurent too. Don' they know nothin'? They's talk in the Treme already 'bout kissin' cousins. When white folks start talkin' 'bout it, trouble comin'. You seen niggers hangin' befo', girl? I has. Seen worsen' hangin's. You tellin' me Maurice Fitzroy got his eye fixed on her? That boy ain't got long to wait, gone disappear soon. They gon' find little pieces of him all over the bayou if the alligators ain't et it all. Her too maybe. But he too mean to kill her easy, he find some bad way to pay her back first for the shame she bring him."

The girl lowered her voice and looked at the ground. "She know. But it's real bad. She *enceinte*. And she scared to death."

"Don't care how scared she is, I won't get ridda no more babies! They come back, hauntin' in the night. Cryin' in the corners. Cain't get no peace."

"She ain't studyin' to get rid of it. Laurent Baptiste goin' to France. Just now they's a man from England visitin' the family, think Miss Evangeline looking mighty sweet, but he goin' home tomorrow. England a long way off from here. She got to act quick. She want a gris-gris make him to take her with him, get married on the ship. She say the captain can marry 'em."

"Unn-uhn! This a *mess*! Where Miss Evangeline at now?"

"At her aunt's. Big party. Her mama busy with the ball tonight."

"This here Englishman, he there too?"

"Yes, ma'am."

"His name?"

"Richard Fairfax."

Mama shook her head and muttered something and sighed. She sat for a minute, working her gums on the pipe, then got up and shuffled to a corner behind the altar. She fumbled in the gloom among her scraps and chicken feathers. She took up bits of this and that and mixed a concoction in a dirty jelly glass. She spat into it, poured it into a brown medicine bottle. "Whut you got the man touched? No good unless you got that."

Delphy took the gold baby Richard had given Evangeline from the handkerchief and handed it to Mama. "Been in his mouth," Delphy explained.

Mama crooned tunelessly to it for a minute, licked on her finger and touched its head. "Richard Fairfax," she said, dropped it into the mixture, and corked it up tight.

She held up the vial. The gold baby gleamed in the murky liquid. "This what she need. He got to drink it. It strong, but you put it in a julep—enough good whiskey and he can't taste it. For twelve hours after she can make him do anything she want. This gris-gris powerful, but you tell her, got to be quick, only work for a few hours." Mama pocketed the ring. She wouldn't sell it; she would make an offering to her mother's spirit.

When Delphy came back from Mama La Bas, Celeste's veranda was filled with lunch guests saying good-bye. Among the cars lined up at the curb the Fontaines' chauffeur paced impatiently by the car. "Miss Evangeline, yo' mama say it high time for you to git home and git ready, Delphy or no Delphy. You leave Delphy behind if you have to and come on home. Yo' mama got enough to worry her with this ball already."

"Just one more minute." Evangeline saw Delphy slip in at the servants' door. "Aunt Celeste, may I have a piece of your stationery?" Evangeline scribbled a hasty note to Laurent and spoke quickly to Delphy: she would dress without her help. She watched her maid slip out of the servants' entrance with the note and a worried expression.

There had been a rainstorm, but by seven the evening had cleared. As dusk fell flambeaux were lit and fireworks burst sparkling across the darkening sky. The colorful floats belonging to the krewes were lined up, and the city's prettiest and most prominent girls were gathering up long skirts and trains, climbing aboard, tripping up rickety wooden steps in satin slippers to their flower-decked "thrones."

A stray firework shot low across the front of the float and they shrieked. Then they smoothed their hair and fluffed their dresses, and the bolder girls pulled illicit compacts from tiny evening bags—"painting" was strictly forbidden by parents at home and the nuns at school—and furtively applied lipstick and powder. When they were all seated and arranged, members of their fathers' krewe handed up their bouquets, bonbons, beads, and gilded doubloons for them to toss to the crowd.

Evangeline Fontaine's coming-out ball was the last party before Lent, and it was going to be splendid. The girls were in a fever of excitement, whispering that Evangeline's father had hired a train to bring a famous dance orchestra down from New York, hundreds of live lobsters packed in ice, caviar, a chef from Delmonico's, and an entire hothouse worth of orchids. As they waited for the float to move, the girls fished tasseled dance cards from their evening bags and compared them, to see who had begged what dances with whom in advance. Between giggles and cries of "He said *what?*" "I knew he was sweet on you!" and groans of "But he *always* steps on my feet!" the girls cast sideways glances at Evangeline, who wasn't saying anything and didn't look at all happy.

The other debutantes stopped chattering to whisper about what was wrong with Miss High-and-Mighty. She had a real grown-up dress from a real Paris couturier, cloth-of-gold, beaded with tiny purple and green crystals that sparkled in the torchlight. It was low-cut too. The girls thought it was a wonder she had been allowed out of her house in anything so daring. "Lo and *be-hold!*" muttered one cattily.

Evangeline didn't need powder and lipstick: her cheeks were flushed just enough to highlight her perfect, creamy skin, and her dark eyes glittered in the torchlight. The other debutantes felt eclipsed and dull by comparison and muttered resentfully that everybody knew the Fontaines' business had lost a fortune in France and that Evangeline's father had been gambling heavily—how come she still got to wear the prettiest dress and have the biggest ball? On top of that, rumor had it that she was as good as engaged to Maurice Fitzroy and would be the first of them to get married. Evangeline was always first.

"Maybe she'll get to go to Paris for her honeymoon!" said one girl with a sigh.

"If she does she ought to stay there!" snapped another girl. "You wouldn't catch me stuck way out at Belle Triste with nothing but Maurice Fitzroy and the alligators for company."

Belle Triste, Maurice's two-hundred-year-old plantation, was named for a giant swamp oak heavily draped in hanging moss that guarded the gateway to the drive and looked like a woman in mourning veils. Long ago an early Fitzroy had died in a duel and a young Fitzroy widow had never shown her face in public again, but wore a mourning veil to her dying day. An air of gloom, or something, clung to the place.

"Sssh!"

"Well, I wouldn't," she went on. "They might be rich, but everybody knows there's something wrong with all the Fitzroys. They get sick or go funny in the head. Some people say it's a curse. Didn't Maurice's father have fits and nobody ever saw him because he had to be locked up in the cellar with a nurse? And what about his aunt who used to wander off into the bayou and one day never came back? They say a slave dropped her on her head when she was a baby—it was revenge because they'd cut her toes off."

"Mama agrees they're strange, but she says it came of marryin' cousins too many times 'cause nobody else was good enough."

"Hush! She'll hear!"

In a lower voice, "And they say Maurice goes wild sometimes, crazy even, he gets this sort of fixed look and turns real mean, that he killed two of his field hands in one of his rages."

"Well, they probably asked for it. My daddy says if the colored hands get out of line somebody has to teach them who's boss."

Evangeline clutched her seat as a firework burst over her head, and the krewe's band exploded into "When the Saints go Marching In." The float started with a lurch that made the girls shriek. As the float swayed above the masked crowds, she fought down the nausea that came in waves. The dress her father had insisted her mother order was too tight in the boned and beaded bodice. The couturier's fitter who brought it from Paris had adjusted it over and over again. She was sure that she had it right, yet Evangeline complained it was too tight, and she couldn't breathe. And tonight everything smelled so! The odor of hot dancing bodies, the cloying jasmine wet from an earlier rainstorm, gunpowder from the fireworks, beer, horse dung, sewers, the levee, all mingling with the greasy clouds rising above oil drums where oysters were frying for po' boy sandwiches. "Po' boy for sale, git yo' po' boy sandwich while they hot! Befo' the parade start!"

Around the float a sea of heads bobbed, merging masked and unmasked heads into a sinister hybrid. What a lot of Loup Garou masks this year, Evangeline thought dizzily. Every time she raised her eyes the lupine, part-human face of Loup Garou, the werewolf who lived in the bayou, leered up at her, torchlight reflecting off human eyes in the slits.

Someone knows...

A few feet away the whispering switched to a fresh scandal about one debutante's unmarried cousin, discovered to be "in the family way." During a pause in the music, Evangeline caught the words "her family...a paper...the judge signed it, it's official, she's crazy and degenerate," "kept under lock and key," and "baby taken away," "disowned," "never come back." Crying and pleading and begging to stay at home, the girl had been bundled into a car and taken away. Probably to the convent they had all heard of, in a distant country parish run by a strict order of Irish nuns who kept leather straps hanging next to their rosaries.

"And that's not all. Guess what our cook says someone told her," and then "Laurent Baptiste" and "They say he had a white girl! In his *garçonnière!*" "No! That can't be true! Who was it? Did they see who it was?"

There was a smothered snicker. "Now that's really crazy! He's colored...what kind of white trash girl would..." As they gossiped the girls tossed doubloons and sweets and strings of beads, waving gaily.

Someone knew.

It was easy to spot Richard Fairfax in the crowd. He seemed intoxicated—by the balmy night, the procession, the bands, the excited crowd...or the strong mint julep Delphy had given him before he set off for the parade.

"Richard!" Evangeline called now. She smiled radiantly as he turned, waved and tossed him a handful of doubloons. Richard caught one, kissed it, and swept her a bow.

"Don't forget our dance," he called.

"Well," said the girl on Evangeline's right, sourly, "you have another admirer. That English officer's certainly good looking. Doesn't Maurice get jealous?"

"Oh, you know," said Evangeline, the smile quickly replaced by her usual bored look, "I have to be nice. He's staying with Uncle Charles who invited him to Mardi Gras and to be an extra man at my ball. He's leaving soon." She prayed for the parade to end.

"Evangeline looks funny, like she's feelin' sick."

At the Fontaines' house the band had been told to play non-stop until the supper interval. Among the dancers and flirting couples Maurice was a brooding presence—withdrawn and drinking heavily, people noticed. Several were asking where Evangeline had gotten to. She had been dancing too much with that English fellow, and then disappeared. Now everybody was looking for her. Her mother was trying to extricate herself from a circle of old ladies all eager to talk to her about their own engagements and complain about "girls today."

"It's the excitement," Solange Fontaine said soothingly to Maurice, glancing over his shoulder for her daughter, drawing him into the circle of ladies so she could make her escape. "A girl doesn't get engaged every day." But she thought Evangeline was taking an inordinately long time to freshen up.

Maurice's eyes narrowed. "Excuse me," he said, "my overseer is signalling me from the door. Forgive the intrusion, Madame, evidently an important matter for him to disturb me in your house." He withdrew and left Solange stuck again with the old ladies.

In her own bathroom Evangeline straightened her clothes and pressed a cold cloth to her head. She had left Richard drowsily happy in a guest room, promising not to rejoin the party but to wait for her at the gate—the julep had worked and she was overwhelmed by the sense her life had veered out of control. She was going to have a colored baby, and she had just seduced another man. She would go to hell—and the Irish convent—unless the rest of her reckless plan worked. Now she had to slip down to the garden for a minute where her note had told Laurent to meet her, to tell him that she knew he was going to France and that she had found a way to join him. Then she had to get back to the ball and go through the charade of the announcement about her engagement. The band was playing away, but they would stop for supper any minute and her parents must be looking for her.

Evangeline opened her door and peered down the landing. No one was about. She gathered up her beaded skirt and crept down the back stairs to the basement. She groped for the handle of the garden door, opened it, and whispered Laurent's name. There was no answer, and she moved into the shadow of the house and peered into the darkness, where she could hear something at the end of the garden. Down by the swamp oak with the hanging moss, figures were moving. A white evening shirt gleamed in the darkness. There was a pause between dances, and over the hum of conversation indoors she heard the crack of a whip and a scream of pain. Behind her she could hear hurried footsteps in the basement, and the door slammed open.

Andre's breathless voice said, "Hurry, Philippe, God knows why, but Maurice is having one of his crazy fits and he's brought his hired men to horsewhip somebody."

"Of all nights," muttered Philippe, "why the hell…" She saw her brothers, in evening dress, running from the house toward the shadows and knew instinctively what had happened. She had to act or it would be too late.

In the dark Evangeline slipped back into the basement and felt about for the old shotgun the gardener kept for killing groundhogs and snakes. She reached into the ammunition box, willing her shaking hands steady so that she could load the gun. Outside someone was shouting and pleading then the crack of a whip and another shriek of pain. She ran out as fast as she could in the hampering dress and down the lawn. The agitated men didn't notice as she pushed aside the hanging moss curtain. Something bloody lay on the ground—no *someone*. He was bent in a strange position, obviously badly hurt. Laurent! Maurice was behaving like a madman, lashing the bullwhip across Philippe's shoulders as he bent to help his cousin. Philippe's evening jacket was slashed to ribbons by the force of the whip, and he staggered and fell.

Andre was trying to wrest himself free from two rough-looking men who had pinned his arms behind him. He shouted, "Have you gone crazy? Why the hell are you taking it out on Laurent? It was the Englishman Evangeline flirted with!"

"Here's her note," snarled Maurice, his face twisted with rage. "My overseer's been watching them for weeks, found it on Laurent's desk at the office this afternoon, real careless of him. At Belle Triste the Fitzroys gave slaves a good whipping if they stepped out of line, after that they got cut. I'll teach this one a lesson, cut him first, then hang him right here in your garden where your whoring sister can watch!" A knife blade flashed.

No one saw Evangeline beneath the hanging moss as she jammed the heavy shotgun hard into her shoulder, as Andre had taught her, swung the barrel at the white expanse of Maurice's shirtfront, and squeezed the trigger.

The old shotgun fired with a violent upward kick, recoiling into her face and bruising her shoulder. It felt like her nose exploded and something warm and wet ran over her mouth. Through a haze of pain she fired again, blindly. Maurice was on the ground now, making a horrible noise. Someone jerked the gun away from her.

Suddenly Solomon the butler appeared, taking charge. The two rough-looking men were gone. Evangeline saw Andre bending over Laurent, and Philippe wrapping a handkerchief over his own bleeding hand. Back in the house people gathered at the lighted windows, peering into the garden.

"What's happening out there? Y'all all right?"

"We've got to keep people away. Get that damn band playing," Philippe ordered thickly. "Solomon, you'll have to help me with Mr. Fitzroy. He's hurt bad."

No one saw Evangeline stoop and snatch a crumpled piece of paper from the ground.

Solomon mopped his brow, then stepped out from under the tree and called, "Y'all can go on back inside now, ladies and gentlemen. If I done told these chillun once I done told them a thousand times ain't no firecrackers allowed in Mist' Fontaine's garden. Like to blow somebody up lightin' them all at the same time. Crazy chillun! Y'all folks rest easy now, just chillun getting overexcited, the way they do at Mardi Gras. We pickin' up the rest of the firecrackers befo' somebody get hurt."

The band struck up, and most people moved away from the windows.

A few guests were still hovering curiously on the terrace and peering into the garden. "Maurice is a regular hero," Andre called, sounding nonchalant, "protecting those pickaninnies from the blast of the firecrackers!"

"Pickaninnies and firecrackers! I declare, niggers got no more sense'n monkeys."

"Andre, is that Evangeline out there? We can see her pretty dress in the dark. What's that girl up to now? Tell her her mama's looking for her."

"We'll do that."

Philippe was giving terse orders, panting hard. "Bandage Laurent up the best you can and get him down to our dock. We've got a ship sailing for Marseille tonight. Get him on it. He's in bad shape, unconscious, but thank God we got here before Maurice used the knife. What was that about Evangeline and a note?"

"I don't know, I always thought his Fitzroy craziness was waitin' to bust out," Andre said. "He's bleeding like anything." He looked up and took in the spectacle his sister made—dress torn, eyes wild, nose gushing blood. "What the hell are you doing here, Evangeline? What have you done! Oh, God!" He turned to Solomon. "Get her upstairs before anyone sees her and causes another scandal. Mama's going to have a fit."

Somebody dragged Evangeline up the back stairs. Delphy's voice said, "Miss Evangeline? I got a poultice for yo' face. Get it on befo' yo' mama see you. She on her way. Andre talkin' to her, 'splainin' this and 'splainin' that to her, drawin' it out so's we got time to git you outta this dress and cleaned up fore she git here."

Delphy worked fast, unclasping jewelry, snatching off stockings and dirty satin slippers, wrapping the blood-stained clothing in a sheet and hurrying off to dispose of it. Evangeline locked the door behind her. She flung open her closet, pushing aside frocks, ball gowns, tea dresses, and dancing slippers until she found her riding boots and a pair of old trousers and the dark jersey with holes in the elbows that she wore when she went fishing at her grandmother's. Delphy was back, hammering on the locked door. "Let me in!"

"Is he all right?"

"Who all right?"

"Laurent?"

"They carried him off real smart. He goin' to France tonight. He alive, just barely. Broken ribs, broken nose, bleedin' hard, but sound like he gon' live. Doctor with Mr. Maurice now. He rantin' and ravin', cain't move his arms or legs. Mist' Andre drug him in the study, empty the decanters all over the floor till everything smell like whiskey, like they drinkin' heavy before whatever was doin' with the fireworks and all. Yo' papa done collapsed in the dining room, yo' mama runnin' back and forth between him and the boys. Oh Lord, Miss Evangeline! Yo' plan, it ain't gon' work! Got the devil in it."

"Never mind the devil! It has to work. Tell the boys they have to keep Mama a little longer, let me get away."

"Miss Evangeline, Englishman got blue eyes, light hair. That baby born, he know where it come from. And they so many people downstairs, runnin' around crazy as chickens, and yo' fam'ly all comin' to see you. You can't get out the house! Ain't gon' work!"

"Hush, I said! I have to think a minute. Go get me some more ice. Just keep everybody away!"

Evangeline tucked her pants into her riding boots, snatched up a dark silk scarf to tie over her hair, turned off the bedroom lights, and opened the window. Andre and she used to scramble in and out of her room from the veranda roof as children, but tonight the ground looked far away and she felt dizzy. Her nose was badly swollen, it was hard to breathe, and she was sure her collarbone was broken. How would she manage? She gritted her teeth.

Downstairs the band stopped playing and Uncle Charles was making an announcement, asking everyone to please go at once. There was a buzz of shocked voices and people began to depart, their cars disappearing down the drive, until the only person left was the tall, fair-haired man waiting in the shadows by the gates, looking back up at the house. Evangeline saw a pinprick of light as he lit a cigarette and smoked it, then another.

Richard reminded himself that she had said best to wait till the house was closed up for the night. He watched

Solomon close the doors, but the sound of the bolt driven home filled him with despair. What if she couldn't get away? If she didn't come he would die. He was on fire with longing for her. She had promised to go if he would marry her, and he'd said they needn't wait for England, the captain could marry them once they were out to sea. Where was she? He thought anxiously of the tide. "We don't want them to have time to follow us," she had said. "Meet me at the gate."

Evangeline quelled another wave of dizziness, aware that she had little time left. Delphy couldn't keep her mother away much longer. There it was, another pinprick of light, another cigarette. Now or never. Summoning the last of her strength, Evangeline climbed out of the bedroom window onto the sloping roof. Mustn't look down. Remember, she told herself, you've done this many times. It's easy. Slowly she dragged herself to the end where a fig tree grew against the house. Thankfully it was bigger than it had been when she was a child. Nearly fainting from the pain in her right shoulder, she used her left arm to let herself down the tree. She dropped to the ground in the shadows, then skirted the drive, a shabby figure in worn clothes with a swollen face. Just before she reached the gates she turned and looked back to her home, with its ornate balconies and sweeping garden, only a few lights showing through the shutters, which were closed now. Then Richard grabbed her hand and they hurried to the river and his waiting ship.

Three hours later the captain performed a hasty marriage service on the bridge as the sun rose, wondering how on earth the girl had come by her blackening eye and swollen nose. He had never seen a shabbier girl or a happier groom. Then the ship began to roll up and down. The bride turned green and rushed to be sick over the rail.

3.

Crowmarsh Priors, East Sussex, October 1938

*A*s she unlatched the churchyard gate on Saturday afternoon, Alice Osbourne saw the handlebars of Nell Hawthorne's bicycle poking up from the weeds where she had propped it against the war memorial with its long list of the village's Glorious Dead and its Latin motto about happy are they who die defending their country. She was shocked by how high the weeds had grown and how unkempt the churchyard looked. Jimmy, the butcher's boy, was supposed to keep it tidy, but since the death of Alice's father, he hadn't bothered. Ivy had crept over the gravestones, while stinging nettles and brambles had taken hold at the back.

Alice felt fragile and insubstantial, as if she was recuperating from a long illness. Six months ago Richard had returned from America, and a stunned, appalled Penelope had rung her from London to break the news. "Darling, such terrible news, I hardly know how to tell you."

"Oh please, Lord, not Richard. Don't let anything have happened to Richard! His ship?"

Penelope's voice sank to a whisper. "No, Alice. He's... he's come back from the United States. He's, well, it's just... I'm so very sorry."

"You frightened me out of my wits. Thank God he's all right!"

"He's married."

"But...that's impossible."

"To an American." Penelope had sounded as if she were being strangled. "Alice, he's bringing her down to Crowmarsh Priors to live. Apparently the girl may be... expecting. Alice, I'm so sorry!"

"But...Penelope, Richard and I are engaged."

Engaged, she whispered as she quickly put the receiver down on Penelope's protests that the news was true. There must be some mistake. Alice had thought it was a cruel, wicked joke. And impossible.

She did not believe it until one afternoon, a week later, she had seen Richard's roadster pulled up in front of Penelope's house. He had jumped out to open the passenger door. Alice's heart was in her mouth as she saw him take the hand of a slender, dark-haired girl and help her out and up the front steps as if she were made of spun glass and might break. Then he swept her up in his arms and carried her over the threshold.

Alice soon learned that they had met in New Orleans, eloped, and been married at sea. Jimmy had told Mrs. Osbourne, who repeated it to Alice over tea in a long, querulous lament. "Mrs. Richard" had indeed come to live in Crowmarsh Priors for the time being. "It's all so shocking! How will Penelope Fairfax ever hold her head up again? I don't know what your father would have said!" she concluded as she always did. It took all Alice's self-control not to bite into her teacup, swallow the pieces, and choke to death on her own blood.

The next day Richard had called on Mrs. Osbourne and Alice at their cottage. Alice answered the door and the color drained from her face. Unable to listen to whatever he had to say she had turned on her heel, leaving him to her mother, and fled out of the kitchen door. She walked aimlessly until it was dark. Richard had left the village next morning, but his wife had stayed behind. Alice came face to face with her in the butcher's. She had dark hair and pale skin and would have been beautiful but for the faint puffiness around her nose. Something about her looked bruised. Like rotten fruit, thought Alice bitterly.

Since then Alice had gotten through the days somehow, going automatically about her daily routine at school, but when she got home her mother couldn't resist a tirade about Richard's behavior. Alice would run to her bedroom in tears. Now she was struggling to hang on to her dignity in public, painfully aware that the village knew she had been jilted for a sly baggage who dressed like a stable boy and spoke with an odd accent.

The future stretched bleakly before her.

Alice let herself into the vestry, breathing in the comforting, familiar smell of beeswax, old vestments, communion wine, polish, mice, and ancient incense. It was a glorious, breezy autumn afternoon and the downs beckoned, but Alice enjoyed having the vestry to herself once Nell had finished cleaning. She undid her tightly knotted head scarf, which made her head look oddly small, and ran her hands

through her hair. It stayed flat and lank, but Alice no longer cared what she looked like.

She put down a freshly ironed altar cloth and took her flowered pinny, with its limp ruffles, from its hook. She tied it on over the drab brown tweed skirt and a twinset her mother had discarded, spread out some newspaper, and took down the brass and silver polish from their shelf. Nell had set out the altar candlesticks and the collection plate, while the silver communion chalice and wafer plate were in their baize bag beside a box of fresh candles.

She shut her eyes, imagining her father putting the final touches to the next day's sermon, trying it out in the pulpit to be sure it lasted exactly twenty minutes, no more. Since his death Alice had continued to prepare the altar for Sunday because no one else in the village had offered to do it. In any case she had nothing better to do on Saturday afternoons. There was a new vicar now, Oliver Hammet, but he was unmarried. Alice sighed. Mr. Hammet meant well, but he was young and this was his first parish. It would have been better if an older man had been appointed. Village gossip had it that Lady Marchmont, who regarded Crowmarsh Priors as her personal fiefdom, had had "a quiet word" with the bishop about Mr. Hammet, who was her distant cousin. When she had been assured that he was "doctrinally sound, very sound" she had demanded that he be given the parish living. As usual she had had her way.

Alice unfolded the rags she had boiled at home and briskly rubbed polish on metal. The problem with Jimmy and the churchyard was the tip of the iceberg. The new vicar was a Cambridge man, as her father had been, but he was not a practical sort of person. He reminded Alice of a distracted owl, a tall, kindly one with glasses. He was wrestling inefficiently with his timetable—his pastoral duties, the parish council, the churchwardens, and the Mothers' Union. He delivered his sermons in a nervous rush, so they were either very short indeed or rambled off confusingly for far too long.

Alice had done her best to help without interfering. She had offered Mr. Hammet tactful but timely hints about the Mothers' Union, the Dorcas Society, and the Sunday school classes and had mentioned her father's twenty-minute sermon limit. He had thanked her profusely, seeming genuinely grateful for her help, but Alice's efforts hadn't made much impact on his chaotic habits. At the vicarage he lived in a muddle of misplaced objects—sermons scribbled on the backs of envelopes, his list of parish-council meetings forever missing. She and Nell had found a lost box of hymnbooks propping up the leaky cistern of the downstairs cloakroom; they were soaked.

After that, Nell had knocked on his study door and told him firmly that he would be wanting someone to keep the vicarage in order and she would see to it. In his mild way, Oliver Hammet had said, "Of course, quite, yes please, most grateful, really, Mrs. Hawthorne, quite happy, whatever you charge" and waved a despairing hand at his study.

Nell told Alice that she had never seen the like: it looked as if a tidal wave of books and papers, church pamphlets, schedules, and hymnals had struck. It overflowed the study and the parlor and was gradually creeping across the dining room into the kitchen. She was always unearthing biscuit tins, half-drunk cups of tea, clerical collars, apple cores, and odd socks. Mice had made a comfortable home in the pantry.

"The state of it!" she exclaimed now, clattering into the vestry with her bucket and rolling her eyes. "I gave it a good bottoming last week, everything dusted, polished, and tidy as you please, and in no time it's a heathen mess again. It wouldn't half give your mother the vapors. It's a blessing she can't see her old home. It's a wife he needs, and the sooner the better." She rinsed her bucket, shaking her head.

This was becoming a sore point with Alice. People in the village kept dropping broad hints about Oliver Hammet's bachelor state and hinting that perhaps she would soon be back at the vicarage, eh? It made her feel quite desperate. She could hardly follow Nell's example and tell him he needed a wife to keep him in order and she was the one for the job. Fortunately Mr. Hammet was absentminded at the best of times, and if he noticed his parishioners' matchmaking hints he gave no sign.

Nell stowed her bucket, mop, and cleaning basket in a cupboard, took off her apron, and hung it on a peg. "As for that garden, it wants weeding. You used to keep it so lovely." She left an opening for Alice to say that perhaps she could spare an hour or two. "Right under his study window, where he has to see it every time he looks up." Alice kept determinedly silent.

Mind you, thought Nell, it was no good getting Alice in the vicar's line of vision these days. She wondered if she dared suggest that the girl's hair could do with a good wash. Or something. It was peculiarly flat today. But Alice looked so dismal that Nell sensed friendly advice would only depress her more. "Here," Nell said instead, handing over a basket, "I've taken some of the windfalls. Your father always said if they were left to rot they'd attract wasps and anyone who wanted them was welcome to them, especially seeing as how your poor mother was never up to using them, not so much as making a bit of jelly. I don't think Mr. Hammet had noticed the apple tree before I mentioned it, but he said, 'Oh, of course, very good of you, Mrs. Hawthorne, please help yourself.' So I did."

"Thank you," said Alice warily, wishing Nell would go home.

Studiedly casual, Nell continued, "Loads this year, never seen so many, and this morning Albert says to me, he says, 'Why not take some to the Osbournes, Miss Alice has a fine way with pastry, always makes such tarts for the Harvest Home, her bein' such a practical young lady. Maybe she could make an extra tart for the young vicar, seein' as how he's got no one else to do it for him.'"

"Thank you, Nell, you're very kind but…"

"Mind, it's the way to their hearts, my girl. My Albert's a devil for pastry. All men are."

Alice gritted her teeth. She wished Nell and Albert and everyone else in the village would mind their own business. She had no more intention of taking apple tarts to the vicarage than she had of sprouting wings and flying over the downs.

"Cheerio then," Nell said and left Alice to her polishing.

Alice wondered how she could convince Nell she wasn't in the vestry to catch Oliver Hammet's eye. It was just so nice—after the bustle of the infants' school all week, then looking after Mummy and listening to her complaints, trying to keep her cheerful at home—to be on her own with the soothing tasks that reminded her of happier times.

The day was so warm that she flung open the window. The late-October sun slanted in from the west, across the fields and the downs beyond. A wasp buzzed somewhere. No children shoved and fought and cried "Miss! Miss!" for her attention, no querulous voice demanded a handkerchief, her comfits, lost glasses, lavender water, a cushion. There was no small, ugly house piled with boxes of Father's papers waiting to be put away. Alice shut her eyes and imagined that she and her father were about to set out for their Saturday walk.

In her mind's eye they had just reached the first stile when the heavy oak door to the church creaked open, then slammed, jolting Alice out of her reverie. Perhaps whoever it was wanted the vicar and would go away. Then her heart sank. She heard the thud of a cane, the unmistakably firm footsteps of authority. A moment later Lady Marchmont burst into the vestry holding a wilting green bundle. "Alice, my dear! Knew I'd find you here. I've brought the last of the Michaelmas daisies for the altar. You might as well put down that candlestick and find some vases at once. I told Gifford to wrap the stems in damp newspaper, but she hasn't the foggiest notion about flowers."

"How kind. They'll look lovely," said Alice, putting down the brass and dutifully producing two tall vases from a cupboard. She held them under the tap, then stuffed in the straggly stems.

"Take them round to your mother after evensong tomorrow. Cheer her up, I expect. No sense leaving them for the vicar to look at. Wouldn't know one end of a flower from another." Lady Marchmont lowered herself heavily into a chair. Oh dear. "And how *is* your poor mother today?"

Alice smiled thinly. "As well as can be expected, thank you."

"Humph! You're looking tired, my dear. All that teaching—children can be so fatiguing. And for what? Children should either be taught at home by a governess as I was or, if they're of the lower orders, be put to an apprenticeship to learn a useful trade. What they're expected to do with all this arithmetic and geography and whatnot when it's becoming impossible to engage a decent housemaid I do not pretend to know. Now, Alice, I've something serious to say to you."

Lady Marchmont leaned forward, both hands on her cane. Alice wondered what would happen if she leaped out of the window and ran—far from her mother and Lady Marchmont, the Hawthornes, the infants' school, the village matchmakers, apple tarts, everyone and everything. Instead, trapped, she cleared her throat and waited for the onslaught. Oh dear, oh dear. Lady Marchmont, please don't say anything at all. Please go away and let me have a little peace and quiet in the one place where I'm perfectly happy just doing what I'm doing. If I concentrate on missing Father I won't have to remember how it felt to be happy, when Richard kissed me, or how we stood with his arm round my shoulders looking out to sea, and him asking how soon we could be married when he returned.

She longed to scream at the top of her voice, "I don't want to remember that Richard married someone else!" Instead she snatched up the gleaming wafer plate, which she had just finished, and pushed a polish-soaked cloth hard against it. Round and round. Harder and harder.

Lady Marchmont didn't notice. "I'll come straight to the point. I very much admire the way you've behaved over this wretched business. You've behaved admirably. *Admirably!* Who could have believed it of Richard! To marry that hussy! No better than she should be, I daresay, being American. And Roman Catholic, Penelope tells me—far worse. But what's done is done. Water under the bridge! Alice, you will marry someone else and be perfectly happy. You'll make an excellent wife for someone, and you simply must buck up and stop moping.

"Your mother, of course, has her health to worry about, and perhaps she's not entirely able to deal with things, but one always feels an interest in a deserving young gel. So I have a piece of news that will interest you. Young Hugo de Balfort is back at the Hall from his travels at last—for good, so Mrs. Gifford tells me, and she had it from the butcher's boy who…well, never mind. Poor Leander de Balfort's health is failing, you know, has been for some time. Naturally he wants his son at home to see to things before they fall into rack and ruin. Anyway, the boy will inherit a handsome property, a shambles now, of course, but nothing that can't be put right provided he does his duty and marries money. Entailed, of course, and as he's the last of the de Balforts, he'll need to marry soon and provide an heir."

"Quite," murmured Alice, vastly relieved there was no question of her penniless self featuring in any matchmaking scheme Lady Marchmont had for Hugo de Balfort, who, in any case, she barely knew.

"The boy should have buckled down immediately after university, getting the place back on its feet, but Leander had old-fashioned notions about the Grand Tour, insisted that in his day, no gentleman could call himself educated unless he'd done it. De Balfort tradition, he said. Humph! If you ask me it was the foreign ideas he picked up on his own Grand Tour that convinced Leander he could improve Gracecourt with cockeyed schemes—Chinese pagodas and such nonsense. Poor Venetia saw her fortune evaporate with his extravagance. Continentals think one must always be improving things to make them pretty, they've no sense of solid English."

Alice murmured something that sounded like agreement and stopped listening altogether. Lady Marchmont was off on one of her tirades about foreigners. Alice decided that when she finished at the vestry she would walk to the de Balforts' home farm for a small pot of cream to go with the scones she had planned for her mother's teatime treat.

Lady Marchmont had hardly paused for breath. "Naturally I did warn him…but to get back to the point, some young friends of Hugo's are staying, down from London for the shooting, though one can't imagine there's much shooting left—the gamekeeper must be nearly eighty. A few pheasants hanging on, I daresay. There's to be a luncheon party next Saturday, after the morning shoot. Naturally one is invited. Since Leander is such an old friend, I said I should like to bring a young companion—so much easier at my time of life—and he of course remembered your father and they will be delighted to see you…"

Alice was horrified. She could think of nothing more humiliating in her present situation as a jilted fiancée than the prospect of being dangled in front of Hugo de Balfort's friends like bait on a fishing line. "You are *too* kind, Lady Marchmont, but I really don't think—"

"Nonsense! They're several girls short."

"But Mummy will—"

"Mrs. Gifford will stay with your mother and see she doesn't need anything. So that's settled."

"But I hardly know Hugo de Balfort, and anyway, they're rather a smart set at the Hall, all cocktails and tennis and fast motors, Lord this and Count that and some Italian artist, not to mention that German singer. I should be absolutely terrified!"

Lady Marchmont waved a hand dismissively. "One need never mind foreigners, my dear. And the clergy are considered as quite the equal of the landed gentry, and your dear father was on friendly terms with Leander; he could hardly avoid knowing the de Balforts because the church is on their land and they were his parishioners, so he wouldn't disapprove of his daughter having lunch at the Hall. A gel will never get married if she doesn't meet any suitable men."

"Still, I would *much* rather not."

"Stuff and nonsense," puffed Lady Marchmont, rising imperiously to her feet. "Your father would insist on your going if he were here. And so do I. Gels need to be out and about, seeing other young people, meeting young men, not moping about in the gloom or running themselves off their feet at their mothers' beck and call. I intend to call for you in the motor at a quarter to one next Saturday."

"But I've nothing to wear," Alice wailed, nearly in tears of frustration and anger.

"And," Lady Marchmont continued, ignoring the look on Alice's face to turn a critical eye on her dull skirt and jumper under the pinny, "for goodness sake put on something blue. It suits your eyes. And perhaps you ought to rinse your hair with vinegar. It does wonders for light brown hair like yours, that one hardly notices otherwise. Just wash it, even. It seems to have gone rather...flat. And one more word of advice, Alice. Remember to stand up straight, my dear. You tall girls forget the importance of posture. *Posture, Alice! Posture!*" She patted Alice firmly on the back for emphasis. "Good day to you, my dear. I'll see myself out."

The vestry door slammed. The daisies drooped dispiritedly over the necks of the vases. In the silence Alice picked up the brass candlestick she had been polishing earlier. The polish had dried to a film. "Bother and damnation!" She stamped her foot. "Hell! Oh *bloody* bother! Bloody hell!" She rubbed the candlestick furiously. Her elbow hit the basket of windfalls and knocked it off the shelf. A cascade of overripe apples hit the floor, to roll and bounce squashily at her feet.

It was the last straw.

Alice bent down, picked one up, and hurled it through the open window as hard and as far as she could. "Damn Lady Marchmont!" she cried. She picked up another and flung it after the first. "Bother bloody Hugo de Balfort!" The rest followed. "Bother his friends! *Bother* Nell Hawthorne and her apple tarts! Pastry be damned! Bloody bloody bloody bother!"

As the last apple flew outside Alice burst into tears. "Damn New Orleans, damn Richard, damn his new wife, bloody damn everything to hell!"

4.

Austria, November 1938

With her long legs tucked under her skirt and a little girl snuggled on either side, sixteen-year-old Antoinette Joseph settled back in the cushions of her bedroom window seat, opened a worn but beautifully illustrated *Fairytales of the Brothers Grimm,* and began to read aloud to her younger sisters. The book had belonged to their mother when she was a child. She put one arm around four-year-old Klara, the other around Klara's twin, Lili. Tanni, as the family called Antoinette, had read "The Sleeping Beauty" to the twins so many times she could have recited it by heart. She let Klara turn the pages for the pictures.

The autumn sun streaming through the window was warm on their backs, and as the princess "fell into a deep, deep sleep," Lili dozed off, sucking her thumb. Tanni put her finger to her lips, winked conspiratorially at Klara, then shifted Lili until the child's head lay more comfortably in her lap. Klara tightened her arm round Tanni's waist and her eyelids drooped too. They often dozed during the day, because none of the three slept properly at night.

Tanni often lay awake with her goose-down quilt pulled up to her chin, listening to her father pacing in his disordered library on the floor below. If she heard her mother sobbing from her parents' bedroom down the hall, she put a pillow over her ears. She always took it off again, because in the room next to hers, Klara had nightmares and Lili had begun to wet her bed. When they cried out Tanni would get up, wake Klara or change Lili's sheets before they could disturb their mother. Then she took them back to her own bed, where she reassured them they were safe at home, safe with Tanni, and hummed lullabies until they slept again. Then she would lie awake, thinking.

Her father was anxious and preoccupied these days. He never played with the twins the way he once had done with Tanni. They never had any fun. Tanni thought wistfully of visits to the cinema or the zoo, or strolls with her parents along the river promenade where an orchestra played in good weather, followed by a visit to the *konditorei*, a magical place of gold mirrors, marble-topped tables, case after case of glistening cakes, and cream-topped ices in tall glasses. The twins had never been inside. The *konditorei* had been the first place in the town to post a "Jews not welcome" sign in the window. Now these signs were up on all the shops and restaurants, and at the cinema and the zoo. *Judenrein.*

Lili and Klara did not understand what being Jewish had to do with ices, walking in the park, or looking at animals. "But *why* can't we go?" they would wail. Tanni didn't understand the why of it either, but the town's hostility was palpable. Not only did it keep them away from all the nice things in town, it now oozed like an evil smell under the solid front door of the Josephs' house, once a happy home, beneath the windows, and over the garden wall.

Her father's wealthy patients no longer came to his surgery, and the few people who still sought treatment did so furtively because they could not pay. Dr. Joseph's consulting room was in upheaval, the heavy curtains down, the shelves empty, his precious collection of instruments and medical texts tossed anyhow. Throughout the house packing cases stood open, partly filled, waiting for china, books, and paintings that had been taken down and leaned against the walls. The Persian carpets were rolled up and tied with stout twine. Dr. Joseph's chess set was scattered. The heavy silver on the dining room sideboard had grown dark with tarnish, and dust balls gathered in the corners. The two maids had left, taking Frau Joseph's pearls, her scent, and a gold bracelet. Her father had refused to call the police, even though the jewelry had been part of his own mother's trousseau.

Tanni's mother no longer sang or played the piano. Neither was she "at home" to her friends on Thursdays. She no longer had her hair washed and dressed each week at the salon. Now she was short-tempered and anxious, her hair dull and straggly, and her pretty Viennese frocks hung unworn on their padded hangers. Lace-trimmed boudoir robes had been crammed into drawers, out of the way, and the once tidy rows of shoes handmade to Frau Joseph's own last were jumbled. Their owner dressed hastily each morning, in old skirts and frayed blouses, and sometimes, Tanni was astonished to notice, her stockings were laddered.

"It is best not to call attention to oneself by dress," her mother whispered apologetically, putting on her oldest hat and taking up the shopping basket. A morning trip to the market was the beginning of Frau Joseph's new daily regime. She and her housekeeper, Frau Anna, who had nursed Frau Joseph as a baby, then Tanni and her sisters, now shared all the work of the housekeeping, cooking, and laundry. Frau Anna was elderly and growing stiff in her joints, so Frau Joseph tried to spare her the hardest tasks.

With her mother so busy, it fell to Tanni to care for her little sisters. Her father called her their "little mother." Sometimes when he did so he even smiled as he used to. Her father, Tanni realized one day, had a great deal of gray in his hair now.

Klara, the clever twin, opened her eyes. "What does *Kindertransport* mean, Tanni? Mutti and Papa whisper it to each other all the time so it must be important, but when I ask, Papa tells me to run along."

"*Kindertransport*," echoed Lili, waking too and sleepily looking up at Tanni. Lili echoed everything Klara said. She adored her twin almost as much as she adored Tanni. Lili had been born second, Dr. Joseph had explained to Tanni, and that meant they had to take special care of her because she was not as quick or as clever as Klara. And indeed, where Klara's eyes were bright and lively, Lili's were placid and guileless.

Tanni was wondering how to answer Klara and wishing she could curl up and have a good long sleep herself, then wake to find everything normal once more, when all three girls heard a commotion downstairs in the hall and an alarming wail from their mother. "No! Dearest Frau Anna, don't leave us! What shall we do without you?"

The girls scrambled off the window seat and flew to the landing where they peered over the banisters at the crisis below, unable to believe their ears. Despite their parents' protests, Frau Anna was insisting she must leave. Frau Anna, who had been with the family since her own husband was invalided while fighting in 1917, who looked after them, made wonderful dumplings, and baked tortes on their birthdays, and who, observing the rabbi's handsome son Anton slip Tanni a small, beautifully bound volume of poetry, had winked as Tanni blushed.

Frau Anna leaving them?

"My husband says an Austrian mustn't work for a Jewish family," she sobbed.

"At least you must take a half year's wages. It's all we have at the moment, and I'm sorry it's not more," Tanni's father urged. "Money is worth less and less every day; buy what you can quickly." Tanni knew Frau Anna and her husband had become very poor. There were so many poor people.

Wiping her eyes, Frau Anna finally took the money, kissed them all, and left.

"It will pass," Tanni's father said to her mother, patting her shoulder as she too wept disconsolately. "It is only temporary, darling. We are all Austrians and our town is too far out of the way for the troublemakers to take much notice of it. Only a few rabble-rousers have disturbed us. Things are worse elsewhere. What, after all, are a few baubles and a housekeeper? We will sit tight, and in the end Chancellor Hitler will call them to order. Then, you'll see, we shall go on as happily as before."

That did not calm Frau Joseph. She and her husband began one of their urgent whispered discussions, their not-quite arguments. Tanni listened intently and heard "*Kindertransport!* You must! At once!"

Frau Anna's departure was the worst of all the horrible things that had befallen them. Tanni left the little girls and fled to her refuge, climbing up in the fig tree to cry alone.

A few minutes later she heard them calling. "Tanni? Tanni, where did you go?"

Perched high in the fig tree, long legs drawn up till her knees were folded under her chin, Tanni hugged herself tight, brooding, biting her nails, and trying not to cry again. Just now she didn't want to be found. Through the last of the leaves she watched Lili and Klara bobbing here and there as they ran about looking for her. Lili's little plaits that Tanni had done that morning were coming undone as she trailed through the overgrown shrubs behind her sister.

"Tanni, stop hiding, play with us. Push us in the swing. Please, Tanni," called Klara.

"Swing," echoed Lili. "Want to swing."

But Tanni was too bewildered and out of sorts to play or be anyone's "little mother" at the moment. She needed someone to talk to, a friend. Her mother had her father and the twins had each other. She had no one. She gave in to a few bitter tears of self-pity, then told herself not to be silly and dried her eyes.

From her treetop hiding place she could see over the high garden wall, with its stout locked door, to the river rushing below and the old stone walls of the town on the opposite bank, its church towers and domes shining golden in the late-autumn sunshine. From here the world looked as it always had. She felt calmer. She was a princess, like the one in the fairytales, surveying her kingdom from the castle tower. Waiting for her prince? Anton? She smiled.

Below her a window opened in the house. "Tanni, please come to the sewing room for a moment," her mother called in the direction of the fig tree.

Tanni wanted to stay where she was and feel peaceful a little longer, but she climbed down the tree and went, dragging her feet along the way.

Frau Joseph and Frau Zayman, the dressmaker, had been closeted in the sewing room for days, working furiously. From time to time the three girls had been summoned and measurements taken, garments basted or tucked. Tanni squirmed as she stood in her shabby old petticoat, which was far too small for her now and increasingly tight across the bosom. Something about the atmosphere in the sewing room stopped her asking for a new one.

"Only sixteen and so tall already," sighed Frau Zayman, increasing the measurement for Tanni's hemline. "It seems like yesterday I made your first school pinafores."

"But I am old enough for the gymnasium, Frau Zayman. It's Klara and Lili who need school pinafores, except they don't go to school any more than I do. I am nearly grown up. Can't you make the hem a bit longer? At my age dresses ought to be longer than a schoolgirl's." To her surprise Frau Zayman nodded and stretched the tape farther. Tanni noticed Frau Zayman's eyes were red-rimmed as if she too had been crying over Frau Anna's departure. Tanni twisted around to see if the tape measure was far enough down her calf.

"Hold still, Tanni," snapped her mother, running a pin into her hand.

School was a sore subject. Jewish children were not allowed in Austrian schools any longer, so their worried parents kept most at home. With no one but Lili and Klara to play with, Tanni moped forlornly around the house, missing her friends, her music lessons, and even geography, which she used to hate. Her schoolbooks and tennis racket lay on her desk and her satchel gathered dust in the corner. Her father had told her sternly to study by herself but was too distracted to notice that she did not. Instead, when she wasn't playing with Lili and Klara, Tanni would lose herself in the book of poems Anton had brought her and dream of love...and Anton's handsome face.

Now, while Frau Zayman fussed with the tape measure, Tanni's spirits fell further. What was the point of having a new dress? They never went anywhere, and Anton, now excluded from the university, rarely left his house. He would never see her in it. Worst of all, Tanni was not allowed to attend the annual *Kinderball*, which was held in mid-December. Her mother sighed. The *Kinderball* had been a sore subject in the Josephs' home. The young people's dancing classes were one of the few activities not specifically closed to Jewish children, probably because the mayor's sister made her living by teaching ballroom dancing and deportment. She knew Tanni longed to go, but she had stopped Tanni attending the dancing classes months ago when she decided there had been too many ugly incidents for her daughter to go out.

Frau Zayman continued measuring. "Such a little waist the girl has. You should eat more, Tanni."

Tanni's mother muttered something about how difficult it was to buy food, and Frau Zayman flushed. For the first time Tanni noticed how thin Frau Zayman looked. She had once been so plump and sturdy, like her son, Bruno. "You've made new winter clothes for Lili and Klara. Such pretty little coats with brass buttons! But what are you making for me with all this measuring?" Tanni tried to take an interest, forcing back the tears that never seemed far away. "And why are those carpetbags on the floor? I thought they were kept in the attic."

"Curiosity killed the cat," said her mother.

"Then what color? Can't I at least see the material for my own dress, Mutti? Please don't make it pink like the last one. Pink with ribbons is for babies, for Klara and Lili. They're only four, and they look adorable in pink, like little bonbons. What I would like is…"

"What?" said Frau Zayman, holding the tape around her bust.

Tanni thought about the sort of clothes a girl might wear to be fallen in love with, by an older boy like Anton who had been at university in Vienna. He must have seen many elegant ladies there. Before the cinema had closed to Jews, Tanni had seen a film where a glamorous American actress danced and danced into happily-ever-after with a dapper hero in evening dress and a white scarf. She knew exactly what she wanted!

Eagerly she told Frau Zayman, "Something gorgeous and grown up and long, in dark blue velvet and silver, perhaps with feathers at the neck, and a little train. High-heeled slippers. A little silk bag for my lipstick and cigarettes. Naturally I would have a jeweled cigarette holder, that I would hold just so." She tossed her head and her mane of naturally curly hair bounced, then struck a pose copied from the film; her eyes rose soulfully, she held aloft an imaginary cigarette holder and sashayed across the sewing room, puffing her imaginary cigarette and blowing imaginary smoke into the air. "The mysterious but charming Miss Joseph, the toast of Vienna, all the young men are dying of love and fighting duels over her." Tanni kicked her imaginary train the way the American actress had, looked back over her shoulder, and fluttered her eyelashes. Her mother laughed and nearly swallowed a pin.

Tanni stopped prancing. She pined for the dancing classes she could no longer attend and especially for their annual cotillion called the *Kinderball*. She adored dancing, and Anton had almost always chosen her as a partner because they were both tall for their ages. He danced wonderfully well. He said all the men in his family did, but that those who were very Orthodox danced only with other men at weddings and on religious holidays—they thought it was sinful to dance with a woman. His father's side of the family had abandoned such old-fashioned notions. They, like the Josephs, were modern Austrians.

Tanni had imagined herself at this year's *Kinderball*— hair up and flowers on her wrist, looking her best—waltzing round and round in her first proper ball dress in Anton's arms. He had promised to attend even though he was really too old. In her dream they whirled, never missing a step, until everyone else at the ball stood back to applaud them. Then Anton spun her outside under the stars and asked her to marry him.

She hadn't seen him in ages, because except for her father, the family never left the house or its high-walled garden at the back except on High Holy Days when they hurried to services at the synagogue down the street. Even then they went quickly. Their neighbors would mutter *"Juden"* and spit at them as they passed.

The atmosphere in the sewing room, which had lightened briefly, settled heavily again. It was impossible to know what to say to the grown-ups. Everyone was so moody and on edge. "Have you had a letter from Bruno lately?" Tanni asked Frau Zayman. "What interesting things has he done in London? Has he seen the king and queen and the princesses driving about? Or the museum of wax people? Do tell us."

It was a conversational gambit that usually worked. Frau Zayman could talk for hours about her adored Bruno and the news in his latest letter from England. Bruno was a plump, solemn boy ten years older than Tanni and much shorter. He was terribly clever, and Frau Zayman, widowed when Bruno was small, had scrimped and saved to send him to England to study. Tanni knew that her mother ordered new dresses they didn't really need to help Frau Zayman with Bruno's expenses and her father purposely ripped linings in his coats or tore his pockets so she could mend them.

Frau Zayman said proudly that the latest news was that Bruno had been offered a teaching post at Oxford, a prestigious award to an outstanding foreign scholar. Then uncharacteristically she fell silent. Tanni intercepted a meaningful look between her mother and the seamstress. Now what had she said that was wrong?

Tanni tried again. "Someday I want to go to London like Bruno," she announced brightly. "I shall see the zoo and the crown jewels and the soldiers riding their horses outside Buckingham Palace. Bruno says there are splendid museums full of beautiful and interesting things, and that afterward, one can take tea at Fornum and Mason—" Why was her mother's best lace tablecloth cut in pieces on the sewing table? "Can I help with the sewing, Mutti? Frau Zayman showed me how to make the tiniest stitches you ever saw, and I would be so careful you'd be amazed..."

"I think," interrupted her mother, stitching part of the tablecloth onto a length of white material in her lap, "we may see Bruno today. Be waiting ready to open the garden door to him quickly when he comes, Tanni." Usually the girls were forbidden to let anyone in. From the garden door, steps led down to the river and a small landing for fishermen's boats. Once they had brought fish to sell to the cook, but now no one called to sell fish to the Jews. Was Bruno coming by boat? Why not by train as he normally did?

Her father rapped at the door. "The rabbi is here with the contract," he said as he opened the door. "Really, my dear, that is nonsense!" he exclaimed, exasperated, seeing what his wife was doing.

"One moment, Herr Doktor!" Hastily Frau Zayman pulled Tanni's old dress back over her head and fastened the buttons at the back quickly.

"Leave us for a moment, Tanni," said her father.

Her mother shook out the voluminous white thing she was sewing, then continued to stitch faster than ever. "It's important; men don't understand," she insisted.

Tanni intervened: this was no time for her parents to quarrel. "I know, I'm to open the garden door for Bruno, but why is he coming, Papa, when he has a new teaching post in England? When everything here is so—"

"He has come back to tell us about it. And now I must speak to your mother and Frau Zayman, Tanni. Run along and—"

"But you already know about it! Why should he come back and tell you?"

"Go," ordered her mother sharply, head bent, sewing furiously. "Your sisters are calling you."

"But I want to stay and help sew whatever is so important—"

"Go!" said the Josephs simultaneously.

Tanni stamped her foot and flounced out. Before the twins saw her she retreated to the fig tree. Nothing made sense. Tears rolled down her cheeks again. After a while she realized she was hungry. She picked one of the figs that still clung to the tree and ate it, although it was a bit withered. She found a better one for Bruno, who liked figs. Below, wasps buzzed over the fruit that was split and rotting on the ground because no one had made jam this year.

The sun was setting, and the high branches where Tanni perched caught the last of its warmth. A breeze rattled the dry leaves. Tanni could smell wood smoke on the chilly air. The late-afternoon shadows lengthened. Once the maids would have lit all the fires at twilight, as delicious smells of supper filled the house. Her mother would have bathed, put on a velvet tea gown, and waited in front of the fire for Dr. Joseph to come in from his surgery. When he had kissed them both he would join her mother in an aperitif before

Frau Anna served the soup and cutlets. After supper Tanni and her father had played chess while her mother practiced a new piece on the piano or read a novel ordered from Vienna.

There was a sharp knock, then a loud pounding that shook the garden door and interrupted her reverie. Tanni started, then began to climb down to open it. The door was overgrown with morning glory and brambles and it took a moment to push them aside. By now the banging was louder and more frantic.

She tugged. "Just a *minute*, Bruno! Don't be so impatient. The door is stuck. There!"

Expecting Bruno, she was startled to find an elderly man with stubble, one of her father's patients, who gasped for breath and spat as he talked. "Hurry," he wheezed, spittle flying. "Soldiers are coming! They say they're setting fire to synagogues and the Jewish shops, looting and breaking windows—shooting even! You must get your father! They talk of driving the Jewish devils out…they are beating some to death."

A breathless Bruno appeared just behind the old man, his spectacles crooked.

"Tanni, it was not supposed to happen till next week, but we must hurry. You know we are going to be—"

But a shocked Tanni had no time for Bruno now. Who was calling them "devils"? Had the old man gone mad? Had the whole world gone mad as well as the Joseph household? Tanni stood staring and motionless, holding Bruno's fig.

"Go," shouted the man and gave her a hard shove. "Run! Run! Tell your father!" His face twisted with fear. Across the river came the unmistakable sound of gunfire. "They are coming! Soldiers!" he howled.

Terrified, Tanni dropped the fig and ran.

She burst into the sewing room where the rabbi was roll-ing something up as her parents and Frau Zayman watched. She had no idea why the rabbi should be in the sewing room. "Papa, there is a crazy old patient of yours who arrived with Bruno, he's raving about Jewish devils," she panted. "You'd better come. And Bruno is here, but even he isn't making sense."

Dr. Joseph and the rabbi hurried out. Tanni's mother and Frau Zayman undid the buttons at the back of her dress again, pulled it off, and slipped another over her head. Tanni's head whirled. Did they think of nothing but fit-tings? Her mother and Frau Zayman tugged and fastened, ignoring Tanni's protests. Exasperated, confused, and frightened, she stamped her foot again and hit at the folds of fabric crying, "Why are you bothering with dresses at a time like this? What is happening?"

"Keep still. This is your wedding dress," her mother said.

"WHAT?"

Something was draped and pinned on her head, blur-ring her vision. Lace. The tablecloth. "Hurry!" her mother and Frau Zayman urged, turning her round, tugging at but-tons. Tanni was blinded by lace and confusion.

"Hurry," said Frau Zayman.

"At once!" thundered her father beyond the door.

"Mutti?" Everything was a blur. They were pulling her along.

"Bruno may take his wife to England," Tanni's mother said in her ear as they went. "Listen to me, this way you will be safe. You are too old for the *Kindertransport*."

Tanni heard Lili's voice asking loudly why was Tanni dressed like that, was she a princess?

"Like a ghost," interjected Klara, "with the tablecloth over her face!"

"A bride, darlings," someone said. "Tanni is a bride."

They told her to stand still, just here, among the packing boxes in her father's study. Beneath the haze of her veil Tanni looked up. She was standing under a sort of wedding canopy contrived from a velvet curtain. Where had it come from?

Frau Zayman asked where the two witnesses were. "There," said the rabbi, pointing to the old man and Anton, whom he had brought along for the purpose. Anton was staring at her in anguish and Tanni wanted to bolt to her perch in the fig tree to stop this happening, but beneath the wedding canopy she was hemmed in by Bruno and Frau Zayman on one side, and her parents on the other.

Lili and Klara were each holding a hand, staring up at her. "What's a bride?" demanded Klara. "I want to be a bride! Can I be a bride too, Tanni?"

"Someday you can," said Tanni, responding automatically from habit.

"Bride," said Lili and smiled adoringly at her sister. "Tanni looks pretty."

"Walk round Bruno seven times, *quickly*!" Frau Joseph ordered. Numbly, Tanni obeyed, her head turning to gaze in despair at Anton from beneath her veil. They could hear shouting in the street, coming closer. In Dr. Joseph's study candles flickered and the rabbi muttered rapidly. They lifted the veil off Tanni's face. Something wrapped in a napkin was thrust under Bruno's foot and Tanni heard glass break. Anton uttered a choking sound. The twins squealed.

"Ssssh," said Tanni automatically, the little mother.

"*Mazel tov!*" cried her mother and Frau Zayman in unison, voices faltering. Other glass shattered in the street while the shouting and the sound of heavy boots grew louder.

"We must go. We must try to protect the synagogue!" said the rabbi over Tanni's father's protests. "Hurry!"

He and Anton ran out of the house, and Tanni's father bolted the front door behind them—but not before Tanni glimpsed a mob followed by uniformed soldiers rounding the corner shouting, "Jews *out!*"

"Hurry," urged her father again and shepherded his family to the back of the house.

But Tanni pulled away and ran back to the window. "Anton!" she screamed. "Oh, Papa, the soldiers caught the rabbi and Anton! Please…what is happening?"

Her father grabbed her and dragged her toward the garden door. When they reached it her mother snatched her from him. "My beloved child," said her mother, hugging Tanni hard. Then she kissed her and bent to prize Klara and Lili away from Tanni's knees. "Darlings, be brave and do as I say."

"Be a good wife. Be safe." Frau Zayman's eyes were huge and frightened in her white face. The crowd began howling outside as more glass broke, more shots were fired.

Tanni's mother thrust the carpetbag Tanni had seen on the sewing room floor into her hands. "Your trousseau. We prepared some things—a bride must always have a few things, we thought there was more time. Go safely to England and be ready to look after your sisters when they come."

"Tanni and Bruno must leave while they can! Go!" Dr. Joseph shoved Tanni toward the garden door. Behind him her mother called, "We will see you in England as soon as—"

"Papa, let Lili and Klara come with me now!"

"No room in the boat," hissed the old man. "Come!"

Her father was dragging the garden door open. "Child, they will be with you soon, God willing. They have papers for a children's train, the *Kindertransport*. It will be better if you are there first, ready to look after them. Promise to take care of them whatever happens. Give me your word, Tanni!" Tanni nodded mutely. "Now go!" ordered Dr Joseph, pushing Tanni and Bruno hard through the garden door. Somewhere nearby an ominous crackling grew louder. Clouds of smoke billowed overhead. There was gunfire, and more glass shattered. A cheer went up. *"Juden raus! Alle Juden raus!"* A woman's scream rose above everything. Above the noise there was a sound of someone pounding on the Josephs' front door.

As Dr. Joseph shoved Bruno after her, Tanni looked back. Her mother was huddled over the twins, gazing toward the front door. Tanni heard more glass smashing. Frau Zayman waved her handkerchief helplessly. "Tanni, Tanni, don't leave us. I'm scared," Klara wept. Lili blew kisses with both hands.

Tanni was frantic. "I can't leave them!"

"Go!" her father roared above the noise and gave his eldest daughter a last hard push. "The mayor promised to protect us—I attend to his crippled son. Go!"

"I promise, Papa," Tanni cried, but the heavy garden door had already slammed, and the old-fashioned iron lock clunked into place. Immediately afterward there was a splash from below as the heavy key landed in the river. With the old man shouting at them to hurry, she and Bruno stumbled down the dark path on the riverbank, acrid smoke choking them.

A small boat was waiting, already untied by the anxious old man. It rocked wildly as Tanni tripped and fell over the seat, banging her shin. There was water in the bottom of the boat, and the skirt of her wedding dress was soaked. As the boat slipped away from the shore she began to shiver and clutched the carpetbag to her as Bruno and the fisherman rowed. Above them orange flames roared into the sky. There was a crash as the roof of the synagogue collapsed.

Panting, Bruno and the old man pulled hard on the oars, and the boat moved slowly away from the bank. Then it caught the river current and went faster. Behind them the town walls, the flames, chanting, and gunfire grew fainter. Soon there was just the night, the dark river, and the red sky, the sound of the oars slapping the water, and the cold. Tanni's wet feet were numb. What was happening to her family? She wanted to throw herself over the side and swim back.

When Bruno looked up he saw that her teeth were chattering and that she was hugging her flimsy veil round her shoulders. At once he rested his oar and made his way to where she was crouched. He took off his coat, draped it round her shoulders, and kissed her brow. Tanni looked at him blankly. Bruno was her husband.

5.

Crowmarsh Priors, March 1939

*A*s he waited for the afternoon train from London to Brighton, the Crowmarsh Priors stationmaster, Albert Hawthorne, sat at the desk in the tiny office and picked up yesterday's papers. He skipped the stories about Slovak separatism in Czechoslovakia, "Cabinet Optimistic over Relations with Berlin," and someone named Goering holidaying in the Riviera. Someone or something called the Baldwin Fund wanted to "get them out." Jews, it looked like. Foreigners, anyway. He skipped that too.

He paused loyally to read the caption beneath the picture of the king and queen in the royal box at the opera house with the French president and his wife. Albert didn't hold with the French. The king looked strained and unhappy— all the responsibility of being a king, Albert guessed—but by his side the plump little queen was beaming beneath her tiara and had one gloved hand raised cheerfully in a wave. He whistled softly at a picture of the new model Daimler and decided to wait until after the train had come through to study the cricket scores in the Test match against South Africa.

He turned the page. A big headline—"Police Arrest Chums of Duke and Duchess of Windsor"—caught his eye, with a photograph of people in evening dress splashing in a conga line through the fountains at Trafalgar Square. The men's evening dress was askew and they appeared to be brandishing champagne bottles, while the women were soaked and looked as if they had nothing on at all. Right at the front of the photo a pretty girl was shrieking with laughter, holding onto a tall, fair-haired man with one hand and holding up her wet skirt so high with the other that there was a shocking view of her legs. In the background the police were closing in. The caption read, "Admiral's Madcap Daughter Arrested Again!"

Albert read on. There had been a society ball at the Savoy, and afterward a party of revelers had gone on to the Café de Paris. Which, according to the police, they had left at dawn, reluctantly—some had banged on the doors, demanding to be let back in. The revelers had stopped taxis, thrown out the occupants, and forced the cabbies to drive to Trafalgar Square, where a number were subsequently arrested. "See the editorial on page ten, 'Scandal of a Modern Debutante.'"

It was the kind of story Albert relished. It confirmed his view that the upper classes were no better than anyone else and that the country was going to the dogs. He tut-tutted as he turned to page ten and read:

There are only three occasions on which a well-bred girl should be mentioned in the papers: when she is born, when she is married, and when she dies. After reading of the shocking behaviour and events of last Saturday in Trafalgar Square, as reported on the front page, Miss Falconleigh's escapades raise issues of public concern. This paper feels it is pertinent to inquire whether her father is competent to command in the Admiralty when, evidently, he cannot command within his own domestic circle.

An unmarried girl's reputation is priceless, easily jeopardised by thoughtless behaviour and any departure from decorum. Normally girls of Miss Falconleigh's age and position in society are strictly chaperoned to guard them from any whiff of scandal. Typically they are not allowed to travel alone with young men in taxis, and nightclubs remain forbidden to any respectable girl, even in our reckless age. Miss Falconleigh, however, has openly cavorted about town and, we regret to say, has been photographed leaving many of London's least salubrious nightspots and most scandal-ridden private parties. Her escorts have included a number of well-known playboys, Argentine polo players, and personal friends of His Royal Highness, the former Prince of Wales.

Her only chaperonage, if it could be called such, has been that of Lady "Baby" Penrose, a former finishing-school chum of Miss Falconleigh, who, though married, is possibly not the most vigilant of matrons, as she is only a year older than Miss Falconleigh. It is to the credit of neither that she shares Miss Falconleigh's taste for notorious establishments. The sad fact is that Miss Falconleigh has been in one public scrape after another since she was presented at Court. Allowances may be made for the fact that she lost her mother when very young, but we must ask why her father neglected to ensure that some respectable older female friend of the family oversaw Miss Falconleigh's entrance into society.

Albert was so engrossed in all this that the London train was pulling into the station before he knew it. Crowmarsh Priors was only a small country station with few passengers coming and going, but his duty was to be on the platform, hat on, whistle to the ready, when the trains pulled in. As he straightened his cap he was reminded that his wife, Nell, would enjoy the newspaper's advertisements for the new spring hats, so he'd best remember to take it home.

He wondered who the sole female passenger was when she stepped down onto the windy platform. No ladies from Crowmarsh Priors had gone up to London today. If they had Albert would have known. So she couldn't be Mrs. Richard Fairfax, who sometimes went up to London, although she was a slender, well-dressed young woman of about Mrs. Richard's age. Far smarter clothes than Mrs. Richard's though. Probably for the de Balforts at Gracecourt Hall, although their visitors usually dashed down from London in their motorcars at the weekend and never arrived by train on a Tuesday.

The young woman had a gloved hand clamped to her head to hold on to her bit of a hat. Her hair flew about wildly as she struggled to hold down the skirt of her costume when the March wind blew rain splattering across the platform. Albert couldn't help noticing she had shapely legs and pretty ankles. He reminded himself that a right-thinking man with a wife and growing daughter had no business ogling strangers' ankles.

On closer inspection he saw that the young woman was a girl, really, for all her finery. She had turned to direct the removal of an extraordinary amount of luggage from the train onto the platform. As the engine steamed impatiently, Albert counted five large trunks, an assortment of grips and several vanity cases, a smart handbag, and a handsome crocodile dressing case.

The guard nodded to him that all the bags were off and rolled his eyes as he gestured at the mountain of luggage on the platform. He reached back into the train and tossed out what Albert was waiting for: a bundle of the newspapers that passengers had left on their seats, tied with string. The guard was a tidy man who would have thrown them away, but Albert thought it was a shame to waste them. "Cheerio then," he called. Then he called, "All aboard," in his loudest stationmaster's voice and blew his whistle, even though, as usual, no one was getting on.

As the train chugged away, Albert fetched the station's ancient baggage cart and rolled it toward the newcomer and her luggage. Her back was to him as she looked in the direction of the village where smoke was curling above a few slate roofs and brick garden walls into sodden gray skies. A row of Georgian houses with fanlights and polished brass on the doors faced the village green. Mrs. Richard Fairfax lived in one of those. There was an old flint church with a Norman tower, surrounded by a graveyard, and behind it the vicarage. Directly across from the church an imposing Queen Anne house with tall windows was visible behind wrought-iron gates set into a brick garden wall. There was a pub, a greengrocer's, a butcher's, and he knew where the red pillar-box stood. The drizzle had driven everyone inside, except Jimmy, the butcher's boy, whizzing past the station turning on his bicycle, and the cows in the next field, who placidly chewed their cuds, regardless of the wet.

A delicate flowery scent drifted to Albert's nose. Unaware that he was doing so, he straightened up. "Let me help you with that luggage, madam...miss," he amended. Up close she was just a slip of a thing. Her full lower lip was trembling and, Albert thought with disapproval, it was rather too scarlet for nature. Paint! And where there was paint, there was powder, he thought darkly. No respectable girl should get herself up like a hussy. Then he noticed the smooth cheek, the defiant little nose, and determined chin. The girl's dark blue eyes met Albert's. She blinked back tears and his heart melted.

"Is this Crowmarsh Priors? All of Crowmarsh Priors?"

"Indeed it is, miss." Albert nodded fondly at the village. To a Sussex man like Albert Hawthorne, there wasn't a better spot in England.

The girl cleared her throat. Something about her was familiar, Albert thought. He was sure he had seen her recently...then it dawned on him. The papers! She was the girl in the fountain! But now on the platform, she looked ladylike, and she certainly had expensive luggage...

She clutched the fur boa that was draped over her shoulders and stared defiantly at him. "Perhaps you could direct me to Glebe House?"

Albert was astonished. She was staying with old Lady Marchmont! Whatever for? he wondered. Lady Marchmont was a widow, had no children, and never had people to stay.

Perhaps the girl was a relative. She certainly didn't strike Albert as the sort who came as a paid companion, like the whey-faced creature with spectacles and thick lisle stockings who had arrived to keep poor bedridden Lady de Balfort company during the last years of her life. Albert shook his head. Lady Marchmont would eat a paid companion for breakfast.

How a pretty girl with such a determined look about her—not to mention rouge—would get on in the forbidding atmosphere at Glebe House he didn't like to think. He was just wondering if he ought to warn her about what to expect when he heard the sound of footsteps hurrying across the station's gravel forecourt. A tall, disheveled young man in a clerical collar dashed onto the platform. He stopped just before he collided with the girl and Albert, and gasped, "Hullo, Albert!" and snatched off a rather unfortunate hat. He apologized breathlessly for being late and said he hoped he had the pleasure of meeting Miss—Miss—er... Lady Marchmont's goddaughter, whom he was supposed to meet.

The girl's sapphire eyes widened as dismay battled with amusement on her pretty face. Her eyelashes fluttered tremulously as she gazed up at the odd young man, who started apologizing all over again, stammering incomprehensibly about urgent parish business, the brasses, the late vicar, and the Mothers' Union.

Albert guessed that he would have babbled for the rest of the afternoon had not the girl cut him short. She moved her crocodile case to her left hand, then held out her right. "How do you do? I'm Frances Falconleigh," she said sweetly. "So kind of you to take the trouble to meet me. You must be

Oliver Hammet, the new vicar. My godmother wrote to me about you."

"Not at all," began the vicar, flushing and hanging on to the girl's gloved hand. "Not at all! Welcome to Crowmarsh Priors! So glad…not at all…really, it's quite a pleasure…too delightful!"

Frances gave a strangled giggle. "You're a perfect angel to look after me when you're so frightfully busy. I don't know what I should have done without you!"

"Delighted to be of service," Mr. Hammet stammered. "Ahem! Er, do allow me to take that, Miss Falconleigh. I'm sure it's far too heavy for you," he said, at last releasing Frances's hand in order to take her dressing case.

"Thank you!" she cooed.

Albert looked from one to the other, his mustache twitching. The little baggage!

Mr. Hammet blushed again. "Er, not at all. My pleasure entirely. Do take my arm. I'm actually a sort of cousin of Lady Marchmont's, distant, of course, very distant. Albert, do you think you might possibly see to the rest of Miss Falconleigh's, er, things?" He gestured toward the luggage mountain, wondering at the amount of things this girl needed for travelling. He simply couldn't imagine. He was acquainted with very few young women. The only child of an elderly vicar whose wife had died when Oliver was a baby, Oliver had attended a boarding school for clergymen's sons and gone to Cambridge with all his belongings in the same two ancient leather suitcases that his father had taken to Cambridge forty years earlier.

"Right you are, Vicar, I'll get Jimmy to bring them round on the cart to Glebe House," said Albert. Mr. Hammet was too busy gazing at Miss Falconleigh to reply—the cat had gotten his tongue.

Frances Falconleigh shifted from foot to foot. "I should have been utterly stranded if not for you," she breathed finally, with a devastating glance at her rescuer, and tugged his elbow to bring him back to the present. "Now I expect Aunt Muriel will be wondering if I've arrived." She steered him firmly toward the station steps. "Mustn't worry her."

"No indeed. Yes, you had better hold my arm quite tightly—the gravel's a bit tricky," said the vicar as Frances's high-heeled shoes slid on the path and she clutched his arm tight to her bosom. The feathers on her hat hid her face, and he didn't see—although Albert did—Frances mouth "Damn!" as her ankle twisted.

Albert watched them go, torn between disapproval and amusement. The girl was clinging to the vicar like a limpet.

He returned to his abandoned paper to check the photos he had seen earlier. Sure enough she was the daughter of Admiral Tudor Falconleigh. Very high up in Whitehall.

Albert shook his head and went back to the editorial. When he had finished he asked himself what the country coming to.

An interesting visitor for Lady Marchmont, he thought.

6.

London, August 1939

*W*hen Tanni and Bruno had landed at Southampton on a gray January morning, they had done their best to neaten their travel-worn appearance, but had seen at once that they were making a far from favorable impression on the lady official at Immigration. She had been cold and stern, reading their documents and passports carefully, as if they must be false. Finally she had sniffed disapprovingly and handed them leaflets in English, printed in large type. She tapped one with her forefinger, then said in clipped, precise tones, slightly louder than necessary, "You are in England now. However you may be accustomed to behave where you come from, you are strongly advised to adapt at once to the ways of your host country. We have prepared a list of things you should and should not do in order to fit in. 'The English,'" she read, "'are naturally reserved, keep themselves to themselves.'"

They did not like, she went on, when foreigners, especially refugees, dressed garishly or wore outlandish costumes. They should do nothing to call attention to themselves. They should dress normally, be modest, polite, and self-effacing, never complain or criticize anything in the country that had so generously allowed them in. Above all they should not put themselves forward for jobs local people wanted. Tanni and Bruno must make every effort to adjust quietly and remember to be grateful. "I hope, Professor," she said thinly, "you appreciate how very fortunate you are to be here."

Tanni had been tired and numb from months of travelling, crowded trains, waiting for papers and permits to be issued, more crowded trains, more waiting for documents to be stamped, long stretches of walking, and finally the rough channel crossing. She did not understand all the words, but the hostile tone was clear enough. She glanced at Bruno, then nodded meekly. She could tell that he was masking his fury at the way they were being treated.

He put a reassuring arm round Tanni's shoulders. "My wife is very tired," he said, then whispered, still in English, just loudly enough for the woman to hear, "All will be well."

"Now, Mrs. Zayman, if you will step over there for a medical examination," barked the woman. They didn't check all the newcomers for disease, just those who looked worst. Fortunately a doctor was on hand to examine them today. If the girl, this so-called professor's wife, had tuberculosis or some foreign disease she would quarantined. "Step over there," the woman ordered, pointing to a curtained-off area where several other wan-looking women were waiting.

Two hours later Tanni had come out from behind the curtain, flushed and confused. Bruno, who had been sitting on a bench, stood up.

"Bruno," Tanni whispered in German, "the doctor says I'm going to have a baby."

He looked at her, stunned. Her lower lip was quivering.

"Bruno, a baby! I want my mother! I don't know what to do!" Tanni's eyes were wide and anxious. Bruno looked for the Immigration woman, but she was lecturing another new arrival at the top of her voice and fortunately hadn't heard Tanni speaking German.

"Don't worry. Both of our mothers will be here soon," he whispered. "We'll all look after you, *Liebling*. Everything will be fine." He had no idea what to do either, but he had to prevent Tanni worrying. "They'll be here soon," he repeated firmly, putting his arm round her again. "They're probably on one of those awful trains, or waiting for a slow official to stamp the passports, but soon we'll all be together in Oxford. The twins will go to school and your father will have patients again. Our house will have a garden where our mothers can sew and you and the baby can sit and listen to the bells from the colleges. We'll all learn to ride bicycles, even Mutti. Everyone rides them in Oxford. You'll see. Everything will be fine."

Tanni felt better and smiled at him. "Our mothers on bicycles! Imagine! I hope the garden in our new home will have a fig tree." Bruno said he wasn't sure they grew in England, but he had seen cherry and plum trees in Oxford. So Tanni imagined herself bustling efficiently round her Oxford kitchen making plum jam while the baby crawled about the floor and Bruno returned home to admire Tanni's efforts and kiss the back of her neck, sending those delicious shivers down Tanni's spine.

But it didn't happen as Tanni had imagined. Bruno took her to the Whitechapel boarding house where he lived in London, where they were to wait for the others to come. But the days stretched from weeks to months, and in March the

Germans marched into Czechoslovakia. Bruno volunteered to translate for the British intelligence service. Someone higher up made a phone call and he was now on leave from the university. He said they had better remain at the boarding house because it was the address Tanni's parents, the twins, and his mother had.

For Tanni life grew more and more confusing. Her body felt as if it belonged to someone else. At first she was sick and terribly sleepy. She would drag herself down the passage to the lavatory to throw up until she was dizzy and shaking. Then her shape changed and she blew up until she felt like one of Lili and Klara's balloons. As Tanni's waist expanded she unpacked the sewing kit her mother had tucked into her carpetbag and let out two frocks.

Bruno had scoured the Whitechapel markets for lemons, the only thing she wanted to eat. He watched, amazed, as she cut them into slices and ate them, peel and all. He was happy about the baby but uneasy about leaving Tanni alone. She understood little English—when people spoke to her she just smiled politely. Bruno was torn between his new work, which ate up so much of his time, and his longing to be with his wife. He was very busy and often out until late at night. When Tanni snuggled up to him in bed and giggled about how large she was getting, he could feel the baby kicking. He grew more and more anxious for the arrival of his mother and the Josephs. When Tanni went into labor a month early, they hadn't come in time after all, not even when Tanni screamed and cried for her mother, paying no attention to the midwives who told her sharply not to make such a fuss.

Once she was back in the boarding house with the baby, days and nights merged into each other until Tanni began to feel that she had always been imprisoned in the dingy room during a dusty, muggy London summer. Time slowed as one day dragged wearily into the next. Bruno was away more and more, and as she didn't like to worry him she told him everything was fine. Really. When he wasn't at home she went back to bed after a grim breakfast of cold toast and marmalade and stayed there, covers pulled up to her chin, moving only to feed or change the baby. Often she would not bother getting up for "tea," as the landlady called the evening meal. If she was hungry she nibbled biscuits from the tin Bruno had brought her.

It became an effort to do anything, even today, when the landlady knocked sharply on Tanni's door and said, "Mrs. Zayman! Letter for you." Tanni held her breath and sat very still in her chair. She hoped the woman would think she had gone out. It was too hard to make the effort of speaking English to her. The landlady had a thick Irish accent, and if Tanni asked her to repeat what she had said, she would raise her voice and broaden her accent. No matter how hard Tanni tried, she never seemed to do the right thing in England.

Even the prospect of a letter failed to rouse her. She no longer cared about letters. When she didn't open the door at once the landlady slipped something underneath it. Tanni heard the rustle of paper, then the woman grumbling as her footsteps retreated down the passageway, which smelled of boiled cabbage and drains. The envelope lay on the floor for some time before Tanni looked at it. When she finally did, she saw it was on thin blue paper, with German stamps and official markings. Her heart skipped a beat when she recognized her mother's handwriting. She put the sleeping baby down and got up slowly. If she moved too fast she felt dizzy. She was sore and tired, though it was nearly four weeks now since she had given birth.

She reached down and picked up the envelope. It was dated months earlier, in April, and looked as if it had been opened, then clumsily resealed. Tanni reached for her sewing scissors and slit the envelope. She took out a thin sheet of paper covered with tiny, cramped handwriting on both sides.

My Beloved Child,

I hope this finds you and Bruno well. And that you have received my other letters but it is hard to know, so I will write again to let you know that after the terrifying night when you left, we are safe and well. Just before the mob in the streets broke down the door we were saved by the mayor and the police chief who managed to divert the crowd—you remember Papa looked after the mayor's little boy and pulled the police chief's wife through pneumonia? But we were saved at a terrible cost. The best they could do for us was to direct the mob to another Jewish house. My only comfort that terrible night was in knowing that you were going to safety, and that Lili and Klara could follow you there.

We had a letter from Bruno that you are to be a mother yourself. Happy news indeed. I long to be there to look after you, but young as you are, all will be well, I am sure. If you feel sick in the mornings a piece of preserved ginger, sucked slowly, will help. Frau Zayman advises drying out some day-old bread in the oven, with a little salt, to keep in a tin by your bed. Eat a piece before you get up. Papa says a few spoonfuls of brandy-and-water if you feel very unwell, and that you must try to have fresh milk and plenty of fruit.

Long before the baby comes we expect to be with you in England! But many things have happened to delay us.

Soon after you left our house was confiscated. We were given only a few moments to get our clothes and a few belongings. There was no time to sell the piano or pack the silver and paintings and Papa's books, so we have lost those too, but they are only things and we must not allow them to become a matter of regret. We are safe and well, if somewhat crowded, living now in Frau Zayman's little flat. Except for her arthritis we are all well thank G-D and I have become very clever at cooking potatoes. We are more fortunate than some, as the Germans have begun to transport those without exit visas for resettlement on the Polish border. We have our exit visas and are only waiting for the girls to leave first. Meanwhile we must wear a yellow star on our clothing, even Lili and Klara, and must not be on the street after dark. From time to time people are arrested.

We long to be away. People queue all day and night for exit visas now. Papa, Frau Zayman and I obtained ours with the mayor's help and will follow when the little ones are safely on their way to you. They should have left on the children's train to England in January, but at the last minute both had scarlet fever quite badly and in the end we feared to let them go. We had to cut their hair because of the fever. Lili was very slow to get better and we debated whether to send Klara alone but thought it best not. Papa has been promised they will have a place on another train soon.

They say it is much safer for the children to go separately without us as the Kindertransports *are sure to get through.*

I confess I do not like it. I could hardly bear to part from you, even with Bruno to take care of you, and the thought of parting with Lili and Klara even for a few weeks, when they will be at the mercy of strangers, is almost too much. Only knowing they will soon be with you keeps me calm and sensible. We wait from day to day for news that their train is leaving. Lili and Klara's two little suitcases are packed and ready in the hall, complete with a favorite doll we managed to save for each. Frau Zayman cut down an old coat of her own to make them warm dressing gowns for England. I am impressing upon Klara every day that when the time comes she must be brave and a good girl like her big sister, a good little mother for poor Lili on the train until they are safely with you. The girls are so excited and happy to think of being with you at last. They miss you dreadfully. They ask if you have enough to eat in England, and I tell them I am sure of it. Food is scarce here and they are often hungry. We struggle to pay for the little we can find, mostly yesterday's bread and old potatoes, sometimes a few cabbage leaves. Most shopkeepers will not sell food to Jews. I saw Frau Anna the other day. She has grown thin like many others, and looked at us with an expression I did not like. I shall be glad to leave. Papa, Frau Zayman and I are prepared, have packed our few things, a little money and some bits of jewelry I managed bring with me. We shall go the moment the girls are off.

The paper runs out, only room to send you our blessings and love. Be well and don't worry, we will all be happy and cozy together in England soon. Try to be brave until then. We send you a photograph of us all, taken by Frau Zayman's kind neighbor who had a camera. He took this one last picture before he sold it and his developing equipment for food. The girls also send you a little drawing so you won't forget them. Klara wrote a message with only a little help from Papa. Love my dearest, Mutti

A blurred snapshot of a couple, two little girls with shorn heads sitting on their knees, and a drawn, elderly woman fluttered to the floor, wrapped in a second thin sheet of paper. At first Tanni thought they had sent the wrong photograph, but after studying it closely she traced the familiar features of her parents in the gaunt couple, her sisters' faces on the little bald heads, and Frau Zayman's in the old woman. She was shocked by their appearance. Then she saw something was written on a scrap of the same thin paper. She picked it up. There were two little stick figures in dresses, with round heads topped with a fuzzy halo of short hair drawn on each, topped with enormous bows. *"Dear Tanni do you miss us our hair will grow back in England lots of love and kisses from Klara and Lili"*

Tanni checked the date on the letter. Third of April. It was late August now! Over four months ago. Suddenly she was overcome with relief. By now they were all in England. She knew at once why they had not found her. The twins had probably arrived first and, not understanding English, had been unable to explain they had lost Tanni and Bruno's address. Her parents and Frau Zayman would have arrived also and tried to contact her, but she had missed them because she had been ill and Bruno had been away. They must have come to the house and asked for Professor and Frau Professor Zayman, and the short-tempered landlady had pretended not to understand and sent them away. Tanni felt a surge of responsibility. It was up to her to find her family and get everyone back together again. All she had to do was find out where they had gone and she would see them soon.

Her spirits sank as she considered the practicalities. She had no idea how to set about finding them in England. She wished Bruno was at home, but he had been away for three days. She never knew when he would return to their little room or for how long, and when he did come back he was preoccupied and she didn't like to bother him. The baby woke and began to cry. She had wanted to call him Johan, after Bruno's father, but Bruno insisted they give him an English name, John, and call him Johnny. She struggled with the English pronunciation.

Tanni sighed, unbuttoned her dress, lifted Johnny out of his cot, and settled back into the old armchair to nurse him. There was so much she needed to ask her mother about babies, like how to get Johnny nursing properly. Her nipples were sore and nursing hurt. If she moved him from breast to breast, he stopped feeding and howled. The landlady complained of the noise so Tanni winced, bit her tongue, and endured.

As Johnny sucked, Tanni looked round her, seeing her surroundings through her fastidious mother's eyes. The room smelled of nappies. Her few dresses and Bruno's spare suit hung in a small wardrobe. There was a layer of grime on the window. Bruno's books were piled beneath it, with her comb and brush and a leaflet about bathing babies on top of them. She often felt like lying down on the unmade bed and waiting for the grime to cover her too, but now the thought of her parents galvanized her. She could see dust balls under the bed. Her mother would be shocked, and Tanni decided she had better give the room a thorough clean.

First though, she should visit her aunt, who was married to a rabbi in Bethnal Green. Tante Berthe Cohen could advise her on what to do next. She was a small, round, kindly woman, not really an aunt but a distant cousin on her mother's side, and Tanni's only friend. She was much older than Tanni's mother, always busy, and had lived in England for twenty years. Rabbi Cohen had known Bruno's father and, although Bruno was not in the least religious, had performed the *bris* for Johnny. Tante Berthe had supported a nervous Tanni though the ceremony and provided honey cake and wine afterward.

Now that she had something to do, Tanni perked up. When Johnny finished nursing she put him down, washed herself as well as she could in the sink in her room, then washed her hair and combed it dry. She sponged Johnny and changed him, then put on her cleanest dress and her hat. She had lost so much weight that the dress was far too big. She must get out the little sewing kit again and take in the seams. She would do that after she had tidied the room and aired the bed, but before she did any of it she would speak to Tante Berthe.

She wrapped Johnny in a crib sheet, picked up her handbag, and shut her door quietly. Hearing the wireless in the sitting room, she tiptoed past to avoid alerting the landlady. Outside she wondered if it was too hot for the baby or whether she should have wrapped him in another layer. Could small babies get a chill even on a hot day? It was so hard to know. If only her mother were there. But soon she would be, Tanni thought, and her heart lifted. What a lovely sunny afternoon it was. She hummed a little song to Johnny as she walked along.

The Cohens lived many streets away, in a small neighborhood in Bethnal Green where the women all wore head scarves and men had long curls of hair under big hats and wore black suits and white shirts open at the neck. There were children everywhere and people were conversing in a language Tanni couldn't understand. She remembered Anton's description of his Orthodox relations, and her heart contracted. No, she mustn't think about Anton now: she was a married woman and a mother.

When Tanni reached Tante Berthe's street she saw two smartly dressed ladies with clipboards, wearing hats, kid gloves, and polished shoes. They looked out of place among the other women in the street, who were mostly dressed in black, with long skirts and thick stockings, their hair covered. The two elegant strangers reminded Tanni reassuringly of her mother. As she drew closer she heard them speaking in the kind of clipped, precise English she had learned at school. She smiled shyly at them, as a large family of black-clad children walked past with their father, who averted his eyes.

One of the ladies muttered, "There are just so many of them! How do their parents tell them apart! And they still won't consider evacuation. The parents don't even speak English properly. Quite, quite stubborn too. The children should be forcibly evacuated, if you ask me."

"Frankly, Penelope, one quite understands why the Germans—"

"Indeed! Come along, we're wasting our time." Both ladies climbed into a black car with a driver.

Tanni hurried on to the Cohens' narrow house. Sweet peas bloomed cheerfully in the small front garden and starched white curtains hung at the front windows.

Rabbi Cohen was busy in his study, but his wife welcomed Tanni warmly, kissing her and making a fuss over Johnny. Then she led Tanni down the passage into a crowded little kitchen sweet with the smell of baking. Several women were crowded together in chairs round a pile of papers on the kitchen table. They looked up as Tanni came in, and Tante Berthe introduced her. The women all had kerchiefs wound tightly round their heads and stared at Tanni's hat, a fetching one Frau Zayman had concocted from the felt of Dr. Joseph's oldest gray homburg, then trimmed with scraps of ribbon and some leftover veiling, and Tanni's brown curls tumbling beneath it. But they smiled when they saw Johnny, reaching to stroke his cheeks and shifting their chairs to make room for her. Johnny fell asleep.

Tante Berthe brought tea in glasses with lemon, a plate of almond cake, and a bowl of dark cherries. Tanni sat politely quiet while the others talked, sipping tea and eating a piece of cake, thinking how delicious it tasted. She was anxious to show Tante Berthe her mother's letter, but the other women were debating something in the language Tanni didn't understand. She stopped listening and waited for a chance to speak. Meanwhile she took a second, then a third piece of cake, licking her fingers with obvious enjoyment. Tante Berthe beamed and pushed the cherries toward her.

Finally there was a break in the conversation, so Tanni wiped her cherry-stained fingers on her handkerchief, then took the precious envelope from her handbag. "Tante Berthe, I need your advice, please. I had a letter from my mother," she began in German. Mrs Cohen said something to the other women, who nodded. With Tante Berthe translating for those who did not speak German well, the letter was passed round for all to read, together with the photo and Klara's carefully printed note.

"My little sister," said Tanni proudly. "She's very clever. But my mother wrote in April and the letter just reached me today. The twins are only five and speak no English. Lili is, has always been a little slow and Klara has to look after her. They must have lost my address before they reached England. I don't know where my parents and Frau Zayman have gone. Since Bruno is away I can't ask him what to do. I thought you, Tante Berthe, and the rabbi would know how I can find them all." Johnny woke and whimpered, and Tanni put him on her shoulder to jiggle him quiet, wondering how soon she could get him home and feed him. "I can't wait for them to see Johnny!"

Tante Berthe's kind face was grave. "My dear…" She hesitated, her eyes darting round for permission to speak. The women exchanged glances. One after another they nodded stiffly. "It may be they have not reached England yet. As your mother says, these are difficult times. We know that many Jews, like your parents, want to leave Germany and Austria, but doors are closing to them everywhere. We are part of a committee trying to help Jews in Europe, and we know the difficulties…"

"Yes, but my family have left and are here now."

A younger woman named Rachel burst out impatiently in English, "Difficulties? Pah! It's impossible! Things are very, very bad in Austria, bad in Poland, worse in Germany. It is hard to obtain a permit to leave, even with a huge bribe. And who can pay a bribe now? The Nazis have confiscated Jewish property, and people who were not poor before are

poor now. So many countries turn their backs. They close
their doors to poor people. It is a little easier for children,
but even for them there are difficulties. My husband liaises
with the *Kindertransport,* finding homes for the children
arriving in England. They are efficient people. If your sisters had arrived you would have been informed, I promise,
so I do not think that they can be here. We are getting word
that the Nazis have arrested many, many people in Austria.
For resettlement..."

"They call it resettlement," interjected another woman,
"when people are forced out of their homes to slave for the
Germans in labor camps, herded like animals, even children and the old..."

Tanni struggled to follow the English. Surely no one
would ever send Papa to work in a labor camp, she thought
uneasily. He was a doctor and highly respected. As for Mutti
and Frau Zayman, what earthly use would they be as labor-
ers? "Mutti didn't say anything about camps, just that people were being moved. But if the letter was written months
ago, they must be in England now. My parents made definite arrangements for Klara and Lili on the *Kindertransport*
in April and my parents had exit visas to follow as soon as
the twins left."

More worried looks were exchanged across the table.

Johnny started to cry in earnest. Tanni patted his back
and her smile faded. She looked from one woman to the
other, and her voice rose with anxiety. "You see, I promised Papa—it was the last thing I said! Bruno and I were
running away and there was no room for the twins in the
boat. He said I had to go first and made me promise to look
after the little ones in England. Now it is my responsibility to

find them. I was so ill with the baby that I...I forgot a lot of things," Tanni admitted guiltily. "It was my fault if someone couldn't tell me the girls had come. There must have been a letter or a phone call, but I was in bed and too tired to get up and they must have thought I had gone away—but now I've recovered I *must* find where they are. We were all supposed to go to Oxford to live when my parents came—perhaps they couldn't find us in London and went to Oxford to look for us." Tears welled up. "My fault..." Her lower lip trembled and tears spilled.

The older women tutted. The poor girl looked awful—such dark circles under her eyes and so thin that her dress was hanging on her. Tante Berthe rose and put her arm around Tanni's shoulders. "Of course it's not your fault, Tanni," she said comfortingly. "The time after a baby is born can be very hard." The other women nodded and murmured agreement. "Take Johnny home, my dear. We will try to find your family. If your sisters were indeed with the *Kindertransport* we should be able to trace where they are."

"And if they were not? So many children, so many..." said the woman named Rachel, her head in her hands.

"Hush," muttered another. "The poor girl is upset enough."

"And Mutti, Papa, and Frau Zayman?"

More looks. "We will begin with the *Kindertransport*—it is easier to trace—but we will do what we can to find your parents and Bruno's mother," said Tante Berthe, patting her hand. "Meanwhile, Tanni, my husband says it is important not to speak of anything we have said outside this house. Not one word. If we are to help Jews elsewhere we must be so careful. The English..."

"The English are as bad as the Germans!" huffed Rachel. "You have no idea how careful we must be to avoid attracting the attention of the authorities. Each of our members keeps different information in her head. No one knows everything so that if one of us is interned or questioned she cannot jeopardize the work of the whole committee."

"Shush, Rachel! Enough already. But Tanni, take care not to speak in German, even to Bruno. They listen everywhere, and if war with Germany comes they will intern people who appear to be enemy aliens."

"Intern?" asked Tanni. "What is that?"

"Detained in a camp, like a prison."

Relief at the prospect of help and hopes of seeing her family soon were now submerged under fresh worry. Tired now and anxious to get Johnny home to feed him, Tanni rose, thanked Tante Berthe, and made her farewells. She walked home as quickly as she could, Johnny howling most of the way, heavy in her aching arms. What if they were put in one of these camps? Would they take Johnny away from her? She hugged him tightly, unable to bear the idea.

When she entered the house the smell from the kitchen of something frying in hot, stale fat turned her stomach. The landlady intercepted her in the cramped passageway. "There's a lady waiting to speak to you. She's in the parlor."

Tanni went quickly into the gloomy little room. A familiar figure of a woman in a smart costume and hat stood up and her heart leaped. Suddenly everything was all right again. Her mother had found her after all. "Mutti!" she exclaimed happily. "Oh, Mutti, I knew you'd come—" She stopped midsentence and her heart plummeted. It was not her mother. She recognized one of the well-dressed ladies she had seen on the pavement on the way to Tante Berthe's.

"Mrs. Zayman?" the woman said uncertainly, checking her clipboard. The girl with the baby looked impossibly young to be married, much less a mother, although judging by what she had seen in Bethnal Green, if she was Jewish, who knew?

Tanni nodded, too stunned with disappointment to speak.

"How do you do. My name is Penelope Fairfax, and I am from the Women's Voluntary Service. The government expects that we will soon be at war with Germany, and for safety's sake we are evacuating mothers and children to the country. It is expected that the Germans will bomb or gas London and the other cities."

Tanni stared at her. What on earth did she mean? "War?" Tanni repeated the unfamiliar English word.

"I'm afraid so. Now, Mrs. Zayman, just sign this form and we can send you and your baby to a safe place away from London."

Tanni struggled to understand. "Away from London?" she asked. How could she possibly go somewhere else? What about Bruno, her parents, and the twins? How would she manage without Tante Berthe? Her head swam. She fought back panic and tried hard to make herself understood in English. "Excuse me, please, but I cannot go, my sisters, my parents, my mother-in-law, they are arriving, I must wait here, in London, for them. We are to go to Oxford when they come. I cannot—"

"Nonsense, Mrs. Zayman."

Cannot indeed! These people seemed to think there was room for every Tom, Dick, and Harry in England, Penelope thought crossly. Already the billets on her list were over-crowded and goodwill was stretched to the breaking point. Also, it was getting late and she had eight more families on her list for whom she needed signatures of consent. She looked at the girl and her baby closely. Foreign, but both looked clean. No sores or coughing, the girl's husband working for the War Office. The baby, unlike most of the scrawny London urchins on her list, was well fed and healthy. With the current shortage of billets, Penelope feared it was only a matter of time before one of her colleagues decided that, as she stayed mostly in her London flat, her own large house in Crowmarsh Priors had plenty of room for evacuees.

She quickly decided to billet this girl and her baby with Evangeline before she was landed with some much nastier children. Her dozy daughter-in-law needed something worthwhile to do. With darling Richard away on active service, Evangeline had too much time to mope. It was time the girl pulled her socks up and got on with things, now that she had recovered from her miscarriage. Whatever could have possessed Richard to elope with the American floozy and break poor Alice's heart? Penelope bit her lip in annoyance. She could never come up with an answer to that question.

She had tried, she honestly had, for Richard's sake, but languid Evangeline was hopeless as a naval wife, and darling Alice would have been a wonderfully sensible and active one, a real asset to his career. "Evangeline reminds one of something rather exotic, like an odalisque!" she had exclaimed once, unburdening herself to a friend. "Or a cat," she added, after a moment. "She's as secretive as a cat." And what was worse, Evangeline was remarkably careless about her dress, never making an effort, wearing any old thing, even Richard's cast-off shirts and pullovers. It came of being American, Penelope supposed. They were an uncivilized lot.

"Too dreadful, darling!" said her friend sympathetically. "How fortunate she's stayed in the country and they've not gone to quarters somewhere like Plymouth, where his superior officers would notice."

"As would their wives!"

Penelope decided to write Evangeline that evening. She would tell her firmly that it was time she pulled herself together for Richard's sake. She must think of her duty and prepare to take in an evacuated mother and baby.

An indignant wail as Johnny woke recalled Penelope to the dingy parlor and her list of billets. "Really, Mrs. Zayman, it gives us no end of trouble when mothers are so awkward about signing." Penelope's tone grew sharper. "And I had better tell you for your own good, the government is talking of internment for German and Austrian nationals, so if I were you I should sign at once, unless you would prefer internment."

"Internment?" asked the girl, jiggling the howling baby.

"A camp, where people have to stay during the war."

"But if I sign this paper I am not going to a camp?"

"Quite!" snapped Penelope, holding out a pen. Her head was beginning to ache. "In fact, you will be going to a rather lovely house in Sussex, much better than you might have expected. Count yourself lucky!"

Two days later Rabbi Cohen came and took Tanni to Victoria Station, promising the ladies' committee would notify her as soon as her sisters were found. "Don't worry,

Berthe and Rachel will see to it." He said Bruno knew where she would be and approved of her going. He and Tante Berthe had talked it over and decided it was a good idea for her to go, especially if it meant she wasn't at risk of internment. He reminded her, in a kindly but serious voice, that she was a wife and mother, that she must try to manage and make the best of things because Bruno's work was very important, and someday she would understand. For now she must look after Johnny, stay well and safe, and keep her spirits up. Tanni nodded and promised, trying to hide her distress. "Good girl!" said the rabbi.

7.

East London, Late August 1939

*T*he man who collected rent from the shabby two-up, two-down houses on North Street, near the London docks, made his rounds on Monday, wash day, when housewives were certain to be in. Those who had the rent money ready watched closely while he counted it and noted it in his little book, then closed the door behind him with relief. Those who hadn't the right amount calculated desperately what excuse they could use to put off payment till next week.

When Mrs. Pigeon went to the door to answer the knock, her face was creased with anxiety. The children in the room behind her held their breaths. Their dad must have found where she'd hidden the rent money again. When he laid hands on it he quickly disappeared to the pub or the dog races, leaving the children to whistle for their dinner. He would come home late and shamefaced, unsteady on his legs, and there would be a loud argument, sometimes the sound of a slap. Next day their mum would turn the house upside down rooting for something to pawn to Uncle. There wasn't much left.

When she opened the door they all stared, open-mouthed, at the person on the step. "That's never the rent man!" exclaimed one child. It was a lady, dressed like the queen in the photos of her in the papers: a smart costume, a hat with little brown and red feathers sticking up at the back, hair nicely dressed under the veil. She had gloves on, a handbag, polished shoes, and shiny legs. On North Street, women wore thick brown cotton stockings, knotted above the knee, and house slippers, even outdoors. "Good morning, Mrs. Pigeon." The lady sounded like people on the wireless.

The children craned for a better view, while their mother stood solidly, blocking the doorway, apron wrapped over her faded housedress and holding Violet on her shoulder. The lady had called before, but after what sounded like an argument Mum had always shut the door in her face before the children got a glimpse of her. This time, the lady quickly wedged a polished shoe in the doorway and spoke in a loud, firm voice.

"Mrs. Pigeon, this time you really must listen! It's not a question of whether war is coming but when, possibly a matter of days. Registration is absolutely vital for all London children so they can be evacuated to a safe place, out of reach of the enemy. But because you refused to register your children, your neighbors followed your example. There are nearly forty children in this street alone. Once the war starts it will be dangerous, if not impossible, for them to travel. The government believes the docks in the east end will be the Germans' first target in London. That's very near North

Street. Any bombs in this area are likely to hit the gasworks, and if that explodes, everything here will disappear in a fireball. The Germans are also expected to use poison gas. It is vital to get the children to safety in time, Mrs. Pigeon, before they burn to death—"

"Oi, *Mum!*" There was a chorus of wails, and Mrs. Pigeon turned to quell her brood with a frown.

The lady seized the initiative while Mrs. Pigeon's back was turned and handed Violet a boiled sweet, which Violet popped into her mouth. People often gave Violet a sweet, and Violet had learned that the best way to get another was to smile angelically. "What a lovely little girl! And a little girl with such pretty blue eyes must be a very good little girl. What is your name, dear? Do you know your name?" The lady held out another sweet.

Violet took it, stuffed it into her cheek as well, and smiled beatifically on cue. "Vi'let."

The lady quickly made a note on her clipboard. "And do you know how old you are, Violet?"

Violet stuck a grubby finger into her mouth to poke the sweets and shook her head. Probably three, the lady wrote. "Do you have brothers and sisters, Violet?"

Violet nodded. "Can you tell me their names, darling? I'll just stay here while I write them down." Mrs. Pigeon turned back, her face like a thundercloud. One of the children nudged another. They waited expectantly.

Violet removed a wet finger from her mouth and confided, "Elsie's cookin' her clothes, we'se 'avin' 'em for our dinner. Mum says ain't nuffink else to sell."

Mrs. Pigeon sighed, defeated. She put Violet down. Without giving an inch at the doorway, she began to name all of the children and their ages. "There's me eldest, that's Bert, who's seventeen, an' 'is brother, Terence, who's sixteen. They was taken on at the docks like their dad was before 'is accident. Bit of luck that was, with jobs so scarce nowadays. Me 'usband's leg got crushed under a load and never mended properly, so with 'im poorly I 'ad a right job to manage until the lads found work. But they're good lads, steady, bring their wages 'ome. We can't do without them wages, missus. My Elsie there's fifteen, finished school and all, she 'as. She'll be goin' out to work. My 'usband's got 'er a place in the glue factory. She starts next week. We can do with her wages as well, keep a roof over our 'eads, all these mouths to feed. Agnes there, she's ten. She's a sickly child. We've 'ad the doctor out twice this year for 'er and I don't know 'ow she's to go nowhere. She can't 'ardly leave the chair. Them's the twins, Dick and Willie. They're eight an' full of mischief. That's Jem," Mum finished, as a baby started to cry. "My youngest."

"Mum!" There was a chorus from the dingy room behind her.

"You lot best keep still if you know what's good for you!" she warned. She sounded sullen, like she did when forced to do something she didn't want to think about, like the time she pawned her wedding ring to Uncle for the rent money. Mum turned back to the door and although she and the lady lowered their voices, they sounded like they were arguing.

Elsie frowned at the visitor, sympathizing with her mother. Everyone knew not to call on a Monday, with all of them wrapped in bits and pieces of Mum's old aprons and other scraps to keep them decent while their clothes dried.

Elsie herself, in a ragged gray petticoat, stirred the wash pot with the broom handle, shoving the rags stained by her monthlies down under the gray suds before her brothers saw them and asked what they were. Dick and Willie, each in a pair of Mum's old drawers they had to hold up with one hand, were fighting over a broken ha'penny top with the other. Their noise had woken Jem, who had been sleeping in a drawer on the dresser. Agnes was huddled under a blanket on the one armchair, whining that the steam and the smell of boiling soap made her cough, but everything made Agnes cough, and mostly the family took no notice.

Violet hadn't been given another sweet and began to shriek loudly for Mum's attention. The lady said, "Good morning, then," rather crossly, and Mum shut the door hard. She turned round with a strange look on her face. "Bloody Germans! Bloody la-di-da. Blackout if you please! Blackout curtains, they say! Curtains! And nuffink in the house but potatoes for dinner—and few enough of them— and the lads and your father home to I don't know what for their tea. Willie, stop larkin' about and get Jem for me, there's a good lad."

"Cor! Mum said 'bloody!'" Astonished, the twins stopped fighting. Their mother was a stickler for "proper."

Willie picked up the baby and made a face. He held the squalling baby at arm's length. "'E's weed over everythink, Mum."

Mrs. Pigeon put down Violet, whipped off the wet nappy, and wrapped the baby's damp bottom in her apron. "Who was that lady? What's that paper say then, Mum?"

She held the paper up to the light. Her lips moved as she laboriously spelled out the words. "Ev-a-somefink. What's that when it's at home?" she muttered. Violet whimpered and reached up to be carried. Mum put Jem on the table that stood in the middle of the room and picked up Violet again. The baby began to howl. "Oh, for pity's sake, Agnes, stop coughin' for a minute, do! 'Ere, Elsie, you're the clever one, read us what it says." She handed Elsie the paper and began to look for a clean nappy. Violet's blue eyes stared at Elsie over her mother's shoulder.

Mrs. Pigeon put Violet down, then unbuttoned her top to feed the screaming baby. "Read it to me," she commanded. "Agnes, you peel them potatoes *naow*!"

Violet stuck out her tongue at the baby.

"Why can't Elsie ever do it?" wheezed Agnes, but dragged herself to the tiny scullery under the stairs and came back with a tin washbasin and a bowl of potatoes.

"Because the less Elsie has to do with the dinner, the better it will be, as you well know, my girl. Them potatoes'll be peeled to shreds. Besides, she'll be the only one of us can make sense of whatever it is, seein' as 'ow you've been too bad to go to school and the twins can't no more read than Jem." Mum tapped the paper the lady had given her. "Tell us what it says then, girl."

Elsie sat down and smoothed the paper on the rickety oilcloth-covered table, and read out slowly,

"Government Eva...evacu-a-tion Scheme

"To ensure the safety of London's children the government has ordered their evacuation to areas outside London considered not to be at risk from the threat of German bombs. Schoolchildren up to the age of fifteen should be registered at their schools, which will oversee their evacuation to locations in the countryside. If your children are not registered and you wish them to be evacuated, the teachers or school keeper will help you. If you do not wish your children to be evacuated you must not send them to school until further notice."

Mrs. Pigeon didn't say anything so Elsie read the notice a few more times, mimicking the radio voice of the lady in the hat. Hoity-toity. "Evacuation." The word had an important, official ring to it.

"Oi, Mum, wot's the lady in the 'at say it was?" asked Willie, none the wiser.

Big square woman though she was, Mrs. Pigeon looked smaller suddenly, her shoulders drooping. Her thin hair was straggling down from beneath the knotted kerchief she tied it up in on wash days. When she finally spoke, her voice sounded as if it were coming from a distance. "It means—it means goin' away, like. They say there's goin' to be a war and the 'Uns'll come bombin' like they did in the Great War. Awful, that was." She rocked Jem. "'Orrible. The fires round 'ere burned and burned. I remember 'ouses and shops an' all'd collapse with people still inside, whole families trapped. And the smell, people burnin'…and the screamin.' …'Orrible it was. They couldn't get 'em out, you see. She came round 'ere twice before, askin' 'ow many of you was under fifteen. 'Well, I can't 'ardly bear to think of it 'appenin' all over again,' I says to 'er. 'It can't,' I says to 'er. 'But it will,' she says, certain as anyfink. 'I fink you can count on it, Mrs Pigeon.'

"And she says I'd go with Jem and Violet, as they're so young, but it might be they'd have put us in a different place

to the rest of you. But that'd mean leaving your dad and the boys 'ere. An' Elsie, I said you was fifteen, 'cause you are, nearly, but that's too old to be evacu-wossname. I don't know what to do for the best."

Elsie discovered something on the back of the notice. "Mum, there's even a list. It says 'ere, 'Children must bring their gas masks in case.' Ugh! 'Orrible! I 'ate wearin' it! And they need 'two changes of underwear, a nightdress or pajamas'—what's pajamas, then, Mum? And 'a bar of soap, toothbrush, toothpaste, a towel, a comb and brush, 'andkerchiefs, a warm coat and jumper, a change of socks or stockings, a spare pair of shoes.'"

"Each, the lady says," said her mother blankly. Elsie did the mental arithmetic to figure how many bars of soap, how many combs and brushes, how many jumpers would be required, and put down the impossible list with relief. "That fixes it then, Mum. None of us can go. We don't 'ave spare shoes or them other things."

There was a moment's silence. Mum looked at the circle of anxious faces. There wasn't one of them she felt she could do without for a minute.

"'Ow 'ot is fire, then?" asked Willie. "We can keep a bucket of water by the door."

"I'm not afraid of no fire," said Dick stoutly. "Nor 'Uns."

"Fire," said Violet and stuck her finger in her mouth.

A bell clanged in the street and a cart rumbled past.

"Wish we 'ad some sausages, though," said Dick, who was always hungry. The others nodded.

Mum looked up. "Them potatoes want boilin'. Agnes, you chop up that bit of cabbage left from yesterday. That bell will be the cat's meat man. I'll get us some bits before them cats 'ave it all. We want a bit of cheerin' up. We'll 'ave it with onion gravy. And we've some mustard powder—we could do with a bit of mustard to perk us up. Elsie, you mix up the mustard."

"No! Elsie makes it lumpy, Mum."

Mrs. Pigeon sighed wearily. "Elsie, wrap a towel round you and get that washin' out on the line. Jem's no dry nappies left." She untied her kerchief, having extracted a precious shilling from the rent money that was hidden there, and reknotted it tight on her forehead.

Out in the street Penelope Fairfax repinned her hat and bit her lip in frustration. She had personally called on Mrs. Pigeon more than once because the woman's neighbors had asked, "And what do the Pigeons say about it all, missus?" and refused to evacuate their children until they knew.

At the thought of the Pigeons Penelope wrinkled her nose. The smell in the house had been terrible, not quite masked by the fug of boiling yellow soap. Those two scrawny little boys had scabies, she was sure of it. The child with the cough didn't sound at all well, and Penelope had been relieved when Mrs Pigeon wouldn't let her in. The one they called Violet was a pretty little thing, though. Lovely eyes. Unusual to see a child like that on North Street. She probably had lice in her head like the rest. Or worms. Or both.

And endless numbers of such children needed to be evacuated from cities all over the country, while the billeting authorities were desperately short of places for them. Penelope thought guiltily of her own spacious house in Crowmarsh Priors. She would have been happy to turn it over to Richard and darling Alice, then move to London, but had felt obliged to remain in the country to help

Evangeline—what a name!—settle in, especially as the girl was expecting a baby. But it had proved impossible to share a house with her daughter-in-law, whose lethargy got on her nerves, and she didn't care to share it with the likes of the Pigeon children either, thank you very much. The very thought of them running amok among the chintz and antiques made her shudder. She congratulated herself on having had the foresight to send the foreign girl and her baby down on the train last week. Now if the authorities learned about her house, she could say that Evangeline had her hands full with evacuees.

Penelope paid no attention to the slip-slap of carpet slippers behind her on the pavement until she felt her arm clutched from behind. A breathless Mrs. Pigeon, anxiety etched into her face, gasped, "Oi, missus, I didn't like to ask in front of the kiddies, but what will become of 'em in this eva-wossname? I don't know what to do for the best, with their father only working casual down the docks, on account of 'is leg, and the two eldest can't leave their jobs, but I don't see 'ow I'm to leave them behind to fend for themselves, only lads they are, and there's me oldest girl, just fifteen, and leavin' 'er alone at that age without 'er mother ain't right."

Penelope sighed. "Mrs. Pigeon, as I've told you already, the government is quite clear that children will be safer outside London. As I explained, they will assemble in the regular way at their schools, and their teachers will accompany each class as they are moved out of London and taken to their billets. You really must put your children first and think what is best for them, as I'm sure you'll agree. Just sign this form while I see about the arrangements."

Wearily Penelope checked her list. Most available billets were already overcrowded, and it was clear that, of those who had signed up for "one nice little girl aged five or six, clean and well behaved," many would have to be persuaded to cope with "six active boys, aged between two and fourteen" or "two girls and four boys, ages unknown." But duty was duty. "You have three who could go to the countryside—that would be Agnes and the twin boys. We've room for three in—er—Yorkshire. On a farm—terribly healthy, wonderful place for children. You could accompany the two youngest, though it might not be to the same place as the other three as spaces are short. However, there is a billet near Scarborough." Penelope knew perfectly well that the elderly couple there had specified "a quiet and obedient little girl of nine or ten." However, they would have to take in Mrs. Pigeon, Violet, and Jem. Perhaps they would warm to Violet, so long as she didn't howl.

Mrs. Pigeon looked blank.

"I'm sure your husband and the two elder boys will fend for themselves somehow. Now, your elder daughter—Elsie, is it? She's left school? Rather difficult as she falls between the cracks, so to speak. Hmm. Normally we can only billet schoolchildren, but it's just possible that your Elsie would do as an under-housemaid for a friend of mine in the country. A certain Lady Marchmont. She's widowed. Quite the backbone of the village."

Mum had no idea about Yorkshire and this Scar-place, but at the suggestion Elsie take up a place as a housemaid, her face lit up. Far more "respectable" than a glue factory. "Elsie go into service? Why," she said, thinking fast, "before my 'usband got 'er the factory place we used to speak of Elsie doin' just that!"

Mrs. Pigeon crossed her fingers behind her back. "Course Elsie doesn't have no trainin'. But, if I say it meself, she don't 'alf take to trainin'." She crossed her fingers tighter. Once Elsie was in the country, surely they'd have to keep her. If there was a war.

A similar thought was passing through Penelope's mind. She knew Muriel Marchmont well—so well, in fact, that the old lady had taken it upon herself to keep Penelope informed about what Evangeline was, and was not, doing. However, her last letter had mentioned she and Mrs. Gifford were at their wits' end since the last housemaid had left to be married. It left an opening of sorts for a girl like Elsie. On the other hand, if that lank-haired girl stirring the wash pot knew one end of a duster from another, Penelope was Queen Mary.

Mrs. Pigeon sensed hesitation and seized her advantage, knowing from experience that advantages rarely came the Pigeons' way. "Elsie'd be out of 'arm's way there. She's a good girl, mind you, is Elsie. But round 'ere you don't like to leave them on their own at fifteen just when boys try to give them ideas and they get their 'eads turned. It'd be a load off me mind to 'ave her there," she urged, "so's I can think about what to do wiv the others. But..." she trailed off, imagination failing her when she tried to see Elsie as an apprentice housemaid, "maybe she wouldn't suit the lady."

"There's going to be war, Mrs. Pigeon. We will all have to make sacrifices," said Penelope crisply, noticing the time. She was overdue at Headquarters with her lists. "If I speak to Lady Marchmont personally, I'm sure she will do her part. I shall register Agnes and the twins at once, and let you know tomorrow where you and the two youngest are to go." She thrust a form and a pen into Mrs. Pigeon's hand. "Kindly sign here. Now if you will excuse me, I am late." She snatched the signed form from Mrs. Pigeon and dashed for the waiting WVS car.

"When are they to go?" Mrs. Pigeon called.

Penelope turned briefly. "On Friday, end of the week. Remember, at school first thing, packed and ready. And don't worry, Mrs. Pigeon, we shall all pull together and it will be fine. Cheerio."

Mrs. Pigeon's shoulders slumped. She'd done it. She hoped everything would turn out for the best. Her Elsie would be settled in a respectable household, out of harm's way, and especially away from that sly boy Bernie that followed Uncle everywhere. She had spotted him hanging about in the street outside their house and suspected he was watching for Elsie. Mrs. Pigeon had learned a thing or two during her own marriage, and she could tell Bernie was a wrong 'un.

And if Elsie went off to be a housemaid they'd have to feed her. That was something. Which made her remember her hungry brood at home. She hurried after the cat's-meat man.

8.

Crowmarsh Priors, November 1939

*T*wo months of living on and off in the middle-of-bleedin'-nowhere Crowmarsh bleedin' Priors with the local police constable and his new wife had convinced Bernie Carpenter that the country was worse than prison. He had never imagined that a place so dull and quiet existed. He missed Bow and Shoreditch. He missed the excitement of the dog track and the bookmakers who deferred to Uncle, the dance halls to which he accompanied Uncle and stood by importantly holding the satchel while they filled it with notes, their protection money, and nodded to "Uncle's boy." He missed the dance hostesses with painted faces and silk stockings, who crowded round Uncle and smelled nice. They brought Bernie ginger beer and tousled his hair and said they were waiting for him to grow up. He missed the street markets where stall owners shouted their wares and tossed him an apple while Uncle checked the stolen merchandise hidden under the carts. He missed "smash and grab" too, with the nighttime excitement of breaking into a shop or a house and scurrying off with a bag of valuables, listening for the lookout to yell, "Fire!" when he spotted the police. But most of all, he missed the little dark room under the pawnshop, the smell of ink, the presses, and making pound notes, doing the watermark over and over again, practicing with the tints on different currencies that had foreign writing and funny old codgers in beards, while Uncle looked critically over his shoulder showing him how the smallest details made all the difference.

"That'll do," was high praise—Uncle never wasted words—and Bernie lived for this fleeting sign of Uncle's approval. And then one day, Uncle drew in his breath and muttered, "By George, you've got the eye and the hand, lad. Something can't be learned—it's in the blood. Couldn't have done it better meself." Bernie almost burst with pride.

Since he'd been in Crowmarsh Priors—he didn't know where it was exactly or he would leave—they'd come to fetch him and then they drove ever so far to somewhere else in the country. Once he got there, though, he had to admit, it was a little bit like old times, which was nice. The geezers there were a funny lot, like they were always half joking and didn't give much in the way of praise, but he wasn't stupid. Way he saw it, if they was depending on a sixteen-year-old boy to make their counterfeit notes and passports and other gear, and paying him to do it, as well as Constable Barrows for his board, then it was their way of saying he had the gift. They talked funny, posh, like, saying one thing and meaning another, but they weren't a bad lot. He'd almost stopped nicking their cigarettes, lighters, and the odd bit of money.

There was nowhere to spend it, was there? When he wasn't wanted he bought a bar of chocolate and wandered aimlessly around the village not knowing where to put himself.

When he spotted the scrawny girl from North Street polishing the door brass at the big house at the edge of the green, he could hardly believe his eyes. What in the name of Moses was the Pigeon girl doing there? He stepped behind a giant laurel bush by the gate and watched her. She rubbed her eyes and swiped the back of her hand across her nose, like she'd been crying. She must have gone into service at the big house. He couldn't believe his luck at seeing a familiar face. Specially her. And her old dragon of a mother wouldn't be around to stop him talking to her.

For days after he had seen her, Bernie hung about outside the gates of the house as often as he dared, waiting for her to come out. They must have kept her hard at work because she rarely appeared. Instead, he saw a large old lady with white hair and a walking stick who stuck her nose in the air all the time like she could smell something bad. There was also a pretty girl coming and going. She had the sort of brownish-red hair that Uncle liked, and she dressed like stars in the pictures, in furs, little hats, and high heels. The gentleman from Gracecourt Hall called for her most days, with a roadster full of friends, and they would speed away, laughing, down the drive. Just the sort of girl Uncle would see set up well in St. John's Wood or even Kensington.

Thinking about Uncle made him sad. Constable Barrows had told him, not unkindly, that Uncle was ill in prison, too ill for anyone, let alone a lad, to visit. However, when Bernie had asked Constable Barrows who the big house belonged to, the policeman lost his genial expression, grabbed him by the collar, and said, "One word of warning, you little weasel. Don't ever think of trying anything at Glebe House. None of your shenanigans there. Lady Marchmont'd have your guts for garters. Put you in handcuffs, I will."

So he'd had to bide his time. Eventually he saw her again. Only the top of her head was visible as she crouched in the tall weeds in the churchyard, behind the old stone tomb with the fellow in armor had his legs crossed, his sword and shield on his stomach. The sound of her blubbering had brought Bernie up short. She had on a black dress, too big for her, a huge white apron, and a little white frilled cap askew on the back of her head. Talking to the dance hall hostesses was easy because they started it, teasing him, like, leaning close and patting his leg. But what did you say to a girl? How were you meant to start? He kicked a loose stone. "Ow," he said loudly, hoping she'd look up. She didn't.

Nothing else occurred to him so he kicked another stone that ricocheted off the tomb. This time she must have heard, because she hiccupped and turned her head. Her nose was running and her eyes were red. There was a red welt on her cheek, as if someone had slapped her.

"Cold day for cryin', innit?" he remarked.

"Bugger off," she muttered and wiped her nose on the hem of her apron, which was wrapped twice round her little waist.

He grinned. He had to watch his language around Constable Barrows and his wife.

Inspiration struck. Constable Barrows's young wife, brimming with enthusiasm for housekeeping in her newly married state, had been horrified by the state of Bernie's paltry belongings, spread out in the spare room, and had furnished him with a pile of her husband's old shirts and handkerchiefs, freshly washed, starched, and ironed. Now he felt for the handkerchief in his pocket. "'Ere, you'll be wantin' this." He moved closer and held it out to her. "Go on, it's clean."

"Was it you washed it?" she asked ungraciously, but took it. Her hands were red and chapped. She gave a great shuddering sigh as she mopped her face.

"Go on, blow," he encouraged her, and she did, a great honking sound.

"I seen you before," he said, squatting down beside her.

"I know," she said dully. "I seen you too. You're the lad what's livin' at Constable Barrows's."

"No, afore that. I mean North Street. You're one of them Pigeons, ain't you?" She nodded. "'Ere, let's get off the ground. We can sit on this." He hauled himself up onto the knight's tomb. It leaned a bit, but it was dry. He held out a hand. She got up, brushed off her skirt and apron, then repinned her crooked cap. "Come on, then. Mind that skull thing sticks out at the end." He scooted over to make room for her. He took out a packet of Woodbines and offered her one. "Smoke?"

"No, fanks." Up close her face was heart-shaped and pale, except for the mark on her right cheek.

Elsie watched him strike a match expertly on the side of the tomb and light his cigarette. Up close his profile was lean and sharp featured as he drew on the cigarette like an old man, holding it between his thumb and forefinger. A shock of brown hair fell untidily over his forehead, almost down to his nose. There was something restless and alert about him—even sitting still his eyes darted about. He reminded her of the ferret her dad had once brought home, having bought it from a man in the pub. It had escaped when he took it out of his pocket to show the children. Mum had screamed as it scampered across the floor, then chased it into the street with her broom.

"You're Uncle's boy," she said, remembering the day Mum had summoned the pawnbroker because she had to sell her wedding ring. Many people living on North Street made furtive trips to Uncle's narrow little shop, but Mum hadn't wanted to go to the shop in case anyone saw she was pawning her heavy gold ring, the last badge of her respectability. Instead she had sent word asking Uncle to call on her. When he came the children had been banished upstairs, but Elsie had crept down and seen Uncle and the lad who carried his case. The lad had caught her eye and winked as she peeked round the corner of the stairs. She had grinned and winked back before Mum saw her and ordered her back upstairs. After that she had seen him loitering in North Street a few times, but Mum had always made sure he didn't talk to her.

"Well, s'pose I am." He looked down modestly. It was like admitting he was the Prince of Wales. In a way he was. In North Street they were proud of Uncle; he was a celebrity, with expensive suits, a motor, and soft-spoken good manners. He raised his hat to the ladies, bought rounds of drinks for all in the pub every Saturday night, patted children on the head and gave them a shilling, wore cologne you could smell a mile off, and was said to keep a fancy woman. No one would have dreamed of grassing on Uncle when the police came looking for stolen property or investigating a bookmaking racket. But forgery was his true business. Uncle was an artist, it was said, not just your common criminal. The local lads envied Bernie his luck in being chosen as Uncle's apprentice. Even the Italian gangs in Clerkenwell, the worst of the worst, respected Uncle.

"'E's looked after me since I was a little 'un. Me dad was gone in the navy, and then me mum died. They was going to send me to the 'ome, but 'cause I used to run errands for 'im, penny a time, Uncle said I seemed like a likely lad and 'e took me in. Told 'em me dad was 'is bruvver."

"Was he?"

"Not really, but they don't care long as they're not bothered. Uncle treated me proper, never lost 'is temper. But he'd keep me up all night learnin' the trade. I'd copy things an' all, pound notes, five-pound notes, till you didn't know which was which. The thing you got to remember is, never make 'em perfect. It's the imperfections marks the genuine ones. 'E said I were a good learner." He cleared his throat. "A credit to the profession, 'e said I was, a great credit. He even said I..."

He stopped. Elsie was gazing at him, wide-eyed. She was a little thing, but it felt nice making an impression on a girl.

"Why ain't you wiv 'im now, then?"

A shadow passed over Bernie's face. "Uncle's in prison again, ain't he? That's why. Sick, too, wiv 'is lungs, somefink. Fevers. Coughs up blood. That's why I'm doing the work 'stead of him." His thin chest swelled. "They say they've never seen anybody good as me—exceptin' Uncle, of course—keep me at it too, they do, I can tell you." He wasn't supposed to talk about it—been warned never to talk about it, or else—but he wanted to keep her looking at him in that admiring way.

"What work? Who says they never seen?"

"The government. I fink." A note of uncertainty crept into his voice.

"The *wot?*"

"Truf is, I dunno exactly. They can't be some kind of gang, can they, if they come straight to the police station? I were in the station at the time...'eard 'em asking for Uncle. Coppers say Uncle's dyin' in prison 'where 'e'—copper nods over at me—'looks like joinin' 'im in no time, 'cause Uncle taught that little sewer rat all 'is tricks. 'E's been caught nickin' from shops, runnin' for the Italians, smash an' grab. Couldn't make none of the charges stick,' the copper says, 'but 'e's Uncle's lad all right. Only a matter of time before we gets 'im sent to an approved school.'

"'Earin' Uncle's so ill they looked at each other and swore a bit, said what were they supposed to do now. One of 'em asked the coppers, innocent, like, did they think Uncle 'ad taught me *all* 'is tricks? The coppers laughed, said I knew as much as Uncle about anyfink criminal.

"The one what 'ad asked said in that case they'd no choice but to give me a try. They showed the coppers some bit of paper and the coppers looked like they didn't believe it. Then one copper grabbed me off the bench, mad as 'ell. He tells me to be'ave or 'e'll cuff me to kingdom come. Then the geezers put me in their motor and we drive up west in London, to a big buildin' with secretaries an' offices an' all. First thing, they 'ad a row with some other bloke, who said not to credit the coppers and 'ow old was I anyway and stop wastin' their time. Finally, to settle the argument, they takes me into a room. Uncle would've thought 'e was in 'eaven— engravin' things, paper, presses, like you never seen. Gave me some passports, some foreign notes, and official-looking papers, said could I copy any of those? I were at it all night, but it were easy. Next mornin' they came back an' took 'em away. They come back, they says 'By George! Bank of England couldn't tell the difference!'"

Elsie was staring, eyes like saucers. He puffed out his chest a little. "They goes off to get a cup of tea, and quick, like, I grabs a five-pound note they'd given me to copy, thinkin' I'd done them enough of a good turn, and skipped out. They sent the coppers after me. Blow me if they didn't find me in Berwick Street market. One copper says to the other, 'They bleedin' want 'im back!' In the end they sent me to live with Constable Barrows, supposed to keep me out of trouble. Now they come get me, I does the work, they pays me, takes me back to Constable Barrows. They don't care what else I do, long as I keep workin' for them. The look on the copper's puss! But can't none of them coppers do anythink about it. Blimey." He chuckled and straightened up. "Uncle would be proud, say I landed on me feet!"

Elsie regarded him steadily. He would swagger when he walked, she was sure of it. She also knew instinctively that if Mum knew he was talking to her, Mum would have her broom out, smacking him into the street same way she'd chased out the ferret. Elsie perked up. For the first time since arriving in the country, her misery eased a little. "What's your whole name, then?"

"Bernard Carpenter—Bernie, really. I know yours already—it's Elsie."

"'Ow old are you, then?"

"Nearly seventeen. Older'n you. But not so pretty."

Elsie tossed her head. "Sauce! Well, I'm fifteen. What's it like at Constable Barrows's?"

He lit another cigarette. "It's all right. You know. They 'aven't been married long so they're still lovey-dovey. And Mrs. Barrows don't 'alf feed you! We 'ave a cooked breakfast with an egg an' all and dinner an' then a big tea with proper bread and butter, sometimes scones and jam, and last Saturday, tinned pilchards! Then," he added as casually as possible, "on Sundays there's a roast dinner wiv beef an' roast potatoes an' Yorkshire pudding, an' there's bread and drippin' for Sunday tea." He drummed his heels on the tomb, a faraway look in his eye. "Bread and drippin's me favorite. You gone into service then?"

"Evacuated to be a 'ousemaid for Lady Marchmont." Elsie sighed and rubbed her right cheek.

"I seen the 'ouse. The old bat in the uniform looks like she's suckin' a lemon."

"That's the 'ousekeeper Mrs. Gifford. She's a 'oly terror."

"And the old lady who acts like she's the queen. Is the girl 'er daughter?"

"Oh, that's Miss Frances. She's Lady Marchmont's goddaughter, whatever that is. She got into trouble in London, 'ad 'er picture in the papers, it was a big disgrace, and they made 'er come 'ere to keep out of trouble, but she's taken up with the crowd at Whatchmacallit 'All. She sneaks out at night when Lady Marchmont's gone to bed. Then they drive to Brighton and go to nightclubs. I sneak down to unlatch the window very early in the morning so she can climb back in wivout 'er ladyship knowin'. She's got ever such pretty things to wear.

"But Miss Frances is a good sort really, the only one's been nice to me, asked me about my family, if they was still in London. When me older brothers wrote last month and said they'd enlisted, I were frantic because I wanted to send a letter to say cheerio and wish 'em good luck, but I didn't know where to send it. I felt bad 'cause Mum wouldn't like them go off wivout all of us all sayin' good-bye. When I told 'er, Miss Frances went straight to the telephone an' rang this person and that person, even though Lady Marchmont was looking at her like thunder, till she turned up their address in the navy. Men send her flowers and chocolates—she gives 'em to me sometimes."

For a minute Elsie was silent. Then she went on: "There's ever such a lot of things in that 'ouse want polishin' or dustin' or puttin' away or gettin' out, and it's scrub this an' wash that an' sweep the other an' make the fires or black the grates...everyfink all proper. I never do things right, and the 'ousekeeper boxes me ears." Elsie rubbed her cheek again.

Uncle didn't hold with hitting women, and Bernie felt a flash of anger at the housekeeper. "Can't you go back home?"

Tears welled up again in Elsie's eyes, "They ain't at 'ome now, are they? All evacuated, that's what. Somewhere called Yorkshire. The people they're billeted wiv were cross because Agnes and the boys didn't bring none of the things they was supposed to, except their gas masks. First thing, they cut off all Agnes's 'air and shaved the twins' 'eads. Nits, they said. Agnes looked in the mirror at 'erself and nearly died of coughin' brought on by cryin'. Mum wrote to me about it, wasn't 'alf cross they didn't tell 'er first, bein' as how she's only in the next town with Vi'let and Baby Jem. Agnes 'ates it where she is, but they say she 'as to make do for the time bein'. The people Mum's billeted with don't like her usin' the kitchen an' their pots and pans, and she and the woman argue about who's to tidy up until Vi'let howls. The man 'as asked them to move Mum somewhere else."

Bernie was at sea with such a litany of domestic difficulties, but he wanted to comfort her. "You and me got to stick togevver and be friends. 'Ere, you said you like chocolate. I got a bit of Cadbury's." Elsie's face brightened. He took a penny bar from his pocket, broke it in two, and gave her the bigger half.

"Ta very much," she said. She closed her eyes as the sweetness melted thickly across her tongue. She smiled in spite of herself.

She looked very pretty, smiling like that, Bernie thought. "That's better," he said, watching a rim of chocolate form round her top lip. He watched as her tongue crept out to lick it off. He wondered what it would be like to lick it off for her, then even kiss her like he had seen some of the men kissing the dance hall hostesses. The thought of it sent a jolt through him. He drew in his breath so sharply that he startled her.

Her eyes flew open. "Chocolate's one of my favorite fings," she said. "It's on my list."

"Your what?"

"I've got a list of fings I like to fink about, when I go to sleep. Nice fings. Lace 'andkerchiefs. Penny buns. Silk stockin's."

"Oh." He thought about this for a minute. "Are people on it?"

"Of course! Mum and Vi'let always was, but lately the boys are too, and yesterday I decided even Agnes is."

"You'd be on my list, if I 'ad one." He leaned closer, unable to resist touching the chocolate shadow on her lower lip with his forefinger.

Suddenly Elsie realized the lad was breathing funny. There was a strange look on his face and that face was now very close to hers. Quickly she jumped off the tomb. "Blimey! Nearly gone teatime. I 'ave to run—got to lay the tea things or Mrs. Gifford'll box me ears again for bein' late. I'll wash your 'andkerchief and give it back."

He wanted to tell her to keep it but, just in time, realized it would be an excuse to see her again. "Ta. Shall I see you 'ere then? Tomorrow?"

"I don't mind." She ran for the big house across the green, her little dark-clad figure merging with the dusk. The apron flapped white until she disappeared though a door in the garden wall.

"Well!" said Bernie. "Well I never!"

9.

Crowmarsh Priors, Late November 1939

I t was a gray November morning, rain beating dis-
mally against the windows, and the morning room
was cold. As usual, Elsie had neglected to lay and light the
fire. Muriel Marchmont sat glumly at her desk, marvelling
that she, who had never had children, now had three girls
on her hands—three girls proving to be Very Awkward
Indeed. Girls these days no longer did as they were told,
and she was quite exhausted with trying to do her duty by
the thankless creatures.

First there was poor, jilted Alice, whose mother refused
to stir off her sofa all day and ordered Alice about until the
girl was as limp as a tea towel. All the useful tips Muriel had
given Alice about how to make more of herself had been
ignored—no wonder the young vicar took little notice of
her. Mrs. Osbourne, dreadful, selfish woman, was too busy
complaining about her health to spare a thought for her
own daughter. Like far too many men, in Muriel's opinion,
the late vicar had married beneath him for the sake of a
pretty face.

Her goddaughter was even more vexing. Frances had been sent to stay at Glebe House because, lacking a mother, she needed female supervision and, her father had stressed, a firm hand: she had been running wild in London with a fast set of unsuitable young men. However, Tudor Falconleigh had failed to explain how Muriel was supposed to chaperone Frances, who now spent most of her time with Hugo de Balfort and his friends at Gracecourt Hall, or, Lady Marchmont suspected, gadding about to nightclubs in Brighton. She had tried to put her foot down, but Frances did much as she pleased.

This trouble with Elsie was the last straw!

Pen in hand and a fresh sheet of monogrammed cream writing paper before her, Muriel struggled to master her irritation and compose her note to Penelope Fairfax.

My Dear Penelope,

I regret to inform you that despite our best efforts for the past three months, Elsie Pigeon falls far short of what is desired in a housemaid. So much so, in fact, that I fear the arrangement must end at once. At first there were the matters of Elsie's intestinal worms and lice—though naturally Mrs. Gifford dealt with those with customary efficiency. But despite her efforts to train Elsie, things have gone from bad to worse.

The girl cannot learn to dust, polish, clean the grates, shine the knocker, make a bed, or sweep a carpet properly. She cannot even wash a teacup without breaking it. She eats nothing but bread and jam, sometimes until she is ill, and cries in the night for "Mum" and "Vilet" who I am told is the youngest of her sisters. However, since we are at war, Mrs. Gifford and I felt it our duty to make the best of things.

*Little did we imagine there could be worse to come. Elsie has
acquired a follower. She has been keeping company with a most
undesirable young man, billeted in the village with Constable
Barrows—in lieu, I understand, of being sent to prison. Elsie
insists he is a friend from the dreadful part of London she calls
home, but all Mrs. Gifford has been able to discover is that he
is an orphan brought up among criminals. The young man
seems to come and go at will, disappearing for days at a time,
and if we are all murdered in our beds I suppose we can thank
the authorities instead of the Germans.*

*So I regret to say that, unless you can make other arrange-
ments for her, Elsie will be on the London train tomorrow.*
Yours ever,
Muriel Marchmont

As she sealed the envelope there was a clatter of heels
on the stairs, then Frances breezed into the morning room
in a cloud of Vol de Nuit, cozy in a ribbon-trimmed tweed
coat and skirt, her fur draped round her shoulders. She was
holding a hat trimmed with blue velvet flowers that matched
her eyes. Rather soigné for a rainy Thursday in Crowmarsh
Priors, thought her godmother sourly.

"I say, Aunt Muriel, I went looking for a biscuit just now
and found Elsie crying her eyes out in the scullery. She says
she's being sent home. Whatever for, poor little mouse?"
Frances looked into the mirror above the empty fireplace
and adjusted her hat to an angle over one eye.

"If you got up in time for breakfast you'd have no need
of biscuits, my dear. 'Poor little mouse' indeed! Elsie, I'm
sorry to say, is on the verge of ruin with some boy who would

be in an approved school if the police had any sense. The housekeeper made a shocking discovery in her room."

"Gracious! What?"

"Silk stockings if you must know, chocolates. Scent!"

Frances turned her head this way and that checking the effect of the hat. It would never do for Elsie to leave. She and Elsie were partners in crime. Elsie crept bravely past a snoring Mrs. Gifford to unlock the front door on the nights Frances had gone to Brighton and sneaked in before dawn. Frances returned the favor by helping Elsie to escape on errands to the village when they spotted her young man lurking near the laurel bush. She had given Elsie a becoming cardigan, two lace handkerchiefs, a bottle of lavender water far too insipid for herself, and some face powder. Then, prompted by a new glow in Elsie's face and an unaccustomed pang of responsibility, she had advised her not to let the lad she was keeping company with take liberties. Elsie had winked and said, "Course not! I'd never! But I lets 'im *fink* he might, next time!"

"Very clever, Elsie darling, but do be careful…"

"Oh! Um, *I* gave the stockings and things to Elsie," Frances said quickly. "She's, um, been doing extra things for me, errands, laundering and mending, you know."

"I had no idea Elsie was capable of anything so useful." Muriel's voice was dry.

Frances tweaked the little veil and pinned her hat. "Well, she's ever so good with my washing. And I gave her the stockings because she admired them so. I've loads, you know, and one of Hugo's friends gave me an absolutely monstrous box of chocolates. Naturally I can't eat them if I'm to keep my figure, and you mustn't eat them with your blood pressure, Aunt Muriel. And I don't think the boy can be as bad all that. Elsie knew him in London, he was brought by his uncle."

"That's not the half of it, according to Mrs. Gifford," said her godmother darkly.

Frances snapped open her handbag and rummaged for her lipstick. "In fact, I think he must be a good sort, really. Because he's doing war work. Although it must be rather hush-hush, because—"

"War work? Preposterous! Whatever gave you such an idea?"

"Because Elsie said he goes off from time to time with what she calls toffs. I thought it was nonsense, then when I was out for a walk last Sunday I passed Constable Barrows's cottage and was surprised to see a motor car pull up, just like the one from the Admiralty that calls for Father. I even recognized the driver, though it seemed odd he wasn't in uniform and pretended not to see me when I waved. I assumed they must want Constable Barrows for something, though why they would send an official car for a country constable I can't imagine unless the Germans really are due here any minute. Anyway, the boy came out, got in, and was driven away. There was another man in the backseat. Curious, isn't it?"

"From what I hear that boy's the dregs of the criminal classes and the girl's a useless baggage. The sooner she's sent packing the better."

"Oh, please, Aunt Muriel! Elsie's a pet, and it would be too dreadful to send her back to the slum they live in. You mustn't! Her mother, younger brothers, and sisters were evacuated up north, her older brothers have enlisted in the navy, so she would be alone at home with her father. Elsie says he drinks and disappears for days at a time. Surely it's your duty to...to Penelope Fairfax, keep her here for a bit longer."

Muriel Marchmont frowned. Poor Penelope was saddled with that dreadful daughter-in-law, and Muriel did sympathize.

Frances rushed on: "When we had drinks at the Fairfaxes' last time Richard was home on leave, his wife told me Elsie's made friends with the foreign girl billeted there." Frances rooted in her handbag again. "And Elsie says she's applied to become a Land Girl now that Hugo and Leander have agreed to take them on at the home farm—the men have joined up or been conscripted. They turned her down at first because Elsie's so young, but she begged them to ask Penelope about it, and they did. Penelope's promised to see to it when she has time. Sending Elsie back to London now will only add to the WVS's problems. Penelope said she had a frightful time persuading people like the Pigeons to evacuate their children in the first place, and now they're tearing their hair out because so many are coming back. People don't believe there'll be any poison-gas attacks."

Muriel threw up her hands. On top of everything else, war was so unsettling for everyone. Normal life had been turned upside down. Girls doing men's work, driving tractors and baling hay! And now there was a foreign child bride who didn't speak English, with a baby in tow, living in the village. So many people had poured into England and no one was bothering to find out if they were Bolsheviks or Jews or anything else dangerous. When Sir Humphrey

Marchmont had been alive he and his wife had seen a great deal of Archibald Ramsay, MP, and had sympathized with the stand his Nordic League had taken on the need to resist the Jewish stranglehold on northern Europe. It was ridiculous of the authorities to discourage the League, she believed.

Now the war had come, she felt a twinge of pity for the women with their ragged head scarves and big-eyed children she saw on newsreels, driven out of their homes by the Nazis with only the clothes they stood up in, but they had undoubtedly brought it on themselves. And she didn't see why foreigners should be allowed to disrupt the domestic lives of people who lived quietly in the country. Particularly when she had shouldered the burden of responsibility for girls whose mothers had manifestly shirked theirs.

She thought of Alice with approval. At least one girl understood duty. If only Frances would stop gadding about and follow Alice's good example. She could learn such a lot from her.

"I'm just off to Gracecourt, Aunt Muriel." Frances yawned, then looked at her little watch. "Bridge, luncheon. Hugo's friends have mostly gone, but we can make up two tables. Leander says it amuses him to have young people around." She pulled a lipstick out of her bag and applied it carefully in the mirror. The prospect of the day before her was not very exciting. In fact, it was exactly like a great many other days, but she couldn't think of any other way of passing the time.

Muriel Marchmont watched disapprovingly as her goddaughter tucked the pretty leather bag under her arm and drew on her pale kid gloves, as if she hadn't a care in the world. It came from a foreign education. She had been expelled from a series of sound boarding schools in Devon and Wiltshire chosen personally by her godmother. Finally, and against her advice, Tudor Falconleigh had sent Frances off to a French finishing school for three years. Frances had stuck it out because he had promised her a shopping spree in Paris if she did. She had returned to England in time for her debut with a near-perfect command of French and equipped with an extravagant supply of day frocks, ball gowns, shoes, and fetching hats that had cost her father a fortune.

Soon, however, she was showing signs that she had inherited from her French mother the dangerous something that turned men's heads, the same unfortunate something that had bewitched stolid Tudor Falconleigh into his too-brief marriage. It had gotten Frances into scrapes in London with all the wrong sorts of men, and now it was having a similar effect on the men in the village, from the vicar to Leander de Balfort. Muriel intended telling Tudor bluntly that their only hope was to get Frances decently married off, before she was utterly disgraced and no one would have her.

She couldn't help noticing, however, that, compared to Frances in her fetching outfits, Alice looked dowdier than ever in her jumpers, pinnies, and too-tight head scarves. She sighed, thinking of the luncheon party at Gracecourt to which she had taken Alice. It had not been a success. Alice had been seated between Hugo and a drawling fellow with a title and a monocle. She had been wearing too much rouge and a drab frock so awful that Muriel had suspected it had once belonged to Mrs. Osbourne. After three nervously downed glasses of sherry, Alice had grown red in the face and talked a little too loudly about her late father's interest in Sussex history, then told a long, rambling story about a gang of smugglers and their underground tunnels.

The titled man had grown bored with the impromptu history lesson and turned to the vivacious girl on his left, leaving Hugo to struggle on with Alice and her history. Hugo, bless him, had pretended to be interested, which encouraged Alice to talk steadily until they left. Muriel had been silent with despair all the way home.

Alice, she had to admit, lacked sparkle. Frances, on the other hand, had far too much. How unfair life was. It occurred to her that Frances was just the person to take Alice in hand. Surely she could work a little change in Alice's appearance. Nothing too drastic—just enough to open Oliver's eyes.

"You should stop gadding about and take on some war work, Frances. Perhaps give dear Alice Osbourne a hand. She hardly stops to draw breath, though one wonders why she has quite so much thrust upon her, poor thing. Teaching, clothing drives, knitting circles, first aid, not to mention nursing that tiresome mother. She ought to be married. That nice young Oliver Hammet should marry too. So suitable, really, a vicar's daughter becoming a vicar's wife. But he...if only Alice looked a little more...a lily in need of gilding, so to speak. Perhaps you could smarten her up, my dear? Oliver would be bound to come to his senses."

To Frances's relief, Hugo's roadster pulled into the drive at Glebe House. "Oh, I know you wanted me to be friends with Alice and I tried, but truly, she's too, too tedious! Can't stick her. Must dash, Aunt Muriel." Frances blew her a kiss and disappeared. The car pulled out of the drive, gravel crunching.

That Hugo was paying Frances what in Lady Marchmont's day had been called "marked attentions" cheered her somewhat, and took her mind off Alice. Such attentions indicated a proposal was in the offing, in her experience. Marriage would steady them both. Hugo would buckle down to his responsibilities on the estate and Frances would soon be occupied with their children. She ought to write Tudor at once to let him know which way the wind was blowing. To avoid delays once Hugo popped the question, Tudor's lawyers might as well look at the question of marriage settlements now. Leander was far too impractical to take the initiative there, but Hugo needed money, and Muriel thought how fortunate it was that Frances would inherit a considerable fortune on her marriage. Leander had never lived up to the responsibilities of the estate, which had been impoverished when he inherited, thanks to his grandfather's gambling and a lifetime's devotion to a series of actresses.

Leander had married well, but instead of plowing his late wife's huge fortune sensibly back into the estate, he had chosen to indulge his aesthetic instincts instead. He had squandered endless sums on flamboyant projects at Gracecourt—hence the Chinese pagoda, the deer park stocked with small Japanese deer that had soon died, the tennis courts, and the latest, a dramatic scheme to redesign a Capability Brown lake as a series of shallow, modern rectangular pools to the specifications of a flamboyant, self-styled "horticultural artiste" with a velvet waistcoat and a foreign accent. Before the shooting luncheon Leander had taken his guests to see them. "Too thrillingly exotic! So modern!" everyone gushed and gave the "artiste" a little round of applause. One of the illustrated papers had even taken photographs for a feature article.

To Muriel Marchmont they just looked big, flat, and strange. "So unnecessary!" she had muttered under her breath. She had noticed that the house was in a shocking state. She had spotted broken panes in the leaded windows, woodworm in the Tudor linen-fold panelling, and the long gallery ceiling sagged under patches of damp. The drawing room curtains were decidedly moth-eaten and there were pale rectangles on the walls where paintings had hung— sold, she imagined, to pay for Leander's ill-conceived schemes and Hugo's fees at Eton and Oxford, then his Grand Tour.

All most unwise, in Muriel Marchmont's opinion. The de Balforts had been at Crowmarsh Priors for centuries, and the business of Leander's life, or perhaps Hugo's now, was to ensure they remained there. It was Hugo's plain duty to marry without wasting any more time and to take an English wife with money and breeding, produce a son at once, and pull the estate together before taxes ate every-thing up.

Frances would inherit her mother's money when she married and the Falconleigh money when her father died. As for breeding, though her mother had been French, the Falconleighs were not to be sneezed at. Frances's great-uncle had been a duke. Muriel Marchmont hated to think that poor Hugo might be forced to look for an American heiress, like Winston's mother. Or that parvenu Nancy Astor. And one American in Crowmarsh Priors was quite enough!

She considered how best to prod the young people along the paths she had chosen for them. Not for the first time she reflected on her will. She had no children and, other than Oliver Hammet, no relatives. She had always intended leaving her money, the house, and her shares to Oliver. Then he could marry Alice. Of course he already had the vicarage to offer Alice as a home. Of course he could marry Alice in the vicarage, but Glebe House was far grander. Besides, Muriel liked to imagine Alice sitting in this very room of a morning, beneath the portrait of herself as a young married woman wearing pearls and court dress, and remembering her fondly. In the fullness of time Alice and Oliver would probably name a daughter Muriel…

As for Frances, Muriel decided it was incumbent on her to leave her jewelry to the future Lady de Balfort, the contents of Glebe House too, except for the morning room furniture and her portrait, of course. At Gracecourt, heaven knew, they could use her things—even the furniture was falling to pieces and the young couple needed to make a decent showing when they entertained. Vicars did less of that, and there was no point in leaving jewelry to Alice, who would look like a donkey in her pearls.

She shoved aside the letter to Penelope Fairfax and took a fresh sheet of cream writing paper. She would dispatch a letter to Tudor at once. And another to her solicitor, instructing him to call on her as soon as convenient, as she wished to discuss a few new alterations to her will.

She had drawn up an inventory of her jewelry after her solicitor's last visit. Where *had* she put it? She rifled through a mass of papers on the desk without finding it. Where, for that matter, had she put her jewel chest in which she kept all but the few items she wore every day? The key wasn't here either. She vaguely recalled hiding the chest somewhere as a precaution, in case Elsie's follower tried to burgle Glebe House. Perhaps her memory wasn't what it had been. But what was?

10.

Crowmarsh Priors,
August 1940

*E*vangeline had come to dread the long nights. She
tossed and turned, awake until the early hours before
she was sucked into an undertow of nightmares until it
grew light. In all her dreams she was back in Louisiana.
Sometimes she was at her old home in New Orleans. It was
silent and dim, the furniture was gone, and each door she
opened led to another empty room while she felt something
stalking her through the silent house, something horrible,
getting closer as she tried to run but couldn't. Sometimes
she was at school, looking out at the world through the convent's little barred windows. But often she was in the country at her grandmother's, leaving Laurent in the gray half-
light before dawn. Mist lay heavy over the cane fields and
smelled of pond lilies. She was late, had to hurry and dress,
Grandmère and the old ladies who never seemed to go
home would soon be up saying the rosary in the parlor, the
servants would be awake—hurry, hurry before anyone saw.

The house was just beyond the hanging moss on the
next swamp oak, then the next, and the next. She began to

run, faster and faster, but she couldn't find the way back in the mist, although she knew it was close because she could hear Inez clattering pots and pans and smell coffee brewing. A mule brayed and a bell rang, but she couldn't see anything.

"Too late! Someone knows," said Laurent, behind her. She whirled round to see who was there. They were coming closer through the mist, until they were close enough for her to see the human figures had Loup Garou faces. She turned to run again, but Laurent's body swung in the hanging moss, blocking her way...

Evangeline would wake with her heart pounding and remind herself all over again that she was no longer in New Orleans. Johnny was crying for his breakfast in Tanni's room. The birds were twittering in the old pear tree in the garden. She would thump her pillows, prop herself up in the four-poster bed with its pink silk coverlet, and steel herself to wash hastily in the cold bathroom down the landing.

Twenty minutes later, still damp, she would put on yesterday's clothes, picking up the ancient gray jumper that had belonged to Richard's father from the floor where she had dropped it next to her boots and trousers. Once Evangeline had been fastidious in her dress, taking pains to match frocks and shoes and jewelry, but now she hardly cared what she wore; in fact, the worse the better.

She went to the kitchen and put the kettle on for tea. She hated tea, but drank it for warmth, and waited for Tanni to come down before she made toast. Then she tried to think how to fill the day while she waited for Laurent to call and tell her to leave at once: this was the day. Her small suitcase was ready, packed with the few good things she owned, ready to go at a moment's notice. It couldn't come soon enough.

At first Evangeline had thought she would go mad in England. She had meant to contact Laurent at once and tell him about the baby. But when she arrived, it had proved harder than she'd expected. Richard had whisked her down to his mother's house in Crowmarsh Priors, and the telephone was in the echoing hall. A barely polite Penelope had come to stay, ostensibly to "help Evangeline settle in," which meant watching her like a hawk. It was impossible to get in touch with Laurent, let alone make any plan to leave, with Penelope there.

After a few weeks, with Richard increasingly away on duty and Penelope's own war work demanding her return to London, Penelope had gone back to her flat near Harrods. Evangeline had breathed a little easier. She had rung Laurent at the Marseille office and told him where she was. They agreed she would join him in France as soon as he found a place to live. "Everything in Provence smells good in the heat, and from up in the hills you can see the sea," he said. "I got my eye on a pretty white house with blue shutters for us there, trying to save some money for it."

"Us? But how can we have the same house?" asked Evangeline, wistfully. She hadn't thought that part of the plan through.

Easy, said Laurent. There were many North Africans in France, with dark skin like *gens de couleur*. They mixed with the white population, intermarried, had children, everything. "Long as you keep clear of the Fontaine employees in Marseille, we'll be fine." It sounded impossible, but Evangeline tried to imagine their new life, their children running about, Laurent coming home each evening. She patted her stomach. She had to tell him soon.

Then she had miscarried at five months and was ill for weeks. When she was up and about again, pale and list-less, she had an excuse to go to London—she needed to see a doctor there, she said. There she managed to contact Laurent in Marseille. Something new in his voice warned her that it was not the right time to tell him about the baby. His voice sounded drowsy. She wasn't sure if he was tired or—could she be imagining it?—wary. She decided to wait and tell him in person.

Evangeline had been surprised by how much she grieved for the baby who would have made them a family. As long as no one knew Laurent was colored and she was white she could not imagine a future for them that did not include children.

"How much longer, Laurent? I miss you so much."

"Not long. I miss you too."

Week after week, Laurent promised they would be together soon. Then summer had ended and a curt tele-gram came from Penelope: she was to prepare a room for an evacuated mother and child. Two days later a tall, dark-haired girl, who looked very young but was holding a baby, stepped off the train at Crowmarsh Priors. The guard handed down to her a huge carpetbag. She looked around wildly as if she didn't know what to do next, and the baby began to cry. Albert Hawthorne, the stationmaster, went to help her. When he learned who she was and where she was going, he chucked the baby under the chin and carried Tanni's carpetbag himself all the way from the station. "She wants looking after," he had told Evangeline firmly as he put the carpetbag down in the hall.

"Good morning," Tanni had said carefully, in English, looking around the wide hall with the light flooding in, the curving staircase, and the Turkey runner on the polished floor. She sniffed. Thankfully there was no horrible smell of boiled cabbage and drains. At the door she had automatically checked for any signs saying that Jews were forbidden. Now she spied a small medallion of the Madonna and Child that Evangeline had scandalized Penelope by hanging in the hall and thought she had better make sure. "Jews are being permitted here?" she asked, shifting Johnny in her arms.

"What?" said the girl who had opened the door. "Why on earth wouldn't they be?" She looked surprised by the question—and Tanni was puzzled by her. She was wearing trousers and some sort of gray knitted thing with holes in the elbows. Tanni wondered if she was the servant, although surely a maid would wear a uniform. It was very odd. "Come on, I'll show you where your room is. Here, give me the baby. Come to Aunt Evangeline, darlin'," she cooed. "What's his name? I got some of Richard's old nursery furniture down from the attic."

Having Tanni and Johnny around distracted Evangeline a little. Waiting for Laurent's phone calls, Evangeline moved restlessly between the house and the garden, keeping busy but never out of earshot of the shrill ring of the telephone in the entrance hall. She filled the long days weeding the garden, playing with Johnny, cooking food she barely touched, writing to Richard. She refused invitations to tea with Lady

Marchmont or for drinks and tennis at Gracecourt Hall and made stilted conversation with whey-faced Alice Osbourne who obviously did not like her but who called to see how Tanni was getting on. Evangeline could see Alice hadn't approved of the Madonna any more than Penelope had, but she didn't care what Alice thought. Alice was just another irritant in the purgatory that was England.

As soon as Laurent told her to come to him, Evangeline planned to put her wedding ring and the sapphire and diamond ring that had been Penelope's, which Richard had given her as an engagement ring—even though they hadn't had time to be engaged—into an envelope with the letter she had written already, saying she was sorry and that he should divorce her. Poor Richard. He had rescued her and he seemed to be in love with her, but it never occurred to her to stay with him. All she could do was look for the gold baby—maybe there was a way to undo the gris-gris—but it was lost. All she could think of was Laurent.

Then war was declared, and autumn set in. Laurent's rare telephone calls usually came late at night, after Tanni had gone to sleep. Evangeline could hear music and laughter in the background. He had made friends with a group of North African musicians who played in a waterfront bar. He often joined them at night after work, he told her, filling in for the saxophonist or the pianist. It reminded him of being back in New Orleans. North Africans looked colored, although they lived among the white French people and no one took any notice. "Not much longer, darlin', just a little harder travelling with the war on. You mustn't come by yourself. I'll come get you soon."

"When, Laurent? I miss you so!"

"Soon, darlin', soon. I miss you too."

Just before Christmas Laurent rang to say that he was now living in Paris and mumbled about lodging with a musician friend. He was looking for a place for himself and Evangeline to live in the city. "You have to be patient, darlin'. Finding an apartment here's not easy—" The call ended abruptly.

Evangeline tried not to be alarmed as the dark days succeeded each other and still she waited. She tried to ignore the war rumbling away in Europe.

One morning in May she dragged herself up from her usual nightmare-ridden sleep, woken by the clanging of the church bell. She was disoriented. She must still be dreaming, she thought, and pinched herself hard.

She was definitely awake, in a strange, rather dirty room, dimly lit by a bar of sunlight falling across a worn but garish carpet. Nearby a church bell was indeed pealing, probably at the old church she remembered having seen on the corner. The window glass had been stuck over with rice paper to prevent it breaking if a bomb fell nearby. A man and a woman were arguing drunkenly outside. A milk van rattled past. There were footsteps in the corridor and someone was talking in a low voice behind the thin partition wall. She was not in New Orleans or in Sussex, but in London, and now she was blissfully awake. Laurent was actually beside her, his warm, naked thigh against hers, a little taller and more solid than she remembered, but sleeping soundly as he always did.

Joy surged through her again as she remembered—the telephone shrilling in the hall the day before—it had been early afternoon and Tanni had nearly answered it. Laurent was in London! Evangeline grabbed her suitcase and rushed for the train, in such a hurry that she forgot to tear off her rings and leave the letter for Richard.

Last night had been their first night together in more than a year, but this time she didn't have to sneak home in the dark. Laurent said no one here knew who she and he were or that he was colored and she was white or that they weren't married. They didn't have to sneak anywhere. Thank you, God, and please, please, let the church bell be ringing because it's a church bell and not because it's signalling a poison gas attack or the invasion.

In the dark she and Laurent had fallen hungrily on each other without pausing to draw the blackout curtains. Their hurriedly discarded clothes lay in a heap on the floor, his hat and their gas masks tossed onto the dresser. His saxophone case was propped in a corner, and her running-away suitcase, beside it, was still packed. She stretched out a hand to replace the cork in the bottle of cognac Laurent had brought from Paris. Then she snuggled back into the crook of his arm and buried her head in his chest.

Now at last they would have a chance to talk about everything, about the baby and how frightened she had been in New Orleans, how miserable after her miscarriage, what had happened when Laurent got to Marseille. How they were going to live now when they got to France. But instinct told her that, first, they had to get used to being together again. It had been a long time. Of course Laurent still loved her as much as she loved him, last night had proved that, but now they could make their plans and the past would be a bad dream. She realized she was still wearing her engagement and wedding rings. She would send them to Richard with the letter today.

But now…she sniffed and sat up again. Coffee!

Laurent's arm tightened. He nuzzled her neck.

"Laurent! Can you smell it?"

"Mmm—Schiaparelli?"

"Even better. Coffee! Oh, Laurent, I bet it's that Italian café down the street. Remember how, back home, the first thing you smelled every morning was coffee roasting? The tea they drink here tastes like dishwater. Sometimes I'd give anything to taste Creole coffee again. With a beignet to dip in it. I was just dreaming—"

"About breakfast?" He yawned.

"Um, sort of. In my dream Inez was making it."

He rolled onto his back, laughing, and stroked her flat tummy. "You always were a greedy chile!"

She stretched luxuriously under his touch. "Mmm, so were you. Remember how we'd eat beignets until we were sick? You ate nineteen once. Way greedier than me."

Laurent folded his hands behind his head and considered. "Inez sure could cook. Waffles. And *pain perdu*. With boudin sausage. Grits on the side."

"*Talmousses,* with cream cheese."

He put an arm round her and settled into the pillow. "Beaten biscuits with country ham. I really liked those."

"And those lumpy rolls they called bullfrogs."

"*Grenouilles?*"

"Yes, those. Philippe said we had to poke holes in the side because they had live frogs inside that would hop down our throats unless we made a hole in the bottom to get them out. We both believed him. It made Inez so mad. 'What's the matter with y'all, pokin' your fingers in my good rolls like that?'" Evangeline's smile faded. "The food's awful in England. I miss Inez's cooking. Do you?"

"I eat pretty good in France." Laurent laced his fingers through Evangeline's pale ones. The family resemblance was strong in the faces on the pillow, their builds, and even their hands with the long index fingers. Evangeline's hair was dark, spilling over her shoulders, while Laurent's was light copper, close-cropped, and curly. His hand was strong and sensitive, a musician's. A lover's.

He played thoughtfully with Evangeline's big sapphire and diamond ring, turning it round her finger. "You sound homesick, well as hungry. Maybe they're the same thing. Me too, sometimes, when it rains and Paris is nothing but wet stones and strange faces and I think about how everything used to be warm and folks saying 'hi' and—but it's different for you. You're a married woman, got other things to think about. Look like your husband takin' good care of you." He gave the ring a last twirl.

"I wasn't really married. Marriage by a ship's captain doesn't count in the eyes of the Church, so I can get an annulment and then we can get married when we—"

"*Us?* Get married?" He stared, looking surprised.

"Well...we can't just *live* together, Laurent." Evangeline thought about the house in Provence—no, Paris—full of children and Laurent coming home to her every night. How could they do that if they weren't married? She blurted out, "But...er...we have to...I almost had a baby, you know— meant to tell you—but then I had a miscarriage..."

"When?"

"Last summer, while you were in Marseille. I guess it was for the best; Richard might have made a fuss about it, thinking it was his and—"

He let go of her, turned away, and reached for his cigarettes.

Evangeline watched him out of the corner of her eye. Something in his attitude made her uncomfortable. Was he upset, thinking she meant she had been pregnant with Richard's baby? That must be it. "It was your baby," she said, testing the waters.

Laurent smiled grimly and struck a match. "And I hear Germans have this theory, mulattoes are like mules—can't reproduce their own kind."

"They've never been to New Orleans then. In Sussex they think I came up to London to see a doctor about why I haven't had a child."

"Thank heaven you haven't. Back home the girls used to get an old colored woman named Mama La Bas to fix it so's they didn't have a baby."

Evangeline took a deep breath. "Let's not talk about it anymore. Tell me what it's like in Paris now. The French must be relieved that the British army's there to protect the border."

Laurent plumped their pillows, settled back, and pulled Evangeline to him. He rested his chin on top of her head and she didn't see the shadow pass over his face. "Paris? You never saw so many desperate folks with nowhere to go. The Germans are coming fast—only thing travelling faster than the Germans are rumors about what they've done in Poland and other places. Maginot Line never meant a damn thing.

Invasion's almost official. People expect Petain will negotiate an armistice. Everyone's so scared you can smell it. Men who aren't in the army have disappeared into the countryside. But for the moment," he shrugged, "there's coffee to drink, and the women still dress up and wear pretty hats and smell good. The clubs and casinos and the Folies are full every night. Folks drink champagne and dance and try to act like what's comin', ain't comin'."

"Can't you leave, come to England?"

"It's OK for me. America's not at war with Germany. Because I'm not afraid to stay in Paris I get work most nights. Even with the Germans coming. Josephine Baker and the Revue Negre were a smash. The French love jazz and blues and swing and what they call 'exotic dancing,' all that shakin' and high steppin' and stuff from the Treme. I've played on records and people buy a lot of those, so I make enough to live on. Like I told you, the Fontaine business is practically finished down in Marseille, and I heard Andre and Philippe are struggling to hold things together in New Orleans since your father died. They write every now and then, asking how I am. They ever say anything to you about, you know, that night?"

"Nobody can understand why I ran off with Richard. Andre's the only one who keeps in touch. He says no one's ever going to forget the scandal I caused. No girl from a decent family is allowed to even dance with him now. He told me Daddy wanted to have my marriage annulled immediately, but Mama persuaded him that would disgrace the family even more, especially if I had a baby. If I ever set foot in Louisiana again I'll be arrested for shooting Maurice. But it doesn't matter. I don't want to go back, ever." Evangeline ran her hand down the livid scars on his back.

He winced, slid down until he was lying flat, then pulled her on top of him. "You're a dangerous woman with a gun, sugar, but you got some sweet ways. Come on, now..."

Afterward they shared a cigarette in their old companionable way. Reassured, she tried another tack. "Why can't you stay here? Not go back to Paris. It's dangerous. Or maybe we could run away someplace else, not England or France. At least we'd be together."

Laurent drew deep on the cigarette and passed it back to her. "Dangerous everywhere—back home, France, here, with the Germans coming, unless the English can hold them off. Which they can't. I can't afford to leave Paris right now. Between the records and playing at the club, I can live. I just have to be careful, don't want to get on the wrong side of the Germans. They don't like colored people. Or come to that, anybody who isn't German. In Paris I mostly say I'm North African, but I got two passports for when the Germans come."

"How do you get back and forth to France at a time like this?"

"I'm pals with some Frenchmen who used to come to the club in Paris. They've set up a headquarters in London, at the top of a pub—the Free French, they call themselves. As a musician and an American I can go back and forth pretty easily, so I have a job as their courier. Pays well."

"Oh, Laurent, couldn't they let me do that too? I'm American and—"

"No!"

Evangeline's face crumpled.

"But I'll come back to England to see you every chance I get. You know I will," Laurent said.

"I know. But it seems so unfair, we've both come all this way to be together, only we can't because of the damn Germans."

After a moment Laurent put his arms around her again. "I know, darlin', I know," he said, chin resting on top of her head. "Let's not talk about it anymore."

The patch of sunshine crept across the carpet and disappeared as the day passed, while they made love and avoided any talk of their old home or their future one.

When they dressed late in the afternoon Evangeline noticed Laurent's socks had holes and his shirt was frayed at the collar and cuffs. At dusk they went out and walked side by side through the streets. They drank coffee at the Italian café, self-conscious and nervous to be sitting side by side, but no one even glanced at them. They wandered through the blacked-out streets, then saw a poster for the new American film *Gone with the Wind* and joined the queue. Afterward they walked back to the hotel through the balmy night, holding hands. "I'm glad we're not in Atlanta," said Laurent, tightening his hold.

"Me too," said Evangeline and burst into tears.

They made love again, then sprawled tangled in the sheets afterward. Evangeline's slender leg was draped over Laurent's as they shared a tooth mug of cognac and a bar of chocolate Laurent had brought. Laurent rolled some cigarettes he said the musicians all smoked in Paris, made from Indian hemp. Feeling mellow, they dozed, and this time Evangeline, wrapped in Laurent's arms, dreamed of nothing.

From below in the darkness of blacked-out Soho the sound of late revelers and a clatter of dishes in a restaurant woke them in the early hours. "Time to get to the pub," Laurent said, yawning. "French boys will be expecting me. I got work to do. But first I brought you some presents." Without drawing the blackout curtains he got up, his spare body silhouetted against the dimming window. He handed a flat parcel and two bags to Evangeline.

She opened the bags first. "What is it?" She felt inside. Sniffed. Tasted. Something stung her tongue. "Oh, Laurent, dried hot peppers! How delicious! English food is so bland I can hardly swallow it." She plunged a hand into the other bag and exclaimed, "Rice!" She hadn't tasted rice in ages. "Where did you get this?"

"Algerian friend in Paris. She's, uh, married to one of the fellows in the band, cooks for us all, they use hot peppers in Algeria like we do back home, make a sauce they put on everything. Now before you open the big one I've got something new I want to play you."

"Oh, good!" Evangeline tossed back her hair, propped herself up, and hugged the sheet around her.

He winked at her. "'Evangeline's Blues,' I call it." Sitting naked on the side of the bed, Laurent ran through some scales, then slid into a slow rhythm, the saxophone soft at first, just touching the notes, enjoying each one before letting it go and sliding into the next, bolder now, the power and the sadness and the sweetness of the music taking hold, until the sound filled the room, and the scattered clothes, the curtains, the dirty window, the faded armchair, the stained wallpaper, the day of lovemaking were all part of it. Evangeline smiled sadly when the last notes faded in the darkness like the feel of a lover's farewell kiss. She wished she and Laurent could stay forever in this room where no one knew or cared about them.

Laurent drew the blackout curtains and switched on the cheap bedside lamp. "Open the other present."

She tore off layers of brown paper. "Oh, Laurent! Your records! Thank goodness Penelope didn't take the gramophone when she moved into the flat! Now I can listen to you every night and imagine you there beside me. You sound better than Glenn Miller!" she exclaimed.

"Wish he thought so too," he said, pleased. "I'd give anything to play in his band. Back home, people buy his records, see my name on the cover. They would know I hadn't vanished without a trace."

Evangeline threw caution to the winds. "Oh, Laurent, *please* take me with you! The French don't care who we are. Or we can go to some other country—Sweden or...or...I don't care, there must be someplace. I don't feel alive without you and I just wait and wait. I'm so *tired* of waiting!"

He sighed. "You're safer here, honey, like I told you. It's not just about us, it's about the Germans and the war. It's getting worse and worse, everywhere. When the war is over we can worry about it. Right now I've got all I can do to stay in one piece, play some music, make a livin'. You've got to be patient. Wait for me where you are. Stay with your husband for the time bein'."

11.

Crowmarsh Priors,
October 1940

*W*ith France under Nazi control and the British Expeditionary Force evacuated from Dunkirk in bloody disarray, the Germans settled in across the channel and launched the Blitz in preparation for the invasion of England.

A month later the bombing seemed to have been going on forever. Every day wave after wave of German planes and their escorts thundered across the channel, darkening the sky over Sussex, then heading north. On their tails black swastikas flashed insolently in the last rays of autumn sunshine.

Sheep grazing on the downs ran in panic, their bleating drowned by the drone of engines. A moment later RAF Spitfires appeared, but the endless German column banked and continued relentlessly toward its targets. Ack-ack fire erupted in the distance. Over Croydon a Spitfire spiraled down from the sky, black smoke billowing behind it.

Albert Hawthorne, hoeing cabbages behind his cottage, looked up, shook his fist, and cursed.

Nell hurried their eight-year-old daughter, Margaret Rose, into the Anderson shelter at the end of the garden and shouted for him to join them. Instead Albert dropped the hoe and wheeled out his bicycle: he was in the Home Guard now. Apron fluttering, she ran after him with his gas mask, muttering that it was all very well for the government with their Home Guard posters, but were the unarmed Home Guard supposed to hoe the Germans to death if they parachuted into the village? She hoped he'd remember he had a wife and a daughter in the shelter and she'd taken the bus and queued for hours in Hurst Green to get sausages for tea, so mind he got home safe to eat them. He pedalled off, marvelling at women's priorities.

He almost collided with Alice Osbourne, now the local air raid warden, who came running out of the church gate still in her flowered pinny. Tucking up her skirt, she leaped onto her bicycle blowing an air raid whistle. Her gas mask swung from the handlebars as she rode off shouting "air raid" sternly at five little boys kicking a football about on the green. They scattered and ran for home.

Alice pedalled hard through the village, making sure no other children were out. There had been so many alarms since the Blitz began that now they no longer took them seriously; air raid alarms were like a new game. When the bombing had begun she and Oliver had devised an air raid signal "ring three times, pause, ring three times, pause" using the St. Gabriel's bell, because they didn't have a siren. Now the War Office had ordered that church bells were only to be rung to signal the invasion had begun. Oliver said it was a sad turn of events. The government had installed a siren in the parish hall, but it was temperamental and didn't always go off.

The knowledge that the Germans were only twenty-five miles away across the channel terrified Alice. It was rumored that bodies in Nazi uniforms had washed up on the coast and that agents provocateurs had infiltrated England and were everywhere. They must try to hold off the invasion, but many people said it was only a matter of time. People were to stay alert and report anyone who behaved suspiciously to the authorities. Alice had taken to calling in at Glebe House to hear the BBC news on Lady Marchmont's wireless each evening—it worked better than the little one at the Osbournes' cottage, and as a warden she needed to keep up with what was happening. Also, it was an excuse to put off going home to her mother. Frances Falconleigh, who had surprised everyone who knew her by joining the Land Army with the young housemaid Elsie, usually returned home on her bicycle at dusk. Frances or Mrs. Gifford drew the blackout curtains, then all five women huddled round the wireless in the morning room.

They heard Churchill's ringing speech that England would "fight them on the beaches but never, *never* surrender." It made them feel oddly heartened. Then weeks later Frances confided her father had told her that Churchill ended the speech with an aside that they'd be fighting on the beaches with empty bottles because empty bottles were all the resources they'd got. It sounded, she added, as if Britain couldn't hold out much longer: the French army had been much larger than England's but it hadn't stopped the Germans overrunning Paris or the French government surrendering.

At this, Alice had closed her eyes in prayer.

Frances had regarded her with disgust. "I wish I had a gun!" she said fiercely. "If they invade I'd be sure to take a couple of Germans with me." Alice stopped praying and stared at her. She had never heard a girl talk that defiant way.

And how could one person fight the Germans? Alice wondered if she would be afraid to die when the time came, and if she would be brave enough to "take a couple with her," as everyone had begun to say you must. Perhaps Frances was right, and they did need guns. Guns! "Sufficient unto the day is the evil thereof," she muttered, which took her mind off shooting Germans and helped her concentrate instead on the people for whom she was responsible.

The new party of Land Army recruits were digging potatoes and picking the last of the apples at the de Balforts' home farm. They worked until dusk, when they caught a bus back to their hostel. Elsie Pigeon could be relied on to get them into the home farm shelter with their gas masks. Although she was the youngest of her group, Elsie was good at bossing people about. Frances was away; she had a day's leave and had gone up to London to see her father.

The air raid siren kept up its piercing wail. It wasn't much comfort to know it had also summoned the Home Guard, which consisted of Oliver, Albert Hawthorne, Hugo de Balfort, the publican's elderly father and uncle, Ted and George Smith, and several farmers' sons in their teens who were due to enlist. They had drilled with broomsticks until Hugo donated Gracecourt's stock of old hunting rifles. Alice wouldn't give two pence for the Home Guard's chances when the Germans came. The enemy had managed to spread the word that anyone resisting the invasion would be regarded as a traitor and executed immediately.

Puffing now, Alice halted to peer into Lady Marchmont's garden. Except for the lavender bushes and the flagstone walk, it had been dug over for a "Dig for Victory" garden. Mrs. Gifford, in her white apron and cap, was following the old lady down the walk to their Anderson shelter, laden with their gas masks, rugs, and a Thermos of tea. Lady Marchmont couldn't move very fast with her cane, but she was nearly there. Alice waved to her and sped by Penelope Fairfax's house.

Evangeline would have Tanni, Johnny, and the three bombed-out evacuee children who had recently been billeted with her down in the musty wine vault where Richard's father had stored his claret and port—Alice and Richard had played "dungeons" there on rainy days. It made a splendid bomb shelter, though—unless the house took a direct hit and buried Evangeline once and for all, which would serve her right. Alice stifled that thought at once on account of Tanni and the children, but she couldn't help thinking of Richard.

Richard and his convoy were in danger somewhere out on the gray Atlantic. In the village hall she had hung a lurid poster—IT ALL DEPENDS ON YOU—to drive home the message that everyone needed to grow food and make do and mend and help the war effort by being as self-sufficient as possible so the country didn't depend on supplies that had to be protected by convoys. The poster showed one such ship, HMS *Gloworm*, sinking in flames after a battle with a German destroyer in April. Every day Alice prayed for all British ships at sea and those who sailed in them—she tried not to be too specific about Richard.

Now she was panting on up the hill toward home and her mother, who got into a frightful state each time the Germans flew over, even though, so far, they had saved their bombs for the cities.

It was twilight by the time she reached the ugly Edwardian cottage, another ominously clear evening, making it easy for German pilots to navigate and good for bombing. The moon was rising over the horizon. To the north, the sky over London was full of silver barrage balloons. Ominously it glowed orange and flashed with searchlights and explosions. Alice parked her bicycle and scanned the countryside with her binoculars, looking for any signs of light that might act as a signal for German pilots—a carelessly drawn blackout curtain, a forgotten autumnal bonfire still smoldering, an absentminded torch user or some idiot who had turned on his car's headlamps. Even Sister Tucker, the nurse, was allowed only a tiny pinprick of a light on her bicycle, and she preferred to do without it, maintaining that her eyes were better in the dark.

She peered into the ground-floor windows behind the overgrown hydrangea bushes and saw with irritation that the blackout curtains had not been drawn. She had warned her mother several times that if she forgot and put the light on they'd be arrested for helping the enemy. She hurried inside, hoping her mother had already gone down to the cellar and lit the lantern they kept there. Their shelter was the old coal store.

Inside, the dark passageway smelled of boiled turnips. "Mummy?"

"Alice? Where have you been? You know how anxious I get when you're off gallivanting. I heard the airplanes, then

I heard the siren. I didn't know what to think! They keep talking on the wireless about poison gas." The sofa rustled as Mrs. Osbourne sat up, querulous, hands clutching at the plaid rug with which she covered herself when she had a nap. Mrs. Osbourne was only fifty-five, but thanks to ill health, real and imagined, she seemed much older. "When your father was alive—" she began.

"No gas tonight, Mummy. If there was, it didn't get me and I'm the miners' canary," said Alice loudly to forestall her mother's litany of complaints. She knew she should wear her gas mask, but she could hardly pedal round the village, then up the hill to the cottage with it on. As for Mummy, she flatly refused to wear hers at all. She said it brought on her attacks.

Alice pulled her mother to her feet. "The village are all in their shelters, snug and sound, and we must go straight down to ours."

"It's so damp down there! I don't know what your father would have said about all this, I'm sure." Alice's mother shuffled her feet into her slippers and took Alice's arm. With her free hand Alice felt for her mother's crocheted shawl on its hook in the hall, which was stacked with boxes. "I'll be glad when this war's over," quavered Mrs. Osbourne, "and you can put your father's books and papers into the coal store, out of the way. This house is so much smaller than the vicarage, and as for storing things in the hall…"

Germans or no Germans, her mother would not be hurried. In fact she seemed to go as slowly as possible. Alice ground her teeth.

Somehow they made it down the stairs, one at a time. In the cellar Alice lit the lantern and settled her mother in her father's old armchair. Then she perched on a frayed ottoman and took up some mending from the workbasket she kept there. The coal cellar was not large and their knees almost touched.

"What does the new vicar do for a shelter?" Mrs. Osbourne asked, arranging her shawl around her shoulders. She made a point of not referring to him by name: he had had no business taking her husband's place.

"The Reverend Oliver Hammet has one of those new Anderson shelters at the bottom of his garden. Some volunteers came from the bishop's office to put it up for him. Funny-looking things—they're a kind of barrel-shaped metal roof and sides, and there's room for two bunk beds inside, perhaps four if people squeeze up a bit. Several people in the village have them, the Hawthornes and even Lady Marchmont. The rest use their cellars like we do."

Alice didn't mention that the vicar's Anderson shelter was now almost impossible to reach beneath the brambles that had quickly smothered his well-meant but hopeless attempt at a victory garden. Oliver had no idea of gardening whatsoever. Surveying the mess, he suggested he might be better keeping chickens or rabbits instead of growing vegetables. Alice had told him that a goat would be a better choice and they had both laughed.

Since then Oliver Hammet had ceased to be a source of discomfort to Alice. The war meant that civil defense procedures had thrown them together frequently and she had realized that although he was a thoroughly kind and good man, she would never feel the slightest romantic interest in him. She sensed he felt the same way about her. She knew Nell Hawthorne still cherished hopes of their marrying in the end, but Alice no longer cared: now she could carry on with her activities at the church without feeling awkward. That, at least, was a relief. But there was no point explaining all this to her mother.

"What other news is there?"

"Hmm...Constable Barrows told me that a shopkeeper in Lewes was caught selling eggs to customers without coupons and nearly sent to prison. Then, let's see, the Mothers' Union is sewing a new banner for the Sunday school corner, and the Dorcas Society were donated some oiled wool so they'll hold knitting sessions in the vicarage parlor three mornings a week to make socks for the troops. Shame you can't go that far, Mummy, because I know they can use every pair of hands. You're good at knitting and crochet. You'd be doing something useful for the troops and you'd have a bit of company."

Mrs. Osbourne had pursed her lips at the mention of the vicarage parlor. She remained pointedly silent. Alice looked up from the mending, changed tack quickly. "The three children evacuated from London settled in well on their first day at school, considering what a dreadful time they've had. Their names are Maude and Tommy and Kipper Johnson. They were bombed out, lost everything they had, and Penelope Fairfax said it was a matter of urgency to find them a place at once so she felt she had to—"

"Billet them at her own house, I heard," Mrs. Osbourne finished for her. "With only that American strumpet to look after them. What can Penelope be thinking of!"

"Mummy, please!" Alice snipped her thread ferociously. "Penelope is too busy to worry about things in Crowmarsh Priors. The WVS are at it night and day, with so many people bombed out of their homes now and using the Underground stations for shelters. It sounds chaotic trying to keep order—all those poor people! Scared, hungry, worried about what they will find when the all-clear sounds. Mothers lose their children and panic, men get into fistfights when they've been drinking, and Penelope said the lavatory is usually just a bucket behind a sheet—sometimes not even that. And one night during a raid a woman gave birth. But Penelope, of course, simply gets on with things and *doesn't complain!*" Alice bit her lip. When she spoke next she tried to sound cheerful, but it was hard work. "So here we are, all safe and sound, Mummy. No fires, no gas attacks, and, so far, no bombs. Mustn't grumble."

There was silence for a blessed few minutes as Alice sewed. She felt exhausted.

Finally her mother cleared her throat and sighed loudly. "It's past teatime. We should have brought a Thermos down with us. Why must you always forget, Alice? I am the last person to complain, but—"

"Have a boiled sweet, Mummy." Alice hoarded her sweets for these emergencies.

The ground under the cellar vibrated. The coast was taking it tonight as well as London, thought Alice. What about "those in peril on the sea"? No safe shelter in the cellar or Underground station for them, just heaving, icy waters. Was Richard ever afraid?

"I will never, never understand why Richard jilted you, Alice. I simply don't know what your father would say if he were alive. If Richard had married you as he ought, we would have been living at the Fairfaxes' house now, instead of that dreadful American and that shiftless gypsy girl with her brat," said her mother.

"As I've told you and told you, Mummy, Tanni's not a gypsy, she's Jewish. Not at all the same thing! She's married to a very young professor who volunteered as a translator at the War Office, so she and her baby need somewhere to live. Sometimes you sound like Lady Marchmont. It's our Christian duty to welcome her and her child, who, I must say, is very well looked after." Alice stabbed her needle into her cotton reel with such force that it snapped. "Here you are. Your nightdress is mended, good as new," she said through clenched teeth. "'Make do and mend,' you know!"

"I suppose I have no choice *but* to make do in this horrid little cottage, have I, with your father in his grave and Richard disappointing us so?"

Alice closed her eyes and prayed silently, *Please, God, either let the all clear come or send a bomb to fall on this house, now, at once and put us out of our misery. Amen.*

12.

London, February 1941

*A*dmiral Tudor Falconleigh put down the latest intelligence report and pushed his chair away from his overflowing desk at the War Office. He rubbed his eyes. Beyond the grimy glass of the window behind him, London lay in ruins. Intelligence reports often contradicted each other, but the pile on his desk contained no good news, only different scenarios for the expected invasion. The RAF lads were throwing themselves as hard as they could against the Luftwaffe, but the latest report warned that the Germans were developing a pilotless plane.

If so, it was the end. The admiral and most of his colleagues believed a coastal invasion by seaborne German troops was coming any day, and they wished the prime minister would concentrate on remobilizing and reequipping the regular army to repel it before it was too late. But Churchill had become fixated with guerrillas and resistance movements, first in Europe and now at home.

He had already diverted resources so Colin Gubbins could set up the Special Operations Executive to parachute British agents behind enemy lines to support the Resistance in occupied countries. It was pointless. The French

Resistance was chaotic: the Communists clashed with the Maquis, who were at odds with local organizations, who disagreed among themselves. It was the same in Poland and Holland. Now Churchill had ordered Gubbins to add to the mess, organizing an English resistance, with Auxiliary Units as its backbone, who would go to ground and sabotage the Germans after the invasion.

The admiral and the prime minister had clashed bitterly at yesterday's War Office meeting over these units—"Auxis," as Churchill called them. They would be trained in the same skills as the SOE: radio telegraphy, laying mines, using explosives, and killing in hand-to-hand combat. The admiral knew it would never work. For starters, they would have to draw on anyone not already called up—call-up evaders, schoolboys, criminals, and the like. There were the reserved occupations, of course, miners and farmers and so on, but there were limits to how many of them could be diverted from work that was essential to keep people fed and the country running. Once trained, Auxis would have to be armed, and in the end, they would be given what amounted to a suicide mission. The admiral thought of all the arguments against it and decided they would have to try again to change Churchill's mind.

As if that weren't enough, he also had to deal with Frances.

The admiral loved his daughter, but he was a man's man and didn't pretend to understand women. Least of all Frances. Girls were a mother's department. Unfortunately his pretty half-French wife, whom he had never understood either, had died three years into their marriage, leaving him in charge of their only child, who was just beginning to walk.

He had known nothing about children, and, until her mother died, Frances had lived out of his sight in the top-floor nursery. He was only occasionally reminded of her presence when he saw her in her pram, with Nanny at the helm, on her way to the park. After his wife died, though, he had felt it his duty to take a closer interest in her. When he visited the nursery for the first time, he was taken aback when the angelic two-year-old in a smocked dress and tiny pearl-buttoned kid shoes had a fearsome tantrum because he had brought her no sweets. He soon learned this dainty creature was headstrong and fearless. Indoors, Frances climbed fireguards and bookcases, fell down a heating vent, and threw whatever she could reach into the lavatory. In the park she was snapped at by strange dogs whose tails she grabbed, and she frequently escaped from Nanny. Once she had tottered into the Serpentine among some ducks—a policeman had rescued her in the nick of time from a watery grave.

Soaking wet, chilled to the bone, scratched by the cook's cat, or bruised after a tumble, Frances never cried, but when thwarted, she threw herself into a fury until the admiral roared at her to behave. Not the slightest bit cowed, Frances roared back. A succession of nannies came and went until, in despair, the admiral turned to his old friend, and Frances's godmother, Muriel Marchmont. She advised a governess. When this too proved a failure, Frances was sent to a series of boarding schools, selected by Muriel. Letters from headmistresses became a regular feature in the admiral's morning post. Each woman regretted that her establishment was not right for Frances, and would the admiral please remove her. All agreed on two things: first, that Frances was remarkably clever when she could be persuaded to work, and second, that she was easily bored, undisciplined, a troublemaker who broke rules flagrantly, and encouraged others to follow suit.

Tudor Falconleigh had dispatched her to the finishing school as a gesture of respect to her late mother, and because nowhere else would take her.

Muriel Marchmont's most recent letter had sat reproachfully on a corner of his desk for some time. He often put off reading her missives because he felt unequal to dealing with a catalog of Frances's misdoings, and also because Lady Marchmont tended to overdramatize things. However, in recent months, she had evidently felt that Frances was beyond her and suggested that she should get married. Then she would be her husband's responsibility.

Now the admiral sighed and slit open the latest envelope. He was relieved to find his old friend considered there was Light at the End of the Tunnel. Frances was being courted by a suitable man. In fact, although the girl had not confided in her, Muriel had felt she should let dear Tudor know without delay that she was as good as engaged to Hugo de Balfort. In the circumstances it was imperative, she wrote, for him to summon Frances to London: "At a time like this, it is a father's duty to have a serious talk."

The admiral's heart sank. A "serious talk" with his daughter always ended in a row and sulks, with the admiral threatening to reduce or withhold Frances's allowance. Still, if Muriel thought it possible that a conversation with her might hasten her marriage to a suitable man, he would have a word. He agreed with Muriel that a woman's proper estate was marriage, and if there was any prospect a conversation would hasten Frances's, the admiral would talk to her. However, he mustn't stir up her rebellious streak because then she would do the opposite of whatever he recommended. He would discuss a financial settlement and leave the wedding arrangements to Muriel, who would know what ought to be done.

If he understood Muriel correctly, Frances's inheritance was important to the de Balforts, who, like many aristocrats, were land rich and cash poor. But in return, his daughter would marry into one of the oldest families in England and gain a title.

Before he could ring Frances, she had phoned him to say she would be coming up to town that week and would like to see him. He would like to see her too, he said— "Give you lunch, m'dear." He had said good-bye and put the phone down. At least where his troublesome daughter was concerned, he had thought, everything would be fine.

When the moment came for that chat, he was less certain. At the War Office he stared at Frances, sitting across from him on an uncomfortable NAAFI chair, ankles crossed demurely, looking frivolous and out of place with the uniformed WRENS bent over their typing. She wore one of her expensive hats with a wispy veil, a smart suit, a fur, and soft gloves. Seeing his expression she said, "Well, Father, I could hardly wear my Land Girl breeches up to town. They're covered with muck. In any case, I wanted to make a good impression on you because I have something important to ask you."

The admiral had smiled indulgently and raised his eyebrows.

"Father, I've had an official letter from someone named Gubbins, who apparently knows you and has heard about me. Not sure why, but that doesn't matter. He asks if I'd be interested in working for a new organization—it's to do with sabotage, either here if the invasion comes or behind enemy lines..." Frances's voice trailed off.

There was silence in the office, the kind of silence that presages a storm. Father looks like a volcano about to erupt, thought Frances. She smoothed the gloves on her lap. She had suspected it would be a mistake to ask him, but at her interview in Baker Street they said that, given his position and that she was under age, she had to have his permission to join them. It came hard to her, but she was determined to keep calm.

Admiral Falconleigh stared at his daughter in stunned disbelief. Who the hell had put her name forward? And why would Gubbins want to recruit Frances? There could hardly be a less likely candidate in England for Winston's crazy organization.

Perhaps she had volunteered—or perhaps not: he couldn't imagine how she could have heard about the SOE, which was supposed to be secret, or the Auxiliary Units, which were also secret. It wasn't clear which one they wanted her for, but either way it wasn't as if they were advertising in the *Times*. He knew that candidates' names were put forward by personal contacts. Which of his acquaintances had suggested Frances? He was sure, however, whoever it was had done so to put pressure on him to drop his opposition to Churchill's plan.

"No, Frances! I forbid it. I will speak to them personally, if necessary. No daughter of mine—"

"Oh, yes, do speak to them, Father! Perhaps they can convince you, if I can't, how frightfully useful secret agents will be supporting the Free French and the Resistance."

"My dear girl, you haven't the foggiest notion about the Free French or any Resistance or Gubbins's organization, but the whole lot are perfectly useless. De Gaulle is holed up issuing proclamations from a Soho pub—no good to anyone militarily." The admiral stopped. Frances would have no idea what he was talking about.

He was wrong. Frances was on the verge of retorting, "I know all about the Free French and the pub, because Evangeline Fairfax told me," but for once in her life she held her tongue. Until she was twenty-one, her father had to give his permission before they would take her. This was not the moment to upset him.

"The Special Operations Executive isn't a more amusing way to help the war effort than working as a Land Girl. It's a cockeyed cowboys-and-Indians scheme that will only get in the way of those fighting for England."

"Actually, Father, a great many people will soon be fighting the war in different ways, and it sounds much more interesting and useful than herding cows. They need wireless operators and couriers and—"

"Aside from being ill-conceived, it's dangerous, it's behind enemy lines, and it's for men only. I disapprove of saboteurs and resistance groups. This SOE is no better than mercenaries! Thugs! Trained assassins! Not quite the thing! Underhand. As I told Winston many times, no gentleman would have anything to do with it, but of course he didn't listen to me. Never listens to anybody. It's risky enough for the men and it's no place for girls. Most unfeminine. Anyway, girls are far too emotional, likely to go to pieces and compromise everyone."

Frances took a deep breath and tried again. "Quite. But Father, girls are also extremely useful in providing backup for the men, organizing passports and ration cards, decoding messages and suchlike, you know. And I can translate. They said they need people who can speak French like natives, and I can and—"

"How do they know your French is perfect? Have you already been speaking to these people behind my back? I tell you again, no daughter of mine will join the SOE or those half-baked Auxi whatnots!"

"But Father, they're the only organizations that have any work I could do—be reasonable! Please, just listen! They know my French is perfect because, yes, I went to see them today, and this darling man asked me questions in French the whole morning. He said he was frightfully impressed."

"For the last time, it's out of the question! And as you're still under age you cannot go without my consent."

"Oh bother!" If Frances hadn't been sitting down she would have stamped her foot. "I'm twenty! If I'd been a boy I would've had a real war job, flying Spitfires or Hurricanes or something. Being a Land Girl is all very well for some, and I thought it would be a lark when I joined up with Elsie— she's Aunt Muriel's housemaid—but looking after pigs and digging potatoes and milking cows and getting all muddy in the fields and wrestling with hay that doesn't want to be baled is so tedious and I can do more—I know I can. I feel wasted. I loathe milking. The cows simply loathe me—and they kick. If I'm to do my bit fighting the Germans I want to do more than hold a milking pail steady."

The admiral's patience was evaporating. He was a very busy man and Frances—as usual when her heart was set on something—was digging in her heels. But it was out of the question. Frances would remain in the Land Army at Crowmarsh Priors no matter how many strings he had to pull to keep her there. Muriel Marchmont was right. The sooner his daughter was married the better.

"I didn't ask you to come up to London to discuss your latest madcap idea, but for an entirely different reason," he began. Frances had opened her mouth and her eyes had the steely glint that presaged an argument or tantrum, but she said nothing. The admiral continued: "As your father and as a member of the War Cabinet, I insist you oblige the country and me by doing your bit with the Land Army. We'll have no more talk about Gubbins's nonsense. Now, to change the subject, your godmother tells me you're seeing a good deal of a certain young man—Hugo de Balfort. A bit of a bright young thing, according to Muriel, and—"

"Father, calling someone a 'bright young thing' is too old-fashioned for words! But I can't imagine why Aunt Muriel mentioned him to you. He's just a pal."

"Indeed? She says he's all but proposed."

"She's a meddling old buffalo!"

"But," he held up a hand, "it's a very sound family. Leander married Venetia What's-Her-Name, earl's granddaughter. Hope of the nation, the landed gentry, especially now. Your godmother's quite right about that. Understand Hugo's health or something kept him out of the forces, but there's nothing, er, to prevent his marrying and, er, having children and so forth."

"What?"

The admiral saw he had floundered into deep waters. "I gather she felt it her duty to confront Leander. She asked him point-blank about the, er, state of Hugo's, um, health. Naturally you, well, babies, children, and, er, all that sort of thing...Muriel has, er, no doubt...apparently Leander told her...and of course she assured him no problem with your ability to...ahem...sons, naturally...keep the estate in the family."

Frances was too aghast to speak.

Her father had gone red in the face and was gazing out of the window. "Title and all that—important to keep it in the family. Marriage, very serious step...leads to all sorts of responsibilities. Er," he stuttered, "children, of course, we've covered that, and there's the matter of money." The admiral felt the ship steady beneath him as he steered away from the rocks. "Your money. To be precise, your mother's money. There will be a good deal of it. We've never spoken of marriage settlements, but they're necessary, we'll put yours in the hands of my legal advisors at once, you young people are too busy being in love to deal with the financial side of things..."

The admiral stopped. The expression on Frances's face did not resemble that of a girl in love. Neither did it encourage him to continue. Heaven help her husband, he thought. Then there was a knock and the door opened to the sound of typewriters clicking briskly. "Excuse me, Admiral." The WREN was holding out a sheaf of telegrams. "Urgent, sir."

She frowned slightly at Frances as if to say, "Why are you sitting there, all dressed up, when some of us have a war to fight?"

He turned with relief to his telegrams and the war.

While her father busied himself with dispatches and barked orders into the telephone, Frances tapped her toe as she stared out the window at gray London skies and rubble. Damn! Damn! Damn! Why did bloody Aunt Muriel have to interfere in everyone's lives? The way she pushed Alice Osbourne at Oliver Hammet was bad enough. But writing to Father about Hugo and discussing everyone's...reproductive faculties? How *dare* she!

Frances was irritated to think that her own behavior had led her godmother to believe Hugo was courting her. Hugo's father, dear old boy, had always been nice to her, and he was a long-standing friend of Aunt Muriel's, so perhaps the two old people had encouraged each other. Frances could see that a man in Hugo's position would be under pressure to marry and produce an heir, but although she had seen a good deal of him, she had always been more interested in his glamorous friends. Hugo himself, though extremely good looking, was actually rather dull.

But life at Glebe House was tedious in the extreme. To escape her godmother's scrutiny, Frances had fallen in easily with the Gracecourt set, who amused themselves shooting, playing tennis and bridge, or dashing off to Brighton for cocktails, dinner, and dancing. But the gay prewar crowd, mostly consisting of minor Continental aristocrats and artistic types whom Hugo had befriended on his Grand Tour, had disappeared since the war began. Hugo was a still a pal, of course, but he was busy with crops and livestock and she, not to put too fine a point on it, was one of his farmhands. There had never been any of what Elsie called "that kind of thing" between them.

Although, now she thought about it, she ran into Hugo quite often in the course of her work—in fact, nearly every day. And he always stopped to talk to her, just being friendly, she'd imagined. Was there more to it?

Frances didn't think Hugo was in love with her or that he wanted to marry her, but if his father was pushing him toward her she didn't want to encourage him. Anyway, since Colin Gubbins's letter and her interview she had been able to think of nothing but his secret organization. It had all been most interesting. The two men and a woman who interviewed her had even asked how she thought women might best fit into the organization.

Frances had said earnestly that in many ways they could be more useful than men, because women were chameleons; it was so easy to change how they looked by changing their clothes and hair. A girl could look anything between fifteen and fifty, pregnant, fat, thin, ugly, pretty, or sick, while men were harder to disguise. Also, in her experience, men usually assumed that women weren't capable enough to do anything particularly important, so they were less likely to be conspicuous and get caught. And of course they could get round men without them noticing. Even Germans.

In fact, she said disingenuously, eyes wide, she found nothing easier than getting round men, unless it was her father. The little man interviewing her had laughed at that, and said it was true and that he quite saw she would be particularly good at it, because she had nearly persuaded him. The woman reminded him for the time being women weren't being recruited to go behind enemy lines. The little man looked serious again and said things might change…

They'd noticed her outfit—made in Paris? Could she tell them what details marked the difference between French and English clothing? What would a French peasant woman wear? An ordinary housewife going about her business in town? Frances had given them a lengthy lecture about the finer points of French tailoring as compared to English and the ways Frenchwomen walked, wore hats, talked to their families, what they ate and even thought.

"Observant," the little man said approvingly and made a note. Had she any serious medical conditions? Could she ride a bicycle? Did she think she could learn to survive on her own in the countryside?

Of course she could ride a bicycle! She was never ill. As for the last…after a moment's thought Frances had grinned and said she probably could. A friend of hers often went poaching when rations ran out and was good at snaring rabbits and pigeons and even pheasants. That seemed like quite a useful sort of skill.

"Have you been poaching, Miss Falconleigh?"

Frances leaned across his desk and looked at him levelly. "Not yet, but I can learn. If I poach a brace of pheasants for you will you take me?"

The little man roared with laughter. "You *are* determined! If we can't get the admiral's consent for the SOE or the Auxiliary Unit, well, we can find you something to do."

Frances nodded. "It's a bargain," she said and held out her hand.

He shook it. "Bargain sealed," he said, "provided I get those pheasants."

Frances had told him she would be twenty-one in November, when she would no longer need her father's permission. Perhaps by then they would be letting women agents join the men behind enemy lines. Now that would be thrilling.

The admiral was still busy. Frances glanced at her watch. She thought how useful it was to have a friend like Evangeline who could do all sorts of surprising things. If anyone could survive in the countryside it was Evangeline. At first Evangeline, with her slow voice and languid ways, had seemed odd, but then, Frances had never known an American, and the fact that Aunt Muriel disapproved of her so vigorously had driven Frances to make friends with her. Sometimes Evangeline borrowed one of the Home Guard's old hunting rifles, which Leander had donated, and went hunting in Richard's waxed jacket. She brought home pigeons—she called them doves—and even pheasants for the whole village. When Frances had explained about poaching, Evangeline had shrugged, clearly unconcerned. Game wasn't rationed, and everyone in the village was hungry for meat.

Frances had been flabbergasted to find that her friend could do more than hunt; she was frightfully clever at making a lovely meal out of what she shot or trapped. She knew how to grill pigeons or rabbit on a spit over a handful of damp apple wood chips. Also, she grew vegetables and kept chickens, and since eggs from your own hens weren't rationed, there was mayonnaise for the artichokes and tomatoes she produced. She baked apples and pears in honey... Evangeline said where she had grown up all the men went hunting and brought game home and girls learned to cook before they got married, so they could make sure their own cooks did it properly. Frances's stomach rumbled. There hadn't been time for breakfast before the train, and the biscuit tin had been empty for ages. Father had promised to give her lunch and she hoped he would remember.

The admiral finished with the telegrams, and the WREN took them away. Frances was fidgeting again. He'd give her lunch, then put her on the train. Before the war they would have gone to the Savoy or possibly the Ritz. A glass of sherry. Oysters. Roast chicken. Trifle. Burgundy. Now, thanks to rationing, the food was dreadful everywhere so they might as well nip into one of the new British restaurants. He knew it would be brown soup, bubble and squeak, then some sort of sweet in a puddle of custard that tasted of dried egg, but they would be in and out in a jiffy and he could get back to the war. Girls! The sooner they got married and stopped wasting their fathers' time the better.

13.

Crowmarsh Priors,
March 1941

*J*ohnny's fretting usually woke Tanni at an early hour, but this morning it was a pair of jays squawking in the pear tree outside her window. She got up sleepily and put on the dressing gown she had made from some old towels Evangeline had discarded for rags. They had been frayed at the edges but a pretty faded blue, and using her coat to trace a pattern on newspaper, Tanni had fashioned a soft, serviceable garment, with deep turned-back cuffs, pockets, and a sash. She had only white thread, but her stitches, tiny and neat as Frau Zayman had taught her, hardly showed.

It's lovely!" exclaimed Evangeline. "I've never had the patience to sew anything. At school the nuns used to rip out my stitches and make me do it over and over."

Flushed with pride, Tanni offered to make her one too, pleased to have a way to thank her for taking them in. A few days later, Evangeline was wearing a becoming pink dressing gown made from an old bedspread. She was so thrilled with it that Tanni asked her if she could rummage through the boxes of old clothes and bedding in the Fairfaxes' attic for more things to alter. "Help yourself. They're not doing anybody any good up there," said Evangeline.

The government was urging everyone not to waste material, and everything related to clothing was in short supply—from needles to buttons, patterns, and zips. There was a rumor clothes would soon be rationed, as well as food. Using whatever odd pieces of material she could find, Tanni made underwear for herself and clothes for Johnny, who was outgrowing everything fast. Word spread round Crowmarsh Priors and the surrounding farms that Tanni could do wonders with old clothes, and before long she was never without the old gardener's basket filled with sewing commissions and a little notebook for recording people's measurements. Albert Hawthorne brought her the newspapers when he and Nell had finished reading them, so she could make patterns. Women brought worn frocks for restyling, letting out, or freshening up with a new collar and cuffs, their men's trousers for new pockets or patching where the seat had worn through, their children's things to be lengthened and let out. Tanni even made two christening robes, finished with beautiful smocking. The women paid what they could afford, or with jam, pies, fruit, and vegetables. In the autumn Constable Barrows's pregnant wife had paid for three maternity smocks and some baby clothes with a precious pair of laying hens donated by her mother: Evangeline's flock increased to four.

Evangeline was grateful for the food that Tanni contributed to the household in this way. Only a few years ago Aunt Celeste's instructions in household management had bored her to tears. Now she struggled to recall everything she had been taught—after all, until Laurent came up with a plan, she was stuck in the village, and they had to eat. Maude, Tommy, and Kipper were always starving, and resourceful though Evangeline became at stretching the rations, feeding four children and two adults—four if Frances and Elsie were with them—was a daily struggle. Besides, her garden and the hunting expeditions took her mind off Laurent.

Tanni saw how hard Evangeline worked in the garden and at foraging to put food on the table, Elsie and Frances on the farm, and Alice with the clothing drives for refugees, knitting for the troops, and first aid classes as well as teaching at the school, and was glad she could be useful too. Color came back into her cheeks and she faced each day confidently, reminding herself that she was a wife and mother, a grown woman with work to do, no longer a frightened schoolgirl.

Now she poked up the embers in the fireplace and put on a log, changed Johnny, and glanced out her window into the long, narrow garden behind the house. Just before Jimmy, the butcher's boy, had joined up the previous autumn, he had helped Evangeline dig up the flowers and shrubs to plant neat rows of winter cabbages, brussels sprouts, and leeks. They had missed some bulbs, though, and between the vegetables crocuses and daffodils blossomed now, bright as stars. She had not noticed them until today. She pointed them out to Johnny, then took him into her bed, pulled the covers over them both, and sang into Johnny's soft hair. Johnny played peek-a-boo, squirmed, and chuckled.

She was so happy! Yesterday she had had a surprise telegram from Bruno. He had an unexpected few days' leave for Passover and was coming today to take her and Johnny to London for a Seder with the Cohens in Bethnal Green. She had seen Bruno only twice since she left London. Both times she had gone by train with Johnny to Cambridge, but had had only a few hours with Bruno before he was called away unexpectedly. She had come home feeling lonelier than ever. Please, she thought, don't let Bruno's leave be cancelled this time. Although he telephoned whenever he could, she had not seen him for so long.

She was also anxious to see the Cohens. They had been interned for months in a camp on the Isle of Wight but had finally been allowed to leave after a tribunal decided an elderly rabbi and his wife were not dangerous enemy aliens or German spies. The Cohens were relieved to be home but badly shaken by the experience. Tante Berthe couldn't understand how the authorities would believe that Jews were Nazi agents. They had been cheered when Tanni wrote to tell them that people were very kind in Sussex and everyone loved Johnny.

Evangeline had taken to the little boy straight away, and Alice had been friendly in her bossy way, calling to see if Tanni needed anything, bringing pamphlets about orange juice and cod-liver oil and an English grammar book. Tanni noticed, though, that Alice disliked Evangeline and barely spoke to her. In the weeks after her arrival Tanni had worn herself out in trying not to upset anyone, and the sadness that had descended after Johnny's birth often gripped her. The English books and pamphlets gathered dust on her bedside table and it was all she could do to give Johnny his orange juice. Sister Tucker looked in as often as her busy schedule allowed, to reassure her that new mothers often felt like that, but Tanni was convinced that the dark feelings must be her own fault.

Then, little by little she had begun to adjust, so that in the last few months she had felt better, more like her old self, and Johnny was thriving. Evangeline and Alice were her friends, even if they weren't friends with each other. She had found a way to make herself useful. She kissed the photo of her family, which was propped against the mirror. Now that Bruno was taking her to London she would be able to ask Rachel where they had gone in England. It was just a matter of time until she was with them again.

The growing bubble of excitement inside her at the prospect of seeing Bruno meant she could hardly swallow her tea and toast. After breakfast Evangeline took Johnny when she walked with the older children to school so that Tanni could get ready. As soon as they were gone, the doorbell rang. It was Alice, on her way to school. She handed Tanni a parcel wrapped in brown paper. Inside Tanni found a pullover and cap she had knitted for Johnny in heavy oiled wool she had purloined from the Dorcas Society's stock. Tanni thanked her profusely and gave her a hug.

As soon as Alice had gone, she bathed, careful not to fill the tub above the four-inch mark painted inside it. Then, wrapped in her blue dressing gown, she washed her hair and rinsed it with vinegar to make it shine.

When Evangeline and Johnny reappeared, she was drying her hair in front of the range. The doorbell rang again. This time it was Frances, in her Land Girl uniform. She held out an elegant dressmaker's box with a French name on it in gold lettering.

"For me?" asked Tanni in disbelief. Frances was so glamorous that Tanni had always been too shy to say much more than "good morning" to her. Frances nodded, with a smile, so Tanni thanked her, opened the box, and gave a cry of delight. Inside, beneath the tissue paper, she had found a cream silk nightdress and peignoir, with lace and wide satin ribbons.

"It'll help keep his, um, morale up, darling," Frances said wickedly. "Take off that dressing gown and try on the peignoir—yes, just as I thought! That cream shade is perfect with your dark hair," said Frances, "and, lucky you, you've more bosom than I have." Tanni blushed—the negligee showed a great deal of it.

"I've got just the thing to go with that," Evangeline exclaimed and ran upstairs. She returned with a bottle of French scent. "Schiaparelli," she said.

Tanni remembered a similar bottle on her mother's dressing table, and the dark feelings hovered, but she decided resolutely that they were not going to ruin the day. She dabbed a little on her wrist. "Bruno will hardly know me!" She giggled.

In her best frock, feeling clean and new, Tanni was in the sun-filled morning room, humming while she put her new things into the carpetbag with Johnny's clothes, nappies, and toys. "What a fine house!" a voice behind her said.

Johnny, who had been about to crawl under the sofa after the cat, paused to stare at the stranger. Then he scrambled to his mother and hid behind her legs.

Tanni was gazing at the solid form of a short, vaguely familiar man with glasses who was taking off his overcoat and pulling funny faces at her son. Suddenly flustered and shy, she felt like hiding too. Then Bruno bent down to sweep a startled Johnny into the crook of his right arm and hugged her tightly with his left. He kissed her cheek. "So," he said. "My family!"

"Oh, Bruno!" She and Bruno had spent so little time together as husband and wife that she was more accustomed to thinking of herself as a mother than as a wife. Now she would have to get used to being married all over again. She thought how much she liked the solid feel of him under his rough tweed jacket.

Johnny squirmed, the cat fled, and Bruno swung his son over his head. Soon Johnny was shrieking with laughter and kicking. Tanni protested that Bruno would make him sick, so Bruno produced a boiled sweet, unwrapped it, and popped it into Johnny's open mouth. There was silence as Johnny sucked, so Tanni, uncertain what to talk about, took a pile of Johnny's clothes out of the carpetbag, unfolded and recounted them. Several times.

"What a lot of things," said Bruno, eyeing the pile on the sofa.

"Everyone's been so kind. My friend Alice, who teaches the children at school, made this." She held up the jumper Alice had brought, one arm longer than the other. Bruno raised his eyebrows and she giggled. "Constable Barrows carved him these animals when he was making some for his own baby, and Evangeline made him a quilt with the alphabet on it and got down her husband's old nursery furniture from the attic. It has rabbits painted on it—"

"Tanni!" Bruno said and swept her into his arms. They were talking softly, absorbed in each other, when Tanni saw, from the corner of her eye, that Johnny had pulled himself up on a side table and his sticky fist had grasped a Limoges shepherdess he had had an eye on for weeks. His mouth was wide open and he was about to test his new front teeth on the frothy china skirt when Tanni swooped.

Just then the black motor that had dropped off Bruno half an hour earlier pulled up, with two figures in the front seat. Tanni fetched a basket that contained a dozen of the household's precious eggs and a pot of honey and another basket with hyacinths from the garden for the Cohens. She kissed Evangeline good-bye, then pinned on her hat. The driver put the carpetbag and hyacinths in the boot, and then Tanni and Bruno got into the backseat with Johnny between them and the basket of eggs on Tanni's lap. The car drove away.

The young man billeted with Constable Barrows was in the front with the driver, but the glass partition was up so Tanni could not hear what they were saying to each other. His profile reminded her of a little English animal that Alice called a ferret. Several times he looked back and winked at Johnny, so Tanni smiled at him. She knew his name was Bernie. Elsie talked about him when she brought potatoes and sometimes illicit tins of beef or fish that she traded for one of Evangeline's game pies.

Tanni had so much to tell Bruno about their life in Crowmarsh Priors when they were alone. Alone! She felt a thrill of anticipation. The sun-drenched spring landscape rolled by, and she and Bruno took turns to point out cows and horses in the fields to Johnny. She glanced at her husband, wondering if he felt the same sense of excitement as they approached London.

But the sight of the devastation the enemy had wrought since she left dented Tanni's high spirits. By the time the car reached Bethnal Green, picking its way through the rubble and the yawning spaces where buildings had been, the sky had grown overcast. Rabbi Cohen, looking older, came out to welcome them with Tante Berthe, who gave Tanni a long hug and made much of Johnny. She exclaimed with joy over the eggs, the honey, and the flowers.

Inside, the house smelled deliciously of soup and baking and something familiar and spicy. Tanni sniffed. Cinnamon. She closed her eyes, seeing the Passover table in her own home, set a day in advance with a damask cloth, the best dishes; for days the kitchen would have been a hive of activity, with her mother at the center of it all. Frau Anna and the maids would have been sent home, exhausted after a thorough spring-clean of the entire house while Frau Joseph, enveloped in a white apron, chopped and roasted, showing Tanni how to add a pinch of this or that, demonstrating how finely apples should be sliced or horseradish grated, and letting the twins pick over a bowl of dried fruit.

Tanni opened her eyes. Tante Berthe was holding out a plate of sugared matzo and almond biscuits. She took one and broke off a bit for Johnny. "Everything smells delicious," she said to Tante Berthe. "Thank you for inviting us." A long table had been wedged into the sitting room at an angle to accommodate as many people as possible, covered in an embroidered white cloth, gleaming china, and glasses. Beneath the smell of cooking Tanni detected bleach and fresh ironing. The rabbi had disappeared into his study with Bruno. Tanni felt herself relax. Thoughts of what would happen when she and Bruno were together and she was wearing her negligee filled her head. In fact, it was hard to think of anything else.

Tante Berthe thought Tanni looked blooming. The WVS woman had been right to send her to the country. Eighteen months ago, when she had last seen her, Tanni was a specter with dark circles under her eyes and hollow cheeks, distraught at having signed a paper that meant she had to leave London where her family expected to find her, or be put in a camp.

"Come, my dear, I'll show you where you're to sleep." She led the way up the stairs to a tiny room under the eaves. A good-natured impulse had inspired her to put her best embroidered linen sheets, often borrowed for bridal nights, on the two narrow beds she had squeezed together, and to tuck Johnny's cot round a corner on the landing. Tanni stroked the sheets. "What lovely work, it reminds me of...oh, Tante Berthe, don't make me wait. What news do you have of Lili and Klara?"

"You must be patient. Rachel is the only one who can answer your questions. She and her family are coming for the Seder, and you can speak to her."

When Tanni opened her carpetbag to give Mrs. Cohen their ration books, the silk negligee spilled out. Tante Berthe smiled to herself. It cheered her to think of young people under her roof—and who knew? Maybe they would begin another baby here. She pinched Tanni's cheek affectionately. She must fatten her up a little, in case...

So many of the Cohens' friends arrived later to squeeze round the table for the Seder that the sitting room was packed. Rachel, with her mother, husband, and four-year-old son, arrived last. She was pregnant and so large that everyone had to move sideways again to make room for her. The candles were lit, and after the Kiddush everyone shifted a little, pretending to recline to drink the first cup of wine. The glasses were refilled, and Rabbi Cohen continued with the Haggadah and the ritual foods: the lamb bone, the matzohs, the parsley sprigs, the slivers of horseradish root. They ate the last with Tante Berthe's special *haroseth*, a recipe passed down on her mother's side of the family for generations, which combined dried apples and dates, raisins, spices, and wine. Rabbi Cohen's voice quavered with emotion as he answered the ritual questions asked by Rachel's little boy, because Johnny was too young. By the time they came to the hard-boiled egg dipped into salt water, people at the table were weeping for loved ones at the mercy of the Nazis in Europe.

Eventually Tante Berthe wiped her eyes and got up to serve the rest of the dinner, which she had spent days preparing. Most of those present had lent her their ration books for the day she had scoured Whitechapel, begging, cajoling, and bullying greengrocers and kosher butchers to get what she needed. Tanni rose to help her.

Soon the table was crowded with dishes, and Tanni marvelled that Tante Berthe had managed to make such a feast despite the rationing. There was beetroot soup with egg drops, gefilte fish with horseradish, chopped liver, sweet and sour chicken, *tzimmis* with short ribs, a potato kugel, and a vegetable kugel. There was an aubergine salad and then a dish of baked apples stuffed with dried fruit and a honey-soaked sponge cake made from matzo flour. Finally Tante Berthe produced plates of tiny macaroons. Afterward everyone joined in reciting grace after meals and then drank the third glass of wine.

Unused to alcohol, even in such tiny glasses, Tanni felt light-headed as they sang the closing prayers and songs. She emptied her fourth glass of wine hardly tasting it, her cheeks pink, then got up unsteadily to help Tante Berthe clear the table. "I'm going to talk to Rachel in a minute," she whispered in Bruno's ear.

"No, you help Tante Berthe, and I'll speak to Rachel," said Bruno firmly, "while you put Johnny to bed. I'll be up soon."

Tanni obeyed dreamily, and Rachel followed Bruno into the rabbi's study. She had been dreading this moment.

"Whatever you have discovered, Tanni has been very ill," Bruno began, "and we must take care that she is not made ill again. She feels responsible for her sisters—she hopes and believes they are England, and it is just a matter of your committee finding where they have been sent. If you know anything, please tell me now. If it is bad news I will break it to her gently. Also, you may have information about which, officially, I must know nothing. You will understand that I must not compromise my position with the authorities, but on the other hand I must help my wife and our families. In return for your help, I promise to assist your committee as far as I can—for example, if you have information that needs to be confirmed there may be ways I can help. I will not say how."

Rachel rubbed the small of her aching back and considered. Bruno did not have to say any more about the need for discretion. Everyone had been warned over and over about careless talk costing lives. She didn't know what he did, but with his languages and his sharp mind, she was sure he was working for Military Intelligence at a high level. Her committee, on the other hand, operated with few resources beyond a group of determined women, out of desperation and on a shoestring, far outside the scope of officialdom, gathering information by any means available through a tenuous network of fragile links composed of family members, neighbors, and refugees from imperiled Jewish communities across occupied Europe. The War Office turned a blind eye. They were unconcerned about Jewish civilians behind enemy lines, but had discovered that the committee's network of informants were sometimes a source of information about RAF pilots missing in enemy territory.

"As far as the Joseph twins are concerned, there is bad news. They are definitely not in England—if they were, we would have found them by now. With some difficulty we traced them to the last *Kindertransport,* which did not leave Austria until June. There were problems when the border guards demanded bigger bribes than had been agreed to let the train pass. By the time the negotiations were completed, the train had been diverted to France, where the children were taken off. They were kept at a transit camp for most of August and then put on trains for Le Havre and the ferry to England. They were due to sail on the day England declared war. That meant the children became enemy aliens and not allowed entry. We think the children were put back on the train at Le Havre, and it went south. They could be anywhere in Vichy, France, probably in a displaced persons' camp."

Bruno grimaced. He knew that those were hellholes, overcrowded with Republican refugees from Spain who dared not return now that the Nationalists had triumphed.

Food and medicine were in short supply; crime and disease were rife. It was no place for two unprotected little girls.

"I know that the Quakers and the Jehovah's Witnesses are being allowed into the camps to help with relief operations—so long as it suits Nazi propaganda—and the American consul in Marseille is sympathetic and helps unofficially as much as he can. Is there information through those channels?" he asked.

Rachel nodded. "The Quakers try to keep track of unaccompanied children so that they can be reunited with their families. So far there is no record of the Joseph girls in the French camps—but of course some children may have died or been removed from the train en route."

"But you will keep looking?" Bruno asked, though he wondered what they could do even if the twins were found alive in a camp.

"Of course, but we are trying to help so many people that it is like emptying the sea with a thimble."

"And Dr. Joseph and his wife—my mother? I have made every possible inquiry through every possible channel. Other than the fact that they are no longer at my mother's flat, there have been nothing but dead ends."

Rachel turned away so he would not see the tears in her eyes. Tears came so easily now at the news she often had to give, news she could not sweeten with any hope. "Our contacts have been able to give us a little information. An elderly man, a relative of one of my colleagues, had been Dr. Joseph's patient and confirmed they were living with your mother, but that the night Lili and Klara left with the *Kindertransport,* the Germans arrested all the Jews in their quarter. If Tanni's parents and your mother were among them, they were probably deported to a German labor camp to make munitions. They say people from the quarter your mother lived in have been seen in Ocswiecim, also called Auschwitz. But until we know for sure, say nothing to Tanni."

"We have American contacts in Marseille who pass funds to the Quakers for the transit camps. I will ask them to keep trying. As for Auschwitz..." Bruno shuddered.

"I know. We will do what we can," promised Rachel, wearily. She repeated it many times each day. They were overwhelmed with people like Bruno and Tanni begging for information about their loved ones.

When Bruno went upstairs, he found Tanni wrapped in her peignoir brushing her hair. Johnny was asleep. She turned to smile at him, laying a finger on her lips. "Johnny was exhausted. His first proper Seder! Now Bruno, tell me what Rachel said! Don't keep me in suspense—I'm sure you have good news."

Bruno's mother had once warned him that the Josephs would not consider a dressmaker's son a worthy husband for their beloved eldest daughter, no matter he had adored her from his youth. But there she sat, his wife, the mother of their son, a welcoming smile on her lips, her hair tumbling over her shoulders, glowing with contentment of a happy evening, his presence, and the certainty of good news. Bruno's heart tightened. He would protect her from unhappiness for as long as he could and tell her only that Rachel and her group still had no definite news. But even that could wait.

He took the hairbrush from her, sat down on the bed, and began to brush her hair, slowly. How soft and shiny it was.

"Bruno! Tell me!" But Tanni shut her eyes and relaxed against him. Bruno put the brush down and buried his face in her neck. She turned and they put their arms around each other. "What did Rachel say?" Tanni murmured, but Bruno pulled her down with him. "Shh, not now, my sweet one. Not tonight. We'll talk about it tomorrow."

14.

Sussex Downs, August 1941

there had been no air raid warning, only the drone of an approaching airplane to alert them just as the village children went out to play after lunch on Saturday when a lone German Heinkel 111 suddenly roared low over Crowmarsh Priors. By the time anxious mothers had dropped the washing-up and rushed out in their aprons to drag their children to safety, the bomber was over the downs, twisting and rolling across the sky to escape the RAF Hurricanes now in pursuit.

Albert Hawthorne thought they must be trying to force the German away from the village and out over the channel before they shot it down, but to his surprise the Heinkel turned back sharply and headed for cover in a bank of dark clouds rolling inland from the sea. Too late.

"Go to it! Get 'im, lads!" Albert shouted as the RAF gunners opened up. Mesmerized, the village watched as the Heinkel veered off course, belching black smoke. Half a minute later it was circling back toward land, wobbling in the sky, tipping sideways and falling out of the clouds, nose down, coming toward the village. Then it dropped out

213

of sight and a loud explosion sounded somewhere on the downs.

The excited children whooped and waved at the departing Hurricanes. "Three cheers for the RAF, then! Hip hip... hooray!" The mothers wiped trembling hands, still wet, on their aprons, feeling faint at such a close shave.

In his study Oliver Hammet had heard the planes through the open window, but the crash jerked him to his feet. Abandoning the next day's sermon, he hurried to unlock the cabinet under the vicarage stairs where the Home Guard kept the de Balfort guns.

At Ashpole Cottages Albert handed Nell his hoe and joined the publican Harry Smith who hobbled past, leaning on his walking stick. The farmers' sons had enlisted and gone, so it was just the three who gathered at the village hall to wait for Hugo de Balfort. Ten minutes later he screeched to a halt in a battered shooting brake. The Home Guard was assembled.

The older children clamored to help find the Heinkel, but their mothers wouldn't let them out of their sight.

In the muggy August heat, the Home Guard set off in their shirtsleeves. The War Office had promised them rifles, but they had not arrived. Hugo and Oliver were armed with the de Balfort hunting rifles and a handful of ammunition. Albert Hawthorne carried a scythe he had honed to razorlike sharpness, and Harry Smith brandished his stout knobbed walking stick, which he called a "fool killer."

If a German plane was shot down, it was the Home Guard's job to find the wreck and either verify that the occupants were dead or, if any German airmen were alive, to arrest them and wait for an ambulance or the military authorities to take them away. War Office directives stressed the danger of allowing shot-down Germans to escape into the countryside where Nazi sympathizers would be prepared to shelter and assist them while awaiting the invasion. The War Office's orders were unequivocal: there must be no escapees. If a German refused to surrender or tried to escape, he must be shot.

Combing the downs was tiring at the best of times, and Hugo's shooting brake was too decrepit to be useful on the uneven terrain, so the men had to go on foot. The downs were bigger than they looked. What appeared to be a gentle rise and fall from a distance became a series of steep climbs and hidden folds, but mindful of their duty, the Home Guard went as fast as they could. From time to time they paused to catch their breath while Hugo scanned the countryside through his binoculars.

"First time one's been shot down so near," puffed Albert. "We're in luck, might actually catch the buggers ourselves. Good sport, I'd say."

Harry Smith gave up, unable to climb any farther on his bad leg. "Sorry, lads," he puffed, red in the face, and collapsed onto a rock bent over his walking stick. "If you find anyone, chase him past me. I'll give the murdering bastard something to remember England by!"

Hugo hurried on ahead of Oliver and Albert. Oliver knew he drove himself hard on Home Guard exercises because he had been rejected for active service. Albert had to fit his Home Guard duties around the train schedules, and eventually he turned back to meet the three forty-seven from London. He wanted nothing so much as to find a

German trying to escape, he grumbled. He'd give Fritz a taste of his scythe, see fear in the man's eyes.

With the exercise he got in the Home Guard, Oliver had become tanned and was easily the fittest of the four, but as the youngest member, he normally let the other men set the pace. As a clergyman, he had not been obliged to join the Home Guard, but with so few able-bodied men available he had felt it was his duty. When Albert was gone he ran ahead to join Hugo, who looked done in, face white as a sheet and panting hoarsely as he swatted away swarms of midges. "It's nothing really, lung collapsed on me when I was a child. Do very well with just the one—army should have taken me." He doubled over, gasping for breath.

"Have a rest." Oliver shifted his gun and put his free hand on Hugo's shoulder. "Sit down. I'll go on ahead and you follow when you've got your breath back."

Oliver hurried on up the steep path at a faster pace. He was enjoying the exercise until he reminded himself that he was supposed to be looking for Germans.

At the top he saw that the downs were deserted, except for a few antiaircraft guns covered with camouflage nets. No one was manning them, and he realized he was on his own as he pinpointed the Heinkel's location by a rising column of smoke, barely visible against the gray sky. He scrambled over a rise toward it.

Moments later he was looking down on a smoldering mass in a green fold of the hills. His hand tightened on his gun as he scanned the downs for anyone running from the wreckage. Could he kill a man—even a German? Oliver had taken it as a matter of faith that, for the present, God and the prime minister were on the same side and he was duty-bound to obey the government's orders. He also felt it would be hypocritical to pray for England's military success when he was too squeamish to confront the enemy.

The smell of burning hit his nostrils and he spotted what looked like two dolls in gray uniforms on the ground. It was the first time he had seen a downed plane outside newsreels. He braced himself for Germans living or dead as he hurried down toward the crashed plane. He prayed that any who were alive would surrender and that he would not be put to the test by having to shoot them.

A fierce blast of heat hit him as he approached the wreck, gagging on the smoke and then a horrible smell. He wadded his handkerchief against his nose, but the stench grew worse as he drew nearer—a horrible mixture of burning fuel, burning rubber, and what he knew instinctively was burning flesh. He thought airmen must be trapped inside—certainly the gunners at the back. The heat was too intense to allow him to get closer and see inside, so he searched for the two figures he had seen from above. Finally he tripped over one and saw the other lying nearby. He guessed they had either been flung from the cockpit, which hung smashed open, or had crawled away from the flames. Oliver bent over, shielding his face and eyes with his arm.

The man he had stumbled over was clearly dead. He lay facedown, singed boots awkwardly pigeon-toed in. His head lay at an impossible angle. The leather cap was split, and something oozed round the edges onto the ground. Oliver was no stranger to death in cottage bedrooms or at the local hospital, but he had never been confronted with it in so violent and deliberate a form. What terror the airmen must have endured as the plane went down. He struggled into the scorching heat toward the other figure.

It moved. The man lay twisted on his back. He had pulled off his helmet, but his hair was gone, burned away from his oozing scalp. As he inched through the blistering heat and the fumes, Oliver could see the man's chest heaving as he gasped for breath. Blood covered the raw head. It had been more than two hours since the plane went down. The man turned his face toward Oliver. There was a hole where his nose had been. Oliver wondered if he had been conscious all that time.

As he looked at the man lying on the ground, any desire Oliver had felt for revenge on the enemy melted into despair and anger that human beings should make such suffering for one another. He wished he had thought to bring some water. He dropped his gun and fell to his knees beside the man.

In the distance the three forty-seven whistled as it left at the station in what was, at that moment, another world. Then there was no sound but the crackle of flames.

The German stirred. He opened a blue eye. His eyebrows and eyelashes had been burned away too. "*Wasser*," he moaned. Oliver groped helplessly for the German he remembered from university—he had read Goethe. The German croaked something else. Oliver caught "*Frau*." The man pawed helplessly at his breast pocket. "*Bitte*," he whispered. Oliver took his hand gently. It felt as if the bones inside were broken. For lack of anything else to do, he began to recite the prayer for the dying.

"*Bitte*," whispered the man again, staring intently at him with one blue eye. "*Fotograf*." He touched his pocket with their clasped hands. At last Oliver understood. *Frau.* Wife. He interrupted the prayer, reached in the man's pocket, and withdrew a snapshot of a pretty young woman with fair hair in braids round her head, sitting on a rug and holding a child. It looked as if they were in a garden or a park, having a picnic. The little girl was laughing and the woman was smiling down at her. He tried to close the man's fingers round the photograph, but they wouldn't work, so Oliver slipped the photograph between the man's fingers and held it there.

"*Kristina,*" the man whispered raggedly, "*liebe Frau.*"

Oliver saw blood trickle from the corner of his mouth. Then he gave a shudder and died.

Oliver felt unbearably tired. He had conducted too many funerals lately, the latest for two brothers crushed when their airfield mechanics' hut took a direct hit. The family had been wild-eyed with grief, and a local farmer's daughter at the back of the church had sobbed uncontrollably on her mother's shoulder. She had been engaged to one of the boys, who had left her expecting a baby. The villagers had condemned her as no better than she should be and cold-shouldered her and her family.

He wanted to rage at God. What is it You expect me to do in the face of all this killing and human despair? I have buried local lads killed by other young men like these two and laid them in the graveyard next to the men from their families who died in the Great War and whose names are on a memorial plaque in the church. Now we will bury these men, and somewhere in Germany their families will weep and there will be more names on other memorials. All across Europe people are killing each other, girls cry over their unborn fatherless babies, and God-fearing people blindly reject the gift of a new life. Eventually all that's left of civilization will be names on gravestones. Why?

As he thought of the scene before him being replayed day in and day out, the slaughter at Dunkirk, Poland, Belgium, France, and everywhere else, Oliver felt an overwhelming urge to lie down beside the dead man and sleep.

A clap of thunder roused him. He glanced up and saw Albert and Hugo coming toward him. Lightning flashed over the coast and the wind blew harder. Time to get off the downs.

"Tonight for once they'll sleep in Hythe—the Civil Defense in London too, while this storm lasts," said Albert. Everyone followed the weather anxiously now, dreading clear spells. Bombing was at its worst then, because the enemy could navigate easily, especially when there was a moon.

"Pray the storm keeps up along the coast," said Oliver, forcing himself to stand as the first drops of rain sizzled on the hot metal. Over the sea he saw more flashes and heard another threatening rumble of thunder.

"Come on. No use standing about up here to get struck by lightning," said Hugo. "I'll contact the police to collect the bodies before any children find them. I'll phone from the vicarage, if I may. Suppose we'll get stuck with burying them."

"Amazin' how Jerry always knows the clear nights to cross the channel," Albert muttered.

Hugo was looking sick. "He got it wrong today. Have you ever thought what we'd do if we actually captured a German and he tried to escape? Could you shoot?"

"If he tried to run away," Albert fingered his scythe, "yes," he said in a firm voice, thinking of Nell and Margaret Rose.

Suddenly Oliver knew with absolute conviction that, having watched the German die, he could not. Whatever happened, even if it were to cost him his own life, he would not kill another human being. He squared his shoulders. His duty was clear. He would continue to pray for the armed forces, but as far as he was concerned, whatever the government's orders, his first duty was to God and the preservation of life. To be certain of something, he thought, even in the most horrible circumstances, was strangely comforting. Like being in quicksand and suddenly finding a rock under your feet. He offered up a silent prayer of thanks.

15.

Crowmarsh Priors, September 1941

ar, thought Muriel Marchmont crossly, was a noisy, inconvenient business. Planes chasing each other overhead, shattering the peace of the afternoon, the dreadful air raid siren, whose shrill summons they all had to obey, no matter when it sounded. And this rationing; coupons and points were so confusing. First it had been sugar and butter and meat, and then before one knew where one was, one needed coupons for cheese and eggs, bacon, and even clothing.

The cook, Mrs. Barkins, had given notice at Christmas and gone to work in a shipyard, of all places. Mrs. Gifford had been obliged to fill in, but cooking was not her forte. Now indigestion kept Lady Marchmont awake at night. And while Mrs. Gifford struggled in the kitchen, the house became more and more untidy. Housemaids were not to be thought of: they had all gone to work in munitions factories or as bus conductresses.

Lady Marchmont thoroughly sympathized with those friends of her late husband who laid the blame for this misconceived war with "foreigners," especially the French and the Poles, who had influenced Churchill. Surely things had reached a point where it was in England's best interests to make peace with Germany. She would have liked to shake politicians until they saw sense. And all the intractable young people for whom she had made such suitable plans. Were any of them prepared to be guided by their elders? Were they the slightest bit grateful? Age made Muriel easily vexed. She hardly knew whether she was more irritated by Frances's refusal to help Alice make herself attractive to Oliver or by Alice's cowed look and pale face. Hugo, she knew from Leander, had not yet proposed, and Frances had gone up to London twice without telling her. As for Oliver...

The last straw had been Oliver burying two dead Germans in the farthest corner of the churchyard. She had rung the bishop to protest that they were most probably Lutheran and as such had no business in an Anglican graveyard. The bishop, who had dealt with Muriel Marchmont before, temporized, hemmed and hawed, said it was wartime and the deed was done, and the Church authorities were not keen on exhumation. Finally he had sent her into a lather of fury by suggesting she pray for her enemies. She had slammed down the telephone, which brought on a dizzy spell.

She had been sadly mistaken in extending her patronage to Oliver. He had forgotten what he owed her and was behaving in far too independent a manner for her liking. Mild-mannered as he was, he had become a figure of authority in the village. The war had matured him. The boyish look had disappeared and he now juggled services, christenings, the Mothers' Union, the parish accounts, visiting the sick, and the Sunday school rotas more or less efficiently with his Home Guard duties. A naturally shy man when he first came to Crowmarsh Priors, he had wrestled for days to perfect a sermon, delivered diffidently with much stuttering. Now, with less and less time to spend at his desk, his sermons were much more affecting because he spoke with simple conviction from the heart, another source of irritation to Muriel, who disliked the low church evangelical streak that had lately been in evidence. Oliver had developed a knack of making a connection between daily and biblical events, which had proved comforting in these difficult times to everyone but herself.

Though a Roman Catholic herself, Evangeline Fairfax had dragged Tommy, Maude, and Kipper to a special children's service, at which she had confided to Frances that Oliver reminded her of the colored preachers in New Orleans: "In a minute he'll shout, '*Amen*, brothers and sisters!'"

Worst of all, Oliver had shown a disgraceful laxity in upholding village moral standards. Several babies had been born to unmarried mothers, the fathers being either away fighting, killed, or missing in action. Oliver had visited them all and, with some difficulty because the girls were so ashamed, persuaded them to let him baptize their children. Muriel Marchmont was shocked when she learned that he planned to do so at the font in full view of the congregation at morning service, as he did the children of lawfully wedded parents. She wrote a furious note ordering him to do nothing of the kind and assumed that that would be the end of the matter.

On the Sunday Oliver had designated for the baptisms, she was astonished to see several girls with babies at the back of the church, looking nervous but at least present. Oliver had preached a most persuasive sermon about new life being a gift from God that should be especially welcome in the midst of war and death. It had had people looking shamefacedly at each other. Several middle-aged women who had lost their sons to the war and were longing to acknowledge their grandchildren burst into tears. Such was Oliver's authority that afterward most of the congregation went to admire the babies. There were offers of outgrown prams and cots, and Constable Barrows promised to carve each child a set of building blocks. The young mothers smiled tremulously, and one remarked bravely that her boy resembled his dad.

Muriel had been outraged almost, but not quite, to the point of speechlessness. She paused in the door, in front of fellow parishioners queuing behind her to shake Oliver's hand. "It won't do! Babies out of wedlock won't do, I tell you. Send them away—lock them up! I won't stand for it, young man!" she spluttered furiously. She ordered him to promise he would never do it again.

Oliver listened patiently. Then he imprisoned Lady Marchmont's gloved hand in both of his and replied for all to hear that it was his duty to baptize every child in the parish as long as he was vicar. "Have a peaceful Sunday," he added.

For once she had been silenced. He had told her publicly that she was wrong! No one had ever dared speak to her like that. Behind her, people grinned at their feet. Lady Marchmont and her tirades were wearing, and they were pleased someone had stood up to her. Aside from the matter of the fatherless babies, she had been particularly nasty to Tanni Zayman because she was "foreign," and everyone in the village was fond of the young woman, whose husband was doing important war work, and her sweet-natured little boy.

How brave of him, thought Frances. She smiled radiantly and winked at him as she trailed out behind her godmother, who announced in a loud voice that she would send for her solicitors the next day to make alterations to her will.

The next afternoon Alice and Oliver were in the vestry, discussing arrangements for the annual Harvest Fayre. There were so few amusements with the war on, and everyone was looking forward to it.

"Every house in the village, except the vicarage, has a victory garden, and competition is dead keen over the biggest vegetables," said Alice. "Nell Hawthorne has a new way of making dried-apple pies for the home-produce table, and we've lots of prizes for the tombola—Tanni has embroidered a sweet baby's cap, the pub has donated a bottle of whisky, Constable Barrows has carved a wooden Noah's Ark with animals, his wife Edith has sewn fifty lavender bags—even Mummy has crocheted a table runner. And there's Shirley Temple, of course."

In the spring the village had clubbed together to buy a piglet. It was being fattened on table scraps and vegetable peelings and was to be butchered and shared out at Christmas. In the meantime the children had named it Shirley Temple, and it had become a pet. "They want Shirley Temple to have a pen at the Harvest Fayre. Margaret Rose Hawthorne has made a ribbon for her substantial neck," said Alice. "Oh, and Nell said that if you don't mind, she'll come and pick the blackberries in the churchyard for jam. It's got terribly overgrown since Jimmy signed up, but looking on the bright side there's a good crop and she can sell the jam with her pies. Goodness, is Mrs. Gifford *running*?"

Lady Marchmont's housekeeper came breathlessly through the church gate, her apron crooked. "Vicar, come quick! It's her ladyship! I've sent for the doctor, but she wants you, Vicar," she panted. "She was gardening all morning in the heat, then after lunch she felt faint. I was clearing the lunch things when I heard her fall. I helped her to bed and sent to the home farm for Miss Frances and the doctor, but she's gone all peculiar in the face, and—"

Oliver grabbed the items he needed to administer Holy Communion and hurried off to Glebe House.

An hour later the doctor arrived and pronounced Lady Marchmont dead of a massive stroke.

Three days later two solemn men in black, one old and one young, with bowler hats and large briefcases, stepped off the morning train from London. Albert recognized Lady Marchmont's London solicitor with his clerk. Over the years she had summoned them frequently. "Last time you'll be needed, I daresay." They frowned at him and marched off in the direction of Glebe House.

At Glebe House, Mrs. Gifford served weak coffee to the two men, Frances, and Oliver, who had been summoned from the vicarage. She started to withdraw, but the solicitor asked her to stay while the will was read. He had advised the Marchmont family for years and had come to dread her ladyship's periodic summonses to Sussex to amend her will. She had always ignored their advice about what was and was not legally possible, and now it was full of tortuous and incomprehensible provisos upon which she had insisted. He settled his spectacles on his nose, cleared his throat, and began, hoping that he could make sense of the bewildering document.

He began with the least complicated provision, a small legacy for Mrs. Gifford and the right to stay on for life in her two rooms behind the kitchen. The solicitor paused. The housekeeper sniffed and said she was glad of the money, but that after thirty years she fancied a change from housekeeping, thank you very much. She planned to take on war work at a munitions factory near Reading.

The solicitor continued. Lady Marchmont had not had time to alter her will before she died, and Glebe House was still left to Oliver, her only living relative. However, he had just received notification that the War Office was requisitioning it for the duration of the war, to use it as a recuperation home for wounded servicemen. The clerk interrupted to explain that, as Land Girls, Frances and Elsie would be allowed to remain in the house since the Land Girl hostel near Brighton was full and no other billet was available in the vicinity. There was something about shares and money for Oliver, while most of the contents of the house and Lady Marchmont's jewelry went to Frances. "Though as far as we know," the solicitor said, looking up at Frances and shaking his head, "there's no jewelry of great value. Surprising really. There was a great deal once—quite valuable. Now there are only her everyday items—her watch, a few rings, some antique brooches. A few items of paste. There should be an inventory, but she was somewhat vague about it last time we asked."

During the reading Frances watched Oliver on the sofa. She wasn't particularly interested in jewelry or furniture. His eyes were closed and she wondered if he was following what the solicitor was saying. If so he didn't look particularly happy to hear that he was now a rich man and the owner of a grand house, even if he couldn't live in it yet. Now he opened his eyes and rubbed them. He seemed to be thinking of something else. It struck Frances how much he had aged since she arrived. He often looked sad and worn with the extra demands the war placed on him. Of course Aunt Muriel had bullied him relentlessly, and he had just had word of the death of a local girl who volunteered to drive an ambulance in London. It had taken a direct hit. Frances knew he had spent hours the night before with the bereaved family.

All of a sudden Frances thought that what he looked was lonely. He was a tower of strength for other people in their hours of need, but did anyone care for him? God, of course: Oliver seemed very firm in his faith. But on a more human level...Frances felt a surge of sympathy and an impulse to put her arms round him. As the solicitor's voice droned on, it occurred to her that he was taller than she was, and if she stood on tiptoe and he bent down a little...her mouth opened as the scenario turned into a kiss and...

The solicitor was staring at her, one eyebrow raised quizzically. Frances dropped her eyes and stared at her knees until at last they reached the end of the will. The solicitor asked if there were any questions, then solemnly accepted sherry and biscuits from Mrs. Gifford. Then he and the clerk packed up their papers to return to London.

When they had gone Frances moved to sit beside Oliver and said, "Since the house now belongs to you, Elsie and I can try to squeeze into the hostel, but perhaps I may store things in the cellar for the time being?"

"Of course, you are entitled to stay anyway, the solicitors said as much. But Cousin Muriel hinted strongly that it would be just a matter of time until you needed them for, er…" Oliver took off his glasses again and polished them with his handkerchief. Frances noticed that his white clerical collar set off the tan he had gotten from walking on the downs and that his eyes, with little lines round them now, were a deep brown. They held hers steadily, looking, she thought, unhappy.

"Mmm," she said. "You mean, she meant me to marry Hugo?"

He nodded. "I think, well, people seemed to expect… think it's…suitable." He polished a clean lens vigorously.

Frances shrugged. "Then they're doomed to disappointment, I fear. For a start Hugo has never asked me. And, speaking of matches she planned…" She grinned.

"I know—oh, I know!" Oliver groaned. He pushed his hair off his forehead and put his glasses back on. "She made it so obvious, and it was frightfully embarrassing at first. Then one day Alice let slip she'd once hurled an entire basket of apples through the vestry window and used every bad word she knew because Nell Hawthorne had tried to wheedle her into making apple tarts for me. We both laughed, and it's been a joke between us ever since. But *only* a joke," Oliver added in his new firm voice. "Alice is a brick, but marrying her would be like marrying my sister. Not at all what I…"

"I wouldn't put it past Aunt Muriel to come back and badger us from beyond the grave. She always wanted to have the last word. Jolly awkward of her, leaving things here and there. Much simpler if she had wanted you and me to make a match of it—that way her house, money, furniture, and jewelry could all stay together."

Oliver looked so taken aback that Frances cursed herself for her ill-timed speech, suddenly feeling that she had gone much too far. "Daft, really," she finished feebly and blushed.

Then he smiled at her and the little lines round his eyes deepened. "Vicars are warned about elderly female parishioners, and I felt I was just getting the hang of dealing with her when she died. If she comes back as a ghost, I shall get the bishop's permission to hold an exorcism. He had a run-in or two with her himself." Oliver patted Frances's hand in a vicarly way, then let his hand rest on hers for a moment. Frances was just thinking how pleasantly warm and strong it felt when he removed it and stood up. "Of course you mustn't think of leaving the house. Nice to think of you living here. Oh, and Elsie too, of course." He looked at his watch. "Mothers' Union meeting at two. Must press on."

Frances sat on in the morning room, absurdly happy that Oliver wasn't going to marry Alice. She felt a sudden surge of sympathy for her. Imagine spending one's days in the infants' school and going home to that dreadful mother afterward. No wonder Alice looked so bedraggled all the time. She would try to be nicer to her.

16.

Crowmarsh Priors, November 1941

*T*he prospect of turning twenty-one soon and being able to quit the Land Girls at last had sustained Frances since her meeting with her father, and had anything been needed to strengthen her resolve, the Wednesday three days before her birthday began particularly badly. At the farm the Land Girl team leader assigned Frances her least favorite job, milking. Grumpily Frances banged the pail on the ground and sat down on the milking stool. She fumbled for the teats, and the cow mooed and tossed her head. "Do shut up and stand still, Queenie," she muttered. The cow shifted, knocking Frances sideways into the straw. Frances picked herself up and slapped Queenie on the rump. Irritated, Queenie kicked Frances hard with a mucky foot and peed over her trousers.

Lugging milk pails back to the dairy she decided to take a shortcut through the bull's pen since the occupant wasn't in sight. Then out of nowhere, the bull was charging toward her from the far end of the field, head lowered. In her hurry to get out, Frances didn't shut the gate properly and the bull ran off down the lane, tossing his head and bellowing. Fortunately two farmers were passing and went after him with a prod and a large forked stick. "Damn!" muttered Frances, sloshing milk into the tops of her boots.

At midday the team leader ticked her off in front of everyone. Frances yawned ostentatiously. The team leader followed the Land Army Welfare Committee's advice for handling awkward moments and keeping team morale up. "Right then! Now we'll have a jolly good singsong over our sandwiches."

Frances snapped. "Not another! It's like a bloody nursery! 'Back to the Land/We must all lend a Hand!' is too stupid for words, and I'll be damned if I'll sing it again, war or no war."

Uncertain how to cope with mutiny in the ranks and trying to hang on to her authority the team leader said, "Right! I shall report you for insubordination!"

"Do. I'm going to the pub for lunch."

Elsie put down her spade. "An' me, I bloody 'ate singin'."

"Elsie Pigeon, I'm reporting you too!"

Elsie made a rude gesture with two fingers and muttered, "Bugger off!" She and Frances cycled off for some cider, leaving several Land Girls snickering and the team leader in a temper.

An hour later and somewhat the worse for wear, they wove back to the farm on their bicycles. Elsie stopped. "I don't fancy goin' back. I'm fed up wiv farmin'."

"Me too, darling. So tedious! Whoops!" Frances wobbled turning a corner and tumbled off. "Ooops!"

Elsie stopped too. "I'm 'ungry. You 'ungry?"

"Always, darling!" sighed Frances, rubbing a bruised leg, light-headed from drinking cider on an empty stomach. Last night's supper, at Evangeline's, had been whale meat. "There wasn't anything else," wailed Evangeline, "even for coupons!" But the whale meat smelled and tasted like fishy rubber that had gone off. Everyone had tasted it reluctantly, then chewed the first bite very, very slowly. Tommy and Maude and Kipper simultaneously spat it out.

"Ugh! Ain't eatin' that no more," said Tommy firmly.

"I'll frow up if I do," said Maude. Kipper looked at his big sister and nodded. "Me too." In the end none of them could stomach it. Even Evangeline couldn't do much with whale meat.

"'Ere. I was savin' this." Elsie grinned and from beneath the pullover in her bicycle basket she produced a packet of ham sandwiches on thickly buttered bread, slabs of chocolate, and American cigarettes. The two girls fell on the food.

"Ham! Oh lovely, *lovely* ham! Where on earth—with rations and all?" said Frances when she was licking chocolate off her fingers. She took a cigarette.

"Bernie," said Elsie.

"Of course," sighed Frances guiltily. Elsie always had treats in spite of rationing, things that were virtually unobtainable since the war started, pressed-powder compacts, perfumed soap, lipsticks, stockings, chocolates, bath talcum, silk underclothes, tinned salmon…

"Bernie's dealing in black market stuff, isn't he? Darling, he'll get caught! The papers are full of dire stories about people who break the rationing laws. Shopkeepers get fined and go to prison just for selling the tiniest bit of butter without coupons. Penal servitude! Months and months of it."

"Bernie? Naaoow, they never," drawled Elsie, exhaling American tobacco luxuriously. "'E's too good at it, knows how to go about it wifout callin' attention to 'imself. Butter. Sugar. Petrol. Whiskey even. You name it, there's a lot of it floatin' about, an' a lot of people can pay for it. 'E knows where to get it, so 'e does a bit of tradin' 'ere and there, this an' that. Lot of it goin' on, Frances. Government can't get their 'ands on everyfink. And anyway they turn a blind eye to what Bernie gets up to. Bernie says they see it as the price they pay for his work."

"Whatever *does* Bernie do, darling, to get away with it? Though I suppose it's the most terrific secret."

"Oh, exactly what he done before the war," said Elsie coolly. "'E's not supposed to talk about it, but he can't help tellin' me. Forgin' an' burglin' and, well, scavengin' after the bombin's mostly."

"What?"

"Before the war the coppers was always trying to nick Bernie and send 'im away. Now 'e 'as a motor to pick 'im up and bring 'im back and they give 'im room and board with Constable Burrows to keep an eye on 'im. They even pay 'im. You got to ask, wot can the government want wiv Bernie Carpenter? Not like they need 'im to fix a dog race or fence a lorry load of cigarettes and jam, is it? The forgin's one thing, 'e told me 'imself. It's like 'e's got a gift for it. 'Nother is, I fink, 'e goes scavengin' in bombed-out buildings, like jeweler's or a bank or a big 'ouse where they might keep jewelry, Bernie goes in quick. 'E's supposed to look for diamonds, crack a safe to get 'em if need be. 'E gets a police guard even to warn people away while 'e's doin' it. I fink the War Office needs diamonds. Dunno for what, but Bernie says some things the authorities get up to you'd never believe. But that's on the quiet, mind. Bernie says it's all right for the people what owned the diamonds, they got insurance an' all."

"Elsie, be careful. Even if he gets away with all this stuff now he's bound to end up in prison eventually. He'll leave you high and dry."

Elsie smoked and thought for a minute. If Mum had been there she would have agreed with Frances. But Elsie was on her own now, and for the time being she was following her heart. She would take care, though. "See, Frances, you don't know 'ow folks like me and Bernie 'ave to live. You only know 'igh-ups and 'ow *they* live. Lady Marchmont and Sir Leander and that 'Ugo—even Alice and her mum who fink they 'aven't much, but they'll always 'ave more'n most.

"You don't know nuffink what it's like round Norf Street, wiv the men out of work and not many jobs anyway, the glue factory smelling enough to make your 'ead ache, me mum skimpin' every day just to feed us our dinner and keep a roof over our 'eads. Always 'ungry, we were, but Mum tried her 'ardest. She sold almost everyfink we owned, even 'er weddin' ring, so's she could pay the rent man. She hated sellin' 'er ring worse than anyfink, always said no matter 'ow bad things got, at least people could tell she were a respectable married woman.

"One fing I learned, you get a chance, any chance at all, not to live that way, you grab it quick. Aren't many chances, for folk like Bernie and me. Bernie, 'e grabbed 'is chance to put somefink by for when the 'igh-ups are finished with 'im and toss him back to Norf Street. An' anyway, what wiv what 'e knows about them givin' 'im orders to do the forgin' an' safe-crackin' an' all, if they makes trouble for Bernie, 'e'll make trouble for them."

"Ah. Blackmail. Good luck to you both, then. And thanks for the sandwiches, they were delicious," said Frances, deciding she didn't really care a hoot if they were black market or not.

They were terribly late back, and the leader was in a frightful sulk. She sent Frances to join the potato diggers in a boggy field where the heavy mud clung to her boots like cement and Elsie to oil the tractor. She ordered the others not to speak to Frances and Elsie the rest of the afternoon. Elsie, feeling the effects of the cider, stalled the tractor when testing it, then drove it into a ha-ha. She emerged swearing and left the tractor on its side. The rest of the team sent them to Coventry, and Frances was glad she and Elsie didn't have to go back to the hostel with them. For the time being they still enjoyed the relative comfort of Glebe House. As usual when Bernie was around, Elsie disappeared the minute work was finished.

It started to drizzle, and by the end of the day Frances was chilled to the bone. Her shoulders ached and there were black half moons of dirt under her fingernails. Scrubbing her hands with hard yellow soap in the cold scullery in the November twilight, she thought wistfully of rose geranium bath salts, fresh white bath towels, manicures, nicely dressed hair, pretty dancing frocks…nightclubs, music, and laughter…now it was all mud, baggy trousers, dreary weather, bad news, gray skies, worry, cold, and Woolton pie and potatoes.

Gazing down at her sweaty jumper and stained corduroy breeches she wondered what idiot at the War Office thought describing Land Girls as "strong, sturdy, and weather-beaten" and giving them outfits to match would raise their morale. And now clothes rationing had been introduced, not that Frances could see it made a lot of difference in the country where clothes hardly mattered, because there was nowhere to go except the parish hall to watch a film once in a while or a dismal dance at the Land Girls' hostel. Soon they would all resemble Alice, in the ghastly outfits her mother discarded and with the tatty head scarf tied on so tightly her head looked shrunken. Or give up altogether like Evangeline who was slim and would have been beautiful if she made any effort. But she didn't seem to care how she looked, with Richard away.

Cleaning her nails with the point of a vegetable knife, Frances reminded herself the minute she came of age she could escape cows and digging potatoes. Evangeline had shown her how to set snares, and Frances had taken the little man his brace of pheasants. He said they would see her after her birthday.

Absently she washed her hands and dried them on the evil-smelling scullery towel that neither she nor Elsie had thought to wash since the housekeeper left. With a war on who minded about housework?

No, what Frances minded, and wouldn't have admitted to a soul, was that she would turn twenty-one on Saturday without any celebration. Of course it was frivolous to think of a party with the war on, but it was too depressing for words to have nothing to mark her coming of age. Frances was a stranger to self-pity, but for a moment tears welled. She brushed them away. She jolly well *would* celebrate.

Why not have a little supper party on her birthday? It would give her and the other girls an excuse to be cheerful and dress up a bit.

But how did one give a party? She had never given a party. She had no cook, no staff to serve, no anything, and she couldn't cook for toffee. But Frances was resourceful. If Evangeline would conjure up something special for a little supper, Frances would offer to look after Tommy, Maude, and Kipper when next Evangeline had to go up to London to see her doctor—the evacuees ran rings around Tanni. She would invite Elsie, of course, and Evangeline and Tanni—Alice too. For men there were Hugo and Oliver and, even though he was so young and cheeky, Bernie. He made it no secret that he thought Frances "a bit of all right." And Frances, amused, thought he was rather a pet—although Alice considered him "not quite the thing," Johnny, and consequently Tanni, adored him, and Elsie was smitten. There were Evangeline's records to play on Penelope's gramophone—perhaps they could dance a little.

And there was one thing she *did* have for her party: drink.

When she had been clearing her godmother's silver and china into the farthest reaches of the cellar to store it before the workmen arrived to turn Glebe House into a convalescent home, Frances had made two discoveries. The first was a stock of dust-covered bottles that turned out to be claret, half a dozen bottles of brandy, and a stone bottle of something labeled "Genever." She brought it all upstairs and cleaned off the dust. The wine and brandy had French labels. She wasn't sure about the genever, but she didn't care. These days drink was drink—a rare treat.

Frances's second discovery had been even more surprising. When she had found the wine, she had stubbed her toe on something wedged under the rack holding the stash of brandy. She shone her torch down and saw brass hinges gleaming dully on a lacquered Chinese chest. She tugged it out from its hiding place and blew off the dust. There was a key in the lock. She turned it and opened the lid to reveal velvet jeweler's boxes of different shapes and sizes. She opened the largest one and gasped. It contained a triple string of perfectly matched pearls with a large emerald and diamond clasp. It was the same one her aunt Muriel wore in the portrait over her desk. Then she found a set of bracelets to match, a pair of old-fashioned diamond clips, rings, brooches, and a man's gold watch with a beautifully worked filigree case and chain, the Marchmont arms on the back. The missing jewelry! Her godmother must have hidden the box there and forgotten it.

Frances adored clothes but had never been fond of jewelry. However, she could see that the contents of the chest were worth a great deal of money. Especially the pearls. Hmmm...for her party Frances decided to fish out a favorite dress she had not worn for ages, an amber velvet tea gown that suited her coloring most becomingly and had little silk slippers to match. What fun to look her best for a change. Oliver had never seen her dressed up. She would even wear the pearls, just this once, in honor of the occasion. Then perhaps Bernie would know where she could sell them discreetly.

Her conscience had pricked. She ought to tell the solicitors she had found the jewelry. She suspected there might be tax to pay. She could ask Oliver what he thought. Then she decided not to. Oliver was so good, he would advise her to tell the solicitors at once. It could wait until after her party.

Next morning cycling off to the farm half an hour late, Frances stopped at the Fairfaxes' to invite Evangeline and Tanni, who was hugely pregnant with her second baby and darning children's jumpers on the sofa. Evangeline agreed to see what she could do in the way of food and said she would ask Margaret Rose Hawthorne to come over and keep Johnny and the evacuees out of trouble so that she and Tanni could enjoy the evening. Then Frances called at the infants' school where Alice was busy putting up new posters in the classroom. "Coughs and sneezes/spread diseases/use your handkerchief!" warned one, and "Is your journey REALLY necessary?" admonished another.

"I wanted to put that one up at the station where Evangeline would see it next time she goes gadding off to London, but Albert Hawthorne says no. He's already covered in posters," said Alice. "But really, Evangeline is so thoughtless." She sniffed.

Still, when Frances issued her invitation, even Alice cheered up and said she would bring Woolton fudge, the latest invention of the Ministry of Food. "Delicious! You'd never guess it's made from carrots!"

"Fancy!" said Frances. All the Ministry of Food's wartime recipes seemed to involve carrots, which Frances detested. How they could be turned into fudge didn't bear thinking about. She suppressed a shudder and cycled away.

On their way to and from the farm that day and the next, Frances and Elsie scoured the damp fields for the last walnuts and chestnuts. All five girls had pooled their cheese rations so that Evangeline could make one of her cheese

puddings. She would use real eggs in it instead of the powdered ones that left a peculiar aftertaste. Bliss!

Eggs from a household's own hens were still not
rationed, and thanks to Tanni's sewing, Evangeline and she
now had an elderly cockerel as well as the hens and a handful of pullets that pecked about in the back garden where
the onions and cabbages and artichokes grew. The eggs
were a godsend. Tanni adamantly refused to eat the odd-
tasting corned beef, wouldn't consider bits of ham or bacon
on the rare occasions they were available, or the dubious
"mince," often the only meat available on rations. Neither
would she feed any of it to Johnny. Sister Tucker clucked and
remonstrated, but Tanni was firm so Sister saw they both
received their full allocations, with a bit extra, of cod-liver
oil and orange juice or rosehip syrup, and milk.

The evening before the party, Frances threw herself into
the preparations. She retrieved some of her godmother's
pretty china and silver from where she had stored them in
the cellar. "At finishing school we had to learn 'table setting and placements,'" began Frances distractedly, hovering
round the table with a basket of cutlery and monogrammed
linen napkins, "but I can't remember exactly what to do, I
never paid much attention."

"Why'd you learn it, then? So's you could train the servants?" asked Elsie with a sarcasm that was lost on Frances.

"Well, actually yes, darling. They said it was frightfully
important to be able to train servants when a girl married.
What if she moved abroad somewhere and the servants
weren't used to doing things correctly? They would get the
forks wrong way round or serve dinner in the wrong order,

not to mention the horrors of getting the seating wrong if someone important came to dine, and—"

"La di dah!" said Elsie, rolling her eyes. She had no idea Frances was so daft. Anyway, thanks to her brief house-maid's training, she considered herself an expert on that sort of thing and enjoyed sitting on the sofa and instructing Frances on the best way to lay the fires in the morning room and dining room, how to polish glasses and iron damask table cloths. Later she got up to help her hide the worst of the mess they had made since the old lady's death, shoving things into cupboards and behind furniture until the house was almost tidy.

"Too exhausting," pronounced Frances finally, "but it looks rather nice, don't you think? No need to actually dust, is there, darling? If we just have the candles and the fire for light, the dust won't really show…"

17.

Crowmarsh Priors, Frances's Birthday

*W*hen Frances finished at the farm on Saturday she cycled home as fast as she could. She was alone because Elsie had stayed behind. After work, through gritted teeth, the team leader had demanded "a quiet word" with Elsie, who had been driving the tractor too fast and nearly run her over. Steeling herself against the cold, Frances took a hasty bath in the tepid four inches of water the War Office allowed. As she watched the filthy water gurgle down the drain, she had a short battle with her conscience, then had another bath. This time the water was more or less clean when she let it out. Shivering, she washed her hair and rinsed it with some flat beer she and Elsie kept in a bottle for that purpose.

By the time Elsie came home and clattered into the kitchen to make sandwiches, her one culinary accomplishment, Frances was wrapped in a dressing gown, with a towel round her head, smelling of hops. She drew the blackout curtains, lit the fires, tipped the last bottle of her godmother's sherry into a decanter, then opened several bottles of claret and left them on the hearth to breathe and warm a little. For good measure she opened the genever and drew the cork on a bottle of brandy. Frances had a swig of the genever to taste it while she huddled close to the fire to dry her hair. The pungent herbal smell and strange taste made her shudder, but it was nicely warming.

The blaze crackled merrily and she had another sip. Then another. She poured some into a glass and drank that too. Her cheeks tingled and she felt much warmer, quite cheerful really. Would Oliver think she looked pretty tonight? she wondered as she tripped back up the stairs. She slipped into the tea gown, which was cut on the bias and swirled gracefully round her hips, making her small waist look even slimmer, then the matching slippers. She peered critically into the wavy old mirror in her bedroom to pin up her hair and fasten the pearls round her neck. She finished by putting on scent and lipstick, thinking how delightful it was to be wearing a pretty dress. Her reflection in the mirror reassured her that she looked like her old self, at least in the dim light. She gave a little twirl and the skirt swished round her ankles.

Someone knocked on the door.

Oliver!

Hurrying downstairs she felt a little dizzy. She clutched the door for support as she swung it open. It wasn't Oliver, but Hugo, in evening dress and a white silk scarf, with a bouquet of roses and a bottle of champagne. "Happy birthday, Frances! How lovely you look! Somehow one forgets Land Girls are, well, girls."

Embarrassed, Frances exclaimed at the size of the bouquet and buried her nose in the fragrant blooms. "Oh, Hugo, roses! They're my favorites. Wherever did you get them in November?" She kissed his cheek rather more warmly than she might have done had she not had the genever, then led him into the morning room, gaily explaining she and Elsie had planned to use the drawing room, then decided everyone would freeze. The morning room was easier to warm with a small fire. "With Alice coming we daren't light one big enough to thaw the drawing room—you can imagine the scolding she'd give us for wasting fuel. You know what she's like."

Hugo gave her a conspiratorial smile, and Frances went off to the larder for a vase.

When she came back with the tallest crystal one she could find, Hugo was standing with his back to the fire and his hands in his pockets. She began to arrange the roses in water, thinking how lovely they smelled, when Hugo cleared his throat and said, "Frances, I've come early because I've something particular to say."

She looked up from the roses. In her slightly inebriated state, his profile seemed wonderfully handsome in the firelight, and it was like old times to see a man in a dinner jacket. Hugo was the sort of man she was used to.

"Frances, I want to ask you...will you marry me? You must have seen how I feel about you—I haven't made much of a secret of it, hanging about whenever you're working. Even the other Land Girls have noticed. I intended to ask you sooner, but then your godmother died, and I felt it wasn't quite the thing. But now that you're of age…"

"Oh, Hugo!"

"Darling Frances, if you say yes you'd make me the happiest man alive. And we suit each other so well—surely you've seen that? I believe we should be very happy together. I'm to tell you from Father that he would be almost as pleased as I, if you did me the honor. It's high time Gracecourt had a new Lady de Balfort and a young family growing up to carry things on. And with the war there doesn't seem to be much point waiting. If you'll have me, that is."

"Oh, Hugo!" said Frances again. She was surprised and flattered. Lady de Balfort! She saw herself by Hugo's side in procession at Westminster Abbey, attending the next coronation, both of them in ermine-trimmed robes and the family tiara on her head! "You've taken me by surprise!"

"You needn't answer at once," said Hugo, leaving the fire and coming closer to put his arms round her. He had never tried to kiss her before.

Instinctively she pulled away. "I don't know what to say." She moved toward the fire and pretended to warm her hands. "I'm sorry, I wasn't expecting…I must think." The vision of herself in the abbey began to fade.

"It's a lady's prerogative to take her time, I believe," Hugo said smoothly. He didn't seem too distressed by her reaction. In fact, he smiled complacently and glanced at his watch. "I found another old hunting piece for the Home Guard, promised to deliver it to Harry Smith. I'll come back later with Oliver. I hope you'll say you'll make me a happy man so that everyone can drink to our engagement. Father said I was to give you special love from him and ask if you can come to lunch on your next free Sunday."

"Delighted," murmured Frances. Her engagement!

The front door shut. Marry Hugo? Doing exactly as Aunt Muriel had wished? Her father would be thrilled.

Frances stood up, took the vase of roses into the dining room, and put them on the table. They made an arresting centerpiece. A new thought reached her addled brain. What if Hugo decided to confide in Oliver? "Congratulate me, old boy. Finally popped the question to Frances, waiting for an answer, you know how girls are, but I'm rather optimistic, hope you'll marry us when the time comes—quite soon, I expect. Trust you'll be called upon to baptize an heir too, before long."

"Oliver! Whatever will he think? Oh, hell!" Frances whispered, suddenly sober.

She heard the knocker again.

This time it was Evangeline with food and Tanni with Johnny, whom Tanni refused to leave behind with Margaret Rose and the other children. Tanni, Frances thought, with a start, looked awful, white and drawn despite her bulk. She handed Frances a thin round apple cake that smelled of cinnamon and admired Frances's dress. Then she settled on the sofa with her feet up while Evangeline laid a sleepy Johnny beside her and covered him with his ABC quilt.

As usual Frances was starving. She followed Evangeline into the kitchen, hovering and admiring the food her friend unpacked and set on the range to keep warm. "In honor of your birthday I sacrificed one of the fowls," Evangeline drawled, unwrapping a clean tea towel to reveal a handsome pie. It gave off a fragrance of chicken and herbs and field mushrooms and had a pastry rose on top.

"Mmmmm," Frances sniffed appreciatively. Next to it was the cheese pudding, golden on top. Tanni had made her special dish, red cabbage with onions and apples, sharpened with vinegar and cloves and garlic, and sweetened with a little honey. It was nothing like its horrible boiled cousin, which cropped up everywhere. For pudding, besides Tanni's apple cake, there was a special treat: two tins of raspberries, discovered in the depths of Penelope's larder. Frances poured them into a glass bowl, the closest she had come to cooking anything. "And what's that?" asked Frances, peeking under the cover of the last steaming dish.

Evangeline grinned. "Dirty rice."

"Oh, darling, how very...thrilling and clever and...um, exotic!" Frances recognized bits of onions and celery, but, "What are those little black bits?"

"Chicken gizzards. It's a New Orleans dish," Evangeline said.

"Gizzards?" repeated Frances faintly, wondering what unmentionable bit of the chicken that might be.

"We used to eat this in New Orleans every Saturday night. Inez, my grandmother's cook, taught me how to make it. My cousin Laurent and I used to hang around the kitchen and Inez would let us help her." There was a sudden catch in her voice.

"Evangeline, you must miss your home. Here you are in England in the middle of a war, and who knows what will happen if the Germans invade. You could be safely home in America with a nice American husband and automobiles and chocolate and no war or rationing or evacuees who wet their beds—"

"But then I wouldn't be married to Richard, would I? And no, I don't wish I was back in New Orleans. Not at all. Never."

She was very definite about it. It made Frances wonder if she could feel as devoted to Hugo as Evangeline was to

Richard, putting up with a war and everything for his sake. She tried to imagine it. Perhaps it was the sex? "Shame Richard doesn't get leave more often, you've only seen him three or four times."

"Three, and only because his ship was in port for repairs," said Evangeline shortly. "It wasn't for long either."

"And I know how much you want a baby…you keep going to see that doctor in London…" Frances trailed off. It had struck her that if she married Hugo, he would want a baby at once, then another. Usually people with titles wanted "an heir and a spare" as soon as possible. Fond as she was of Johnny, she couldn't imagine having a baby of her own any time soon. Couldn't imagine *wanting* one. All that growing fat and then actually giving birth—such a messy business and no end of agony! And then there was the sex part. No, somehow she was altogether disinclined to imagine sex with Hugo.

"You never know what might happen when the war's over," said Evangeline. "But I better warn you, Tanni got another letter today from those people she knows in London. It's upset her and she's trying not to say anything about it tonight because she doesn't want to spoil your evening. She says you've been so kind to her."

Frances was conscience-stricken. All she had done was given Tanni a spare negligee.

In the morning room, Tanni had gotten up to stretch, her hands on the small of her back. "Genever!" she cried, recognizing the bottle on the sideboard. "Wherever did you get it? My father used to make his patients take it after meals. It tastes horrible."

"I know, I tried it while I was dressing," said Frances, making a face. "Warming, though. Like some?"

Tanni nodded. "It's practically medicine, so it'll be good for the baby." However vile it tasted, genever was a reminder of home. She turned away so Frances would not see her smile fade.

After the Passover Seder, Tante Berthe, who was still upset by her internment, had warned Tanni never to speak German, not even in private, because you never knew who might overhear and report you as a spy. Tanni must be especially careful, she had added, not to offend any of the people in the village where she was living.

According to Tante Berthe, nowhere was really safe for Jews now. "Internment," she said, in a frightened whisper, was what the Germans were doing in Europe to them. Who knew what else happened? The British might even decide to follow the Germans' example—Rachel said because of the labor shortage, conscription for women was coming and people, especially the upper classes, were beginning to say there should be peace with Germany. Tanni knew that was true—she had heard Lady Marchmont say it. It was just as well that Tante Berthe had never met her.

Bruno had reassured Tanni over and over again that his job as a military translator meant that he, and Tanni and Johnny, would not be locked up in a camp, but after the Cohens' experience Tanni believed nothing was certain, no matter how kind Evangeline, Alice, Frances, and Elsie were.

Tante Berthe had also warned her that with the baby coming, it was not good to worry, but Tanni found the trying not to worry was even more of a strain. Although she kept everything to herself, her mind was as swollen with worries about what she must and must not do, or say, as her stomach was with the new baby.

Frances poured glasses of sherry from the decanter on the writing desk, then handed Tanni a generous quantity of genever. Tanni closed her eyes. It smelled worse than she remembered, but she gulped it down. In no time she felt light-headed and more relaxed.

A little later Alice arrived, her hair arranged inexpertly in the new "victory roll" style. She had with her a plate of lumpy gray slabs. "Carrot fudge!" she announced proudly.

"Too delicious!" exclaimed Frances, trying to look delighted but surreptitiously parking the plate behind Tanni's apple cake.

Alice had discovered an ancient lipstick while she was tidying her mother's room and now applied it in the mirror over the fireplace. Then she craned her neck to check the effect with her new hairstyle in the candlelight. It looked better if she stepped back a few paces.

Evangeline had brought the gramophone and records, lively new music that she said was called "swing" and slower, moody sounds she referred to as "jazz," explaining they had been recorded by a friend in Paris. In a change from her usual slapdash attire, Evangeline had raided the trunks in the attic and found a beaded dress that dated from Penelope's youth. She had also dug into the jewel box Richard had given her for some amethysts that had once belonged to Richard's grandmother, unaware that he had once promised to have them reset for Alice. The overall effect was striking, and for once her beauty was apparent.

Seeing the jewelry on Evangeline, Alice took a sharp breath and tossed down her sherry in one gulp.

Elsie came in with a new red silk scarf draped dramatically over her shoulders, then flounced out again. She returned, brandishing an ebony cigarette holder, with two platters of inexpertly trimmed sandwiches covered with damp tea towels. "I made these meself. Surprise! Tinned salmon!" she announced triumphantly. "And... fish paiste!" she said less certainly. Bernie had sworn blind that Frances would like it. The toffs where he worked had made quite a carry-on when a consignment of it turned up at their offices. They'd assured him it was "quite the thing." He told Elsie it cost the earth, that he'd tried it, and it was disgusting. Toffs didn't 'alf 'ave strange tastes. Elsie had licked it off her fingers in the kitchen and gagged as the nasty little black things popped fishily in her mouth. Bernie was right. It tasted like the fish Mum bought cheap on a Monday, past its prime. She whipped off the tea towel.

"Bloater?" asked Alice, wrinkling her nose at the fishy smell and squinting. "Hasn't it gone a bit black?"

"Elsie darling! Caviar!" gasped Frances.

Elsie told her it was a present from Bernie, who had sent his apologies. She whispered to Frances, "'E's been sent for, urgent."

Dressed up, bathed, and looking forward to a special dinner, the five young women relaxed. They felt glamorous and worldly sipping their drinks and listening to jazz and waiting for the men. For the moment they stopped thinking about responsibilities and rationing, shortages and aching backs, drawing out the enjoyment as long as they could. They finished the sherry and Frances said they might as well have some of the wine.

Tanni drank more genever. Now that she was used to the taste it wasn't so bad.

A cozy, cheerful glow settled over them. "Whatever can be keeping Oliver and Hugo?" they asked each other from time to time, but they were a little tipsy and hardly cared.

All at once they had their answer. The air raid siren shrilled, and they heard planes approaching in the distance. Alice, whose cheeks were flushed with unaccustomed alcohol, muttered, "Damn! They must have been warned to stand by for Home Guard duty. Shelter, everyone! I have to run." She threw on her coat and left.

"Bloody Jerry!" muttered Frances. "Come on, we ought to go to the shelter—or down to the cellar, at least," she said. "Otherwise Alice will—"

"To 'ell wiv' Alice! We shan't all fit in the shelter, anyway, not with Tanni so big. I'm stayin' put for once," said Elsie defiantly, lighting another cigarette. "To 'ell wiv Alice and to 'ell wiv the Jerries!"

"Let's have another drink, then," said Evangeline, in no hurry to get up either. Now that she had a chance to sit down, she realized how exhausted she was after all the cooking, then wrestling a screaming Maude and Tommy and Kipper into the bath before they went to bed, something they loathed, mistrusted, and resisted. Their family had taught them that baths in winter were unhealthy. Margaret Rose Hawthorne was sensible for her age and would get them down to the shelter in the wine cellar.

If only Laurent had taken her to France straight after she had come to England. She tried not to think about what she had overheard the drunken little Frenchman in the Soho pub say to him. Not realizing that Evangeline spoke French and could understand every word, he had nudged Laurent knowingly and referred to the North African girl with two children who depended on Laurent, so much so that he could never stay long on his rare trips to England.

"Just a joke, darlin'," muttered Laurent in her ear later. "You know I love you…"

Evangeline closed her eyes, waiting for drink to blot everything out. She knew in her bones that the North African girl had been more than a drunken Frenchman's joke. Laurent was what they called at home a "hot-blooded man," and there had been no word from him for months. She tried to rein in her imagination but failed.

"So, it's unanimous!" said Frances, brandishing the wine and genever bottles, then refilling everyone's glass. For the next hour the four stayed put, drinking, daring Jerry to make them move, getting hungrier.

Alice returned to giggles and drunken bravado. She was chilled to the bone in her thin coat and huddled by the fire, shivering with a caviar sandwich and a large brandy since they had finished the sherry. There was a full moon and the ARP had rung to say there had been heavy raids over London, Birmingham, and Exeter. Though the all-clear had sounded in the village, the Home Guard had been ordered to stay on duty.

At last Evangeline said they had better eat or the food would be ruined. They went into the dining room and filled their plates, admiring Frances's carefully laid table with Hugo's roses in the center, opening a little in the warmth of the fire. Frances poured more wine, and they lifted their glasses to each other.

The evening wore on. They moved back to their places round the morning room fire for coffee, rather weak coffee, but no one cared. They felt warm and pleasantly full for once. They had eaten most of the food, drunk all of the wine, smoked all of Elsie's cigarettes, and finished an entire bottle of brandy. Frances pulled the cork from another with a loud "pop" and they all laughed uproariously. Chestnuts roasted on the hearth. The fire crackled, and from time to time they took turns to crank the gramophone. In the background the jazz was lovely, if somewhat melancholy.

"No reashon to leave this to go shtale," said Frances, tipping more brandy from the second bottle into everyone's glasses. They were all rather drunk now, especially Tanni, who had gotten through most of the genever by herself.

"Poor Oliver and Hugo, shtill on duty," Alice said dreamily from the depths of her armchair. She supposed she was tiddly. It felt nice.

The clock struck eleven, then midnight. No one moved. Frances was glad that Hugo hadn't come back, and it was just as well that Oliver hadn't either. She was now finding it too much effort to get out of her chair. The bottle was now being passed around by leaning in each other's direction.

"Blimey, Tanni, you've bloody finished that gen stuff," exclaimed Elsie, suddenly spotting the empty bottle rolling on the floor. The tip of Tanni's nose was red and she had gone quiet, staring into the fire.

"Lordy," said Evangeline and hiccupped…"You shouldn't of done that…"

"Don't care," muttered Tanni, propped in a nest of cushions. She was eating the last of the carrot fudge.

"Me neither," said Evangeline.

Alice hiccupped too and raised her glass. "To...end to the war. God shave the king. The prime minister...and...and...abshent friendsh...thoshe in peril on the sea." They drank.

"You next, Frances...'s your birthday."

"To...Evangeline...lovely shupper, Tanni'sh new baby...Johnny and Elsie and Bernie and Oliver...to the war's end of course. And to...end of the blackout and clothing coupons and no more whale meat *ever*...dancing at the Shavoy...gardenia corsages...Madame Vionnet...Parish!"

"Hear hear!"

"Amen," said Evangeline, brooding drunkenly on the Algerian woman and not in a mood to toast anything.

"Elsie?"

Elsie stood up unsteadily.

"To me promotion! Leader said."

"The leader promoted you?" Frances was incredulous. The woman had recently accused Elsie of being a German saboteur because she was so hopeless with farm machinery and animals.

"I'm 'ead rat catcher now, aren't I?" Elsie said proudly.

This was greeted with shrieks of laughter and hiccups, "Head *rat* catcher?"

"Well—there's only one for the time bein'—me—but when there's more I'm to be rat catchin' team leader. Fancy! Me own supply of poison and all. Arsenic! Cyanide! Talent for destruction, she said I 'ave, might as well use it on rats because I'd used it on everyfink else. Wait till Agnes and Mum and Vilet and Jem and the twins 'ear."

"Congratulations!"

"Well done, Elsie!"

Tanni began to cry. The others stopped laughing. Bewildered, they looked at each other, then at Tanni. Then, one by one, they got up, somewhat unsteadily, and gathered round her. Alice asked, "Is it the baby? Oh, Tanni, you aren't due for...weeks!"

"Maybe...we...ought to—um—ring Sister Tucker?" asked Frances reluctantly, realizing that Sister Tucker would be scandalized to find them all, especially the expectant mother, drunk as lords.

The genever had sapped Tanni's usual restraint. "Not the baby." Her face crumpled and she burst into tears. "It's the...the twins!"

18.

Crowmarsh Priors, Frances's Birthday: Into the Small Hours

"What...is...she...talking about?" asked Frances, struggling to sit upright.

"Must have been something Elsie said. She should have known better, sho thoughtlesh of her!" said Alice accusingly.

"Do shut up, Alice!" said Frances, who was trying to think clearly and finding it difficult.

Elsie perched on the arm of Tanni's sofa, patting Tanni's shoulder and glowering at Alice. Alice didn't know nuffink about people, she thought. Tanni was the only person Elsie knew who understood when Elsie talked about missing Mum and the others. Bernie and Frances meant well, but neither of them had much family to miss. Evangeline clammed up if you mentioned hers, and as for Alice—the less said about Mrs. Osbourne the better. Now it occurred to Elsie for the first time that, besides Bruno and Johnny, Tanni might have a family somewhere too, even though she'd never talked about them. And now she was crying about some twins.

"'Ere, Alice, you're the sort as always 'as a 'ankerchief. Tanni needs one." Sullenly Alice groped for it and passed it to Elsie.

"There, there," said Elsie, bending over Tanni. "Blow yer nose, and tell us wot's the matter."

Curled in an armchair, Evangeline was finishing her brandy. "Elsie, you weren't to know, but Tanni pinned a photo over her bed. Two women, a man, and two little girls who look alike. Family, I think. I gather they're all missing. Her aunt Bertha...warned her not to talk about them—said she'd be arrested if she did."

"Who'd arrest Tanni?" demanded Elsie indignantly. "And where is her family missing from?"

"Tanni, try to calm down—not good for the baby, you know. Tell us about it. Won't let...anyone...'rest you," said Frances.

The look of concern on everyone's faces was too much for Tanni. She blurted out, "Evangeline's right. I mustn't... yes, I will tell you." She reached into her pocket for an envelope and unfolded Rachel's letter. "From London. Some friends there are trying to find what has become of everyone." She wiped her eyes. "They can't find my parents or Bruno's mother in England. They were supposed to come, but they've disappeared in Austria, probably arrested and sent to a work camp in Poland with all the Jews in their neighborhood." Tanni gave a sob. "But Lili and Klara, my little sisters, were on a special children's train coming to England, now they're probably in France, in a displaced persons' camp...if...they're not dead!" She started to cry again.

"Who?"

"Are they supposed to be in England?"

"Wot's this all about?"

"Elsie, *hush up* and let Tanni tell us!" ordered Evangeline.

"Tanni, stop crying," Frances said sharply. "Where in France?"

Tanni found the place in the letter with her finger. "It's called Gurs."

"Wait. Let me see if Aunt Muriel had a map. My geography's fuzzy." Frances went unsteadily into the room that had been Sir Humphrey Marchmont's study—which had been kept as he left it—and returned with an ancient Baedeker. She turned the pages, clumsily hunting for a map of France, thinking what a bit of luck it was that the Home Guard were still on duty and it was just the five of them. Tanni would never have said anything with the men around. She found the page and put the book on Tanni's lap.

Evangeline and Alice came across to lean over Elsie's shoulder to see the map on Tanni's lap. Tanni peered at it. "Here," she pointed to the place on the map not far from the Spanish border. "My friends learned that when Lili and Klara's *Kindertransport* was turned away from England it went here, to Gurs, where there is a big displaced-persons' camp. First it was refugees from the Spanish civil war. Many Spanish people stayed, but the camp is now full of people fleeing the Nazis who thought they would be safe. When the children arrived in Gurs the Germans had not occupied France."

"How on earth did you find them?" asked Evangeline.

"Some Americans, Quakers, I think, keep records of the names and ages of all the children who are without their parents. My friends sent them money and told them that the Joseph family in England were hunting for twin girls who should have been on the train. The Quakers finally sent word there was no record of Klara and Lili Joseph in Gurs, alive or even dead. They always noticed twins because for some reason the Germans had several times sent the police, the Milice, to the camp to find any twins and they always took them away.

"Then the Quakers heard that a priest had snatched several children as they got off the train, before the guards saw. They have probably been living with local people. They tried to learn if Lili and Klara had been kept from the camp, but they had to be careful and it took a long time. Finally they heard that twin girls might be living with an elderly couple in a village some distance from the camp. The priest finally admitted he had placed them with his sister and her husband. One had been slower than the other and he thought their name badges had said 'Klara' and 'Lili.' The Quakers are willing to help, although they are not supposed to, because the Germans have ordered that Jews, even children, who are not French, must be turned over to them. Informers are everywhere and the priest, the Quakers, and those hiding Jewish children are at risk of being arrested themselves and shot."

"I didn't think the Germans controlled that part of France yet..." said Frances.

"The Vichy police—the Milice—help the SS. They do what the Germans want. They take people from Gurs and send them to another camp at Drancy, near Paris. From there, the prisoners are taken to a prison in Poland, at Auschwitz."

Her voice faltered. Rachel had not minced words in her letter. They would keep looking for her family but Tanni must be prepared for bad news. "My friends say Auschwitz, where my parents and Bruno's mother are, is very bad, that terrible things happen there, more than anyone knows…the Germans say they will eliminate all Jews from Europe, from the face of the earth, even. If my parents, Bruno's mother, are there, God protect them. But it sounds as if Klara and Lili are not. Yet."

Evangeline twisted a strand of hair. The Free French she knew in London talked about Auschwitz and the other German camps with horror. Some of their members had fallen into Nazi hands and two had escaped with stories that were almost too terrible to believe. Evangeline had been appalled by what she heard. She had asked if the British government knew about the prisons. The Frenchmen had snarled that the British were not interested in anyone's hides but their own.

Now Evangeline nodded. "I think the news is censored to avoid scaring folks any more. Everyone would just give up otherwise."

"Is that true that no more foreign children can come here now?" demanded Alice.

Tanni nodded.

"S'outrageous. We mustn't stand for it." It was unlike Alice to question authority. "Bloody won't stand for it, I say!"

The others were even more astonished to hear Alice swear.

"Perhaps Father would know if's a way to get round the law…" Frances mused, trying to focus. "But knowing him—" she broke off.

"He'll prob'ly say rules is rules. What then?" Elsie knew that the admiral came from the class who made the rules, and made them to suit themselves. If they didn't fancy a law they changed it. People like Bernie and herself broke it and went to prison. Anyway, what came of the government's bleedin' rules? Bernie had shown her a newspaper story about a ship full of refugee children torpedoed en route to Canada because the law stopped them coming into England.

"Good fing your Agnes and Vi'let and them others are in Yorkshire and not on that, innit?" Bernie had said, meaning to be comforting. The ship had been the *City of Benares*, Elsie remembered. Many children had drowned while their ship burned and sank. She had felt a wave of such hatred for the Germans that she nearly choked. And she hated the British officials who had sent the children to sea. No difference between them, really.

Suddenly Elsie was grateful to Evangeline's bossy mother-in-law for persuading Mum to take her family out of London. Bernie had been right: even if they were all separated, the little ones were safe in Yorkshire near Mum, away from the bombs and German fiends who torpedoed children. Even if Agnes had her hair all cut off, it wasn't the same as being taken away by the Germans or drowned. She shivered—Mum would have said someone had walked on her grave.

Evangeline tried to think of something to cheer Tanni up. "Maybe the girls will be all right. Lots of French hate the collaborators. The Free French in London send the Resistance supplies and guns and Resistance people rescue our pilots if they're shot down and get them home before the Germans capture them." Then Evangeline remembered something else she had overheard. "Maybe the Quakers have got them out of France. An organization called something like Secours des Enfants smuggles Jewish children over the Swiss border. And there's the Chemin de Liberte, which goes over the Pyrenees into Spain. It sounds like a long walk over a mountain pass, but people do it, it's not impossible. Maybe they—"

Evangeline's familiarity with wartime France was surprising. "How do you know so much?" Alice demanded.

"Er, at the, um, clinic last time I was in London, one of—one of the nurses was married to a Free French officer and, er, we chatted."

"'Careless talk costs lives,'" Alice snapped, quoting a War Office poster. "And I can't see why this nurse would talk so much." She imagined Evangeline being arrested as a spy and smiled.

"Even if the Quakers could get them away before the Milice find them," said Tanni, tracing the route with her finger, "Klara might be able to walk through the mountains to Switzerland or Spain, but Lili is weaker and slower. She depends on Klara for everything. And Klara would never leave her." They must believe I abandoned them, she thought sadly.

The clock in the hallway chimed one. Alice had taken up her knitting, but her eyes weren't focusing well and she kept dropping stitches. There was a silence while everyone thought. The small fire flickered in the grate, shifting the shadows on the walls.

"Isn't there anything we can do?" asked Evangeline when she came back carrying Johnny. "I mean, to help the girls escape some way?" She thought of her own desperate flight from New Orleans.

"They need a way out of France, which is a problem with the Germans everywhere. And then a way to get into England, which is a problem because it's illegal."

"What about unofficial, like?" asked Elsie. "Could they get into England wivout anybody findin' out?"

Alice stabbed her knitting needles viciously into the tangled mess that would have to be unraveled in the morning. Too much brandy had given her a headache. She was fed up with the war. The War Cabinet didn't have to sit knee to knee in the coal cellar with her mother, night after night. Bother the War Cabinet! And bother Mummy, she thought, forever whining, "What would your father have said?"

The familiar refrain went on and on in her head. "What would your father have said!" She was tired of wondering what her father would have said if he were there on every single occasion, including this one...she felt sleepy, but the refrain echoed in her head "What would your father have said?"

She wanted to snap that she knew exactly what her father would have said!

"Black Dickon's gang used that for forty years," he would say, pointing to a spot where the mouth of an old smuggler's cave tucked into the cliff. "It's just visible at low tide, large enough for a low boat to slip in unseen. Right under the excise men's noses."

Alice! Her father was beside her. *You can't have forgotten, right under the excise men's noses.*

"But...Defense Zone now," Alice muttered.

We drew maps, said Alice's father firmly and was gone.

"Yes, Father, maps," Alice said.

Alice was as dotty as her mother, Frances decided.

Evangeline raised her eyebrows. "Tea, anyone?" she asked and disappeared into the kitchen. She came back with a tray and cups.

"Smugglers," said Alice, taking hers, "did it."

"Alice, we've all drunk more than we're used to. Have your tea. Did what?"

"Pay 'ttention," said Alice. "Another way into England, well, there is one. Smugglers' tunnels. Used to be a lot of smugglers along this coast. They brought in things from France, like lace and brandy and tobacco, so they didn't have to pay duty. If they were caught they were hung—that's how serious it was. Anyway, my father had an old book about the parish, and a famous smuggler named Black Dickon had a cave...excise men never found it. Apparently they could just get a boat in it at low tide, but otherwise when the sea comes in the entrance is blocked. The smugglers unloaded inside and used tunnels to carry the contraband away from the coast."

"Alice, that was a long time ago—"

"No, listen! Father and I found it! We used to go for a walk together every Saturday afternoon and we found it at low tide. He became quite excited, made maps to work out where the tunnels might have led because the parish book said there was an entrance in our churchyard. Father thought it possible, and that probably the de Balforts had been in on the smuggling, because Gracecourt was such a fine house."

Elsie's eyes narrowed. "Can you smuggle fings from France today? Like people?"

"Dangerous. Although...it must have been dangerous all those years ago when the king's soldiers hanged the smugglers they caught. And the government must think it's possible, because there are loads of posters up, warning Germans might get past the coastal defenses and to be on the lookout," Alice replied.

It was amazing what you learned when people assumed you didn't understand French, Evangeline thought, saying, "Hand me the map. Somewhere off Brittany, the Resistance operates escape lines. They pick up RAF pilots right under the Germans' noses and take them across the channel. It's got an odd name." She ran her finger along the Brittany coastline. "Here! Plouha. It's got high cliffs. Could the Resistance be persuaded to send two children along with some English pilots, do you think?" asked Evangeline.

"Evangeline, the children are hundreds of miles away from there," said Frances impatiently.

"True, but the Resistance needs money and a lot of other things, ammunition, guns, medicine, and radio transmitters," said Evangeline thoughtfully. "For enough money, they'd do anything."

"Money! How much? And where would we get it?" asked Alice.

"That's the problem..."

"Not necessarily," said Frances. "There's Aunt Muriel's jewelry. The solicitors thought she'd lost it or sold it, but she'd hidden it. I found it in the cellar and it's mine now. She left it to me. Look at these—they're worth a fortune." She unclasped the pearls she was wearing and passed them round. "And there's more—bracelets and diamond clips and things. Even a tiara. They'd be worth thousands if they were sold. That should be enough."

"But even if we could contact the Quakers and even if they agreed to take the girls away from Gurs, how would they get to the coast? Would the Resistance take them all that way? And even if someone agreed to bring them across the channel, how would they get them past the authorities into England? We couldn't ask RAF pilots to break the law by smuggling children in, and anyway, I daresay they'd be met by the authorities."

"And once they got here, it would be impossible to hide foreign twins in Crowmarsh Priors," said Frances, thinking ahead. "Everyone knows everything. Where else could they go?"

"I know a place no one would notice—no one likely to tell the authorities anyway!" exclaimed Tanni. She was remembering when she had visited Tante Berthe in Bethnal Green before the war and seen two well-dressed Englishwomen staring at a line of black-clad children following their father. Penelope Fairfax's friend had commented on how alike the family of Hassidic children looked and wondered how the family could tell them apart.

But it was Penelope's casual comment, "Sometimes one can quite see why the Germans..." that had made Tanni's blood run cold. Now it gave her an idea. "In London where my friends live, there are whole streets of large Jewish families. Many are very old-fashioned and dress their children in long, dark clothing. The English see only the clothes and think all the children look the same. Two more children would fit in without the authorities noticing—as long as they could get identity cards and ration books."

"Nuffink easier than laying 'ands on ration books, Bernie says, not even worf forgin' those 'cause so many go missing from the post office. You can buy 'em on the cheap."

"But would any family take the risk? They'd be arrested if they were caught, Tanni," said Frances.

"Well, what about the people hiding the twins in France now? They're at risk of being shot," said Tanni. "A rabbi I know always says to save a life many things are permissible, and this would save two. So I'm sure someone would be willing. I'll have to ask carefully and not mention any of this to Bruno yet," she added. There was a new note of firmness in her voice. "In fact, it is better that he doesn't know." In case he forbids it, she thought. She had never had a secret from Bruno, but now there was no choice.

"How would we get them from Crowmarsh Priors to London? The train wouldn't be safe. There's Albert Hawthorne, for one thing. He knows everything that goes on."

"Bernie's ever so good at getting things when they're wanted. 'E can get a car and petrol and 'e will too if I tell 'im. Never mind restrictions. Oh, don't turn up your nose, Alice! 'E'll see the girls up to London safe and sound, if 'e knows what's good for 'im. See to their ration books too, 'e will."

"If we could get them there before anyone saw them…" said Frances slowly.

They looked at each other, then everyone stared at Alice. "Do you think the smugglers' tunnels still exist?" asked Frances.

"Probably."

"If they do," said Evangeline, "can people can still get through them?"

"If they haven't collapsed. It was a long time ago."

"Mustn't get ahead of ourselves," said Frances. "We don't know where the tunnels are, whether anyone would agree to bring the girls, whether—"

"When you're desperate, you find a way," said Evangeline with feeling. She whispered to Frances so that Alice couldn't hear, "We could ask the French people I know in London whether they would take the jewelry in exchange for bringing the children."

Frances nodded. Then she said aloud, "Alice, did you keep your father's maps?"

"I think so. We must have. We've boxes and boxes of his papers stacked in the hall at the cottage. Mummy's been after me to sort them and move them to the box room. We trip over them every time there's an air raid. But one thing at a time," said Alice primly in her best schoolmistress voice. "I'll find Father's maps and try to work out where the cave is. And we need to find out if there really is an entrance to the tunnels from the churchyard. Even if it's there it may have collapsed, so someone will have to go down and see and I don't know who could—"

"At home I loved caving with my brothers and Lau—If you find the tunnels I'll go down on a rope and see what they're like," Evangeline volunteered. "I don't mind. I've done it lots of times."

"Do we tell anyone else?"

"No! If Tanni's not going to tell Bruno, we shouldn't say anything to anyone else. Not even Bernie. One step at a time."

"Shouldn't we mention it to Oliver? If we're prowling in the churchyard he's bound to wonder what we're up to."

"No," said Frances, "better not. He would want to save the children, of course, but he's awfully conscientious. He might disapprove if it's illegal. And it must be. Let's not tell him until we have to. Unless we're very, very careful we'll all go to prison, and then there'll be no one to help Lili and Klara."

Tanni felt guilty. Tante Berthe would be aghast if she knew what they were discussing. But she had to do something, she *had* to. The baby kicked and she squirmed on the sofa. Suddenly something else was happening...

"Tanni! What's the matter! Oh...oh dear!" exclaimed Frances.

Tanni's face was screwed up and she gripped the armrests hard as a fierce contraction took hold. She let out a deep groan, "Oohh!" A stain spread on the sofa as her water broke.

"Now we must send for Sister Tucker," exclaimed Frances.

"That'll be the baby comin' all right!" exclaimed Elsie. "Took Mum the same way—'er waters broke all over the place, and next minute Vi'let were there, 'owlin' 'er 'ead off! Alice, ring Sister Tucker—quick!"

19.

London, November 1941

The night that Frances celebrated her birthday and Tanni went into labor, the German bombers that had disturbed the birthday party in Crowmarsh Priors flew on to hit London hard. The sirens screamed across the city, and in the streets firewatchers and air raid wardens hurried to their posts, while ordinary people rushed from their homes or the pub into the nearest Underground station, clutching children, bedding, and gas masks. The rattle of ack-ack fire opened up on the approaching planes, followed by the first pounding explosions on the outskirts. As they came closer, people pushed harder to make their way into the shelters. The air raid wardens blew their whistles violently in a bid to prevent panic.

Arc lights sliced up through the night sky between the silver barrage balloons as the bombers flew over and building after building disintegrated in an avalanche of masonry and broken glass. Flames erupted and devoured whatever was left inside, seeking a whiff of gas from a damaged main or a store of paraffin.

From the east, over the docks, there came a roar so loud it drowned out everything else. London shook. A warehouse where rum was stored in barrels had taken a direct hit, and a river of flaming liquor spilled into the street. A gasometer was damaged and a lone repairman went up swiftly, silhouetted in the searchlights as he fought to stop it exploding.

Even deep underground they felt the reverberations. At her WRVS canteen post on a platform Penelope Fairfax tried to smile calmly as she poured tea and doled out buns or cigarettes. She hoped the two lads who had come in drunk and arguing wouldn't overturn the lavatory cubicle again. It smelled terrible already, a fug of unwashed bodies and urine, with cigarette smoke and dust shaken loose by the bombing. It got in one's hair and nostrils and made everything gritty. Wearily Penelope wiped her hands again on the damp tea towel they used to mop up spills. She felt sticky and badly in need of a bath.

The hurricane lamp in a far corner went out. Children whimpered in panic. "Miss, oh, miss, the lamp," called a woman urgently, panic in her voice too. They were all afraid of the dark—anything could happen: people were robbed, girls raped, and the rats came out, searching for crumbs, scurrying over the sleepers.

"Just coming! Soon have it lit, don't worry," she called, picking her way past bunks filled with people lucky enough to get a ticket for them, then over whole families camped on the filthy floor, playing cards, gossiping, or asleep rolled in blankets. She attended to the lamp and the children calmed down. How could so many children still be in London? she wondered as she picked her way back to the canteen. They had tried so hard to get every one to safety. Some of the mothers recognized her and wouldn't meet her eye: they had had enough of the billeting and brought their children home.

Back at the canteen Penelope nudged her coworker and nodded in the direction of a pimply boy standing at the entrance. "That Communist lad Ted's got in again tonight." He was holding a pile of printed sheets and arguing with a man who eventually told him to shut up because people were trying to sleep.

Ted ignored him and began his whiny singsong chant: "*Show* your solidari'y wiv the working class, *support* our Russian brothers-in-arms on the second front against Fascist Nazi imperialism. *Buy* your copy of the *Mornin' Star*, the voice of the workin' class, what's really fightin' this war," chanted Ted. "Fraternal unity in the struggle! *Support* our Russian comrades…"

There was a chorus of "Shut up! Worse'n bleedin' 'Itler 'e is!"

"Let the workin' class 'ere get a bleedin' bit o' sleep!"

"*Show* your solidari'y wiv the workin' class…"

"I'll give 'im solidarity!"

There was a scuffle, then a loud "Ow! Bloody 'ell!" the sound of paper ripping, and then silence.

They didn't sound the all clear until long after the bombing had stopped, to keep people off the streets while the worst of the damage was cleared and the emergency services hunted for survivors. It went just after dawn on Sunday morning. People asked each other if they were all right and then warily climbed back up the stairs, anxious to get home but fearing that home might not be there.

"What the Jerries don't bomb the bloody looters'll 'ave while your back's turned," muttered a weary woman pulling her three grubby children up the stairs. "They nicked my sister's sewin' machine—it were brand new. She saved three years for it to start 'er own business makin' curtains and cushions an' that."

The woman next to her shook her head and tutted in sympathy. "Looters is as bad as the Germans, I say. Worse, stealin' from their own."

Squaring their shoulders to prepare for the worst, both women came round the corner and saw their street. Their jaws dropped. Gone. Everything was gone.

Until last night the area had been a rabbit warren of small terraced houses, home to hundreds of people. Now it was a landscape of destruction, a few walls with blown-out windows still standing in a wasteland of smashed bricks, bits of window frame, chunks of roof and chimney, blown-apart stoves, shreds of carpet, split cushions, the odd table leg, a pram with the wheels torn off, a hairbrush, toys, a man's boot with the laces ripped out, shattered chamber pots and someone's cat, dead, its teeth bared in a grin. The cloud of smoke and dust still rising from the bombed houses was so thick that it hid the broken glass that crunched underfoot. A smell of gas hung in the air.

"Put out that cigarette!" barked the ARP warden at a dazed man in pajamas. "You'll send us all sky high!"

The shovels and pickaxes that had chipped at the rubble since daybreak continued as the day wore on. Somewhere a child cried intermittently, though not as loudly as it had cried that morning, or even an hour ago. There were still faint cries of "Get me out! Oh, please, get me out!" and "Over here." A gray blanket of fog set in while the diggers struggled to pinpoint where the voices were coming from.

276

But they carried on with a superhuman will, hauling up the dead and the nearly dead. But the triumphant shouts of "Ambulance, over here!" grew fewer and fewer as the day wore on.

Now furtive figures darted through the gloom, stooping and digging, well away from the emergency workers. They paused from time to time to lift something from the rubble, anything from household goods to jewelry—not likely in this street—to broken light fittings and pieces of electrical flex, which was in short supply and particularly valuable now. When the warden saw them, he chased them away. "Looters!" he muttered, "at a time like this! They'd steal the knicker elastic from a corpse and sell it."

"How many do you suppose are still down there?" asked one of the rescue team, who had been digging since daylight. His arms were shaking uncontrollably but many people were missing.

A time bomb detonated in the distance.

"There was more earlier," said another rescuer shortly, lifting his tin hat to wipe his brow. The afternoon was drawing on and the dull, smoky light would soon go. He was listening for the child he had heard below, focused on getting it out. He had four of his own at home and kept thinking what if…

Their shift was over, but the rescuers carried on doggedly. A girl from the mobile canteen handed them steaming mugs of cocoa. "Just let us know when you can get water and milk down to anyone trapped below," she said quietly. Not "if" but "when." "Have it for you in a flash. A drink helps them hold on a little longer."

"They wanted to come back," said the warden, angrily, to no one in particular, and swung a pick with all his might at a slab of brick wall that had fallen across two houses that lay in ruins. "Evacuated with the children, they were, to the countryside and all, but when nothing happened at first they got fed up, wanted to come home. Had to look after the old man, missed their homes, missed the neighbors. They and the kiddies were safe, but oh, no, *that* wasn't good enough! They had to come *home*! So they packed up, came home, and brought the kiddies. And then Jerry turned up."

"Quiet!" snapped the digger.

The child cried again, feebly and briefly, and a woman groaned something that sounded like "Help the kiddies. Get us out. Please get us out," somewhere below the brick slab the warden had just split.

"It's all right, dear," shouted the warden. "We know where you are now. Just another few minutes and we'll have you out. Nearly there." He was hoarse from shouting to mounds of bombed building. "You'll be 'avin' a nice 'ot cup of tea before you know it. Brewin' up now, they are. Come on, lads," he shouted, so she could hear him, "mustn't keep the lady from 'er tea. Nearly there, my love. How many of you, do you know?" Keep her talking.

"My baby! Where's my baby? Please find my baby!" another woman cried, shrilly, somewhere down the street.

"My baby! My baby! My baby!" echoed down the street.

The tired diggers were joined by the ambulance driver, a strapping young woman from Yorkshire, who silently took the shovel from the man whose arms could no longer lift it and began to dig. "It's all right. You rest a bit. Me family's all miners. Diggin's in me blood," she said stoutly when he protested. "Can you tell where the child was crying from?" she whispered to the warden, shifting a smashed wardrobe. Clothes fluttered inside.

"Just hereabouts," he muttered, gesturing at the side of the mountain.

"Baby! Baby! Baby!" The shrill voice was cracking. An older woman came from somewhere and put her arms round the distraught mother, who collapsed, sobbing and unable to walk. Another woman hurried forward to help, and they half supported, half carried the limp figure toward the canteen at the end of North Street. The canteen girl wrapped her in a blanket and put a strong cup of tea with two extra spoonfuls of precious sugar in her hands. The woman clutched it, spilling tea as she rocked back and forth.

It was the word "tea" that had brought Mrs. Pigeon round again. She had been talking to someone just now about tea. What had she said? The last thing she remembered, she had been getting the tea...it was terribly dark. Was it because of the blackout? There was a buzzing noise that came and went, sometimes it sounded like people talking and she had heard them say "tea." She tried to turn her head, but it hurt...darkness and pain. Everywhere, inside of her, pressing on top of her...everywhere. She heard the buzzing and wanted to shout again, but she was too cold and sleepy. She whispered, "Sausages." A treat for tea, sausages.

"Did you hear that? Somebody moaned near my foot. Lend us a hand and we can shift this slab now. Hello, can you hear us? We're coming for you, nearly there now. Don't give up—call out if you can."

Mrs. Pigeon looked into the darkness for the voices. She couldn't tell whether they were above her or below her. She tried her best to call out again, but something kept filling her mouth. She choked.

"Hello," came the voice again. "Let us know where you are. How many?"

But she was drifting, thinking of how the butcher on the corner had waved them in, said he'd kept a few back, and seeing as how Mrs. Pigeon and the kiddies had just come home an' all...he'd wrapped them in a piece of newspaper with a wink, adding an extra one at the last minute "for the little girl"...what little girl?

Violet.

Jem and Violet—where were they? They ought to be sitting at the table where she'd left them, plates ready...waiting for her to cook their tea. Then they had to get to the shelter because the siren thing had gone...but...the room had heaved sideways and the ceiling had come down...she spat to clear her mouth and gathered the last of her strength to shout, "Three!"

"Listen, was that someone saying 'Three'? Calling 'Jem,' asking if he can hear her? Good, found her now, just here... We're coming, love. We're coming. Kiddies, yes. Yes, we've got your kiddies safe here. Names? Vi'let, yes indeed."

The warden looked at the other diggers in a way that dared someone to contradict him. No one did. They had to keep her hopes up if there was any chance of getting her out alive.

The ambulance girl saw small fingers reaching through the rubble. Relieved, she reached down to grasp them. "Hold on," she urged. She gave them a squeeze and a small severed hand came easily out of the rubble. She reminded herself fiercely that the people trapped down there counted on her to help them. She wasn't going to be sick now. Keep digging. Be sick later. She choked down rising bile with a mighty force of will and concentrated on lifting the debris, piece by piece. Then she uncovered something with a bow in its hair—a little girl. She dug out the rest and found a smaller child. A boy. She laid what was left of the children to one side, covered them quickly, and set to help heave away a broken beam. The little boy was still warm. Debris rattled over their feet and they could see the woman now, by the gleam of her eyes, in the faint light. She seemed to be conscious. They had to keep her awake, they knew, keep her talking.

"Come on, lads," said the warden, "nearly got her now. Easy, missus, this lass from the ambulance has a stretcher. You're safe now. Can you talk to us, tell us your name?"

The ambulance girl and the driver dug as hard as they could to free the woman's legs.

"The kiddies—Vi'let. Jem. Did you find the kiddies? They was with me...on the train all day, comin' 'ome... nuffink to eat all the way from Yorkshire. 'Ungry after the train...I stopped at the butcher on the off chance—sausages...no sausages in ever so long...siren went, but I only stopped for a minute to get their bit of tea. Thought we 'ad time...never had the sirens in Yorkshire...Vi'let!" she wailed. "Where's Vi'let? Where's Jem? 'Ave they finished their tea yet?"

"Easy, dear. They're fine. You'll soon see them." Slowly they eased the woman from beneath a broken beam and onto a stretcher. "Soon, love."

She was soaked through. Looking back into the hole where she had been the warden saw the gleam of water.

"Main's burst," he muttered. Sometimes people survived the bombing only to drown in the rubble.

The ambulance girl tucked a blanket round the woman. "The children are dead," she mouthed over her shoulder.

"They mustn't 'ave a cold tea again. First sausages we'd seen in months. I only stopped a minute..."

"That's right, dear." The warden was waving the ambulance back to where they stood. Where the hell was the man with the morphine?

"Where we was billeted, such a carry-on when I used 'er kitchen, called us dirty. Most nights the kiddies and me, we made do with bread and marge instead of a cooked tea... ooh...can't feel me legs, nor my arms neither. Why's that... oh. Oh! That hurt...I'll be all right long as I know the kiddies is safe...let me tell them..."

Suddenly Mrs. Pigeon felt sleepy again. The fog made it hard to see, and it was getting dark. Long past teatime... Jem and Vi'let were hungry...the girl in the tin hat was leaning over her, saying something to her, shouting, but from a distance. Bossy boots...no older than Elsie, ordering her to do something or other. It sounded like "keep talking to me," but she was fed up with being shouted at...the woman with her la-di-da house in Yorkshire shouted, "Filthy! Like filthy gypsies!" The kiddies were so happy when she'd said enough was enough and they'd go home today...sausages! Bit of luck. Their favorite. Sausages...

A minute later the ambulance girl extricated her hand from the woman's and felt for a pulse. "She's gone." She covered the gray face with the blanket and helped lift the stretcher into the back of the ambulance with the two dead children. No need to hurry. She sat down in the rubble and rested her head in her hands. The canteen girl brought her a mug of tea. "Drink this, love. Plenty of sugar in it."

"Like this every bloody night," muttered the warden, looking off into the distance. His jaw clenched and he looked at the ambulance girl. She'll soon get used to it, he thought. It was getting dark again. He prayed the Germans wouldn't be back, but mostly he begged God to help the antiaircraft gunners to blow every last German plane out of the sky and to help the RAF bomb every last city in Germany and every last German in it to smithereens.

"'Allo, what's this?" muttered his mate. He was in the hole from which they had pulled the woman out. He'd found a newspaper parcel. He opened it gingerly. "Crikey! Sausages. Bit dusty, but…no need to let them go to waste." He slipped them into his pocket.

The ambulance girl watched him. Then she thanked the canteen worker politely and managed a glassy smile. "I'm all right. Back to work." She drank her tea, then tried to stand up, doubled over onto her knees, and vomited.

20.

Crowmarsh Priors, December 1941

It was a sober, frightened congregation that attended morning service in Crowmarsh Priors. The previous Sunday, Japan had bombed the American base at Pearl Harbor, and four days later Germany had declared war on the United States.

The church was packed. Oliver was gray and sharp-featured, as if he had not slept for a week. There had been more German planes in during the night and heavier bombing over London and Birmingham, with many more civilian casualties. Rumors abounded that German airmen had parachuted into the countryside and were hiding, waiting for the invasion. Anything seemed possible. It felt like the end of the world had come.

Ever since the telegram with the news of the death of her mother, Jem, and Violet, Elsie had been fierce, uncommunicative, and red-eyed with grief. She had howled like an animal, cursed the Germans, and refused to be comforted, even by Bernie. Oliver had had the sense not to offer religious platitudes. Now Elsie sat in church, face set, with

Frances on one side and Evangeline on the other, each gripping one of her hands. Maude, Tommy, and Kipper sat on Evangeline's other side. Maude and Tommy had said their parents was chapel so they weren't going to no church, but Evangeline had insisted and, for the first time ever, threatened to box their ears if they made a fuss. Tanni was still in bed recovering after giving birth and feverish with an infection.

Now Maude and Tommy squirmed and kicked each other, but Kipper, feeling anxiety in the air, laid his head quietly against Evangeline's arm. A deathly pale Alice frogmarched her mother down the aisle. It was the first time Mrs. Osbourne had been seen in church since her husband's death, but today Alice made no allowance for her ailments or nerves. Land Girls from the hostel had crowded into a pew at the back. They had chapped red hands and anxious faces. In frocks and hats they seemed vulnerable and young. Even the team leader came.

Hugo de Balfort read the lesson in a grave voice.

When it was time for Oliver to step into the pulpit, he said that today he would not preach: they would just pray. As well as the usual prayers for the king and queen and the government, the armed forces, the bishop, and the country, Oliver said special ones for local people serving in the forces or volunteer services—Richard Fairfax on his destroyer escorting supply ships across the North Atlantic, those nursing at the North African front, Penelope Fairfax in the WVS in London, all of the men and women serving far away from home, working in factories or driving ambulances.

There were a few smothered sobs.

Lastly he told his congregation to keep faith with each other, with all those for whom they prayed, and above all with their Creator.

One member of the congregation rebelled. As she looked about her at all of the heads bent in silent prayer, Frances felt only rage that the Germans could terrorize the world like this. At war, are we? she thought defiantly. Very well, she intended to fight the bloody Nazis. She bent her head, but not in prayer. She swore a solemn oath to God if God was listening, and if not to the devil himself, to seize her opportunity to train as an agent, for the Special Operations Executive or the Auxis, whichever would do the most damage to the Germans. She had been told to attend a second interview with the little man in London at Christmas, and that if they accepted her she would go immediately for the first stage of her training: her absence from the farm would be less noticeable when all of the Land Girls had Christmas leave. And as for Tanni's family...now they all realized that, for people like Tanni's family, the war wasn't about inconvenient rationing, ugly blackout curtains, and unpleasant Land Girl jobs. In the cold light of day she realized what a far-fetched plan they had devised to help Tanni's sisters when drunk, but Tanni was depending on them now—and Oliver's words about keeping faith with one another had hit home. Well, even if the Auxis or the others accepted her she would find a way to keep her promise. She'd cross that bridge when she came to it, she decided. Helping Tanni would be a kind of battle against the Nazis.

After the service everyone was subdued, but kept a stiff upper lip for the sake of the rest. Alice nudged her mother firmly into the queue to shake Oliver's hand.

Frances walked out of church, then paused to wait for Hugo. She was meant to have lunch with him and Leander at Gracecourt. She had accepted the invitation the day after her party, too distracted by the birth of Tanni's baby and a racking hangover to make an excuse. Now she realized that to both men it would appear a luncheon to celebrate her and Hugo's engagement.

Hugo had a word with Oliver, then came over and took her arm possessively.

"Hugo, I must speak to you at once."

"Frances, darling, could it possibly wait? I've suddenly been summoned to a meeting of all the Home Guard units in the area, and I shall have to join you and Father later. Then we can tell him…"

"Hugo!" Frances turned to face him. "It can't wait. I have to tell you that I can't marry you. I'm terribly, terribly sorry. I'm fond of you, but I'm not sure I feel quite—oh, I don't know—in love enough to be very good wife material. And with the war on, well, I just don't…"

Don't need a husband who wants to know where I'm going and what I'm doing, she thought.

"I see."

She was uncertain whether he was angry or offended. "In the circumstances I oughtn't to lunch with you and your father. I'm so sorry if you're disappointed, but it's for the best."

"Frances, do please have lunch with Father. I shan't be there, and he's been looking forward to it. I can drive you—I must go home and pick up a few things for the meeting," he said stiffly.

"You needn't drive me, I'll go on my bicycle," said Frances. "I must change first anyway. Oh, Hugo, I wish we might stay friends."

"Do you?" He looked at her intently. "Then so do I. And I shan't lose hope. Perhaps I might change your mind one day."

Oliver called him, and Hugo shouted, "Coming!" then turned away before Frances could say anything else.

It would be horribly awkward alone with Leander today.

At Glebe House Frances changed her hat for a head scarf, donned her godmother's old mac, and cycled off in a drizzle. She was in a bad mood by the time the towers of Gracecourt loomed into sight, in the middle of the vast sweep of park.

She found Sir Leander alone. As she hung her wet mac on the fireguard he said, "Kind of you to keep an old man company, my dear," and poured them a glass of sherry.

The small sitting room off the long gallery that Sir Leander used as his study was cozy. Two logs blazed on vast Tudor firedogs and the linen-fold panelling glowed. Beyond the curtains the park was gray and wet. Looking out of the window Frances saw that the tennis courts were overgrown and abandoned, and the box bushes along the brick path needed trimming. The rectangular pools Sir Leander had been so proud of were only half full. It was hard to remember Gracecourt before the war, when it had been the scene of such gay times, tennis, lunch on the lawns, summer cocktails in gardens strung with paper lanterns, weekend house parties when Hugo's cosmopolitan friends had come to shoot pheasant.

There was an awkward silence. Sir Leander, now confined to his wheelchair, looked terrible. He turned to face Frances, who was perched on the sofa. "Not often I get to lunch alone with a pretty girl these days." He raised his glass. "Here's to the good health of you energetic Land Girls. In my day no one would have worked women so hard. Doesn't seem right, you having to clear ditches, do all that rough work, war or no war."

"The cows are the worst part," said Frances lightly, wondering how to tell him tactfully that she had refused Hugo.

He saved her the trouble. "Now, my dear, I'm going to come to the point. Hugo was here for a few minutes a little while before you arrived, and I understand you have turned him down." He raised his eyebrows.

Frances nodded.

"But I hope and trust that you will change your mind."

"I'm very fond of Hugo of course, but with the war on, everything's so unsettled..."

Sir Leander shook his head. "He told me what you'd said, and I encouraged his belief—his hope—that you would come round. You know, young women often believe a lot of twaddle about romance and being swept off one's feet, that sort of thing, but it's really not sound, my dear, not sound at all. Of course Hugo's terribly fond of you, but in these troubled times young people, especially in a family as old as ours, need to take a longer view. When it's a question of a certain position in society, continuation of an ancient, distinguished family..."

Sir Leander had always been kind to Frances, taking an almost fatherly interest in her, marking her out for special attention and small courtesies even in the days when other, more prominent women guests had been present. Frances had become genuinely fond of him and now she stared at her lap feeling awkward and wishing she hadn't made an old man unhappy. She looked up suddenly and saw that, despite his frailty, Sir Leander's demeanor was haughty and aggrieved. He looked at her keenly. Oh dear.

"I speak for your own good, my dear, *in loco parentis*, as it were. I realize that your father may have been too busy to… ahem. But let me remind you that in marrying Hugo, you would become mistress of a fine estate, and after my death, you would be Lady de Balfort, secure in the state that is what all women are meant for, marriage and motherhood, in the highest station of our society. Your father entirely approves. His solicitors and mine have already discussed marriage settlements. Forgive my bluntness, but if you felt you could be tolerably happy with Hugo I should like to see the two of you married before I die, and I should like even more to know there was an heir on the way to ensure the future of the estate."

This was too much! Frances stared stonily into her glass, feeling she could cheerfully have strangled all the solicitors with her bare hands.

Sir Leander continued: "The admiral's no time for beating about the bush, and he rather feared you had hatched some madcap scheme for doing *intelligence* work or some such thing." He chuckled as if the idea was preposterous. "Surely not? He and I agree it's hardly a job for a girl, and he assured me, he put his foot down."

Frances seethed.

"Think it over, my dear. Now, if you've finished your sherry, my cook has left us something on the sideboard in the chafing dish—probably quite dreadful, with all this rationing and whatnot. We'd better go and eat it, though. I can manage, thanks very much."

He led the way in his wheelchair.

In the long, dark dining room, with its rows of family portraits, the polished table was laid for two with ancient Limoges and crested, if tarnished, silver. Something was steaming over a spirit lamp. It did indeed smell dreadful. Frances took the plates and spooned onto them brownish lumps in a thin gray gravy. There was a dish of limp boiled cabbage and another of carrots.

"Corned beef rissoles, I think," muttered Sir Leander. "Promise me, if you do change your mind about Hugo and become mistress of this house, the first thing you will do is engage a housekeeper who understands plain cooking."

In despair, Frances helped herself to mustard.

"Fortunately," her host said with a smile, lifting a dusty bottle left open to breathe at his place, "a few bottles of Burgundy in the cellar—laid down long before the war. Thought we'd have one today to celebrate your engagement, but if that's not to be the case, at least it will help this travesty of a meal go down."

The wine was lovely. Frances managed to cut her rissoles into tiny pieces and hide them under the cabbage. The excellent wine had given her a warm glow. She fetched the pudding from the sideboard—spotted dick and custard— and gamely ate a bit, trying not to notice how dried eggs made things taste of dried egg no matter what you did. Sir Leander poured the last of the wine.

There was a small fire in the grate, and the French clock on the mantle ticked musically. The small dining room was one of the oldest rooms in the house and still had leaded windows. Frances lit the spirit lamp again and made them a jug of ersatz coffee. Then she excused herself.

"You remember where the cloakroom is, of course?"

"Yes, thank you."

She headed for the downstairs cloakroom next to the gun-and-boot room at the far end of the panelled passage with more de Balfort portraits on the walls. She peeped into the little gold-and-white salon on the way. It had been Hugo's mother's private sitting room, and Frances had spent many delightful evenings there before the war. It had always been her favorite room in the house, its full-length Venetian mirrors, painted ceiling, and view of the park beyond.

Now, like the rest of the house, it was somewhat the worse for wear. A pane of glass in the french window was broken and patched with cardboard, and the parquet floor was warped. The ceiling had a dark patch of mildew. The de Balforts must be short of money. Aunt Muriel had always been highly critical of Sir Leander's extravagant schemes, and now Frances thought that perhaps she had been right. Why had he not spent the money on keeping the house in order? It was in a dreadful state.

She continued down the passage to the cloakroom, opened the door, and squealed. Something large and black was blocking the lavatory. She peered cautiously. It was a dead bat. She shut the door and went back down the passage toward the grand staircase. There was a bathroom on the landing. A whiff of tobacco smoke told her that Sir Leander was having his after-lunch cigarette. She wouldn't disturb him by mentioning the bat. She tiptoed past the half-closed dining room door and up the wide staircase with its worn

Turkey runner. Halfway up a noise from somewhere higher in the house stopped her dead in her tracks.

The housemaids' rooms were in the attic, but they had all left for factory jobs. Now there was only the aged cook, who was too old for the factory and always had Sundays off to visit her sister in Brighton. Hugo was at the Home Guard meeting and Sir Leander, unable to climb the stairs to his bedroom on the first floor, now lived on the ground floor in the butler's old quarters. She listened harder and tiptoed up to the landing. Something was moving about on the second floor where Hugo had told her the day and night nurseries were.

"Hello?" she called. The noise ceased. It must have been a rat. Or had squirrels got in? Frances listened for another minute but heard no more. She went on to the bathroom. It was covered with cobwebs and full of old books and broken chairs, but at least the Victorian plumbing contained no bats. And it flushed. She washed her hands with a scrap of desiccated soap and looked for something to dry them. She remembered that airing cupboards were usually positioned next to the hot water pipes. A heavy gilt picture frame was leaning against the stretch of wall behind the bath, but she could just make out the outline of a cupboard door. She nudged aside the frame and opened it, but there were no towels, just a broken radiogram, a rusty oil tin, and a large torch.

Frances wiped her damp hands on her skirt. She picked up the torch, wondering if they had forgotten where it was and needed it, but put it back, not wanting to explain how she had found it.

When she went to join Sir Leander in his study, the warm glow the wine had imparted had worn off and she was cold. The old man was sitting with a tartan rug over his knees, looking pinched and done in. The wireless was on in the corner and she could hear Beethoven. Outside it was getting dark.

"Sublime music," said Sir Leander. "German. This war is a sad business. Should never have happened, you know."

"It's getting late and I should be off," Frances said. "I'll draw the blackout curtains for you first. I hate leaving you on your own, though, Sir Leander. It's the cook's day off, isn't it? Is no one else here?"

"No, we always hope Mrs. Jones doesn't go off leaving something to burn or catch fire in the kitchen. Not as young as she was and getting forgetful. Never know how she manages the journey to Brighton. The buses are so unreliable— can't use their lights to see where they're going, just creep along. Shame Hugo isn't here. Perhaps you'll see him on his way home. Will you remember what I said, my dear? And reconsider?"

"Of course. Thank you for lunch." Frances pulled the black drapes across the windows. "I'm sure you understand...I need to think...getting married is such a serious decision, isn't it?"

"Very," said the old man, staring into the fire. "Everything in the future depends on it, my dear. Absolutely everything."

21.

Crowmarsh Priors and Sweden, January 1942

At the end of the third week in December Bruno had a week's leave for Christmas and hurried down to Sussex, anxious to see his new baby daughter, who was now almost a month old. He had been worried when he heard that Tanni had given birth at Glebe House after a party. He had rung at once, and Evangeline had told him there had been a problem with the birth and Tanni had been ill afterward, but the baby was fine.

When Bruno arrived he rushed upstairs to find Tanni better but still tucked up in bed, looking pale but pretty in a faded pink bed jacket and her dark hair tumbling over her shoulders. Her face was thinner and somehow less girlish, but her eyes lit up when he came into the room, kissed her, and told her how much he loved her. She insisted on sitting up with her sewing basket to hand and stitched away at things she had promised villagers, feeding the baby and reading to Johnny. They had named the little girl Anna.

Bruno made himself useful, carrying meals on trays to Tanni and seeing that she ate them, helping an overworked

Evangeline, playing with Johnny and the evacuees, and, whenever he had a free minute, scooping up Anna, sleeping or not, to sit with her in the rocking chair Evangeline had found in the attic. He was entranced by his small daughter, who stared at him solemnly from the crook of his arm. "She has your eyes and my nose," he said to Tanni, stroking Anna's downy little head. "Are all baby girls so beautiful?"

He was amazed at how people from the village called to admire and coo over Anna, bringing outgrown baby clothes, nappies, and toys. Margaret Rose Hawthorne begged to hold her, and he let her, but hovered nervously. "Awww, she's so little," exclaimed Margaret Rose.

Even the vicar came. Bruno was taken aback to see a him in his clerical collar bending over the cot, but when Oliver smiled and held out his finger, Anna curled her tiny fingers round it. Babies seemed to like Oliver; even the fussiest ones at the baptismal font calmed when he held them. "What a fine baby!" he said. "This dear child is cheering up the whole village in a very dark hour indeed. Am I imagining things or does she have her mother's eyes?" Bruno warmed to him at once.

Too soon the happy interlude was over. Ten days after his arrival, Bruno kissed Tanni, Johnny, and Anna while they were still asleep and left Crowmarsh Priors in the dark. Though Bruno didn't smoke, on the way they stopped for him to buy a packet of Players from a shop that had opened early, then motored on to Norfolk. The car stopped at a windswept airstrip where they waited until a military vehicle pulled up and a man in handcuffs accompanied by an armed guard got out. He and the others were given breakfast in a hut—powdered eggs scrambled into a watery mess, sausages, heavy gray buns, and lukewarm tea. Bruno usually made a sandwich of the sausage and the bun. He was never hungry so early, but he ate those breakfasts, awful as they were, because he knew it would be a long time before he got another meal.

Afterward the three passengers boarded the waiting Norseman aircraft with two pilots on board. No one spoke as the propellers roared and the small plane taxied down the runway creaking and rattling. The light flickered off and on as the plane lifted and climbed sharply, bouncing through air pockets. Bruno hoped they wouldn't run into a snowstorm, although he knew the plane could land on ice or water if it had to. He wanted more than anything to be back in the warm bed with Tanni, Johnny, and Anna but forced himself to focus on the job ahead.

The weather grew worse as they flew north, and Bruno sat back, bracing himself. The plane was not made for comfort, and the passengers—Bruno, the man in handcuffs beside him, and the military guard—were all bundled against the piercing cold in heavy coats and scarves.

The man beside him looked steadily away from him through the window. He had a thin, haughty profile, stern eyebrows, and an unblinking fixed expression. He had not touched breakfast.

Hours later he turned to Bruno. "Sweden. We are headed for Sweden judging by the time we've been flying." It was a statement, not a question.

"Near Sweden," corrected Bruno.

"Ah, so I thought. The coast. The island where your government and mine exchange prisoners of war. Secretly, of course. One spy for another. *Quid pro quo,* as you English say. Though you are not English yourself, but Jewish." The haughty face smiled mirthlessly. "One can always tell. Something…inferior in the face. They send my Jewish interrogator to escort me to the exchange as one of their subtle insults. The English understand the nuance of insult better than any other race."

Bruno regarded him impassively. The man was an Anglo-German with important connections in aristocratic circles. He had had a job in Military Intelligence, where he had been spying for the Germans for years, eluding detection. He had even had access to Churchill and passed confidential information to his superiors that had resulted in the loss of untold numbers of lives before he had been traced and arrested.

"The British spy for whom I am being exchanged—I must assume he is someone important?"

Bruno said nothing.

"You will not tell me his name, naturally. Perhaps it is one of your girl spies? Your Special Operations Executives? Not one of their little wireless operators, I expect, or a decoder. They are expendable, and in any case we normally shoot them ourselves after extracting all the information they can give us. A few are remarkably brave, of course. But for me, there will be someone important. Ah, well, whoever it is, I shall be in Berlin soon. We'll meet again when the Fuhrer decides the time has come for the invasion. There are many more like me in England, waiting for the final victory. And we shall be victorious."

The man fell silent and Bruno waited, silent too. Finally his ears popped, a sign that they were descending. The plane banked and circled over a small island in the midst of an endless expanse of water. The ground was dusted with snow. The man looked out of the window, smiling, craning his neck for the sight of the plane bringing the man to be exchanged for him and take him back to Germany. He was vain and longed to know how the British gauged his importance. A crudely marked landing strip ran the length of the island, but otherwise it was bare and deserted save for rocks, a few pine trees, and a hut. No other aircraft.

"So we're first, and they're late," he muttered, "which is discourteous, but the bad weather explains it, no doubt."

Still Bruno said nothing.

The Norseman bumped hard as it hit the ground and taxied down the runway to a stop. The prisoner peered again at the bare, empty island and then at the sky. The pilot and copilot got up and stretched. The pilot opened the door, and a blast of freezing air swept in. The pilot and copilot stood on either side of the open door, waiting. "Come on. This way."

The man looked at Bruno, the pilots, and the guard. "But the other plane is not here. Where is it?" he demanded. No one said anything. He looked from one to the other. Slowly realization of why he was there dawned on him. His face crumpled in disbelief and shock. The blood drained from his face and his lips formed "No!" but he didn't say it.

Instead he turned to Bruno again. "May I have a cigarette?" It sounded like an order.

Bruno took the packet of Players from his breast pocket, opened it, and tapped one out. The man raised manacled hands to take it. They shook only slightly as Bruno struck a match.

They all waited in silence as the man smoked. He finished the cigarette and ground the butt under his heel. "I am ready," he said, standing up straight. The military guard led him down the steps of the plane, and the pilot and copilot walked on either side of him, heading for the clump of pine trees next to the water.

Bruno followed them down the steps, stretched, and stamped his feet in the cold. He had been present at the prisoner's interrogation and knew that he deserved what was about to happen. He thought of his mother and the Josephs, the hell they must be enduring. If they were alive. Of Lili and Klara, just a few years older than Johnny, wherever they were. What if Johnny and Anna...no, he could not bear to think of his children in Lili and Klara's situation.

That was the reason he could do his job. He had escorted a dozen enemy agents to this bleak island for the same purpose. The next time he came here, how he hoped it would be with whoever sent those clear weather reports to the Germans.

A volley of shots echoed in the cold silence. The military guard and the pilots returned without the prisoner. They nodded to Bruno. "It's done." Briskly they refuelled the plane from the supply in the hut and, with the propellers whirring, turned it to face down the narrow runway. The little aircraft gathered speed and, at the last possible moment, lifted, up and over the bare rocks, climbing slowly. Bruno thought of his mother and the Josephs in some German work camp, wishing he could believe that today's act of justice would help them.

22.

A Training Camp, January 1942

From below no one could see the two men standing in the rain on the castle battlements. They were looking through field glasses, observing the new recruits, who had spent the morning practicing with explosives and now were being put through commando training. They were taking it in turns to recover heavy containers, the kind that would be dropped behind enemy lines with ammunition and equipment, from the icy waters of the lake that had once supplied the castle with fish.

Both men's glasses paused on the same recruit. "Ah, Miss Falconleigh!" exclaimed one. "Tudor will be furious, of course, when he finds out. Where does he think she is? And how is her training coming along?"

"He thinks she's in Reading on a Land Girl Welfare Committee. Her reports are excellent, and the training's going very well," said one, watching a slim figure slithering beneath a muddy hedge. He sounded rather pleased. "Surprising aptitude for it, though you wouldn't think it to look at her, pretty little thing like that. If they send her behind enemy lines they'll make her plainer with dowdy clothes and a country girl's shoes. She convinced us of how useful that might be."

"The most unlikely people have a talent for this sort of work. You'd never think it to meet her in the street, but she's not afraid to handle weapons and runs well. Quick mind too. Observant and keen to do something active."

"Fortunately she's matured a bit since the first interview, but we're still concerned that she's a bit young. And she struck us as a bit…a bit…"

The other man smiled. The first speaker had been the "little man" of Frances's first interview. That he had committed himself to a pretty girl for a brace of pheasants was a standing joke in the organization.

"Tudor had quite a time with her. Dreadful school reports! Ringleader, troublemaker, expelled from everywhere. Scandalous photographs in the broadsheets as a debutante. Unsuitable escorts, arrested for madcap pranks…"

The first man nodded complacently. "Her type is out for adventure. But she has intelligence, determination, and speaks perfect French. Just needs to learn a bit more self-discipline, how to take orders, that kind of thing. She wants a posting to France, but we decided not to send her yet. She's our youngest recruit, a bit of a firecracker, might get overenthusiastic, endanger other agents on the circuit. The Old Man decided she needs a longer probationary period, so we'll assign her to the southern Auxi mission after her mock exercise, see how she gets on. She went to Wiltshire for Auxiliary Unit training. Booby traps, sabotage. More explosives. She's got a cool head, kept her nerves steady."

"I hope her hands are equally steady. Auxi Units use those sticky bombs, God help them. Awkward things, enough nitroglycerine to stop a tank, but hard to detonate through the metal cover. Regulars won't touch 'em." He thought for a minute and added, "Ought to suit Miss Falconleigh, though."

"She'll go to Beaulieu for the final leg of wireless training, then home for her mock exercise we assign all recruits for their final test. Jerry has plenty of help from this side of the channel, and the Old Man's worried about whoever is helping the German pilots with their navigating. Not sure how. Perhaps lights in the blackout. Another bugger is sending weather reports to the Luftwaffe on the French coast, signalling the all clear for a raid. Haven't found him—or her—yet either, but when I think what he's responsible for, I'd gladly shoot him myself. We call him Manfred. The Auxis down there are looking, but Manfred could be a whole cell, or just one German agent who slipped in."

"So you plan to send her back to Sussex to help look for Manfred?"

"Wouldn't go quite as far as that. Doubt there's anything suspicious in Crowmarsh Priors. It's too small...but still, it's in a sensitive location, close to the Coastal Defense Zone. They say Lord Haw-Haw has a nephew in Brighton, and the Nordic League always had a lot of sympathizers among the county families down there. Before the war a lot of the country house set there had German friends, Nazi connections. We're keeping a close watch on them, but nothing has turned up to suggest they're active fifth columnists. But even if they aren't personally involved, Intelligence is worried about what mischief their German pals might have got up to before the war, information they might have collected about the area, possible landing places, and so on. 'Off for an afternoon walk, old chap, just take my camera, amateur photography, so jolly.'"

"We're assigning Miss Falconleigh to practice her surveillance skills at the de Balfort place, Grace-something-or-other, for her mock exercise."

"She been told yet?"

"Not yet. As I said, she expects to be posted to Europe. But the Old Man says she should carry on as normal for the next few months, keep her eyes open and report anything that seems a bit off. Something's decidedly fishy down there, and you never know, she might turn up something."

The first man exhaled. "If the Auxis *do* find Manfred, he ought to be taken alive for questioning, of course, but it may not be possible. Anyway, he's likely to be a nasty piece of work, and he'll know what the stakes are. So, lessons in silent killing tomorrow. A few tricks from the Shanghai Police."

"Jolly good. From what I've seen so far, I think she'll like that almost as much as the sticky bombs. What about parachute training?"

"In a few months, just in case we have to drop her in France sooner than planned…" He didn't finish the sentence. The other nodded. And neither mentioned what they both knew: that when a female SOE operative behind enemy lines was betrayed, arrested, or killed, they had to be ready with her replacement. A trained Auxi like Miss Falconleigh could be held in reserve against just such an eventuality.

23.

Auschwitz, March 1942

*O*n good days after work, the guards did not set the
dogs on anyone for sport or choose a prisoner to run
to death. Instead they drove the inmates back into the com-
pound and tossed in a few loaves of stale bread for them to
fight over. Icy winds blew through the cracks in the walls,
and the prisoners lay hungry and shivering in their bunks,
trying to hang on to life and the last vestiges of their human-
ity. Some achieved this by retreating into their past lives.
For others a happy memory provided them with a respite
from hell, but for more it intensified the horrors of their
existence.

Dr. Joseph was one of those who sought escape in his
only comfort, that all three of his children were safe in
England. He told the story over and over. His eldest daughter was married to a good man, a professor, who had taken
her to Britain and safety. He had put his younger children,
twin girls, on the *Kindertransport* and sent them to Britain
too, where they lived with that sister, who had always been
like a little mother to them. The twins had missed their train
in January 1939 through illness but, thank God, they had
recovered and by a miracle he had managed the impossible

by getting another place on a train that left in the summer of that year. His children were together and safe.

He dwelt on that to stop himself thinking of his wife in the women's block. He caught a glimpse of her now and then, her shaved head and gaunt cheeks…he remembered how she had looked on the day he proposed, then on their wedding night, as a pretty young matron in a coat with a fur collar and muff made by Frau Zayman, smiling down at five-year-old Tanni.

Poor Frau Zayman had been ill with pleurisy, coughing and feverish in the sealed railway car en route to the camp. There had been nothing to eat or drink, and she had not been able to lie down. She had breathed her last crushed into a corner.

A man who had failed to get places on the *Kindertransport* for his own children wept. A new prisoner inquired politely if the married daughter had children yet.

"We heard that my Tanni was expecting," said Dr. Joseph, dreamily, "just before we were taken away. The baby will be three this summer. We do not know whether it is a boy or a girl."

"Congratulations," several men whispered in the darkness from the crowded bunks. "May the mother and the baby be well and the baby have a long and distinguished life."

"Ah, to know your children are together in England, safe, with enough to eat and learning, even playing, perhaps. Milk. Sunlight. It must be a great comfort," another man murmured. It was unimaginable here.

Not all of the camp prisoners were lying in their bunks, despite the late hour.

A work detail was awake in another building, this one brightly lit, where the doctor was still at work. His archrival, Ernst Schafer, had failed in his expedition to Tibet to find a lost tribe of pure Aryans, and now the doctor's eugenics program had finally been given the go-ahead. It was a great coup for him. He had always thought that Schafer's theory was rubbish, but so long as Himmler had taken an interest, it had gotten the man out from under the doctor's feet. When Himmler had finally lost patience with Schafer he had looked to the doctor's experiments as the best means of assuring the supremacy of the Aryan race.

But the program was not producing results as quickly as he had promised, Himmler was increasingly impatient, and the doctor was increasingly worried that he was no closer to satisfying Himmler's demands. For the time being he procrastinated, hiding behind "procedures" and "evaluations," recording every detail of the experiments in his old-fashioned handwriting, then drawing up specific, lengthy criteria for the next. He insisted that patience and precision would pay off, and it was now a matter of selection of specimens. But the answer had eluded the doctor—so far.

Meanwhile he kept assuring Himmler that, given a little more time, his proper scientific methods, not madcap adventuring schemes, would achieve the desired result. His aim was beautifully simple: to establish scientifically the preconditions for giving birth to twins, which would enable German women to reproduce twice the number of babies. Aryan reproduction would double at the same time as inferior non-Aryans were eliminated. The doctor hinted to Himmler of the vast breeding camps he envisaged, stocked with carefully selected Nordic women, mothers of the pure master race that would fulfill Germany's destiny, all bearing two perfect children at a time. So efficient!

The Fuhrer himself was taking a keen personal interest in the project.

But hints and promises had to be fulfilled. The pressure was mounting, and the anxious doctor had considered expanding the research to triplets and even larger multiple births, before concluding reluctantly that the undoubted efficiency of such births was outweighed by the risk of weakening the Aryan genes by spreading them too thinly among several babies. Twins were the safest bet. In any case there was a shortage of triplets and other multiple births in the camp on which to conduct satisfactory experiments.

Tonight the doctor was just finishing. The teenage Gypsy boys, fine healthy specimens and identical twins, lay dismembered on the bloody operating table. The doctor pondered the number of differential tests he had made, comparing how the systems of identical twins dealt with toxic substances, whether one had superior resistance, and so on. He would write up the results in his usual meticulous way once he had examined the organs, but he felt a faint anxiety as to whether he had been able to establish any important new criteria before the specimens had died. Perhaps if he used anaesthetics they would have lived a little longer, which would have allowed him to conduct a wider range of tests.

He needed to look at what "identical" meant from a different angle. He frowned, thinking, while he scrubbed his hands and changed his bloodstained white coat, leaving the inmate doctors to dispose of the mess. Four thin prisoners in lab coats shuffled forward. When the trains of deportees arrived, doctors were ordered to step forward. They always did so voluntarily, expecting to be assigned medical care of the prisoners. Instead they were put at the doctor's disposal. They were less trouble and more efficient than ordinary prisoners when they cleaned his laboratories, but more than one had responded badly to his refusal to waste anaesthetics on experiments. One had even killed the specimens. The guards had dealt promptly with him as an example to the others. The doctor sighed over the wasted experiment.

Perhaps a fresh approach to twin births...he had had a supply of twins made available to him, mostly Jews, culled from displaced persons' camps and ghettos, schools and hospitals, in every country Germany occupied. The subjects were housed in a special children's wing of the camp. The supply of twins, however, had now dwindled to nothing, and the majority had been boys. What he needed were twin girls, to study the development of their reproductive organs.

Then he had a brainwave. It occurred to him that it would be valuable to conduct experiments on the parents of the twin child specimens. Though this presented him with another practical difficulty: the twins in the children's house had been separated from their parents before they arrived at the camp.

He felt slightly squeamish about conducting experiments to benefit Aryans using Jewish specimens, but even Jews, wily as they were, weren't smart enough to foil conclusions reached through proper scientific methods.

The doctor turned to his assistant. "We have reached the next stage in the research, and for that I require twin female children *and* their parents. It is a matter of the highest priority. Extra bread for any prisoners who can identify parents of female twins."

One of the inmates cleaning the experiment room raised his eyes. "Bread," he whispered to himself. He thought of his fellow prisoner Dr. Joseph, whose bunk was below his. Dr. Joseph had not stepped forward when all the doctors had been ordered to do so.

The inmate had been arrested at the same time and almost on the same street as Dr. Joseph and his wife. Out of kindness he had not told Dr. Joseph that he knew the June train bearing Dr. Joseph's twin daughters had not reached Britain before the Germans invaded Poland and war was declared. He knew that because his own son had been on it, and, he had thought, safe in Britain, like Dr. Joseph's daughters, until, to his horror, his son had appeared in the men's block at Auschwitz. At Gurs they had selected the men and boys for deportation first, sent them to Drancy, then finally on the cattle car to Auschwitz, the boy had told his anguished father. Two months later his son had died of pneumonia, aged twelve.

In the unlikely event that Dr. Joseph's twins had been so fortunate as to reach England, then they were beyond the reach of the Germans until the invasion, when their fate would be sealed. If they had not and were still alive, they must still be in Gurs unless they were already at Drancy. There would be records, of course. The Germans were meticulous.

If the girls were in either place, they would eventually fall into German hands, if they were not in German hands already. It was only a matter of time before they died or were sent to one of the larger concentration camps as his son had been—and his younger children. So, he rationalized, it wouldn't matter if he informed the doctor of their existence and that of their parents. All he could think of was bread.

He knew that Dr. Joseph's wife had been taken to the women's camp. The inmate had seen her there across the wire. She was emaciated and probably tubercular, but she was alive.

To ease his conscience, the inmate weighed up the advantages to the Josephs. If he told the doctor about them and their daughters, the authorities would soon find the girls if they were in a French camp. They would be brought to Auschwitz without delay and the Josephs would be reunited in one of the cells in the medical-experiments block.

He knew that there was no hope for anyone in this place of horror, but for a little while the Joseph family would be together, and as subjects of medical experiments they would be given soup and porridge, maybe even an onion or some boiled cabbage. And he himself would have extra bread...

So he would not be increasing the Josephs' suffering if he exchanged the information for bread. Quite the opposite. For a time their lives would be better. Until the end. He did not think too long about what always happened in the end.

He would do it.

As the prisoners shuffled out of the door to empty their buckets of dirty water, the last inmate paused in front of the doctor's assistant and asked permission to speak. He had information that parents of twin girls were here in camp and that the children could be traced.

The doctor listened and made notes in his precise hand-writing. He smiled. He would give the order for extra bread when he had all four of the subjects safely in his laboratory. But that would not take long. Given the Fuhrer's interest in the project, he would soon have the Joseph children if they were at Drancy, at Gurs, or even in the vicinity of the displaced persons' camp. Meanwhile he ordered the Joseph parents brought to the experimental wing and given blankets and soup.

24.

Crowmarsh Priors, January–May 1942

*W*hen Frances went away over Christmas and stayed away for weeks afterward, Oliver missed her. When he saw she had returned his heart lifted. After morning service on that first Sunday, he kept hold of her hand while he asked if what he had heard was true, that she had been assigned to some committee in London?

"Yes. Land Girl welfare thing. Father's volunteered me." Frances rolled her eyes. "You can imagine the sort of thing—are we doing enough to keep Land Girls' spirits up, encouraging their moral welfare? We need to keep them on the straight and narrow, apparently. Especially now the Americans have arrived with, um, all sorts of things like chocolate and Coca-Cola. Some of the girls are being—er—led astray."

"If there's any pastoral assistance I can give, if I can be any help at all," he said earnestly, still holding her hand, "please let me know."

Frances dropped her eyes. "Thank you. It's good to know I—we—can call on you."

Frances had been told to use the Land Girl Welfare Committee as cover to explain her absences. It was part of an agent's work, but she hated lying as she gazed into Oliver's clear brown eyes. Honesty was so deeply engrained in him that it would never occur to him to lie about anything. What would he think of her if he knew?

Her thoughts turned to the mock exercise she had been assigned. It was the final test for all recruits, and Frances had been hoping for something daring, such as blowing up a target under the noses of the authorities. Instead, she had been sent home to Crowmarsh Priors and ordered to carry on as a Land Girl, but do keep a close surveillance on the de Balforts and to make regular reports of any of their friends and acquaintances who visited. It was very tedious indeed: there were no longer any visitors at Gracecourt. Also, it would be uncomfortable to make ostensibly social calls herself to keep Hugo and Leander under surveillance, particularly as it involved seeing Hugo, whom she would much rather avoid. Worse, Oliver might get the idea that she was encouraging him—as indeed might Leander and, above all, Hugo himself. Frances, who had always cut up rough at the slightest hint of discipline and having to do what she disliked, thought "Bloody hell!" But she bit her lip and followed orders.

Meanwhile Frances, Evangeline, Elsie, and Alice were determined not to let Tanni down. Evangeline said the plan was no more outlandish than other plans that had worked. No one thought to ask her what she was talking about. Elsie was still beside herself over the loss of her mother, Jem, and Violet, and for her, fighting the Germans was personal now. She took out her fury on the rats, but she had plenty to spare. Even Bernie was alarmed by the new steely glint in Elsie's eye.

Only cautious Alice held back: she said the plan had been conceived in a moment of drunken madness, and she was sorry, but really, they must see it was completely irresponsible...

The other three gave her no peace, and finally Frances exercised her considerable powers of persuasion: "Alice, darling, of course you're right, and perhaps it is rather daring, but what else can we do? We might be sentencing the children to death if we do nothing! Do we want that on our consciences? Anyway, we're friends—one for all and all for one, as we used to say at school." She had used the motto freely during her school days, when she was inciting her friends to wild escapades that had invariably landed everyone in trouble. Alice, on the other hand, had been a model pupil. "We can't possibly do it without you," Frances urged. "You are indispensable, Alice! You're the only one who can find the tunnel!"

"Oh, all right," said Alice finally, against her better judgment but worn down by flattery. She had never been included in the "one for all" thing at school, never had friends, and never felt in the thick of things. She only hoped they would not all be arrested.

"Besides, we need your good sense, Alice, to keep us steady!"

Alice suppressed a little smile. She could quite see that. She felt important already.

Oliver was startled when Alice told him that she, Frances, Evangeline, and Elsie had decided to tidy the appallingly overgrown churchyard. Faith manifested itself in the most unexpected ways, he thought.

From his study he watched in amazement as they tackled the area around the Great War monument first, where it was just possible to see that a patch of ground was now bare near eight new graves, all with jam jars of snowdrops propped against homemade markers. Elsewhere, only a few weathered headstones were visible above the blanket of nettles, brambles, Virginia creeper, and ivy that had taken hold, then climbed up the sides of the church and the squat bell tower.

Alice unearthed a pair of rusty clippers from a drawer in the vestry, and as a miserable January gave way to an even colder and wetter February, Oliver grew used to seeing one or another hacking away when she had an hour to spare and it wasn't too dark to see what she was doing. Alice came after school when she didn't have a knitting session, a first aid course, or air raid warden work, or on Saturday mornings after she had sat with her mother for a bit. Evangeline nipped in for a few moments snatched between the children, the garden, the chickens, and her hunting expeditions. Even Elsie surprised him by stamping into the church in her work boots demanding, "Where's them clipper things, then?" Frances came on Sunday afternoons, when the Land Girls were off duty. Oliver offered to help her once or twice, but she had said no, firmly, she knew what she was doing.

Sitting at his desk now trying to compose his thoughts for a Lenten sermon, his attention drifted to Frances, who was there now. He watched her slim figure bending, clipping, and tugging. She paused occasionally to swear when she ran a thorn into her hand. She had a neat waist, he thought, and a pretty shape even in those trousers and that baggy jersey. The thought made him smile. He did not think of himself as a man who noticed women's figures...

Bruno came home on unexpected leave for a few days at the end of February, and Tanni, though happy to see him, was nervous lest she give something away and was almost relieved when he left.

Progress in the graveyard stopped when it snowed heavily in early March. When it finally thawed Elsie stomped in with her case of cyanide and pushed about in the undergrowth. "Huntin' rats," she said to Oliver.

"Don't rats do most damage where food's stored? Pantries and barns?" asked Oliver, puzzled. "Do you find many in churchyards?"

"Everywhere, rats are, you'd never credit it," Elsie the expert assured him. "Burrow around, rats do, graves an' that. You want to get them in the spring, er, when they're nestin', you know. 'Scuse me, must get on. P'raps people ought to keep out of the churchyard on account of the danger."

"Well, no one's ever been attacked by rats here," said Oliver mildly.

"But there's poison and 'orrible traps and such like all over, 'idden. Cyanide! Very dangerous, cyanide. Don't want any of the kiddies gettin' hurt. Or poisoned and dyin' a 'orrible deaf," said Elsie darkly.

"Oh dear! I'll put up a notice."

By the end of March the strain was wearing Tanni down. Rachel had written to her with a brief update that, if their information was correct, the Germans were sending large numbers of children to Auschwitz. Now that Germany and America were at war, the American Quakers in charge of the relief work in southwest France were being arrested, and the helpful American consul in Marseille had been recalled. Rachel was doing what she could to find someone in Gurs who could verify that twins reportedly living on a distant farm were Lili and Klara, but the weeks went by with no word.

One day Evangeline returned from London to tell Frances that a colonel in the Free French had agreed that, for a price, the Resistance would transport the children, if they could be found, along one of the rescue lines used for the RAF. However, they might not be willing to do it until midsummer when farm vehicles and loads of straw would make it easier to hide two children and move them across France to Brittany.

Then out of the blue Richard wrote to say that he had a fortnight's leave at the end of April. He and Evangeline would go to the coast and have a proper holiday.

The others were thrilled for her. "This will stop you moping, darling!" exclaimed Frances.

But Evangeline seemed oddly subdued at the prospect, though the others bustled round to help her get ready.

Frances took a critical look and said, "Really, Evangeline, you have rather let yourself go."

Evangeline was surprised when Tanni voiced her agreement. Her English had improved as her confidence had grown, and she sat a protesting Evangeline down in the kitchen and trimmed her unruly tumble of dark hair with the sewing scissors. "Much better! I know you don't care how you look, Evangeline, but think of his morale!" she exclaimed, admiring her handiwork. "Now for your nails!" She handed Evangeline the nailbrush. Later she cut up an old pillowcase to make a fresh collar and cuffs for Evangeline's least shabby frock.

Frances ransacked Glebe House for something suitable to give Evangeline and came up with two precious sets of lace-trimmed silk knickers and chemises. It was now against clothing regulations to use silk or sew lace on underwear, but Frances said she didn't see how anyone could check. Evangeline protested she had everything she needed, but Frances overrode her. "Darling, it's practically your honeymoon. You had no time together after you got married because Richard went straight off to sea. Women's underwear these days is too gray and dreary and dreadful for words. Sometimes I can't bring myself to wear it at all."

"Frances!"

"Well, I can't—it scratches dreadfully. And here's a hat, a rather fetching one, I think! You're *not* to meet Richard in that disgraceful old trilby that belonged to his father." Frances presented her with a hatbox. "And gloves. They were Aunt Muriel's, and she'd had them since the Flood, but at least they're kid. Here's a pair of stockings—and a petticoat." Tanni tucked the nightdress and peignoir Frances had given her into Evangeline's case, with a bottle of whiskey from Bernie, sent via Elsie, who was going to move into the Fairfax house and help Tanni with Maude, Tommy, and Kipper while Evangeline was away.

Evangeline thanked them all, but said, "I really shouldn't be leaving you with so much work…"

"You'd think she had honeymoon nerves," said Frances to Alice. "Don't people get over those?"

"How would *I* know?" snapped Alice.

Next morning, with Richard's train due at eight, everyone but Alice gathered in the Fairfax hall waiting for Evangeline to come downstairs, to make sure she had not backslid when getting dressed. They were all surprised how smart and trim she looked. She glanced at her reflection in the hall mirror— a sleek, dark-eyed stranger stared back, one she hadn't seen even when she met Laurent in London, an Evangeline she had thought she had left behind her the night she ran away. She blew a kiss to them all, picked up her suitcase, and set off for the station, leaving five-year-old Kipper in a howling tantrum because she was going away. Elsie had to put him in a headlock to keep him from running after her.

She walked slowly, but she was still too early for the train. She waited nervously on the platform, listening for it and trying to remember what Richard looked like.

When it pulled in, a tall naval captain got off. Evangeline waved and walked slowly toward him. "Richard?"

His weather-beaten face broke into a smile and he came striding toward her.

"Darling! You're even more ravishing than I remem-bered!" He swept off his cap and kissed her hard right in front of Albert, then swept her up and swung her round in a bear hug on the platform until she was breathless. The hat Frances had lent her went flying. "Richard, put me down!" Evangeline gasped but couldn't help laughing. He did so and took her case, then Evangeline repinned her hat and smiled nervously at him as they waited for the next train. He seemed older than she remembered and exuded command.

He put an arm round her and looked down hungrily at her upturned face. "I keep thinking you'll disappear like you do in my dreams."

"Nonsense!"

They stepped into a carriage and Richard swung Evangeline's case into the overhead rack, then made sure she had the window seat. He checked their tickets and put them into his pocket. He had made all the arrangements for their holiday. Evangeline sat back in her seat with a magazine he had brought her, unsure what to do with herself, but thinking what a novelty it was to be looked after.

"Every day I think how brave you are to be in England, my darling, when you might be safe in America with your family."

"No," she said quickly, "I don't want to be there, I want to be here."

"I'm a lucky man. Now," he said, taking her hand firmly, "letters are all very well, but lots don't get through, and then there's the censor. You can't imagine how I've longed to hear about everything you've been doing at home."

Evangeline had dreaded being cooped up for two weeks by the sea with a man who was almost a stranger, and at first, with Richard watching her so intently, she could only smile stiffly and give brief answers. She mustn't think of Laurent—she *must* put him out of her mind for now! But it was evident Richard really wanted to hear all about her and Crowmarsh Priors, and in the effort of telling him, somehow, her reserve melted and she began to relax. When she was with Laurent she was always on edge, wrestling with jealousy or worried about what he was doing with the Free French. After their lovemaking, they talked about Paris or the band: he was preoccupied with his own precarious existence, less and less interested in Evangeline's life in a small English village, with her garden and the evacuees.

By the time they arrived at the guesthouse, Evangeline felt that the fortnight would be manageable. It was clean and comfortable, and the gray-haired lady who ran it had a son in the navy. She gave the Fairfaxes her best room, decorated in a faded toile print, with a sea view and a four-poster bed. She winked at Evangeline and said that most nights she could manage "a nice bit of fish" for them if they should fancy a quiet supper in.

The nice bit of fish often turned out to be a lobster or a boiled crab, which she served them in the small parlor, on a table laid by the fire with the blackout curtains drawn. Every night Richard asked if Evangeline wouldn't prefer to go out to a restaurant or a nightclub, but she insisted she was most comfortable curled up next to him on the sofa, listening to the wireless and chatting, much nicer than a smoky, noisy nightclub, she thought. She spent most of her time with Laurent in places like that.

Richard didn't want to talk about life at sea. He wanted to know about everyday things in the village and was entertained by Evangeline's tales of Tanni and Johnny and of Anna being born in Lady Marchmont's morning room and of how Evangeline went hunting on the de Balforts' land because it was so hard to manage on rations and there were still pheasant and rabbits to be had, and even wild ducks on the ornamental lake. Fortunately the gamekeeper had died, so she hadn't been caught.

"Poaching! You?" Richard roared with laughter. She told him how Kipper trailed after her like a puppy, about Elsie and the rat catching, and how Lady Marchmont had tried to marry off Alice to the vicar and Frances to Hugo.

A shadow crossed Richard's face at the mention of Alice. "Darling, I have a confession to make. I'm afraid I was once terribly unkind to Alice. We were engaged. Then somehow, when I met you, that was it for me. I was bewitched or something."

Evangeline put her hand across his lips. "Ssh. I know. I hadn't been in Crowmarsh Priors long before Lady Marchmont was dropping hints, and I soon figured out why Alice hated me. But...nothing that happened to either of us before matters now," she said, suddenly wishing it could be true. Everything was just so...so normal, so happy with Richard.

They went for walks. After so long at sea, Richard noticed everything, was thrilled to see the first crocuses and daffodils. And every night they made love in the big four-poster. Evangeline was shy at first, but to her surprise it was wonderful. Richard paid as much attention to her in bed as he did out of it, and night after night she lay happily by his side after he had fallen asleep, feeling oddly content and secure. The nightmares disappeared. When she guiltily tried to conjure up Laurent's face she found she couldn't, so she curled up against Richard and laid her cheek on his shoulder and went to sleep.

One morning as they lay luxuriating in bed for a last few minutes before braving the chilly bathroom down the passage, Richard said, "Darling, have you thought if there were another baby? I know you had a dreadful time of it before, but my mother says a miscarriage doesn't mean there won't be children later. I can understand that perhaps, with all you have to do at the moment, you'd prefer to wait. It's just that, well, with the war, things are so uncertain, we may not meet again for some time."

"Would you like a baby, Richard? Really and truly?"

"A whole nursery full, my darling."

"Let's try and see what happens," Evangeline murmured eagerly.

Three days before Richard was due to return to his ship, there was a phone call at teatime. Grim faced, he packed hastily. Evangeline watched, stunned, retreating behind her customary dreamy mask so that he wouldn't see her misery. She didn't want to send him off worrying and didn't want him to go. Ever.

But he had to. That evening they stood together on the railway platform. Evangeline, whose bright smile hurt her face, would take the morning train next day. As they waited Evangeline rummaged in her handbag for a handkerchief she promised herself she wouldn't need until Richard left. She felt something in the bottom and held it up. Her eyes widened. "Oh, Richard, it's the gold baby! I kept it...for luck. Take it for luck now."

He slipped it into his pocket. Then he put his arms round her. She leaned against him, and neither said anything while the train approached. As it pulled in Richard took her face in his hands. "I want to remember you exactly. Do you know? When I got off the train in Crowmarsh Priors I had forgotten how beautiful you are. I can't think how I managed that." He kissed her on her forehead quickly, then got onto his train and was gone. Evangeline returned to the guesthouse and went to her room, where she collapsed onto the four-poster and cried.

While Evangeline was gone, Alice had kept thoughts of Richard and Evangeline at bay by keeping busy. The afternoons had lengthened, and there was an hour of daylight school and her mother's teatime. She found a pair of gumboots left in the cottage by a previous occupant and, when the weather allowed, went for long walks, tramping through the muddiest fields and coming home at twilight to a litany of complaints. She stayed up long after her mother went to bed, rummaging through her father's papers to find the old parish records and his map. Eventually she found both and pored over them late at night. Intriguingly the records mentioned an entrance to an old smugglers' tunnel in St. Gabriel's churchyard beneath a grave, but nothing specific. The next day Alice went to see if anything looked likely among the mounds and headstones that were emerging as the undergrowth was hacked away. Nothing did. Finding the grave with a tunnel, if there was one, would be like looking for a needle in a haystack. And how on earth would they know if they found it? Would the tunnel be under a coffin? Even Oliver would be suspicious if they started digging up the dead.

By early May they had only just cleared a path to the oldest side of the church behind the bell tower, but that was all. Alice wanted to give up, but the others wouldn't let her. So she went over and over it in her mind—if you started at St. Gabriel's and ended on the beach...but she had only a hazy recollection of where the cave entrance was, and anyway, there were coastal defenses, mines, and barbed wire, so unless they could find the beginning of the tunnel, assuming the army hadn't found it and blocked it off... Alice heartily regretted mentioning the wretched tunnel at Frances's party, but Tanni had heard that Lili and Klara might have been found, Elsie remained determined, and Frances wanted to keep her promise, while Evangeline had come home from seeing Richard as keen as Alice was to keep busy.

"I'm a bloody fool," Alice muttered, having tramped miles to get as close as she dared to coastal signs that warned, "Danger MINES. Keep Out." There had been a slope and a narrow inlet, which she remembered had been invisible until she and her father were peering down into it. He had pointed to a dark place. "See that? It just looks like a submerged rock, but watch while the tide goes out," and sure enough, Alice had seen the rock opening at the waterline. She despaired of getting close enough to find it again, but she felt sure it wasn't far away. She and her father had walked to the cave and back between lunch and teatime. She racked her brains. It had been an early lunch, she recalled, during the summer holidays. Say two hours there, another two back...home by teatime. She began to time her routes to the coast.

One Saturday afternoon she passed the pruning shears to Elsie just before two. She had a blister and knew there would be hell to pay for leaving her mother to manage lunch on her own. Now she had to polish the altar brasses, but first she unwrapped a sandwich she had brought with her and sat down beside the church gate to eat it. They weren't getting anywhere, she thought.

Elsie plunged into the undergrowth to hack away. She heard thrashing, then Elsie's squawk. "Ow! Caught me foot in them bleedin' vines!" followed by "Bloody 'ell" and a scraping noise. "'Ere, you'd better look at this," Elsie called.

"What is it?" Alice got up and went to her.

"The tomb with the bloke lyin' on top is under them briars. Me and Bernie used to sit on it and talk when we first come 'ere, before I went to be a Land Girl. Think it's sunk a bit. Cor, what a thicket—like it's been wove round it. You'd not know it was 'ere now," said Elsie. "There's a skull stickin' out on the end, on a neck, like—a long one, like a snake. Creepy if you ask me, but I s'pose that's what they liked in them days…anyway, I was lookin' to see if it were still 'ere and caught me foot on that bramble and fell. I grabbed the skull and somefink shifted, but I can't see what it was."

Alice took the pruners, clipped back some runners, and edged through the tangle. Elsie showed her the stone panel with the skull, which grinned up at her. There was a large gap between the panel and the corner of the tomb. She tried to think what her father would have done. She took hold of the skull and noted how neatly it fitted a hand, how her fingers slid easily into the eye sockets and her thumb through the grinning mouth. Peculiar, but…Alice pulled. Nothing happened.

"I think I pushed it when I tripped. Try pushin'," said Elsie.

Alice pushed. Nothing. "'Arder," urged Elsie.

Alice leaned and pushed with all her might, twisting the skull as she did so. It rotated with a scraping noise. She twisted again, and the panel came open, releasing a blast of cold air and a rotten, fetid smell. "Phew!" said Alice, stepping back.

"Blimey!" said Elsie. "Do you think we finally found the tunnel or somefink?"

"I bloody well hope so," said Alice and bit back the urge to add, "Some*thing*, Elsie, not some*fink*!" She was forever correcting the evacuee children, even though she herself had recently taken to swearing rather dreadfully. "Let's come back tonight with a torch. We can pile the clippings round it so no one will suspect..."

"'Oo else you fink would care?" Elsie muttered.

From his desk in the study window Oliver watched, puzzled, as the two women put back the briars they had just cut away. Why on earth would they do that? The door opened behind him. He looked round to see Nell Hawthorne in her overalls, her hair tied up under a knotted scarf, who had come in ready to attack the cleaning. "Those two are certainly hard at it," he remarked, nodding at Alice and Elsie who were dragging yet more cuttings back to the place they'd just cleared.

Then he noticed Nell looked distracted and upset. "Come in."

She wiped her eyes.

"Nell, whatever is it?"

"I thought you'd have heard, Vicar! Albert just came to tell me that Mrs. Richard caught the eleven thirty to London this morning in a dreadful state. He heard her calling and he held it up for two minutes, though it's against the rules. Said he would never have done it but he could tell by her face it was an emergency. She called to him that someone had just telephoned her with news that Mr. Richard's convoy was torpedoed by one of them wolf packs of German subs last week. It did for the ships and most of the men, but a few were rescued. Mr. Richard's alive, but Mrs. Richard said he's burned bad. He and the others was out in all weathers half dead until an American ship spotted their lifeboat. He's been taken to a special hospital near London for burns."

Oliver remembered the dying German pilot and was too horrified to say anything, so Nell went on, "Seeing the girls out there with their minds on gardening makes me think Tanni must be the only one besides Albert who knows yet, and she's got her hands full with those five children. I'd better tell Elsie and Miss Alice. Unless you'd be good enough, Vicar."

Oliver nodded. "Of course. At once." He stood up.

"And to think," said Nell, starting to cry, "only last month Mr. Richard was home on leave, and him and his wife went off on the train, happy as larks, according to Albert. That poor girl and his poor mother! Sometimes, Vicar, I get so angry about this war. I pray God will strike Hitler and all the Germans dead, though I don't suppose I ought to. Anyway, I suppose if He wanted to He'd have done it by now and saved a lot of misery."

25.

London and Crowmarsh Priors, May 1942

*A*t the hospital a haggard doctor ushered Evangeline and Penelope into a side room. He was kind but didn't mince his words. Richard had extensive burns and had nearly died from exposure before an American destroyer rescued him and the few other survivors. At first they hadn't been sure that he would live. For eleven days Evangeline and Penelope kept watch by his bed in a curtained-off area in the critical ward full of bandaged, groaning men.

Once they were past the worst, the doctors still couldn't say how fully Richard would recover. He was unlikely to see again, and at the very least, once he was allowed up, he would need a wheelchair. Now he lay bandaged and under a tent of covers, sleeping or drowsy with morphine.

The nurses brought cups of tea and cut the insignia off Richard's ruined uniform, which they gave to Evangeline with the few things they had found in his pockets, including a little lump of gold. The nurse peered at it, thinking it looked almost like a baby. A charm. She had seen many talismans men carried, and though this one looked worthless, she knew better than to throw it away. She put it in the little pile of possessions with his comb, his pay book, and a damp wallet with a photo of Evangeline in it.

Evangeline and Penelope kept their voices bright and steady in case he could hear. From time to time Penelope got up, went to the lavatory, and cried. Then she bathed her eyes and returned to her chair. While she was away, Evangeline would lean close to Richard and whisper to him that he must try, that she believed he had survived for her, and now that he was back on dry land she wasn't going to let him go. "Please, Richard, get better. I love you." Then when Penelope came back she would straighten up. Sometimes she silently prayed the rosary, and occasionally she ran to the lavatory to throw up.

If Richard woke, asking for a drink, Evangeline held the straw to his lips and tried to smile, forgetting at first that he couldn't see. She stroked his cheek where there were no bandages.

Anxiety for her son had aged Penelope. Her hair had gone gray and she seemed to have shrunk inside her uniform. But she needed to be cross with someone, so she turned on Evangeline, who was as careless as ever about her appearance and who had arrived at the hospital breathless and perspiring in her gardening clothes, without having brought so much as a comb. "I must say, Evangeline," she had snapped, "most wives with a husband in hospital would make some effort to look nice. Other women manage to keep tidy and smart even with clothes rationing." Evangeline had stared at her aghast, and Penelope suddenly remembered it didn't matter, that Richard wouldn't see how any woman looked—perhaps never again. She fled to her refuge in the lavatory.

After days spent sitting by Richard's bed, snatching a few hours' sleep in shifts, Matron told them that they should be getting on with their lives, now that he was out of immediate danger, and that it often helped—here she lowered her voice—injured men to know that the world went on and their sacrifice hadn't been for nothing. Also, of course, the country needed every pair of hands.

"Would you like to come down to the country for a while? I'm sure the WVS will give you a few days more," Evangeline urged. But Penelope declined, remembering the chaos that greeted her on her last visit to the Crowmarsh Priors house with five children living at her home. She preferred to keep busy in London and go home at night to her orderly flat, exhausted enough to sleep deeply, sometimes undisturbed even by air raid sirens.

Now Evangeline bent over Richard and whispered that she had to go home and carry on but would be back as soon as she could. Meanwhile he must get better. She was going to take him home as soon as she was allowed. Would he promise to do whatever the nurses told him? "Richard, I know you can hear me, and I shan't go until you promise," she murmured. Finally he nodded. Evangeline cast a look of despair at the nurses, one of whom said at once, loudly and brightly so Richard could hear, that Evangeline wasn't to worry and her husband was mending quite well, as much as could be expected. They would see her again soon.

When her train pulled into Crowmarsh Priors, Albert hurried to open the door and helped her onto the platform. "There, there," he said helplessly. Evangeline, who had managed so far without breaking down, suddenly clung to his arm and lost her rigidly maintained self-control. "When the nurses...the critical ward is so...so...they're trying so hard with Richard...so brave...oh, Albert!" He helped her to a bench where she sat sobbing until the flood of tears stopped and she could set off for home.

When she got home Kipper threw himself at her and clung to her like a limpet. Frances, Elsie, and Alice arrived after work. "Oh, darling," said Frances and gave her a long hug.

"Bastards!" hissed Elsie.

Tanni shooed the children into the garden with a promise that she had hidden sweets for them to hunt, then made tea.

"I have to go back next week," said Evangeline wearily, "but all I want right now is to think about something else, anything but lines and lines of beds with poor injured men in them. How are we getting on?"

Tanni got up and dragged something from the sofa. "Look what I made while you were gone," she said. Now pregnant with her third child, Tanni had stitched together a kind of tent from blackout material big enough to screen the growing pile of brambles they were stacking around the de Balfort tomb. They needed their torches to see what was inside the entrance, but in the blackout the faintest glimmer of light at night would give them away.

They had also needed rope, but it was impossible to get hold of any, even at the farm. Before Richard had been injured Evangeline had suggested they could tear up sheets and plait them into long strips, then sew them into a rope. But where on earth were they going to get sheets now that everything was rationed?

Elsie had come up with the answer. A huge pile of bed linen had been delivered for use when Glebe House became a convalescent home and was stored in the scullery. They could jolly well help themselves to some.

Tanni had balked at theft of government property, but Elsie had hauled it all over to the Fairfaxes one evening in a wheelbarrow. Thereafter, as soon as the five children were in bed, Tanni had cut up the purloined sheets and, for the next week, plaited and sewed late into the night. She had prayed that Bruno wouldn't find out.

Alice looked at the rope and also thought about how stealing government property was a crime but decided she didn't care. She wasn't the bloody government's watchdog. "I think I found where the cave is," she said, "but I can't get past the barbed wire to see from the cliff above. The signs say it's mined anyway."

"Well done, Alice," they said, perking up. "Do tell!"

Alice described how she had set out for her evening walk, altering her course a little each day, looking for a slope and a narrow inlet..."We won't know for sure unless we go down the tunnel," she finished.

They waited for a night when storm clouds brought an early darkness and a heavy rain kept everyone indoors. Wearing oilskins, Evangeline and Frances crossed the green with the rope Tanni had made. Alice left her mother a flask of cocoa and a cold supper of potato pie, then cycled off into the rain, with complaints about her mother's digestion and her own unladylike behavior ringing in her ears.

Evangeline was wearing one of Richard's oldest pull-overs under her oilskin. Alice recognized it and burst into tears.

Frances patted her shoulder. "Do shut up, darling, and concentrate."

Elsie was the smallest and, to her horror, had been assigned the job of going with Evangeline. She was terrified of being underground. She watched Evangeline knotting one end of the rope round her waist. "I 'ope you know what you're doing," she quavered.

"I've done it lots of times," said Evangeline confidently. "Elodie Le Houèzec. It's fun. Come on."

Elsie peered into the black hole. "It's dark down there and it stinks to 'igh 'eaven! An' anyfink could be down there, lurkin'."

"Elsie, don't be a coward. I need you in case I can't get through a narrow bit. You might be able to."

"Wiv'out you? By meself? Bloody *'ell*!"

"What do we do if anyone comes to investigate?" asked Alice. "We're bound to be arrested. Practically everything's against the law or amounts to helping the enemy these days, so this probably is too. What if someone's watching?"

"It's midnight and it's pouring. Who could possibly be watching?"

"Come *on*, Elsie," said Evangeline. She shone her torch down and they saw worn steps carved into one wall and a series of niches occupied by ancient coffins in the other. They averted their eyes and concentrated on the steps.

"Those look a bit narrow. Men's feet must have been smaller two hundred years ago," said Alice, peering over her shoulder.

"I'll go first," said Evangeline.

Elsie followed her carefully down the first few steps. "It's freezin'."

"It's too late to go back now," said Evangeline below her. "Remember, watch out for steep drop-offs, and if you see a puddle or a pool of water, don't put your foot in it. It might be deep. Just keep close behind me."

Alice and Frances watched as the pinprick of light from Evangeline's torch disappeared into the dark passage. Elsie and she were to go for as long as the first torch lasted then come back using the second torch. If there were forks Evangeline had said they would retrace their steps to the entrance and find a way to mark their route. If they got lost they might never find their way out…

Evangeline and Elsie went as quickly as they could along the narrow, twisting passage. "'Ow' d'you suppose they got smugglin' up them steps?" asked Elsie and shrieked as something flapped over their heads.

"Only a bat," said Evangeline, waving her torch about. "They hate the light."

"You didn't say nuffink about bats," Elsie quavered. She kept looking back over her shoulder, thinking it was horrible having all that black behind them. The walls were closing in, and something brushed her hair as it flitted overhead into the dark. "Ow! This is like 'avin' a nightmare!"

"No, it's not," said Evangeline. "Come on, you're not scared of rats—think of all the girls who'd throw up their hands and scream at the thought of one. You're head rat catcher! Anyway, bats are a good sign. Means there's a way out so they can fly out at night to find food."

"They bite people!"

"No, they don't."

"'Ow do you know?"

"Because at home, growing up, I spent time on my grandmother's plantation. We had everything out there, bats, alligators, cottonmouths. I only had my older brothers to play with, and I wanted the boys to take me with them when they went hunting and fishing. They'd have left me behind if I'd made a fuss about a little thing like a bat."

"What's that big dark thing? There!"

Evangeline's beam swept over a black gap in the wall. There was a swoosh as more bats flew out of it and they looked in. "Looks like another cave, with something on the wall." The torch beam picked up something circular, then glanced off something pale. Both girls screamed.

Skulls grinned up at them and other bones were scattered about with something that looked like rags. Chains set into the rings in the walls had rusted.

Evangeline crossed herself automatically. She said shakily, "Alice told me the smugglers kidnapped excise men if they couldn't be bribed. They must have chained them up down here. No one could hear them above ground and no one knew where they were." She shuddered.

"Knowin' what I know about rats, they must have eaten the...bugger this! Let's go back, Evangeline! Please!"

"You can."

"Not by meself! Bloody 'ell! Prob'ly them excise men's ghosts are waitin' to get even."

"The Germans are worse than ghosts, and they're real. Now hush! Other people got through here, and we've promised to help Tanni because no one else will. What if it was your sisters?"

"I'd like to catch them German pilots when their planes crash an' all, an' drag 'em down 'ere, chain 'em up, and leave *them* to be the rats' dinner," Elsie whimpered as they went on step by careful step. "'Ow long we been down 'ere?"

"About an hour and a half."

"Can't we go back now?"

"No."

"Bugger!"

The floor was slippery with bat droppings, but the ceiling of the tunnel was higher now, and they could feel air moving.

Recently Elsie had been going through a moody patch. A few days earlier she had had a frightful row with Bernie, who had slammed the door of the official motorcar and disappeared in a huff. Now, to distract Elsie, Evangeline said, "I saw Bernie was back after your argument. He looked quite the gent—a suit, overcoat round his shoulders. He even tipped his hat when he saw me. Looked like he'd had a haircut. Did the two of you make it up?"

"No."

"Why not?"

"'E wants us to get married."

Evangeline halted in her tracks. "Married? Elsie, you're way too young—and Bernie can't be much older."

"Nineteen, 'e is. He finks 'e's nineteen anyway. Though it's possible, 'e says, 'e's a little older. 'E don't know for sure. 'E's got the War Office finkin' he's older. 'E says you got to make 'em fink you're old enough to know what's what."

"But that's too young to get married."

"'Ow old were you when you married Richard?"

"Well, eighteen, but..."

"And you said you 'adn't known 'im long—a few days by the sound of it. I've known Bernie three years. Near as dammit."

"Are you, um, having a baby?"

"No." Elsie giggled. "Bit of luck I'm not, really, but just at the—you know, moment when—anyway, Mum comes into me 'ead, talkin' about respectable, and I says 'no.' Drives Bernie wild it does. Me too. Don't know 'ow much more of that either of us can stand. No, reason I were cross wiv Bernie is, 'e's asked me to marry 'im on account of a wife can't testify in court against her 'usband, which would be a 'andy fing, from 'is point of view. 'Is words exactly."

"That's no reason to get married! Even if they turn a blind eye now, sooner or later all that black market stuff will land him in prison. What will he do when the war is over and they treat him like a common criminal?"

"Well, that's exactly what I fought. 'Wife testifyin,' I says! 'Ow much, I says, of 'is proposin' was 'im wantin' us to get married and 'ow much was it 'im not wanting to go to prison? Bernie looks all confused and starts mumblin' about will you or won't you. So I says, 'Bernard Carpenter,' I says, 'even if I says yes, there's conditions. There's to be no more of the burglarizin' an' scavenging when the jewelers and the toffs are bombed—I don't care 'ow bad the War Office needs them diamonds. Looting bombsites is disrespectful. No goin' back after the war to the safe blowin' an' muckin' about with them gangs, especially them Italians in Clerkenwell. Mum always insisted on being respectable. She said then people can't look down on you, no matter what class you are.' I says, 'I owe it to Mum.' Course Bernie cut

up rough at that, said, "Ow's a leopard to change 'is spots?'
and more to the point, "Ow's 'e to make a livin' and take
care of a wife and all?' but I looked 'im in the eye, didn't I,
and told 'im straight, 'Bernie Carpenter, it's all or nuffink
wiv me. All or nuffink. Either you turn over a new leaf and
turn your hand to a respectable line of work or I wouldn't
marry you if you was the last man on earth.' So 'e went off
cross, like. Couldn't let 'im see I was worried sick 'e wouldn't
come back, could I?"

"Are you in love with him?" Evangeline had a catch in
her voice. "It's just that sometimes you think you're so in love
you'll die unless you can be together and then when you are,
you find you were wrong. You have to be careful when you're
in love, because you never know where it will take you."

"Don't I know! Mum was in love wiv me dad once. Look
where that got her, into a right dickerment, she used to say,
so I'm not rushin' into nuffink."

"Good," said Evangeline, who was in a predicament
herself. Once again she counted the weeks since her last
period. She had last seen Laurent five—no, four—weeks
before Richard had come home on leave. Laurent had been
rushed, even more so than usual, and they had only had
a few hours in the afternoon before they had hurried to
the Soho pub. Laurent had had a furtive, distant air, which
made Evangeline feel she must have done something wrong.
He smoked a lot of the sickly sweet cigarettes he said all
the musicians used. They gave Evangeline a headache and
made her dizzy, but Laurent had been cross when she said
so and refused to smoke them.

At the pub Frenchmen swarmed everywhere, and
Laurent was summoned to de Gaulle's room. The president

of the French government in exile, he had just returned from North Africa, and Evangeline had gathered there was an important meeting about German successes there. Before it began, Evangeline had cornered the colonel about bringing Lili and Klara. Laurent had remained closeted with the others, and she had left and taken a late train back to Crowmarsh Priors.

Then Richard had come back…*Please let it not be Laurent's baby.*

Behind her Elsie was rattling on about Bernie. "An' another fing. 'E says 'e wants to look after me, but actually, I fink it's 'im what needs the lookin' after. So it 'as to be me decides a few fings straight off. If 'e's going to be my 'usband, a 'usband off down the pub like me dad or wiv them gangs and specially a 'usband in prison's no good to me…"

There was a faint but definite sound, a low, rhythmic roar.

"Oh, Elsie, it's the sea! The cave must be—!" But just then the torch dimmed and flickered.

"Uh-oh, this one's going out." Evangeline sighed. "Time to go back. Mustn't take any chances. But…" she sniffed… "I can smell fresh air and the sea. Alice said she thought that when the tide comes in," she pointed the dying beam at the walls, "the water level rises in here. We don't want to be caught when that happens."

"Evangeline!" exclaimed Elsie, forgetting the cold and the bats and her love life. "We done it! We bleedin' done it!"

26.

Auschwitz, Late Spring 1942

*T*he doctor was furious. Imbeciles! Four months had elapsed since he ordered the Josephs brought to the medical wing, fed and treated for tuberculosis, but in all that time the fools had failed to locate the Joseph twins. Instead they had brought him two forty-year-old women, twins to be sure, Austrian and from the camp at Gurs, but how had such an idiotic mistake occurred? It had been a specific, direct order to find two seven-year-old girls named Lili and Klara Joseph.

He had been told some nonsense about the records not showing any Joseph twins in the camp. The doctor had raged and pointed out their names—Lili Joseph and Klara Joseph—plainly written on the *Kindertransport* manifest. And now the Fuhrer was demanding every day to know when the breeding program would begin. If the doctor did not produce a result soon...

He threatened to have every tenth man in the unit shot unless the Joseph twins were located immediately. Obviously they were somewhere in southwest France. It was clear that Frau Joseph would not live much longer, and he would have to begin searching all over again for parents of twin girls.

Meanwhile the forty-year-old sisters were sent to a secondary breeding program, an experiment the doctor wrote up with as much obfuscation as possible, buying himself a little more time. Both women had died. He had begun what he called "preliminary work" on the Joseph parents in the meantime.

27.

Bethnal Green, East London, June 1942

*I*t was late on Sunday morning but the blackout curtains were still pulled tight across the front windows of the narrow terraced house at the address Tanni had given them. Two young women in siren suits stopped in front and squinted at the number.

"This is it. Oh, Evangeline, my head hurts like the devil!" moaned Frances. They had spent the previous evening in the Coach and Horses pub, the Free French headquarters in Soho, where Evangeline seemed to know a great many men who all asked after someone called Laurent. She had introduced Frances to a short French colonel with soulful dark eyes and a large black mustache. Evangeline had smartened herself up a bit, and Frances was looking particularly fetching: she had done her nails and hair and worn one of the pretty prewar frocks from Paris that Tanni had shortened to show off her legs. The Frenchman had leaped gallantly to his feet and bowed. He had recognized couture at once and was greatly taken with Frances. He had sat with the two women at a corner table for hours, ordering brandy and more brandy and becoming quite emotional toward the end of the evening when Frances disengaged his hand from her knee where it was trying to creep upward and insisted they had to go.

"A hangover's a small price to pay, Frances. Look, you got heaps of information out of him. Plus, if I remember his parting words right, he has never met such a woman, he adores you, his heart is eternally yours, and he's going to put Paris at your feet when the war's over. And he'll be waiting for you this afternoon in the pub..."

"Oh my head! My poor head! Longest evening of my life! But I'll have to string him along somehow so he'll act as a go-between with the Resistance. It'll be a bit tricky holding him to his promise without actually...if Tanni only knew what we've been through! Come on."

Evangeline knocked on the door and the curtains parted briefly. Someone had been waiting for them. Then an elderly woman in a kerchief and an apron opened the door a crack. "Quickly, come in."

"How do you do? We're Tanni's friends. I'm Frances Falconleigh, this is Evangeline Fairfax, and you must be Mrs. Cohen," said Frances, trying to see in the dark hall after the brightness outdoors.

"Ach!" groaned the woman, rubbing her forehead. "Come." She led the way to the kitchen at the back of the house. "Please sit down. Rachel will be here in a minute. It is she who knows everything." The kitchen faced into a cramped back garden and was a little brighter. Mrs. Cohen bustled, moving a "Make Do and Mend" pamphlet and a pile of jumpers with holes, then busied herself with a kettle, muttering to herself in a language they did not understand. Finally she handed them tea in little glass tumblers. "I am sorry. I am so worried I forget my manners. You are welcome here."

Evangeline put down the roll of papers she was carrying under her arm, and Frances stood Tanni's carpetbag on the floor.

"A little something to eat?" asked Mrs. Cohen.

Both girls shook their heads. "No," they said with feeling. "But thank you."

"The rabbi and I heard your husband was badly hurt," said Mrs. Cohen to Evangeline. "I am so sorry. Will he get any better?"

Evangeline gazed at her tea. "The doctors aren't sure yet. I'll see him later—it's my day to visit him at the hospital. We all hope he's improving, but it's a slow process. I expect Tanni told you that the house Frances lives in has been requisitioned for wounded soldiers. It's close to the one where I live now with Tanni, her children, and some evacuees. The doctors say Richard can be transferred to the convalescent home as soon as it's ready and it'll be better for him than living in our house because it's being specially fitted out for patients and it's quiet. He can't stand noise now—his nerves are still mending."

Mrs. Cohen shook her head sympathetically, and then, hearing footsteps outside, she scurried into the hall to open the door. She came back with a younger woman in a head scarf whom she introduced as Rachel.

"The rabbi is away," Mrs. Cohen whispered. "I didn't tell him, Rachel—you told me to say nothing, but it's so hard keeping a secret from him."

"You're right not to tell him, Berthe. He needs more worries? Let's get on. I should be at the office and can't stay long." Rachel put down her gas mask, yawned, and accepted a glass of tea. "I'm sorry. I'm so tired. Give me a moment to remember what we found out about the Joseph twins... there was something new...I have to remember so much and our records are in a muddle." She smiled apologetically at Frances and Evangeline.

"Tanni Zayman's family?" Frances prompted. "Her parents, Dr. Joseph and his wife? Her husband's mother, Mrs. Zayman? Lili and Klara Joseph who should have arrived in England three years ago but didn't? If you only knew how desperate Tanni is..."

"Yes, the Joseph sisters. We believe they have been found. We had made contact with the American Quakers at the Gurs camp before Germany declared war on the US. Technically the Quakers are nonpartisan, but the Germans are suspicious of pacifists and tolerate them only because they can use them for propaganda purposes, to say that the Quakers run relief operations in the camps. It is one of the lies the British government chooses to believe."

Mrs. Cohen wound and unwound a spool of thread, muttering prayers under her breath.

"We told Bruno months ago that either the girls had died on the train or that they never made it to the camp for some other reason. Then we learned that a priest had hidden some children with local families. For a long time we could not find out where, until one of our contacts cycled out to an isolated farm where he had heard an elderly couple had twins. He reported seeing the girls, aged six or seven. The old couple insisted they were their granddaughters. Our friend was worried because the old people would be arrested or shot if they were hiding Jewish children, and the children would be shot too, or deported. We had passed on the information that the girls' family in England were looking for them, and in any case, our friend knew that if word had reached him of the children's whereabouts, it wouldn't be long before the Germans came. He urged them to let him take the girls and hide them elsewhere, but at first the couple refused. It turned out the priest is the old lady's brother. But finally the couple gave in."

Rachel drank some tea.

"The area is under Vichy control now, but the Germans are expected to extend their demarcation line south at any minute. The Nazis are rounding up all French Jews and are searching for foreign Jews who have taken refuge in France. They are already combing the area around Gurs for children from the *Kindertransport* manifest who are not in the camp, but we are hearing rumors of something else too. A doctor at Auschwitz may be conducting medical experiments in human reproduction on prisoners. We heard there is a special order to seek out twins and rewards offered for any found. Our friend was right that it is only a matter of time before the Joseph girls are discovered or betrayed."

"God forbid!" Mrs. Cohen put her head in her hands.

"May God forbid," echoed Rachel.

"So we need to act before the Nazis find the children or those helping them. Can the Quakers hide them a little longer," Frances asked, "until we can make arrangements to get them out of France?"

Rachel considered. "They have to be careful to act only as neutral humanitarians. Anything more will jeopardize the small amount of good they are permitted to do. Nevertheless, some are less neutral than they were, and those are a link through which we have sent money to the Resistance for medicine, guns, ammunition, wireless sets," she said. "It buys us information and favors in exchange. They can sometimes help someone escape if he or she is important enough to justify the risks involved, and like the airmen shot down over occupied territory, they can be smuggled along escape routes, with the help of local Resistance networks, to pick-up points on the French coast and then taken back to England. But do not forget that the price is not just money. The Germans execute civilians in reprisal for Resistance activities. But the Quakers would probably agree to do what they could to help get the girls to the coast, if there were some prospect of reuniting them with their family. The Resistance, however...I'm less sure they'd be willing to use their escape routes for children—but, for enough money, who knows? But even assuming the children reached England, then what?"

Frances said, "We have a plan..."

Rachel stopped her and looked at Mrs. Cohen. "Berthe, I am sorry, but it would be best if you would please leave us by ourselves now. It is for your own protection that you should not know what is said. Then, if the authorities ask you, can truly say you know nothing."

"But, Rachel!"

"For the rabbi's protection too, you must be able to say you know nothing."

Mrs. Cohen sighed and left the room.

"First, we can pay the Resistance to bring the girls along the escape route to the coast and then across the channel," said Frances steadily.

"The authorities would only send them back!"

"Only if the authorities knew of them."

"But the Costal Defense Zone is impenetrable."

Evangeline spoke up. "No, it isn't, which is why the government are so worried about Nazis slipping through. We've found a way into the country people used hundreds of years ago, through an old smugglers' cave on the coast and a tunnel going inland. We believe the authorities don't know it's there—there's no official map. Just this." From the roll of papers she pulled out Alice's tracing of her father's map and spread it on the kitchen table. "This was drawn twenty years ago by a vicar in our village, an amateur local historian who died a few years ago without showing it to anyone but his daughter."

"So?" said Rachel, bending over to look.

Frances pointed to a spot on the Sussex coast. "The smugglers went back and forth to France from here."

Evangeline explained how they had discovered and explored the tunnel, then pointed out how it ran to St. Gabriel's and was still usable if the children could be brought to the coast.

"It seems a bit far-fetched," Rachel muttered, "although… in some cities Jews are escaping through the sewers. Once that would have seemed far-fetched too." She bent over for a closer look at the map.

"Did this ever work?" she asked dubiously.

"Very well. The government never stamped out the smuggling gangs—the industrial revolution came along and men stopped making a living by sea. This is probably the only map in existence. And it was quite as dangerous when the smugglers used it—the coast was crawling with troops and excise officers ready to hang any smugglers they caught. The smugglers still got through."

"So here is the cave on our side, but where on the French coast? The Germans are everywhere."

The time Frances and Evangeline had invested in charming the Free French colonel had paid off. Frances said, "We know sea rescues of the RAF take place from Plouha where the cliffs are steep, like they are at Dover. Right under the Germans' noses."

Rachel was wavering, they could see, but she said, "Crossing the channel in a small boat is dangerous, nearly impossible—there are mines and submarines. The captain, probably a French or Spanish fisherman, would have to weigh the risks and decide what he can and cannot do. There is no guarantee he will not turn back or land elsewhere on the coast. And you say the children will come out at night from this tomb, here?"

"That's right."

"And then what? I suppose there will be a car waiting to pick them up, full of petrol despite regulations?"

"Actually yes, and it's better if you don't know who is helping us." God bless Bernie and the black market, thought Frances.

Rachel gave a small, wry smile. "I understand. And then?"

Evangeline took a deep breath and explained how Tanni suggested the children could be hidden. Ration books would be provided.

Rachel stared at her, dumbfounded at such a simple solution. Then she nodded. "Tanni may be right. My sister... perhaps...let me think...we must make sure no one knows who the girls are or where they come from, then no one could give them away..."

She thought for a minute. "My sister Judith and her husband, Dovid, have a large family of ten children in Tottenham. Berthe does not know Judith and rarely leaves this Bethnal Green neighborhood now, so she is unlikely to hear of the girls being in the Jewish community in Tottenham. I will ask Judith if she and Dovid would be willing to take in two children, knowing nothing about them, not their names or where they come from. Only Tanni and we will know who they are and where they are."

"But there is a risk—will they take it?"

"Yes, for Jewish children. I think so. Dovid's cousins in the Lodz ghetto have been taken by the Nazis, and he...it helps that they do not know who Tanni is. If either is arrested they can say they took in two children whose parents went missing after a bombing raid. I think Tanni is right. For once the authorities' lack of interest in Jews will help. Now, you say you have money. How much?"

"Not money, not yet, but we have these..." Frances lifted the carpetbag onto the table and pulled out a towel-wrapped bundle. Inside were three old-fashioned black velvet jeweler's cases. She undid the brass clasps and Rachel gasped. It was Lady Marchmont's splendid triple string of pearls with the emerald and diamond clasp. Frances opened the two smaller cases to reveal the matching earrings and bracelet. The pearls glowed against the black satin of their case, while the emeralds and diamonds winked and sparkled.

Rachel, whose family had a shop in Hatton Garden, knew immediately that they were worth a fortune. She hadn't expected anything like this. "They aren't stolen? If we're caught there will be enough trouble without that. They must be worth thousands."

"They're mine. I inherited them. And there's more in the bag. I'm on my way to show them—or a few of them—to a man I met last night, a colonel with the Free French who belives agents in France will help us for enough money... it's better that you don't know more. We'll offer them part now, the rest when the girls are here."

"It's a dangerous plan, but I cannot imagine there will be another way to rescue these children. It is worse to abandon them if there is a chance. So we must help, risk or not. Tell Tanni to be brave," said Rachel.

"You know she's pregnant again? The nurse says it's too soon. Anna was only born last November, Bruno had leave in February, and now this baby's due in October. She hasn't been very well," said Frances. She closed the jeweler's boxes and returned them to the carpetbag.

Rachel stood up. "We'll be in touch as soon as we have some answers. And one more thing. Tanni may see her sisters briefly when they arrive in your village, but then they must leave at once. After that, Tanni must not know their whereabouts in London or the name of my sister and her family. It will be sad for the girls and for Tanni, but you must make her understand the risks for them—and for Bruno—if she or he knows anything. It must be enough for her that they are safe."

Frances and Evangeline promised they would make her understand. "Good luck, Rachel."

"Good luck to you too."

As the front door closed behind them they heard Rachel exclaim, "Two lives! And there are hundreds of thousands..."

Evangeline went to the Underground while Frances walked down the street, bustling now with everyday activity.

She was more worried than she would admit about the part of the plan that involved hiding Lili and Klara so openly. However, she tried to see the busy street through the eyes of the authorities. She caught snatches of conversation in what she assumed was Yiddish. There were women in head scarves tied like Rachel's, with shopping baskets and children. In fact, children were everywhere, dressed in black and carrying satchels. The boys wore little caps on the backs of their heads and had side locks. The girls had on thick stockings like their mothers wore and skirts that came nearly to their ankles. Frances began to smile as it dawned on her that the SOE controllers couldn't have bettered Tanni's simple plan. Among the close-knit Jewish community in Tottenham, Lili and Klara might be newcomers, but Rachel had assured them the community would close ranks to protect them, and to outsiders, two more little girls in thick stockings and black dresses would blend into the background.

Frances found a tube station and bought a ticket. She would have to find a place to change out of her siren suit into her pretty frock, fluff out her hair.

Two hours later, glamorous once more, she tightened her grip on the carpetbag and entered the smoky gloom of the Coach and Horses. She paused dramatically and tossed her hair back. Every male head swivelled, and the colonel strutted forward importantly before any other man could waylay her. "Ah, ma chère, Mees Falconlee!" He put a proprietary arm round her waist to lead her to a table.

Frances flashed him an encouraging smile as she sat, calculating his mood. The colonel ordered wine and offered her a cigarette, which he leaned forward gallantly to light for her. Frances let her hand rest on his, as if to steady it, then drew it away almost caressingly. Frances licked a speck of tobacco off her lip and the colonel began to breathe more quickly. This was going to be a game of cat-and-mouse, and she had to calculate carefully how far flirting would take her, then at what point she should reveal the jewels they were prepared to exchange. She feared what would happen when the colonel finally "persuaded" her upstairs as part of the bargain. She would try her best to get him drunk but if the worst came to the worst, the lessons of the Shanghai Police were fresh in her memory. She hoped it would not be necessary to put them into use.

At the same time, Evangeline emerged five Underground stops to the north, near the hospital. A one-armed man was selling small baskets of strawberries at the entrance and she bought one for Richard: he couldn't see flowers, but he could taste the strawberries. He had been moved to a side ward, and on her weekly visit Evangeline spent the day at his side, reading to him, smoothing his sheets, giving him sips of water, and telling him the latest bits of news from Crowmarsh Priors. But no matter what she did, Richard remained passive and unresponsive.

"Shock," the nurses assured her. Most of the time he slept, and then Evangeline sat quietly, wondering what she was going to do. A doctor at the hospital had just examined her and confirmed that her nausea and dizziness were due to pregnancy. When she asked how far along she was, the doctor was exasperated. "How long ago was your last period!" he exclaimed. "All you need to do is count backward."

Evangeline had chewed her lip. She still couldn't remember whether her period had come before or after she had last seen Laurent. Unaware of her dilemma, the doctor advised her not to tell Richard yet but wait till he was stronger.

She had persuaded Frances to wait till tomorrow to go home because Laurent was coming to London tonight, and hard as it would be, Evangeline knew she had to face him, possibly for the last time. He was her cousin, her only link to her old home and family, and she had loved him for so long—and so dangerously—that the realization that she no longer loved him had come as a shock, and a liberation. Still, she worried for his safety, going back and forth to France. And she wasn't sure whether to say anything about the baby. He would be furious, but if the baby was obviously colored…

No, she wouldn't tell him. If the baby was obviously colored, she couldn't count on Laurent.

At six she walked slowly out of the hospital toward the tube, still not certain what she was going to say.

Later, in a dim café in Soho, Evangeline and Laurent drank beer and ate the day's special, Mock Duck. "This tastes like a duck would taste if it was made out of potatoes and old turnips," said Laurent. "Awful. Less to eat in Paris, though." He looked different—thinner and older, no longer a boy. He had wolfed his "duck" and its puddle of gravy, then finished Evangeline's. For pudding they had stodgy jam roly-poly. "That's awful too," muttered Laurent, making a face and drinking more beer. "When are they moving Richard home?"

"Soon. When Lady Marchmont's house is finished there'll be a place for him to recuperate. There are too many stairs at Penelope's for him, and we're crammed already with three evacuees and Tanni and the children. But we should talk about..."

Laurent interrupted curtly. "I've got a job to do, honey," he exclaimed impatiently. "They keep me busy, back and forth to France, can't tell you about it exactly, got to live. Don't keep askin' to talk about it!"

Laurent jiggled one leg under the table, a nervous tic he'd developed. "One day to the next is all I can manage. They've given me French identification papers, but the Nazis are good at detecting fakes, especially in Paris, and I had a scare last time I was there, Gestapo stopped us, looking for somebody...they decided my papers were in order, but they arrested some guys behind me for having false documents. When he heard what a close shave I had, de Gaulle called a pal and had him get me a new set—there's some young fellow at the War Office—they say he's the best, so far no one's been able to spot his fakes. But you know..." he shrugged.

"Laurent, I have to tell you..."

A drum roll and a clash of cymbals on stage drowned the rest of what she said.

Laurent perked up and changed the subject: "You worry too much. Wait till you hear this band. They use me sometimes if one of the musicians can't play. One has a brother plays with Glenn Miller, says he can get me a job when they come over to play for the troops. How about that?"

He took out cigarettes for them both and lit Evangeline's, then his own. Evangeline stared down at her empty glass, trying to decide when to get up and leave. When Laurent slapped the table she jumped. The tempo had picked up. "Come on, sugar! Let's dance and forget about the damn war." Suddenly eager, he yanked her out of her chair, swung her onto the floor, and spun her away.

Three American GIs in Ike jackets sat in the corner watching the dancers. When their beer came they tasted it and grimaced. It was their first night in London. As their eyes got used to the gloom one drawled in a flat Georgia accent, "Son-of-a-bitch, y'all look at *that*!" He nudged the soldier next to him. "That's a *white* girl for sure. And she's dancin' with a *colored fellow*!"

"Where?" said his friend from Nebraska who had been sizing up two single girls at the bar. He squinted at Laurent. "Him? Looks white to me."

"A high yellow, we call 'em. Some white blood, but you can always tell a nigger! Back home, he wouldn't be dancin' with her long, I promise you that. Be dancin' from the end of a rope."

Evangeline felt dizzy as Laurent spun her away, spun her back, and hugged her tight. "Just follow me, honey," he said into her neck and kissed her ear. "It's like old times again, and your train isn't till tomorrow. We got all night."

No, it wasn't like old times, she wanted to scream. It never had been like old times ever since she'd followed him to Europe. She couldn't regret saving him from Maurice, but her heart was no longer his. She wanted to be in the hospital where Richard lay. She wanted to turn back the clock and be in a seaside boarding house, curled on the sofa with him, she wanted to see him striding toward her on the railway platform, holding out his arms to scoop her up, not caring that Albert Hawthorne was watching. She wanted to talk about the baby they were going to have…she wanted to run. Back to her life.

When the dance was finished, Evangeline snatched her handbag from the table and did exactly that, without looking back. Laurent was busy clapping and shouting for an encore, and then the musician whose brother played with Glenn Miller was pulling Laurent up onto the stage. She knew it would be some time before he noticed that she had gone.

28.

Crowmarsh Priors, July 1942

The wedding about to take place that sunny afternoon was a distraction and a welcome relief from
the horrors of war. With most of the young people called
up, with handsome Richard Fairfax lying half dead in his
bandages in the hospital, with the Germans on their way,
and the mute testimony of the bare earth over new graves
in the churchyard, Crowmarsh Priors heard the dogs of war
howling at its gates.

But today, everyone was in church, wearing their best
clothes, and there was the usual sense of happy anticipation as they waited for the bride to arrive. No one minded
that she was late; they luxuriated in a rare feeling of normality. People said the things to their neighbors that were
always said on these occasions. Not necessarily important or profound things, just normal things, soothing
platitudes and timeworn sentiments appropriate to the
occasion.

"What I say," whispered Nell Hawthorne to the butcher's
wife beside her, "is that a wedding is a wedding and young
people will be young people, war or no war. You have to
wish them the best, and though he's a good enough lad at

heart, he wants keeping on the straight and narrow. She'll be the making of him."

The butcher's wife nodded in agreement. "Takes you back to your own wedding, doesn't it?" she whispered back.

There was a buzz of similar conversation, and ladies' hats bobbed as they looked round and admired the decorations. The old church looked lovely. Alice, Frances, and Evangeline had arrived at dawn with armloads of flowers and greenery culled from the last vestiges of flowerbeds and from the countryside to decorate the church. Now a handsome pair of tall Limoges vases that had belonged to Lady Marchmont stood on the altar, spilling over with jasmine, roses, and ivy, while crystal pitchers of cow parsley and honeysuckle filled the deep window alcoves, turning the ancient church into a sweet-smelling bower of green and white. Tanni had made strips of a worn-out sheet into white bows for the end of each pew and tucked a bit of baby's breath and ivy into each.

To everyone's surprise Mrs. Osbourne, who had once played the harmonium at weddings conducted by her late husband, had been cajoled and flattered by Nell Hawthorne into resuming her place at the instrument. She was wearing a feathered picture hat that had not seen the light of day for years and watching for the signal from Oliver to begin the wedding march. Meanwhile she was playing "Jesu, Joy of Man's Desiring," her particular favorite, over and over again. They had played it at her own wedding. The dusty feathers on her hat quivered tremulously as she threw herself into the music, trying different keys.

Margaret Rose Hawthorne, sitting beside her mother, shivered with anticipation. Weddings were so exciting!

Someday, her mother had said, it would be her turn. She had begged a white ribbon from Tanni to put round Shirley Temple's neck and had sulked when Nell nevertheless firmly refused permission for the pig to be tethered to the church-yard gate.

Standing at the altar in his vestments, Oliver craned his neck to see if Elsie and her bridesmaids had arrived on the porch yet. Bernie was fidgeting nervously in front of him, hoping he hadn't done something to make Elsie change her mind. He had come back from London after their row two months ago, lonely and miserable without Elsie. He was determined to ask her to marry him properly. He could see now that he had gone about proposing the wrong way—he should never have mentioned criminal proceedings. Elsie was particular about some things, owed it to her her mum, she kept saying. Anxious to get it right the second time, he had shamefacedly made inquiries among his colleagues about how you did it. The toffs had explained what men usu-ally said on these occasions and said it was the usual thing to have a ring to the ready for when the girl went all fluttery and said "yes." Bernie had had no idea you needed a ring as well, but he returned to Crowmarsh Priors equipped with beautiful antique sapphire and diamond engagement ring and a speech he had practiced over and over: Would Elsie do him the honor of becoming Mrs. Bernard Carpenter?

He had spoken his piece and held out the ring. Elsie stared at it, then at him open-mouthed. To his horror, she had stamped her foot and said, "Bernie Carpenter, I wouldn't marry you if you was the last man on earth! Mum would turn in 'er grave, she would!" Then she had stormed off, muttering darkly about lootin' and safe-crackin' and prison and Mum being right and, inexplicably, something about ferrets. She never wanted to see him again and good riddance.

It had been the worst moment of Bernie's life. Bewildered and frightened, he had run after her and said all right, he could see she didn't want a 'usband what was always in prison, but he wasn't a reformed man until she married him so she'd better marry 'im quick. Meanwhile he planned to have just the one engagement ever in his life and the toffs he worked for said to do it proper you needed a ring and— Then it dawned on him that Elsie thought he'd stolen it. Honest, he hadn't done no lootin' to get it, no dodgy deals; he'd traded some Polish airmen "a bit of paperwork" for the ring. All legal and aboveboard. It was the same work he did for the War Office, and since the Poles and the War Office were on the same side fighting Germans, that ought to be all right, oughtn't it? No gangs! Bernie emphasized, no safes, no looting, no burglary involved. 'Specially, he added, no looting of bomb sites, out of respect for how her mum and Jem and Violet had died. Besides, he said, as something else occurred to him, he loved her and he didn't think he could do without her. So would she marry him? Please?

Mollified, Elsie quickly reconsidered. Whatever he promised now, something told her that Bernie and the law would never be friends. For once she wished she knew what Mum would have advised. On the one hand she had no intention of leading Mum's life, or worse. But Mum was dead. If she married Bernie it would be up to Elsie to keep him on the straight and narrow. For a moment she wondered whether she was up to the job for the rest of her life. But as she gazed into Bernie's anxious face, she decided perhaps she had learned a thing or two from her mother about keeping men in line, so perhaps she was. Finally she gave him a smile, said, "All right then, Bernie, I don't mind if I do," kissed him, slipped on the ring, and sighed. "Fancy! Me engaged!"

Elsie seized every opportunity thereafter to call Bernie "me fiansay" and Bernie felt proud, though he didn't know what the word meant, exactly.

Now, fiansay or not, Bernie wondered if someone could stop the old woman playing the same tune over and over and over. Hot and self-conscious, he ran a finger round the inside of his collar, which felt too tight. He wasn't sure what you were supposed to do standin' up front like this with everybody starin' at you. Probably laughin' behind their 'ands too. He didn't know why they had to make you so nervous. It was all very well having Constable Barrows as his best man—something else the toffs said you needed—but he wished Uncle was there.

Bernie hadn't known much about getting married and vaguely assumed you just ran off to Gretna Green and did it. But, oh, no!

Constable Barrows said you were supposed to go speak to the girl's father first and ask permission to marry her. Then you had to speak to the vicar and get a license and there were the banns…Bernie scratched his head and said the first was a mite difficult, as no one knew where Elsie's dad was. He hadn't been seen for years and was probably dead in the bombing or died of the drink. Constable Barrows had considered and said, "In that case better speak to the vicar," so he and Elsie had done that. And that part had gone pretty well, considering. Next thing he knew Elsie didn't have any spare time for him, the women were busy chasing a dress for her to be married in and Tanni was sewing like blazes. Something called a trousseau.

He nudged Constable Barrows. "'Ere! A bit awkward, innit, standin' in front of everybody, waitin'. Shouldn't Elsie be walkin' down the aisle by now?" he muttered. What if she changed her mind at the last minute?

"They all do this, lad," said Constable Barrows with calm authority. His wife, Edith, had assured him men had no idea, *no idea at all,* of the last-minute crises with hairpins and veils and garters and bouquets on the most important day of a girl's life. He smiled at Edith in her best hat, holding the baby, looking sweet and plump and unconcerned in the front row on the groom's side of the church. She was chatting happily to Nell Hawthorne and the butcher's wife.

"Feels like we've been standin' here ages. What if she isn't comin'?"

"She'll be here, lad, don't you worry."

"That tune is gettin' on me nerves," said Bernie as Mrs. Osbourne added more riffs and began to hum quaveringly along. "Must 'ave played it a thousand times already."

Oliver looked down at his vestments and tried not to smile. Bernie and Elsie had turned up on the vicarage doorstep and abruptly demanded he marry them. Bernie had been so nervous he blundered into his joke that if Elsie married him she couldn't testify against him in court. Elsie had flashed him a stern warning look, and to Oliver's surprise cocky Bernie went quiet as a lamb. Oliver had asked about baptism and confirmation and things they had never heard of, until their eager eyes glazed over. Finally Bernie leaned forward, desperate to get the upper hand of this wedding thing in Elsie's eyes, and said, "That's all very well, but oughtn't vicars to stop immorality in the parish? Unless you marry me and Elsie there'll be immorality every chance we get."

Elsie blushed but nodded defiantly.

Trying to keep a straight face Oliver thought, oh why not. Elsie was the only thing likely to keep the boy from a criminal career, and if he didn't marry them there was bound to be another illegitimate birth in the parish before long. The old saw "Strike while the iron was hot" crossed his mind. He bent church rules in every way these days, so he would bend a few more to marry them. When the bishop eventually heard of it there would be trouble, but the bishop had his hands full of more urgent matters at the moment, and Oliver was beginning to think too many church rules got in the way of Christianity.

The girls had pitched in to help Elsie. Wedding dresses couldn't be had on clothes coupons. "Even the War Office hasn't suggested a Utility Wedding Dress, darling!" said Frances. Alice, so active in clothing drives, recollected a lady welfare officer named Barbara Cartland had collected a supply of wedding dresses from her society friends that could be borrowed by service brides. Alice tracked them and sent off Elsie's measurements. The frosty reply came that the dresses were available only to girls in the military service, not the Land Army. Furious, Frances made a phone call to her father and threatened to ring every half hour of the day and night and tie up his line unless he did something. The admiral muttered he would see what he could do.

The day before the wedding a large cardboard box that had obviously been posted many times before arrived by special post. Tanni spread a sheet on the floor and she and Evangeline carefully cut the string, saving it for use later. They gasped as they unpacked an elegant white *peau de soie* dress and veil, done up in layers of tissue paper. "Worth," whispered Frances reverently, reading the label.

Wondering about the bride who had first worn it, Tanni made Elsie try it on at once. "It's a perfect fit except you're so short this hem must come up," she said. "Hold still while I pin it." She had already done the same with the negligee and peignoir set Frances had given her, which she, in turn, lent to Evangeline when Richard was on leave. The negligee and peignoir were now pressed and folded with a sprig of lavender in a smart overnight case lent by Frances, waiting for the weekend's honeymoon in Eastbourne.

On the afternoon of the wedding Albert Hawthorne, who was to give Elsie away, was waiting for the girls in the shade of the laurels at Glebe House. "You can do with the practice," Nell had said briskly. "Someday Margaret Rose will be wanting you to do the same for her." She brushed his best black suit and polished his shoes until they shone like patent leather. Albert took out the gold pocket watch his grandfather had received for seventy years' service as stationmaster in Crowmarsh Priors and, with a sense of ceremony, draped the chain across his waistcoat. Might as well do the thing properly.

He arrived well on time and waited and waited, then began to shift from foot to foot. What the blazes could the girls be doing? If the trains ran late as weddings the whole country would grind to a halt.

Inside, Tanni and Alice and Frances, who had afternoon leave from the farm, fussed around Elsie, removing pin curls from her hair and draping a towel round her shoulders while they powdered her face. Elsie was almost shivering with excitement and her eyes sparkled. Evangeline, looking lovely in a drop-waisted 1920s frock she had found in the attic, chased the four older children to give their hair a final brush. At five months pregnant and already large in her maternity smocks, Tanni had tried to beg off being one of the bridesmaids, but Elsie wasn't having it: she insisted she needed all her best friends to stand up with her, so Tanni wore an everyday pink cotton smock, freshly laundered and with a lace collar made from an antimacassar tacked on. She said she would probably have to hold Anna so she wouldn't scream, and Elsie responded, "The more bridesmaids the merrier," so Tanni had dressed Anna like a miniature bridesmaid in a pink smocked frock with her little bit of dark hair brushed up and tied in a large pink bow on top of her head. Barely able to sit up without wobbling, she was resplendent in Richard's old pram, decorated with a spray of honeysuckle and white ribbon. She nibbled her bare toes, watching the proceedings solemnly.

"Stand up and let us slip the dress over your head, slowly does it." There was a rustle of material and a swishing sound as folds were patted into place. "Hold still…there! That's the buttons done! Now the veil. No, pin it here. And here." They fussed and turned Elsie this way and that.

"You can look now," said Alice finally, leading Elsie to the full-length mirror in the hall.

Elsie caught her breath. Agnes and the twins would have been gob smacked, and as for Mum—whatever would she have said! Born on North Street, behind the glue factory—now look at her! Grand as grand could be—all silk and lace, a train that dragged behind like she was a queen, four bridesmaids, and even Johnny dressed up as a little pageboy to hold the ring on a pillow until it was time for Bernie to put it on Elsie's finger. The pageboy had been Alice's idea. And all this grandeur went hand in hand with being a lawfully wedded wife! And she was about to be properly married in a proper church! Given away! She didn't even understand what was going to happen, even though the others had explained it all, as if they went to weddings every day of the week. Her stomach fluttered nervously. Like Bernie, Elsie had never actually been to a wedding, just seen the pictures in the papers. But one thing was certain—it was respectable.

There was even a wedding cake for after. It was a surprise to Elsie to learn you needed a cake on top of a dress and everything else. The girls had pooled their month's sugar and butter rations and in the larder was a small wedding cake Evangeline had made, decorated with real roses that she had brushed with egg white and sprinkled with sugar. And Bernie had some bottles of champagne that the toffs had given him. So he said. Today, Elsie wasn't going to ask.

Elsie's engagement ring winked encouragingly on her finger.

"We ought to go before this lot get dirty again," said Evangeline, marshalling the overexcited children who were chasing each other round the garden and pulling up Johnny's pageboy socks again. "Don't want Bernie thinking you've changed your mind."

The bridesmaids put on straw hats trimmed with fresh flowers and bits of ribbon. They had bare tan legs, but had carefully painted a seam up the back of each other's calves with a piece of burnt cork. They gave each other a last-minute inspection to make sure their "seams" were straight.

"Ready."

"The bouquets!" exclaimed Frances, running back to the scullery for five small posies of roses and Queen Anne's lace stuck in jam jars of water. "Here," said Alice wistfully to Elsie, who looked like an overexcited child, "loop the train over your arm, like this, while you walk to the church."

They walked outside, and Albert offered his arm to the bride. Clutching it with the hand holding her flowers and her train in the other, Elsie looked up at him, and her smile suddenly went wobbly and tears brimmed in her eyes. "Thinkin' about me mum, ain't I? Wish she could see me," she sniffed, "she wouldn't 'arf be proud."

Albert blessed Nell for the extra clean handkerchief she'd known he would need. He handed it to Elsie. She dabbed her eyes, blew her nose, and returned it. "Fanks. Don't want me intended to see me comin' down the aisle with red eyes, do I? There, I'm ready."

Afterward everyone agreed it was a shame there was a ban on ringing the old bell at St. Gabriel's when the happy couple came out of the church, but it had been a lovely wedding. Bernie said, "I will" several times more than he needed to, and in the wrong places but very earnestly. Oliver preached a wedding sermon about being in the midst of life at this time of rejoicing and, to impress the seriousness of the occasion on the bride and groom, who were whispering endearments, emphasized that the church regarded marriage as an indissoluble union. When he pronounced them man and wife and told Bernie he could kiss the bride, Elsie threw herself into Bernie's arms.

They all trooped across the green to the Gentlemen's Arms for the wedding breakfast. A grinning, relieved Bernie's hand was wrung by the men. Constable Barrows slapped him on the back and said, "Well done, lad!" and Harry Smith in his role as publican stood him a couple of brandies. Besides the bottles of champagne there were jugs of beer and shandy, lemon barley water for the children, and plates of sausage rolls, thin cucumber sandwiches with the crusts off, tinned salmon with salad, and a raised pie Evangeline had managed that was mostly vegetables but with enough hard-boiled egg for each slice to have a pretty yellow and white round in the middle. Fairy cakes had been contributed by Nell Hawthorne and Edith Barrows. Everyone cheered as Elsie, flushed with happiness, and Bernie cut the wedding cake and a tiny piece was handed round to each person with a glass of champagne.

Nell Hawthorne nudged Edith Barrows and looked significantly at Evangeline in her drop-waisted dress. Both women smiled. "You can always tell," said Nell. "A baby's the best thing that could have happened. It will take Richard's mind off things a little when he comes home. She's so good with all those children that aren't even hers!"

When the time came Elsie didn't want to throw her bouquet, but Nell Hawthorne said firmly now she was married it was only fair to give another girl a turn. "Like Alice Osbourne," she whispered purposefully. There must be *someone* for poor Alice. Nell turned Elsie and her train around until Elsie's back was to the guests. Just in time Nell spotted Margaret Rose preparing to spring forward and catch. Nell shook her head firmly, mouthing *"Don't you dare!"*

"Aww?" wheedled Margaret Rose.

"No," said Nell firmly. Margaret Rose sulked away. Making sure her daughter was out of range Nell ordered, "One, two, three, *throw!*"

Elsie pitched the flowers back high over her head and pivoted to see who the lucky girl was. "Oi, Frances, you caught it! You're next then!" she shouted gleefully. Frances looked quite startled, as if she hadn't intended to catch anything.

"Know who that'll be, don't we," she heard Albert Hawthorne say, winking at Nell and nodding in Hugo's direction.

Frances considered throwing the flowers back to Elsie.

"Better think of getting changed, you're off on the train soon," said Frances as the last of the sandwiches was eaten and the last toasts made.

"I hate to take the dress off—this has been the best day of me life!"

"Tanni's got your going-away outfit in the saloon bar. Harry says you can change there, everybody's outside in the sunshine. Come along, Mrs. Carpenter."

Elsie beamed. "*Mrs.!*" she whispered.

Albert Hawthorne confided to Nell that he was looking forward to getting home to a cup of tea and taking off his shoes. They pinched.

There was a little procession to the station to see Elsie and Bernie off. Albert led the way with the bride and groom, and the other girls followed clutching small paper parcels, the skirts of their summer frocks blowing in the breeze. The children scampered about, playing tag. When the train pulled in, it was crammed full of servicemen who leaned out the windows and cheered when Albert said, "Just married! Let the bride and groom on, lads!"

Tanni and Evangeline and Frances and Alice undid their parcels and threw flower petals over Elsie and Bernie as they got onto the train, and everyone was waving as it departed. Then Albert went on ahead, anxious for tea and his armchair, leaving the others to wander home more slowly, enjoying the warm evening and the sunset and the glow left by the wedding.

Behind the others, Alice ran back to the station platform and quickly stooped and gathered a handful of petals from the floor. She wrapped them in her handkerchief and stuffed it into her pocket. "For luck," she whispered. "Mine."

29.

Crowmarsh Priors,
August 1942

*A*fter their three-day honeymoon, Elsie and Bernie returned to Crowmarsh Priors to live at Glebe House. Housing was in short supply, with so many people bombed out, so a young couple had to take what they could get. Bernie was thrilled by the idea of living anywhere so grand, and neither of them fancied being squeezed in with another family. With Bernie away so often, Elsie thought it would be nice to have Frances for company.

But soon after, workmen finally arrived to turn Glebe House into the long-promised convalescent home and from then on the place rang with hammering, sawing, and welding. "Soon have it done," the foreman told Evangeline, knowing she was calculating how long it would be before she could get her invalid husband back to the village. Frances, Elsie, and Bernie had to shift quarters. They were turned out of their bedrooms but told they could stay on in the huge attic, which was up a steep, narrow flight of stairs and no use to convalescents. Frances and Elsie began shifting Lady Marchmont's things stored there to clear space up there for their possessions and bedroom furniture.

In the middle of the commotion, Frances had been summoned away. "Bloody welfare committee!" she had groaned, putting down the telephone on a coded message. "Land Girls' morals are in tatters, thanks to American GIs with their nylons and Hershey bars. Committee headquarters are flooded with complaints from furious parents demanding we chaperone the girls more closely. Too tiresome, but I must go."

So Evangeline and Elsie were left to sort out the attic to accommodate a married couple and a single Land Girl. They piled Lady Marchmont's trunks and boxes in the middle as a kind of barrier wall and arranged two makeshift bedrooms at opposite ends under the eaves. "Still, it beats the hostel," said Evangeline, trying to shove a wardrobe into place as part of the barrier. "If you and Bernie take that end you'll have privacy behind this thing, a big window, and a nice view of the downs. He'll be surprised to find it all ready when he gets back—even if Frances is at the other end. I'm sure she'll put a pillow over her ears."

"Will you stop messin' about wiv that wardrobe, Evangeline, in your condition!" Elsie grabbed her friend's arms and sat her on a mattress.

Evangeline was wearing a smock now, which Tanni had made her. She patted her swelling belly. "It's starting to kick like mad. Richard felt it when I was at the hospital last week and actually gave a sort of laugh. I'm so glad I told him. The doctors were wrong to say I mustn't. It's made such a difference to how he feels...is it beginning to cloud over, do you think? It's supposed to rain." Evangeline was torn between happiness and anxiety. Who was the baby's father?

Elsie leaned out of the window. "Maybe. A bit. I 'ate all this waitin' about—months it's been, and two false alarms. Goin' all the way down that bleedin' tunnel and nobody there. Worryin' that we got no idea where the kiddies are, just know that they got away before the Germans came lookin' and shot the old people wot looked after them. Murderin' buggers. Wish we'd 'ear sommink, just whether or not they're, you know, still alive..."

"I wish we could think of somewhere better to keep them than a cold passage full of bat droppings while we wait for Bernie to bring a car." *And I wish I knew who my baby's father is.*

"Evangeline, that's nuffink compared to the rest of it!"

"I suppose not. It wouldn't be so bad if Tanni could see them, but Sister Tucker insists she has to stay in bed now until the baby comes. It seems cruel—those poor children won't understand what's happened, probably scared to death. Then up to London under a blanket and more strangers, but we can't risk anyone seeing them."

"At least Tanni'll know they're safe and she'll see them eventually. That's the main thing."

"Hello, are you up there?" Alice called from the bottom of the stairs. She sounded breathless.

Evangeline and Elsie looked down into the stairwell. "We're moving things, any news?"

Alice ran up the stairs. "The workmen are having their tea." She lowered her voice anyway. "Rachel just phoned. She's had another message the twins are on their way."

"Really? She's said that twice before and the messages were wrong."

"It's certain this time, the local Maquis took them from wherever they've been hidden all summer."

"They're right under the Germans' noses," fretted Evangeline. "We have to trust some pretty rough characters, and there's no certainty we can rely on them. The Resistance colonel Frances and I met in London was incredulous, then furious that we wanted them to bring two children across the channel. Asked did we take them for nannies? He refused point-blank until Frances showed him some of her jewelry, said she'd hand over more when the twins arrived. He changed his tune then, but warned that the men he knew would abandon the twins if there was any risk to themselves. He was plying Frances with champagne he'd bought under the counter, hoping she'd finally go upstairs with him, so she told him that was part of the bargain, once they brought the children, and that did the trick."

"Did he tell her how they planned to get the girls to the coast?"

"He wouldn't say much about how, it was clear he didn't like it. He called some of his friends over and his friends didn't like it either, said two children would jeopardize their operations and they'd have to drug the girls to keep them quiet. Frances didn't like the sound of that, but they were adamant that no one would risk being shot for the sake of two unimportant *enfants,* no matter what Frances was paying. If worst came to worst, if anyone betrayed them or even if they just got fed up, they would abandon the girls to the Germans and their prison camps."

"Maybe it isn't such a wonderful plan, after all," said Alice, who had had cold feet right from the start.

"It's the only plan if the alternative is leaving them to die in a German camp," snapped Evangeline.

Alice remained skeptical. "Do you guess these camps really exist? You never hear about them on the news. If they're as bad as Rachel says, you'd think someone would have noticed. Oh, I know, I know, Evangeline, we don't hear everything on the news. So we stand by and wait. Again! I don't know why we let Frances talk us into this."

"Of all times for Frances to go away!" grumbled Elsie. "What's she do on all them committees anyway? What Land Girl welfare! I ask you!"

"She expects to be home in a few days. Hope she's in time, because I can't go down the tunnel any longer and she can. If Frances isn't back, Elsie'll have to manage on her own."

There was an alarmed squawk of "Bloody 'ell!!"

"But we're ready as we'll ever be, aren't we?" said Evangeline, stretching her back, which ached. Her mind returned to the baby. If it was Laurent's there was a chance it would be quite fair-skinned, he was half white. Or more, because his mother had white blood too...

"Blankets, dry clothes, handkerchiefs, first aid kit, brandy for the boatmen, sandwiches, and a flask of cocoa." Alice went over the list again, although they knew it by heart.

"I fink we got everything except the sandwiches and the cocoa, and there's no sense in makin' them ahead. 'Ow's Tanni today?"

Tanni was trying to pretend she was fine, but it was clear to all of them she wasn't.

"Not too well. Sister Tucker didn't care for her color and is worried that her ankles are so swollen. Worry is bad for her, and naturally she's worried sick. Upset too that she can't see the twins." Evangeline chewed a fingernail. What if the baby looked white but had that telltale coppery hair?

"She'll be fine as soon as this is over."

"Evangeline, are you feeling all right?" asked Elsie. One minute her friend was glowing, the next she looked like she was in another world and didn't hear when you spoke to her. "Evangeline! Are you listening?"

"Fine. Why?" She was obsessively calculating for the millionth time when her last period had been.

Below in the front hall a door slammed and someone ran up the stairs. "Hello—anyone up there?"

"Frances! You're back early."

"Just in time, Frances! Rachel phoned, wait till you hear..." They all began to talk at once.

Frances knew she looked remarkably fit and tanned for someone who had been stuck in a London office with the old biddies of the Land Girl Welfare Committee. When Alice commented she said, "My Land Girl glow," and hoped it sounded plausible. In fact, she was fresh from parachute training at a Manchester airfield. Her practice jumps had been too thrilling for words and she had hoped that finally she would be sent to France. But to her dismay and annoyance Frances had been sent back to Crowmarsh Priors.

But there was one compensation: her mock exercise had become real. There had been a briefing at the training camp. Military Intelligence was redoubling its efforts to find "Manfred" on the south coast. Auxi agents in southern England were on red alert after a panicky report that two German airmen had escaped when their plane was shot down over Kent. One was believed to be a senior member of the SS, with orders to assassinate Churchill and the king. There had been similar alarms ever since the start of the war, which had proved false, but alarms could not be discounted when invasion remained a real possibility.

Military Intelligence had drawn up a comprehensive list of possible fifth columnists with real or suspected German connections or sympathies—anyone with whom German agents or spies might shelter. Its accuracy was doubtful—the list did not discriminate between those people known to have had pro-German, if not pro-Nazi sympathies before the war, or to have attended Oswald Mosley's rallies, and those, like Alice Osbourne's father, on the grounds he had twice travelled to Germany as a student and had drunk beer at the *Oktoberfest* among German students who had included several now prominent Nazis.

The little man who had interviewed Frances looked grim as he ordered her to step up surveillance in her area. "What we do know is that before the war, the country house set invited a mixed crowd for weekend house parties that included their Continental friends. We know some Nazis were among their guests, and these would have had an excellent opportunity to reconnoiter in the area, gather information that would be useful for a German invasion, photograph the area where the coastal defenses are now. You know the sort of thing, 'Walk before tea? Jolly splendid scenery on the coast—I think I'll take a few photographs, hobby of mine.' For now keep your eyes open for anything suspicious, and if there's nothing, eliminating suspects will save our time."

To Frances's chagrin, she had let slip that Hugo de Balfort had proposed to her and she had turned him down.

Her superiors had made a joke of it. "She'll probably marry him eventually—very suitable, though she complains he's been damned persistent, won't take no for an answer. May as well keep her watching Gracecourt. We'll be able to eliminate the de Balforts from the list right away and stop her pestering us to go to France."

Since the Auxis were stretched thin in the south, Frances was to extend her surveillance over a wider area, and her Land Girl Welfare Committee was the perfect cover. "Manfred's down there somewhere," the little man reminded them. "We need to comb the countryside."

Then, to Frances's alarm, they stopped joking about Hugo. The Old Man had suggested marrying him would provide her with the best cover of all. Frances's eyes took on the steely look her father knew so well. She would stay in Sussex but she would *not* marry Hugo. She could always divorce the man later, they said, placatingly. The Old Man did not like being thwarted.

The possibility she would be ordered to marry Hugo struck her as absurd at first. Then it forced her to recognize something else: she was in love with Oliver Hammet.

Frances knew that that no matter how much Oliver liked her—and he did like her, she could tell, very much indeed—and for all his breaking of minor rules of the church, he was a clergyman. She remembered the sermon he had preached at Elsie and Bernie's wedding about the permanence of the marriage bond. If she married Hugo it would put her beyond Oliver's reach forever. He would never accept that those whom God had joined together could be put asunder, except by death. He would feel bound to follow the Church's position on divorce, even if it broke his heart and hers. If she married Hugo she could never marry Oliver.

She wouldn't let the damned Germans and their war ruin her life that way!

The minute she was finished she grabbed her things and fled the training camp just as someone came with a message the Old Man wanted to see her...

Now, in the attic of Glebe House, when she should have been paying attention to Alice, Elsie, and Evangeline, who were all talking at once, she was listening fearfully for the telephone. She knew that when he learned she had gone, the Old Man was likely to roar an order at her down the line. How could she refuse a direct order?

"Frances! Are you listening?" Alice demanded. "Oliver wants to..."

Oliver!

Below in the hall the telephone shrilled. What could she do if it was the Old Man?

Oh, Oliver!

She felt trapped until a crazy idea occurred to her, and she knew that if she hesitated she would never act on it. She must go now, before she lost her nerve.

Alice had started for the stairs and the phone. "Don't bother, I'll get it," said Frances, racing past Alice. "Then I'm going out for a walk to clear my head."

"A *walk*? Now? But Frances, you've only just come in and we have to tell you—"

She wasn't listening. She threw a cardigan round her shoulders, ignored the telephone, and walked as fast as she could to the vicarage. Her knees felt weak and Frances, who was never normally at a loss for words, had no idea what she was going to say. She was terrified.

If she paused to knock, she might reconsider, so she didn't. "Oliver," she called, opening the door. "Oh, Oliver, please be at home, I so need to talk to you."

"Up here," he called from the study. "Be down in a jiffy."

But Frances was already running up the stairs. "I need you to do me the greatest favor in the world! You're the only one I can trust to help me."

She dashed into his study as he stood up behind his desk. "What can I do for you?"

For a minute as she looked into his steady brown eyes she couldn't say it. Then she thought about Hugo and the wedding night. "What if a person needed to get married very, very quickly? At once, even. Is there a special license?"

"Yes, the bishop can sort out an immediate license if necessary." A look of sadness crossed Oliver's face, and Frances rushed on: "I want to ask you something...a girl doesn't normally do this...but you might want to, and if you did want to it would have to be now, right away. Unless you do it soon it may be too late. It will save me from a great deal of misery and allow me to keep...doing something important, without losing...something that is also important And...and...if you think for a moment you don't want to you're too honest to... agree to..." Tears sprang to her eyes. "The thing is, would you trust me even if I couldn't tell you everything?"

Oliver wondered what on earth was upsetting her so. She was making no sense and she was almost crying, nothing like her usual insouciant self. "Frances, as long as it's legal I'd do anything you wanted." He came round the desk and stopped himself from putting his arms around her. Vicars mustn't do that with upset parishioners. Even if the vicar loves the parishioner more than life itself.

Frances gulped. She gazed up at him, her sapphire eyes wide, and blurted out, "Oh, it is legal, but it has to be kept secret."

"Very well. You know vicars are bound to keep the secrets entrusted to them, so I promise to keep any mysterious secret of yours, whatever it is."

"But you would have to trust *me*...and not ask me questions."

Oliver had no defenses left. "I'll trust you till the grave and beyond, if necessary. I'll do anything you ask of me. Anything. And never ask questions."

"Well, don't promise till you know what it is." She gathered her courage and blurted out her request. She held her breath. Immediately she wanted to take it back because she had probably ruined every hope. Oliver's face was transformed by disbelief. Then joy. "Do you want this? Truly?"

She nodded. "Yes, so much! But only if you..."

"Oh, Frances," he said, reaching out for her. "It's like being offered a miracle. If you only knew. Yes, a thousand times, yes."

Late the next day there was a knock on the Old Man's door. "Come in," he said, "and while you're at it, where in hell has Miss Falconleigh got to? Get her on the telephone at once. Sent for her yesterday but she'd flown."

The man who had entered was fidgeting. "Out with it!" barked the Old Man.

"It's Miss Falconleigh, sir."

"About time! Well, what about her? Gone to keep an eye on the de Balforts, has she?"

"Sir, yes, actually there's something else—"

"What is it, man? There's a war on in case you hadn't noticed and we've not got all day!"

"She's eloped, sir."

"Ha! Followed orders, married that Hugo fellow, has she! Excellent! Knew we could count on her!"

"Actually, no. It seems she's married the local parson. Ahem! Our Miss Falconleigh is now Mrs. Oliver Hammet. Most awkward, sir. Makes it impossible for her to marry Hugo de Balfort."

The Old Man expressed himself with fury and a great many expletives for the next fifteen minutes. When he was told that Mrs. Hammet had said the vicar agreed that their marriage should remain secret for the time being, he was not placated. Married or not, she should not carry on as before while awaiting her posting to France.

30.

Crowmarsh Priors, September 1942 and After

"**B**limey, wot you doin' ere?" demanded Elsie. She had returned to her and Bernie's part of the attic to find her sister unpacking a shabby suitcase. Agnes's things were strewn everywhere. "You're supposed to be in Yorkshire! Billeted."

Agnes looked up sulkily. She had gotten taller and her skirt and cardigan were several sizes too small. "Aren't you glad to see me?"

"'Course I am," said Elsie. "You're my sister. Look at you, taller than me!"

"Well, I'm fifteen now so I'm not billeted no more, am I? Them people in Yorkshire, they was caught, wasn't they? They just had me and the twins, but they was sendin' in billetin' forms to get the allowance for six evacuees. So the magistrates sent 'em to prison. Serves 'em right too."

"But—"

"Me and the twins was sent to another billet, but they was full to burstin' already and it was 'orrible. They told me where you was and that you was married an' all. 'No more billets for me,' I says. Twins aren't 'appy neither. Can I stay wiv you? This 'ouse must be bigger'n Buckin'am Palace, so there ought to be room for me and the boys."

"Well, I'll 'ave to see about the boys but...'course you can stay."

"Won't be for long. I'm thinkin' to take a factory job to keep meself. I met a lad at the station, when I changed trains in London, givin' out leaflets about the Russians and the eastern front. We got talkin' an' 'e showed me where to get me ticket and I 'elped 'im wiv the leaflet things for a bit, waitin' for my train. 'E says nuffink easier than gettin' a factory job in London, and if I've been up in Yorkshire it'll do me good to be wiv workers and comrades in London, where that 'urban prole...prole...oh urban wossname' is."

"Agnes, you got to be more careful! You mustn't go takin' up wiv every strange Tom, Dick, an' 'Arry in the station!"

"'Is name's Ted." Agnes scowled defiantly. "An' I'll speak to whom I please!"

All of a sudden Elsie felt much older, more like Mum than she would have thought possible. She sighed. "We'll make you a bed on the floor 'ere in our room for the time bein'. Rest of the house is requisitioned. They're turnin' us into convalescent 'ome, for the wounded. Can't 'ear yourself think for the poundin'," she said as the workmen resumed hammering somewhere in the house. She gathered up Agnes's things. "'Spect you'll be wantin' a barf."

"But it's only Tuesday!" exclaimed Agnes, who bathed only on Saturday night.

"That's all right," said Elsie grandly.

"La-di-dah!" muttered Agnes under her breath. "A barf on Tuesday! Don't mind if I do."

Next morning Agnes looked a bit brighter for a good night's sleep, being cleaner, and some clothes of Elsie's that were much nicer than her own, if a bit short still. She insisted on following Elsie when she went off to her rat catching and stuck close by until, exasperated, Elsie said she was going to get poisoned too unless she gave her a bit of room.

That night Agnes was there in the room when Bernie returned. He was not best pleased. "Can't you put 'er somewhere's else?" he muttered. "Ovverwise, how we s'posed to... you know..."

The next day Elsie went round the village, knocking on doors to see if anyone had a space for Agnes. The Barrowses offered their box room temporarily but not for long as Edith was expecting again. Agnes collected her things and went off grumpily, muttering "A copper! You're jokin'!"

"It'll 'ave to do for the time bein', Agnes. There's a war on."

As October approached the workmen completed a fire escape outside Frances's window in the attic. As Elsie and Bernie were wrapped up in each other they never noticed when she slipped out nights to join Oliver or that a visitor climbed up to her room when she was in. Even during the day she was often to be found wherever Oliver was. She said someone had to distract him from what had gone on in the churchyard.

Meanwhile Hugo had become very tiresome indeed, hanging around her during the day, inviting her to go for a drink at the pub, offering to give her lifts whenever he had one of the farm vehicles. One day when she refused, he cornered her in a barn and begged her again to marry him. He did not take her rejection kindly. A few days later he burst unexpectedly into Oliver's study and found her flushed and

Oliver distracted. Thereafter he found excuses frequently to call at the vicarage on Home Guard business.

"He suspects something," thought Frances, so next time Hugo invited her to have a drink with him she agreed, and even flirted a little, to throw him off the scent. It backfired. Hugo took this as encouragement to propose again, and this time he didn't trouble to hide his fury when she turned him down. He stared at her coldly and told her it was plain who his rival was.

"Rival? What on earth do you mean?" bluffed Frances.

"Oliver Hammet, of course."

"Really, Hugo, how likely am I to become a vicar's wife?" said Frances coldly, then stalked away.

Tanni was a bundle of nerves, hollow-eyed and jittery. Sister Tucker told her not to think of getting out of bed and not to pick up Johnny or Anna. Evangeline, who was getting bigger herself, had her hands full trying to cope with all of the children and was exhausted by the end of the day. When Alice came round one afternoon with Woolton pies and pallid turnip jam, she burst into tears. "What would we do without you, Alice?"

Alice patted her on the back. She had never got over her dislike of Evangeline, but it was her Christian duty to forgive.

Evangeline was too pregnant now to go hunting, but hungry as they were, no one could face whale meat or the indeterminate "poison mince" available at the butchers. Frances surprised them all by going out into the fields and coming back having snared some pigeons fat from harvest grain; Evangeline stuffed them with windfall apples and roasted them.

In fact, Frances realized her hunting expeditions were excellent cover and an excuse to roam with a weapon. Military Intelligence had narrowed the radius in southern England from which they believed Manfred's signals were being sent, and she was under orders to search country houses whose location near the coast made them a convenient hiding place for any Germans who slipped into the country. She had been issued an official firearm. "He's there somewhere. Keep looking," she was told.

Though she thought it was pointless to include Gracecourt and said so, her superiors disagreed. The Old Man's revenge, thought Frances crossly. But whenever Hugo was on Home Guard duty with Oliver, she broke in and made a methodical check of all the rooms and outbuildings, but found nothing. Afterward she hurried back to Glebe House, yawned ostentatiously for the benefit of Elsie and the sharp-eyed Agnes, and disappeared to her end of the attic. Then she would slip off to the vicarage or wait for Oliver creep up the fire escape steps to her. Their time together was so precious that they never wasted it sleeping. They were blissfully happy, if very tired.

"Darling, I look forward to the day when we can behave like a respectable old married couple," said Frances one night. "It'll be so lovely to get up and have breakfast together. I never imagined anything so simple could be something I'd look forward to. I can actually make tea and I can probably manage toast for you."

"Won't it? Vicars don't normally climb into their wives' bedrooms like thieves. Rather fun, this, though it is a bit short on sleep. The bishop would be horrified. I'm not sure being married is meant to be this...this jolly!"

"Bother the bishop!"

Twice she nearly had an awkward confrontation. One night in early October Hugo came back to Gracecourt unexpectedly and nearly caught her climbing out of the cellar. Hugo called, "Hullo? Anyone there?" several times. She flattened herself in the shrubbery, held her breath, and prayed Hugo didn't have a torch…that made her remember the upstairs bathroom and the airing cupboard in which she had found one. Perhaps she should check it next time.

A week later she was back. She had seen Hugo cycle off, so she climbed in through a back window and slipped upstairs. In the bathroom the gilt frames were gone and the airing cupboard door hung open. She crept closer and felt inside to see if the torch was still there. It had gone. Instead there was a radio set. Frances frowned, thinking what an odd place to keep it, then jumped as she heard the front door bang shut and Hugo call to his father that the meeting was postponed. She slipped down the back stairs and out through the window she had left open, and was creeping outside under Sir Leander's study window when a heated argument broke out.

"I tell you she is!" Leander was pounding the floor with his cane. "There's too much at stake. It's your job…persuade her! I've been in touch…they'll deal with Hammet, get him out of the way…"

Frances stopped thinking about the radio. It sounded like she and Oliver were in serious trouble. "They'll deal with Hammet" could only mean the bishop and the church authorities. Someone must have noticed the amount of time she and Oliver spent together and complained to the bishop that the vicar was having an affair with his parishioner.

Then there would be an almighty fuss about why they were keeping the marriage a secret, and Frances would have to think of a way to avoid revealing her Auxi status to everyone but especially to Oliver, who still didn't know.

Bloody hell!

Frances strained to hear Hugo's response, which was something like "Hold on, I've...something else they'll pay for." Frances wondered why the church would be paying Hugo for information, that seemed off a bit, but mainly she was worried about how to warn Oliver about the bishop without explaining how she knew.

Rachel rang and said she'd heard Tanni was expecting twins. Definitely, she said. She felt it in her bones. They ran in Tanni's family.

It was the signal they had been waiting for: it meant "tonight."

Alice took the message. She rushed her mother through tea and hurried back to the others. She found Frances had gone off on one of her rambles, Agnes was hovering around Elsie as usual, and Evangeline was lying down. She got up and helped Alice to cope with the children. They could have a bath holiday just this once, she said, as long as they went to bed early.

"Not unless we have a washin' holiday too!" demanded Tommy and Maude.

"Washing too," Evangeline agreed, too tired to chase them with a soapy cloth.

"An' no brushin' teef!"

To make matters worse, the previous night's Home Guard meeting at the village hall with two other local Home

Guard units had been postponed to tonight. They would be coming and going just across from the churchyard. The girls would have to be very careful that they weren't seen.

"Bloody 'ell! What'll I do about Agnes? She never goes back to the Barrowses' before bedtime," muttered Elsie to Bernie. At least he was home and could fetch the car he had hidden in a disused barn straightaway. That meant the girls could go straight to London while it was dark. By morning they would be safe.

First, though, they had to deal with Agnes. Elsie was desperate to give her the slip to collect blankets and make the flasks of cocoa.

"'Ere," said Bernie. "Give 'er these." He produced two little tablets.

"I can't poison me own sister!"

"It's not poison, it's sleepin' pills." Bernie looked sheepish. "I got some from…a man I know when Agnes was sleepin' in our room…"

Elsie kissed him, and when Agnes came in a few moments later, she gave her a large mug of cocoa, with the pills dissolved in it.

By nine o'clock Agnes was snoring, her head on the kitchen table. "Best get her upstairs," said Elsie. "You take 'er shoulders, I'll get 'er feet."

"Not our room again!" said Bernie.

"Look, if she's comfortable she'll sleep better. Stands to reason. Put 'er in our bed. We're not likely to need it tonight. And we can 'ardly carry her to the Barrowses, can we, like she was drunk or dead or somefink."

By nine thirty Agnes was tucked up in Elsie's attic bedroom, dead to the world. Bernie told Constable Barrows she hadn't been feeling well and Elsie wanted to look after her.

Then Elsie, Bernie, Alice, Evangeline, and Frances gathered in the churchyard. Bernie had hidden the car a mile down the lane behind a hedgerow. The Home Guard meeting had ended, and Hugo de Balfort was the last to leave, looking around him as he walked away. Then the village was quiet, tucked up behind its blackout curtains. It began to rain—a blessing.

They were all on edge. Alice kept checking her watch. Finally she said, "Low tide in two and a half hours. Frances, it's nearly time you and Elsie started down."

"Right."

"Blankets an' sandwiches and fings 'ere in this bundle."

"We don't know how long it'll take to get them back from the entrance. They may have been drugged and we'll have to carry them."

They tried not to think about what might be happening to the children as they got closer to safety. Alice had told them what the parish record said about how the smugglers towed contraband in barrels under the water. The idea of the twins lying drugged in the bottom of a boat dodging mines in the channel was bad enough, but if they had to be dragged under water...they might suffocate or drown, like unwanted kittens, if anything went wrong.

When it stopped raining, a nearly full moon was emerging from behind the heavy clouds as they unwound their ropes and checked their torches, emergency candles, and matches. "Oh, no!" The rope was tangled and had to be unwound. "I wonder if anyone can see us with this moon," Alice said.

"Everyone's probably asleep."

When Elsie checked the lever, the tomb slid easily open. "Glad this 'as got easier to shift. First time we tried it, it wouldn't 'ardly budge."

"Concentrate and keep calm," muttered Frances. "Damn this bloody rope!" She had told Oliver she could not see him tonight—it was one of those times when he had to trust her. In that case, he had said, smiling at her, he would get some sleep, he was exhausted. Frances hated to think of him sleeping alone.

Then, after twenty minutes of frantic picking at the knot in the rope in the darkness, unbelievably, they heard the drone of planes coming toward them from the channel.

"Oh, no! Oh, bloody hell!" said Frances. "They're coming straight over us."

They all looked up. "Keep your faces down so the light doesn't shine on them! Get down!" ordered Frances, and they flattened themselves in the shadow of the church waiting for the planes to pass overhead and hearing distant anti-aircraft fire from Brighton.

Closer and closer the planes came. A bomb fell on the downs, then another, and another. The earth shook. "Why're they dropping bombs on the downs? They normally fly on north!" The earth shuddered.

"I'll have to go back. Tanni and the children need to get down to the cellar and she'll never manage on her own." Evangeline ran off as fast as she could.

"Bernie, you get home with Elsie," Alice ordered. "Agnes will be terrified if she wakes up." Elsie and Bernie needed no urging and ran for Glebe House where Agnes was sleeping in the attic, the most dangerous place.

Alice watched them go. She knew she had to get home to her mother, so she didn't pause to think of the danger. With the ground shuddering beneath her feet and flashes all round her she sprinted for her bicycle hidden in the bushes and leaped onto it. She could be home and back within an hour.

Frances raced for the vicarage as the planes roared closer. "Oliver!" she screamed. "The shelter! Hurry!" But Oliver was already at the door, shouting, "Frances!" just as the first plane flew low overhead. He grabbed her and pulled her inside, then under the staircase just as the explosion knocked them off their feet and shattered the vicarage windows. "The church," said Oliver in disbelief, his arms tight round his wife. "Why are they bombing the church?"

On the floor Frances clung to him, burying her head in his shoulder. He held her tight, bracing her against another explosion. The ground shook violently as another bomb hit the churchyard. They heard glass shattering, and the bell pealed incongruously once as the tower crashed down. Masonry and gravestones were flung into the air and thudded back to earth.

The planes went as quickly as they had come. Frances and Oliver touched each other gingerly as they pulled themselves to their feet. "Close," Frances breathed. Both were shaking and stunned. The vicarage door was off its hinges, and there was plaster everywhere.

Outside they clutched each other as they gazed at the devastation.

The church was in flames. "The tower," gasped Oliver. He could hardly believe his eyes. Masonry and stones lay scattered and broken across the churchyard.

"Oh, no," said Frances, faintly, peering at the place where the knight's tomb had been. "Dear God, no!"

Oliver held her shoulders. "I hate to leave you, I know how shaken you are, my darling, but I must make sure no one in the village is injured or dying and needs me."

"Of course," said Frances faintly, sick at the thought that the old tunnel might not have been strong enough to have withstood the bombs. "Yes, go, darling. I'm a vicar's wife. I understand." As an Auxi with demolition training she understood all too well. But she had to be sure.

"Oh, Frances..."

"Go on!"

Oliver hugged her quickly and hurried off.

She made her way toward the flames. The knight's tomb was covered with rubble although most of the tower had collapsed onto the other side of the church, where a Victorian stone angel now lay on its face. Frances gritted her teeth and began to tug at chunks of masonry. She had to try to get to the children. Desperation lent her strength, and finally she managed to heave and lever the last of the heavy pieces off the tomb. The handle with the skull was still intact, but the top lay open.

She found the rope that they had untangled before the bombers went over. Then a torch. She tied the rope around herself and fixed the other end to the tomb. She tested it to make sure it would hold, then lowered herself down the narrow steps. She was used to the tunnel now and moved quickly, flashing the torch ahead, up and down the walls, checking for damage. There were intermittent showers of dust and earth, which she knew meant the tunnel was unstable. She swore softly and hurried on.

When she reached the alcove where the smugglers had left excise men to die, the torch beam picked up the small metal trunk from Evangeline's attic in which they had stashed an emergency supply of blankets, chocolate, candles, and matches. The light flickered and her torch went out.

She groped her way to the alcove opening and felt for the trunk, rummaged in it, and found a candle and the matches. Something scurried past her in the dark, and she imagined she could hear breathing. "Bloody hell," she muttered, but the thought the children might be stuck farther along left her no choice but to keep going.

The path sloped down now, but Frances realized something was wrong. Before, she had been able to hear the sea and feel the movement of fresh air at this point. But now... she could not hear the sea and there was no breeze. Sure enough, she soon saw that a pile of rocks blocked her way. It nearly reached the top of the passage, but she dug uselessly, shouting "Lili!" "Klara!" desperately over and over. The only answer was a rattling noise of small stones from overhead followed by an ominous trickle, then a cascade of dust. There was nothing she could do now but go back. High tide would soon fill the cave, seeping in over the barrier. She could hear the water now on the other side.

By the time she reached the stone steps she had no strength left to drag herself up. What were they going to say to Tanni? Clutching at straws, Frances decided to contact Rachel before they said anything. Their only hope was that tonight had been another false alarm. Holding the plaited rope she began to climb slowly up. Halfway up, she heard Elsie call her name.

Bernie leaned over to haul her up the last few steps, and Frances collapsed onto the ground. Far below in the tunnel they heard a rumble that all three knew meant it had collapsed. "Thanks, oh, Elsie, there was a landslide and I couldn't...they weren't...oh, God!" Frances started to cry. In the distance Constable Barrows was shouting something, and Elsie and Bernie left her to see what it was, and above all to keep him away from the tunnel. When Frances had pulled herself together and blown her nose, something occurred to her. She went home and rang the special number she had been given.

"There's something odd here, not sure what is going on exactly, but it might have to do with Manfred. I'll be there in the morning to explain," was all she said. Next day, before anyone else was up, Frances left a note she had to attend another Land Girl welfare meeting.

31.

Crowmarsh Priors, November–December 1942

*T*he ugly little Edwardian cottage at the top of the hill where Alice and her mother had lived was nearly empty. On a dismal November afternoon Alice was alone in the bare front bedroom where the blackout curtains hung limply, packing up the last of her mother's things. On the night that the Germans bombed St. Gabriel's, she had gotten home as fast as she could, but it had been too late. She had rushed into the dark, silent cottage, finding her mother in bed, covers pulled up to her chin, dead, her face frozen in a rictus of terror. What, indeed, would her father have said? Alice knew she would never forgive herself.

In shock, she had stumbled back to the front door and seen St. Gabriel's burning. The vestry, she mused, must have been a tinderbox of dry wood and vestments. The bomb had narrowly missed the vicarage, and Oliver might be... Then the full horror had struck her. She knew at once that the tunnel had collapsed.

For a long time afterward Alice had been numb. They all had. She continued teaching and with her war work but she had lost all sense of purpose. Now she emptied her mother's cupboard and drawers automatically, her progress slow. She kept having to stop because she was crying. Poor Mummy. Poor children.

But she had nearly finished. Into the last box she put a few mended nightdresses and two dressing gowns with frayed sateen cuffs, some seashells her parents had collected on their honeymoon, a half-empty tin of talcum powder, a collection of prayer books, a set of lace doilies. The feathered picture hat. As she tied up the box Alice thought that she, too, was fated to die alone in some dismal bedroom with just a few faded mementoes of a life even less momentous than her mother's had been.

She sat down on the bare mattress. She had hated leaving the vicarage because that had been her home, but now, looking around the bleak room, she felt nothing. She would be gone to London as soon as Christmas was over. Every time she passed poor shattered St. Gabriel's she remembered the happy hours she had spent there. Now it was gone, and Richard lay injured in a London hospital. It was time to leave Crowmarsh Priors.

Penelope, with her endless list of contacts, had been a brick, getting Alice work with the WVS and finding her lodging with two elderly sisters who had a spare room at the top of their house in Connaught Square. She had even come up with a replacement teacher for the infants' school, a middle-aged woman who had taught before her marriage. She had been widowed in an air raid—the same night Alice's mother had died and many other people, Alice had learned. Penelope, who never complained, had been shaken enough to tell Alice that she had had a narrow escape. The sirens had blared and there had been a horrible accident at the East End Underground station where she was on duty. The police had tried to force too many people in. A great many people had been killed in the crush, though Alice wouldn't see anything about it in the papers: the authorities didn't want the incident reported lest it stop people going to the shelters.

Alice wondered how the world could hold so much sadness.

As Tanni had lain in bed worrying about Lili and Klara, she had been frantic when the first bombs dropped on the downs. But as the planes came closer she forgot everything but the need to get five sleepy children down to the cellar. In her panic she had picked up both Anna and Johnny. By the time Evangeline had gotten back, Tanni was in labor. Sister Tucker had come as soon as she could, but it was too late. Tanni had given birth to another little girl, who had cried once and died in her mother's arms. Sister Tucker gently took the little corpse from her and said she was sorry. Tanni did not seem to take in the sad news. She did not cry or show any emotion. Sister Tucker made Tanni as comfortable as she could and said shock could do that to a person, that sometimes people blotted terrible things out of their memory altogether.

Next morning, with Tanni still alarmingly unresponsive, Evangeline tried frantically to contact Rachel and the Cohens in London to tell them about Tanni, the baby, and the bombs, but when at last she managed to get through, the telephone operator said there had been heavy bombing in the East End again, and many exchanges were out of order.

She also wanted to contact Bruno, but only Tanni knew his whereabouts and she was drifting in and out of a stupefied sleep and didn't seem to know anything. An overworked Sister Tucker had been called away on other emergencies and Frances was gone, leaving Alice, Elsie, and Evangeline helpless and frightened.

Ashen-faced, they tried to decide what ought to be done about the baby, whose tiny body lay wrapped in a linen napkin in the cold dining room. "We have to do something."

Finally at dusk, they gathered by Tanni's bed, and Evangeline bent over her and said gently, "Tanni, darling, we're all so sorry, but we have to bury the poor little baby. I know this is hard, but you need to tell us, if you can, if there is anything special we need to do for a Jewish baby. Does she have a name? Constable Barrows offered to make a coffin and a little marker for her grave."

"What baby?" Tanni had whispered. Then Tanni just lay staring at the ceiling, her lips moving silently. She refused to eat or say anything else, either to them or to Sister Tucker, who had called, gray with fatigue, to check on her. There was no question of Tanni getting up for the burial, Sister Tucker said. She gulped down a cup of tea and told them they would have to manage as best they could.

The next day passed and there was still no response from the Cohens. Finally Evangeline went to the vicarage and told Oliver the baby had to be buried even if they couldn't get in touch with Bruno, and did he know if there were special rites?

Oliver rang the bishop, who promised to try to contact a rabbi. He found one in Portsmouth, which had been bombed, so the rabbi had his hands full there. He would try to come to Crowmarsh Priors, he said, but with petrol rationing and the uncertain bus service it might be some time. The only other thing he could report was that the rabbi had said that a Jewish burial should take place within twenty-four hours of death. The bishop told Oliver he was sorry but that as it wasn't the child of Christian parents he didn't think there was anything Oliver could do. Angry for once, Oliver slammed down the telephone.

"What should we do?" the girls asked each other wearily as the afternoon waned. They trooped back to Tanni's bedside. "Tanni, we thought we'd bury her in the far corner of the garden, where there are still some rosebushes and that funny old sundial. Darling, can you just say if you agree?"

Tanni remained silent.

There was still no word from Bruno, Rachel, or the Cohens.

"How much longer can we wait?" they asked each other as it grew dark. "The burial is supposed to take place within twenty-four hours and already it's past that."

"We must give the poor child a name," said Alice. "We can't just bury her without one."

"What about 'Rebecca'?" suggested Evangeline.

The next morning in the cold dawn light, just a little over forty-eight hours after Rebecca Zayman's birth, Alice, Evangeline, Elsie, Bernie, Oliver, Agnes, the Barrowses, and the Hawthornes stood round her small grave as it was filled in. Constable Barrows stepped forward, bent down, and placed a smooth stone with "Rebecca Zayman, 28th September 1942" painted on it. Oliver recited the Twenty-third Psalm and asked them all to pray silently for Tanni and Bruno. Tears rolled down the women's faces. Oliver bowed his head, heavyhearted with longing for Frances.

Oliver had tried desperately to track down Bruno but met a stone wall of bureaucracy. All anyone would say was that he was "unavailable." Five days later, when he finally reached him, Bruno said he would come at once and arrived within hours. He hurried to Tanni's room, then spent more than an hour at the end of the garden. He came back with red-rimmed eyes and said that, in the circumstances, he had no choice but to take Tanni to a sanatorium until she was better. There was a place close to where he was based, so he could visit her often.

Evangeline helped him dress her. She had packed some of Tanni's things into the old carpetbag and was about to ask if Anna and Johnny might go to the Cohens for a few weeks when her own baby was born, but Bruno pulled her out of Tanni's room and told her some grim news. The Cohens, Rachel, and her husband and two children had been killed in an accident at an air raid shelter, when the police had forced too many people too quickly down the stairs, the crowd had panicked, and people had been crushed to death.

"Oh, Bruno, how awful!" said Evangeline, realizing it must be the same incident Penelope had witnessed. She said nothing about Johnny and Anna, though she wondered how on earth she was going to manage five children and a newborn baby. And she certainly couldn't add to Bruno's problems by telling him what she thought had happened to Lili and Klara.

The girls hugged an unresponsive Tanni good-bye. "Get better, darling," whispered Evangeline. Then Bruno put his arm round his wife and steered her into the car. They waved sadly as the car with Tanni and Bruno pulled away.

At long last the doctors told Evangeline that Richard could be moved to Glebe House now that it was ready. His condition had improved a little: most of the bandages were off, and he had surprised them by regaining sight in one eye. When he arrived, Hugo came to see him. Richard was in a wheelchair now, and when Evangeline wheeled him into the visiting area, he reached forward to shake hands. Hugo seemed taken aback.

"I say, old chap...lost for words, really." They chatted awkwardly for a quarter of an hour, then Hugo looked at his watch, muttered something about the Home Guard, and left. Next day he sent word he and his father were both in bed with chills and unable to visit anyone for the moment.

Richard had made an effort for his visitor, but talking tired him. The only person he responded to was Evangeline, and he loved to feel the baby move inside her. The doctors told her it was a stroke of luck that Crowmarsh Priors had its own convalescent home. His nerves were still mending and in no state to cope with a noisy houseful of children, but in time...well, they would have to see.

Elsie looked after the children while Evangeline was with Richard, but much of the time Evangeline had to manage on her own. She was busier than ever now there was her baby to prepare for and no Tanni. It was due the first week in January, and Evangeline hoped that, after the birth, she and Richard could make a fresh start. Somehow.

Before she knew it, it was nearly Christmas and she was late getting the winter cabbage in, utterly necessary if they were to have enough to eat. She dug ferociously in the garden, wearing an ancient pair of trousers that, in happier days, Tanni had altered with laces on the sides to make room for Evangeline's expanding belly. She swung her spade and felt a warm trickle as her water broke.

That afternoon Sister Tucker arrived, and she sent Tommy and Maude running to fetch Alice after school. Sister Tucker said someone had to let Richard know, but Alice snapped that Elsie could do it.

Evangeline was in labor for two days and fought the contractions, terrified by what might happen if the baby were born with Negro features or coloring. Eventually, however, she gave birth to a son. She lay still, pale, exhausted, and frightened, while Sister Tucker bustled efficiently then handed her a tightly wrapped bundle. "We're a few weeks early, Mummy, but we're very well all the same," she chirruped.

Evangeline hardly dared look, but when she did, the baby's eyes were blue, and his hair, of which there was a great deal, was brown. A tiny pink mouth opened in a yawn, which quickly turned into a howl. Evangeline too began to cry—with joy and relief. She was sure he wasn't Laurent's. "There, there," said Sister Tucker, "all over now and he's lovely. Have you thought what to name him?"

"Please...will you tell Richard?" murmured Evangeline, "and I would like to call him Andrew. I had a brother named Andre..."

"That's the first anyone's heard of any brovver!" Elsie remarked when she heard.

When Frances returned, she, Elsie, and even Alice took it in turns to sit with Evangeline, who, like all new mothers, was expected to stay in bed for at least a fortnight. Nell Hawthorne brought some broth and plumped her pillows and cooed over the baby, while Edith Barrows had made her custard and jelly from her own mother's recipe to "get Evangeline's strength up." "It's like we're repopulating the village!" Edith said, patting her own large bump.

While Evangeline was recovering, Elsie made Agnes help with the scrubbing, the laundry, and minding the children while a resentful Agnes complained bitterly that Elsie had turned into a right bossy boots.

The one topic the four young women avoided was Lili and Klara Joseph, but they had a permanent reminder of what must have happened in the shell of the church: the remains of the tower stood open to the sky, surrounded by masonry, broken glass, smashed wooden pews, and roof slates. The impact had wrecked many graves, so headstones and marble slabs mingled with the other debris. The knight's tomb was still in its place, but had sunk almost out of sight. There was no way now to reach the entrance. The only faint hope was that the boat bringing the little girls had not reached the cave as expected, though with mines and military sea patrols, the possible reasons why didn't bear thinking about. But if there was some other reason and the girls weren't dead, where could they be now?

Frances said that they could try the Free French to see if anyone in their network of contacts might know. But at the moment neither she nor Evangeline could go to London.

Christmas brought two visitors, of whom one was Penelope: she wanted to spend time with Richard and admire her grandson. The other was a gangly lad with acne who slouched off the train. "It's Ted!" exclaimed Agnes, joyfully. "I wrote to 'im, didn't I? Told 'im where I was," she informed Elsie. She was living with Elsie and Bernie again because the Barrowses' baby was due any minute. As Frances was often away, Agnes could sleep on her side of the attic.

When Ted arrived he established himself in the garden shed at Glebe House, almost before anyone realized he had done so. In return for a camp bed and a spirit lamp he helped Evangeline with the gardening and odd jobs, talking nonstop. He wanted them all to become socialists. The longer he stayed, the more convinced Elsie was that Ted had driven his family mad with his politics and they had thrown him out. He lectured and hectored everyone: Oliver about religion being the opium of the masses, Albert about solidarity with the working class, Frances and Evangeline about suppressing the workers and imperialism, and Alice about social revolution and why the Church was a bourgeois tool of oppression.

When he harangued Bernie about the inherent flaws in the capitalist system, Bernie snapped, "'E's drivin' me round the bleedin' twist! Woss 'appened to me peace and quiet, eh? Like a bleedin' circus round 'ere. We get married so's we can be togevver, then Agnes is 'angin' around in the room wiv us, an' now we got bleedin' Ted! Either 'e goes or I break 'is jaw to shut 'im up."

"Bernie, I got to keep an eye on Agnes. Ted's always goin' on at 'er about free love—I 'eard 'im—next fing you know, she'll be in trouble an' 'e's not the marryin' kind. Where'll she be then? I'll tell you where, back wiv us wiv a flippin' baby! I owe it to Mum to look after 'er. Blood's ficker than water."

"Glad I never 'ad no bleedin' family!"

"Bernard Carpenter! You 'ave so got a family! You got me, 'aven't you?" Elsie put her arms round Bernie's neck. "Always will too, if you know what's good for you." He relented and gave her a kiss. It was hardly the perfect moment for her to tell him that he was, in fact, about to have more family than he expected. She had had a letter from the people who had taken in her brothers: they had had a fire, so they and seven children were now living on top of each other in a neighboring family's tiny two-up, two-down cottage, the only accommodation available at the moment. Since Elsie was now a married woman they were sending the boys to her.

She put off telling Bernie as long as she could, which wasn't long because she discovered the boys were due to arrive on the weekend train. "At least you'll be together for Christmas," wrote the woman whose house had burned down. Elsie groaned.

"Wot we need," she told Bernie, when she finally confessed that the boys were on their way, "is a 'ouse of our own. And for once, I don't care how you get it if so long's we can all be togevver."

"Only on condition that Ted don't come too," said Bernie firmly.

And he did find them a house, which was a miracle with housing in such short supply. It was at the end of a once-genteel terrace in Eastbourne. Shabby and near-derelict, it nevertheless had a number of bedrooms, a double drawing room, and bells everywhere for summoning a now nonexistent maid. It had an odd assortment of furniture left behind by the previous owners, who had had an overwhelming fondness for red velvet, chandeliers, mirrors, and brightly patterned carpets. "Blimey, it's a palace, innit, velvet curtains an' all!" exclaimed Elsie, gazing at Bernie in wonder. "However did you find it? No, don't tell me!"

So Bernie didn't tell Elsie it had been a brothel Uncle had owned. On his shady solicitor's advice Uncle had registered the title to the property in the name of Bernard Carpenter, who, unbeknownst to the land registry, had been a child at the time. Shortly before Uncle went to prison, he told Bernie what he had done, knowing the boy was too much in awe of him to ever try to deprive him of this property. Now, though, Uncle had died, and the former inhabitants had moved on to greener pastures in London. Bernie reasoned it hadn't been requisitioned because the authorities didn't like requisitioning brothels, so it must be his to move into.

Agnes balked at going to Eastbourne, insisting that she would stay on in Elsie and Bernie's room at the top of Glebe House. But Elsie wasn't going to leave her alone with Ted. She obtained a transfer to rat catching in Eastbourne with Agnes as her assistant.

"I'll miss you," said Evangeline sadly, "'specially with Alice leaving too and Frances away so much."

"I know, I hate to fink of goin', but what else can we do? I owe it to Mum to look after the boys and Agnes."

After Christmas Evangeline and Alice waved Elsie, Bernie, Agnes, Dick, and Willie off to their new home. Before long Ted appeared in Eastbourne, much to Bernie's annoyance, and stayed.

The day after the planes bombed Crowmarsh Priors, uncertain whether she should have mentioned it earlier, Frances went up to London, sought out the little man, and asked his advice. She hadn't thought anything of it at the time, but she had found a radio in the airing cupboard at Gracecourt after having lunch with Leander a year earlier, which might or might not be odd. And she was being hounded by Hugo who was increasingly persistent with his marriage proposals. She had begun to think him deranged. No sooner had he accused Oliver of being his rival than Frances had overheard him telling Leander that "they would deal with Hammet." She had thought Hugo had meant the church authorities would discipline Oliver for having an affair with a parishioner, but could he have gotten wind of her marriage? She thought it unlikely, because Hugo had seemed merely jealous, but then the church was bombed, a most peculiar target, surely...there was no point in their bombing an isolated church and a few hills.

"Hmmm. Perhaps Hugo is just madly in love with you," said the little man.

"No, he isn't. That's what makes it odd. Men have been in love with me before—you needn't raise your eyebrows, most girls have had men in love with them at some point—and men in love don't behave in this, this intense, unpleasant way. Hugo is practically snarling his proposals. Something is decidedly 'off' with him."

The little man said they mustn't jump to conclusions, but now she must watch Gracecourt and both de Balforts as closely as she could. If Frances was right, it wouldn't be only the de Balforts who were involved, and she mustn't give the game away before they could spread a net to catch everyone. "And Frances," he warned as they parted, "never forget for a minute how dangerous collaborators are. They have everything to lose."

Frances stayed in the village for Christmas instead of going to her father. She disappeared on long rambles into the country and came back with pheasants, rabbits, and even a small roe deer once. Poaching provided her best alibi. In training they were told that when they had to lie, they should stick to the truth as far as possible.

Alice had been ordered to report for duty in London early in the New Year. On New Year's Eve, after the children were asleep, she came to say good-bye to Evangeline and Frances. She was wearing her new WVS uniform for the first time. She had lost weight and the uniform's skimpy skirt showed off her slim figure and long legs. Its tailored style suited her. She had made an effort for the first time in months, manicuring and buffing her nails, applying lipstick—a going-away present from Elsie—and under the jaunty WVS cap, her hair was arranged in the victory roll she had finally perfected. She looked a different person: efficient and capable but unexpectedly glamorous, like a forces' pinup in uniform.

Over the last bottle of wine from Lady Marchmont's store she and Frances and Evangeline chatted. Frances had been devoting her few spare moments to help Oliver at the makeshift chapel Oliver had arranged in the vicarage dining room so the village had a place to worship. "So good of you, Frances," Alice remarked.

Frances made a self-deprecating face. "You were always the mainstay of St. Gabriel's, and someone's got to help Oliver keep the parish together when you're gone," she told Alice.

Evangeline stared at her. She thought Frances was a most unlikely candidate to fill Alice's shoes, but she and

Oliver always seemed to be together now, and when they weren't, each was looking for the other. Odd.

"Anyway, darling, since you're leaving us, I've a little present for you." Frances changed the subject. "You never know what might happen or who you'll meet in London. If the right man comes along, I daresay you'll need this." She handed Alice the crocodile dressing case Albert had seen her holding on the station platform the day she arrived in Crowmarsh Priors.

"Oh, *Frances...*" breathed Alice. She stroked it and then opened the catch. It was the most exquisite thing she had ever seen, let alone owned. Inside it was beautifully fitted in silver and mother-of-pearl, with a brush and comb, a manicure set, a sewing kit, a crystal powder bowl with its own large puff, holders for three lipsticks, and two Lalique scent bottles, each half-filled with Vol de Nuit. There was a mother-of-pearl-handled toothbrush, a little box for tooth powder, a padded drawer for jewelry, and a clean handkerchief edged with lace. In the back a mirror swivelled out on a clever little hinge. "Oh, Frances—I've never owned anything so pretty!" she said. "When I die they'll find it and say I—that I...had...a friend..."

"Let's not be morbid, darling. No tears! Something in my bones tells me you're going to meet a wonderful man soon and you'll need this for a wedding trip. Promise to write and tell us all about it when it happens."

After she had gone, Evangeline and Frances finished the wine and gazed into the fire. "You and Oliver," said Evangeline after a while, "you're in love with him, aren't you?"

When you have to lie, stick as close to the truth as you can. "Yes," Frances said. "I know what you're thinking, that it doesn't make sense, but, Evangeline...no one must know. It must be a secret for now. Please, say nothing."

"I can keep a secret," said Evangeline. "You've no idea."

"If you're my friend, keep it, and please, don't ask me anything else. But if anything ever happens to me—a bomb falls on me or something—promise you'll look after him. He's got, I mean, he let drop, he's got some sort of heart condition, it doesn't show, but he does."

"Promise."

"Feels like this war's gone on forever, doesn't it?"

32.

West London, August 1944

*A*lice had struggled all day to get a grip on herself, but felt she had lost the battle. That morning she had gotten out on the wrong side of bed to find a
gray, damp day, unseasonably cold. She hadn't been able to
concentrate properly, as if the atmosphere oppressed and
smothered her every thought and movement. She felt irri-
table and longed to be somewhere that wasn't cold, dark,
dirty, and dangerous. Somewhere the sun was shining and
she could have a proper bath instead of a hasty wash from a
tap in a bathroom with a broken window.

Now the day was nearly over—no doubt to be followed
by another equally dreary tomorrow. She concentrated on
arranging biscuits in neat circles on a cracked platter. She
straightened the teacups, waited for the tea urn to bubble,
and wondered why she had volunteered again to play hostess for another church social when she hated them—especially when she was exhausted and would rather be in bed.
Never again, she promised herself.

Suddenly one of the dreaded V2 rockets whooped over
the church. The ominous sound drowned the gramophone,
the chatter stopped, and everyone in the hall froze. There

had been no warning sirens and no time to run for the air raid shelter. You were all right as long as you could hear the noise. It was when you couldn't that it was dangerous, because that meant you were directly beneath it.

"Under the tables, everyone!" Alice shouted just as they heard it hit. Another followed and fell close by, probably intended for Paddington Station. The third whoop stopped suddenly, and the rocket brought down half the ceiling with a thud and put out the lights. Alice crouched, eyes shut tight and seeing again the little boy lying dead in the street yesterday after a direct hit. She had picked him up and asked the neighbors, dazed survivors, who he was. Nobody knew. She had kept a stiff upper lip, of course: she had tucked the little corpse into an ambulance, then got on with directing stunned people who no longer had homes to temporary shelters and hot food.

When the raid finally ended the church hall was full of fragmented plaster, broken glass, and people asking each other if they were all right. Someone produced a torch. The urn lay in a puddle on its side, surrounded by broken cups. The blackout curtain rails were askew across the broken windows, and they could see searchlight beams across the sky. "Extinguish that torch!" someone ordered, and the tiny gleam of light disappeared.

Alice felt limp and was choking and gasping for breath, throat gritty with dust. Somehow the tall American airman who had been talking to the vicar had an arm round her shoulders and was trying to help her up. But Alice wasn't sure she could stand. She felt so weak she wanted to collapse in a heap. Tears pricked her eyes. Mustn't cry, she told herself sternly. It would never do for the WVS to give way. They had to set an example and carry on. She was just tired, she muttered to the airman. They were all tired—Ellen, Judy, and the vicar too. Suddenly she realized how comforting it felt to have a man's arm round her in the dark. She was shaking.

"You're the first girl I met over here could quote the scriptures," he said in her ear.

From the number of very white teeth Alice could see in the gloom, she grasped he was smiling. He had an odd way of talking, as if he was in no particular hurry to say what he had to say. "I beg your pardon?" she said.

"You just said, 'Sufficient unto the day is the evil thereof.'"

"Did I?" Her colleague Ellen had warned her that she had been talking to herself. I am turning into an eccentric, bitter woman, like Mummy, she thought. The knowledge weighed her down like another wartime burden. "Well, those were rather close! Still, we must count ourselves lucky; remember that others are worse off." She had tried for a brisk tone—why had her voice wobbled? *Deep breaths, my girl. You've lasted this long,* she reminded herself.

"If those bombs had fallen any closer we are the ones that'd been a lot worse off. Ma'am," he said in that slow voice. The "ma'am" was respectful, but he had managed to keep his arm round her shoulders. It felt nice and strong. Weakly, Alice decided to let it stay for a minute, just until she stopped shaking and collected her thoughts. But she continued to shake.

The man put his other arm around her and held her tightly to him. "It's all right," he said. "You English are some-thin' else. That rocket scared the daylights out of me and

I'm in the air force. You're just a gal, and gals've got a right to be scared. I bet you been through this lots of times since the war started, and still here you are tryin' to act like everything's normal. It isn't, but it's all right now."

After a short time the shaking wore off and Alice began enjoying the warm, solid feel of the man close to her. Then she reminded herself that Americans had a shocking reputation; she shouldn't encourage advances. He was probably married anyway. First Richard, now this fellow...who seemed kind. They were all married. Alice sighed, fought back self-pity, and began to pick glass out of her hair. She sniffed, and something splattered onto her jacket.

"You're bleeding," said the airman. "Hold still." He took out his handkerchief and held it to her nose.

"It's only a nosebleed—I'm hardly a war casualty," she wanted to say briskly. Instead she quavered, "Thank you. Oh, no! I've bled all over the front of your uniform!" She wished the earth would open and swallow her, bloody nose and all. First the rockets, now this, on the first occasion she had talked to an attractive man in ages.

He was grinning now. "That's all right. Have a good cry if you want. Go ahead, I'm used to it. Women always feel better after a good cry, least that's what my sisters tell me. And I have five. Somebody's always crying, getting something out of her system. I'm Joe Lightfoot. US Air Force." He wetted his handkerchief in some of the spilled water from the tea urn and gave it to her. And you?"

"Oh. Yes." Sniff. "How do you do?" Sniff. Alice mopped at her face and eyes and dabbed at her nose. "I'm Alice Osbourne. Women's Volunteer Service. How long have you been in England?"

"Six months. I fly a bomber, missions over Germany, helped back up the invasion on D-day. Pretty busy. Had a weekend leave, so I decided I better see London. Boy, those trains are crowded. I got to London, and it's all so dark. I didn't know what to do until I stopped to ask directions and I saw the sign says y'all were havin' a social tonight and servicemen were welcome. Been watching you from across the room, moving around, organizin' things like you're in charge. This your church?"

"Sort of, now I'm in London. I help out sometimes." Watching her? Dismayed, Alice brushed hard at her uniform. She must look terrible. Perhaps it was a good thing the lights were blown out. Why, oh, why hadn't she remembered her lipstick? She hadn't had a bath in days. And why couldn't she think of anything to say? She fell back automatically onto a familiar topic. "My father came here as assistant vicar when he was first ordained. Then they gave him his own parish in the country where—"

"Your daddy was a what?"

"A vicar."

"So you're a preacher's daughter! Well, Alice, I come from a churchgoing family myself, where all the firstborn sons are named Joe. Officially I was baptized Joseph Lee Lightfoot the Fourth. Don't know what denomination this here church is, but my family's all Southern Baptist. You bein' a churchgoin' woman, I thought I better mention it and get that out of the way."

Alice had never heard of Southern Baptists. "Oh?" she said faintly.

"You feelin' better? Good, I'll keep talking. I come from the country too, a little town called Goshen, Georgia. 'Bout a hundred miles from Atlanta. You've heard of Atlanta, haven't you?"

She nodded. She had no idea where it might be on the map.

"My family've had a farm there since before the Civil War. Daddy's branched out a little, has him some stores that sell feed and hardware. Had about ten between Goshen and Atlanta by the time I shipped out. Wants me to come back and help him run the business, seein' I'm the only boy. Promised me two hundred acres to build my own house when I do."

What, Alice wondered, were "feed and hardware"? And how much land would you have to own to give away two hundred acres? Just for a house? What *could* America be like? "I'm rather hungry," she said. "I don't suppose any of the biscuits survived? I forgot to have lunch and I'm a bit light-headed. Usually I'm much calmer."

"I bet you are. Here, have a cookie. Less see, this plate looks the cleanest...shame it's too late to invite you to dinner, but the officers' club is closed by now and probably most of the restaurants. You live near here? I was thinking maybe we could have dinner tomorrow, if you're not busy, that is," Joe said. He handed her a plate of biscuits that were somewhat the worse for wear. Alice ate them anyway. They tasted dusty, but she didn't care: she was famished.

"They do some good steaks at the officers' club. Where do you live?"

Steaks? Alice almost fainted at the idea. Other than poison mince she hadn't seen beef in years. "Quite close to here," she said. "If the house is still standing, I'm billeted with two old ladies, who rather discourage callers." It occurred to Alice that she was nearly twenty-eight and, aside from her father and boarding school, had spent her whole life living with older women, starting with her mother. She was uncertain what to say next. Should she agree to have dinner with him? He seemed nice enough, but American servicemen were known to worm their way into a girl's good graces with charm, chocolate, and cigarettes. She didn't want to give him the wrong impression...but on the other hand, she didn't want to put him off either.

"They discourage callers," she said again, without conviction.

Joe chuckled. "That's OK. I know how old ladies are—real strict sometimes. Lotta old ladies in Goshen. I'll walk you home anyhow. They can't object to that when it's so dangerous out there. Besides," he said, taking her hand, "I need to know where to pick you up tomorrow so's we can have that dinner and I can see you in the light before my leave's over. Check that you're as pretty as you looked before the lights went out. Daddy says if a girl's pretty and knows her scriptures that pretty much covers all the bases."

What on earth was he talking about? What bases? Then Alice caught her breath. Pretty? She hoped her face at least was clean. Never mind the scriptures right now.

"Oh," she said, flustered. "But I-I really ought to help clear up..." Across the hall Judy and Ellen were sweeping up broken glass and sending her resentful looks.

"Aw, come on. Quick." He took her hand. "Bet you clear up all the time." He guided her outside firmly. She didn't protest: he was right, she did clear up most nights, and it was rather lovely to be rescued from it.

Outside the rockets had destroyed an office building and a clothing shop, while a block of flats nearby was in flames. The fire watch were shouting and the pavements were covered with rubble, bricks, and broken concrete, as well as slippery with water from the fire hoses. Alice tripped and half fell as she picked her way over broken masonry.

"Here, allow me," Joe said. The next thing she knew he had picked her up and was striding easily through the mess. She put her arms round his neck. What a night! After a minute she said, "You can put me down now, we're past the worst. This is my square. The old ladies live just there, on that far corner, next to the fish-and-chip shop."

He set her on her feet, but she was oddly reluctant to let go of him. "Fish and chips—that's like fried fish and french fries, isn't it? Will they be open? Everything looks kind of dark."

"I can smell them."

"Come on, then. You haven't eaten tonight, and I can't have you fainting on me."

Ten minutes later their hands were full of greasy newspaper and Joe was looking for a place to sit down. "Do you have to go in right away? Or can we sit here on this bench and eat before it gets cold?" he asked. "Will you be chilly?"

"No. I'll be fine," said Alice cautiously, listening to check for background noises. Behind the bench the dark square was a mass of trees and shrubbery that usually rustled with courting couples or prostitutes and their clients. Although Joe seemed nice—very nice, in fact—Alice was anxious not to give him "ideas." Wasn't she? Suddenly she was unsure. What would she do if he did get ideas?

They fell on their fish and chips. Joe had wanted something called ketchup, whatever that was, but Alice had liberally doused their fish and chips with vinegar and salt instead. "No ketchup," she said. Afterward she felt much better. Joe put his arm round her again and they sat for a while. Alice was relieved–still no noise from the undergrowth—the rocket, she guessed—and relaxed. She found herself smiling into the darkness. "What *is* ketchup?"

Joe laughed. "Tomato sauce." He pronounced it "tomayda." "I can't imagine life without ketchup. Everybody in America eats it!" He looked up. "There's a few stars out—not as many as back home, though. I miss the nightime noises, the dogs barkin' and the cattle, owls…crickets. You miss living in the country?"

"I didn't think I would, but I do. When my mother died I thought I couldn't wait to get away, find different war work. I was a teacher and wanted to feel more a part of things—do my bit in a more active way. Oh, I don't know what I wanted."

"Are you married?" Joe asked bluntly. "Or engaged or just in love with some fellow in the forces?"

"Oh! Well…" Oh, why beat about the bush! thought Alice. "No, I'm not married. I was supposed to be, but the man I was engaged to went to America and came back married to somebody else. A complete surprise and rather dreadful at the time. His mother fixed up my job with the WVS. And here I am."

"Lucky for me," said Joe. He tightened his arm round her shoulders. "Means I got to meet you. I wasn't sure if the reason you didn't say whether or not you'd have dinner with me tomorrow was because there was someone else. Just so you know right away," he said, leaning closer, "I'm not married either. But if this war made me realize one thing, it's that I'd like to be. Every time you go up in that plane you think, maybe this time I won't make it back. Lot of pilots haven't. I don't want to die without having been married or had a chance to leave a child of mine on earth. And where I come from the two go hand in hand. So when I found a long-legged, pretty churchgoin' gal, I thought to myself, maybe this is the Lord's way of sayin' 'Don't waste time, Joe, she's the one...'"

He had turned and his face was very close to hers. Alice wanted to say that this was all a bit quick for her, but something told her to be quiet, shut her eyes, and *don't move.* Joe kissed her—in a nice way that left room for her to pull away if she wanted to, yet it was still a kiss that meant business. Alice felt breathless and wondered if he would think she was a shameless hussy because, somehow, she couldn't stop kissing him back.

Hours later a tired air raid warden coming off duty passed the bench where Alice and Joe were sitting. He saw them nuzzling and laughing, holding hands, comfortable with each other, sweethearts, clearly. He saw the girl yawn and heard her say, "All right, eight tomorrow night. Now I really must go." But she didn't move.

The warden turned up his collar against the drizzle and smiled for the first time that day. Good luck to them, he thought, good luck to us all.

Three days later, on Monday, the telephone rang in the Fairfaxes' hall.

"Evangeline, I can't talk for long, but guess what? I'm getting married...Thank you. Next weekend...An American airman...Yes, it is rather sudden...from Georgia, I think it's called. I'm going to live there after the war. Do you know it? You must show me where it is on the map next time we see each other...Very happy indeed...What? What did you say happened? Can't quite hear you, Evangeline...Burned down last Sunday! Gracecourt? Not another bomb! Oh, his cook's fault...I bet she went off to her sister's and forgot things on the stove...Sir Leander dead! Oh, how dreadful, poor old man. And Hugo?...I see. Yes, I shall certainly write to him in hospital. Unbelievable. Be sure to tell Frances, won't you? I've tried and tried to phone but can't reach her...In London again? You haven't seen her since the fire?...Well, when you do, tell her she was right about the dressing case, I'm taking it on honeymoon and will think of her being right. Good-bye, Evangeline."

Alice rang off. More bloody bad news! She squared her shoulders. She couldn't *wait* to marry Joe and go to America. Her life was going to start all over again in a brave new world where they would go to the Southern Baptist church, people talked about "tomaydas," ate ketchup, and drank Coca-Cola. Joe was already asking what kind of a house she'd like and talking about Joe the Fifth. She had an engagement ring with a huge diamond flanked by two smaller ones that Joe had bought for her in Hatton Garden. She thought about her husband-to-be and smiled happily. She was pretty when she smiled.

33.

Crowmarsh Priors, 8 May 1995

here were jealous mutterings at Albion Television when Katie Hamilton-Jones was promoted overnight from lowly researcher to presenter of the *Heart of England VE Day Fiftieth Anniversary Special*. Unkind comments were made about the fact she was only a recent graduate, the shortness of her skirts, her long blonde hair that she was in the habit of tossing dramatically, her father's connections at the network, and rumors that she was sleeping with the producer. Ambitious Katie ignored them. She had been elated. But when the big day arrived she was nervously pacing the village green in Crowmarsh Priors and her confidence had evaporated. Her notes were a meaningless blur and her knees were almost shaking with stage fright.

While the crew set up their equipment she took deep breaths and tried to calm down. She walked around, checking angles for the best shots with Production back at the studio. She wanted the older cottages with their low walls and front gardens, the Queen Anne mansion, which had been turned into a convalescent home during the war, set back behind a high brick wall, and across the green, the pretty Georgian terrace and the Norman church. The Gentlemen's Arms pub with its red, white, and blue-planted hanging baskets and bunting.

Behind her the lane, only one car wide, was just visible, twisting and dipping through the hedgerows. Beyond it the downs swelled, dotted with sheep. With a bit of maneuvering, the cameras could block out the row of ugly 1960s houses behind the pub so that viewers would see the quaint Crowmarsh Priors of fifty years ago.

"Testing, testing. Can you hear me in the studio, Simon?" she asked into her headphones for the umpteenth time.

"Don't worry, if you get stuck we'll talk you through it. Be professional. Five, four, three, two, one," said Simon. "You're on."

Oh hell! Deep breath. Big smile. Professional. "Welcome, ladies and gentlemen, to this special edition of *Heart of England*! As the nation pauses in remembrance on the fiftieth anniversary of VE Day, I'm Katie Hamilton-Jones for Albion Television, and we hope you'll join us as we report live all day from the village of Crowmarsh Priors in Sussex." She made dramatic sweeping gestures with her hand to indicate the village behind her.

"Stop flapping your arm," growled Simon and the editor, simultaneously in her earpiece.

Rattled, Katie clutched the microphone with both hands and continued, "If London is the beating heart of Britain, country villages like Crowmarsh Priors are its lifeblood. Today, with the birds singing and sheep grazing on the hills above me, this peaceful village in Sussex looks like a picture postcard, with its village green, its country pub, and its cottages all basking in the early morning sunshine. On September 3, 1939, the inhabitants of countless villages like this throughout England heard the grim news that war had been declared with Germany.

"Today's special edition of the program pays tribute to the people of Crowmarsh Priors and to villagers in all parts of the country who lived through England's darkest hour. VE Day marked the end of a terrible time, and this fiftieth anniversary will be solemnly remembered by the people who lived through it. Today we will join the village in a special service of remembrance at the parish church, just one of many services of commemoration across England. Afterward the service will be followed by a fete on the village green and we will be speaking to people who remember when war came to Crowmarsh Priors."

It was going pretty well, and Katie felt more confident. If she was this good on her feet, perhaps she should have gone to the Bar after all. She tossed her hair back and spoke directly into the camera. She hoped her mother's friends were watching. "We'll be speaking to a number of special guests about their memories and experiences, including two elderly gentlemen who will tell us about being in the Home Guard and some of the residents of the Princess Elizabeth Convalescent Home for the War Wounded here in the village, that handsome building over there," Katie pointed to the Queen Anne house, "that was requisitioned by the War Office when its owner died as a place for wounded servicemen to recuperate.

"But today's program is mainly about the women. The women who stayed at home are the ones we rarely hear about, those women who kept the home fires burning even while they added the burden of war work to a busy life. They were wives, daughters, sisters, and mothers, who worried about loved ones fighting far away in the armed forces, and at home, they braced themselves against the long-expected German invasion. Those women maintained a stiff upper lip, 'kept smiling through,' and otherwise 'did their bit' while they raised their families and were the mainstay of their communities. This program pays tribute to those unsung heroines, and our featured guests today are four women who lived right here in Crowmarsh Priors.

"They were four young women, girls, really, who became wartime brides. Their lives were shaped by the conflict, and adversity drew them together. Now they are elderly ladies, but today they are reunited in their wartime home for the first time in over fifty years, to relive their experiences of England's darkest hour and reflect on the war's impact on their lives. For many of our older female viewers, this will bring back wartime memories of their own."

Behind Katie the camera picked up a silver Mercedes turning sharply onto the green and parking at an angle. After a moment a woman got out of the driver's side and the door slammed shut with a solid *thunk*. The camera homed in on her: short, tubby, and elderly but splendidly dressed in a purple flowered silk outfit, with a large, glittering diamond spray brooch pinned to her substantial bosom, a many-stranded pearl necklace, mauve court shoes, and matching stockings. She opened the car's back door and retrieved a picture hat of the same fabric as her dress, a silk handbag, and lavender kid gloves.

The cameraman muttered, "It's that Lady Moneybags. The one paid for the church getting restored and everything." Katie squinted at her. The patroness of today's events,

Lady Carpenter, was a dead ringer for the Queen Mother, dressed as if about to launch something. She gushed, "Our first war bride has arrived! That's Lady Carpenter, Sir Bernard Carpenter's widow, who has just got out of her car. Lady Carpenter is the youngest of our four war brides, and it's thanks to her generosity that the historic parish church of St. Gabriel's has been restored and the celebration is taking place today. She's here bright and early to make sure everything is in place for this special day, this very, very special day, um…because she was…the special…um…arrangements. Um…" Shit! She was blowing it.

Back in the studio Production was panicking too. Katie was losing it. "Stay calm. Talk about the church, keep the flow smooth," said Simon firmly in her earpiece.

Fortunately Katie was quick on the uptake and, despite her moment of panic, knew her stuff. "Speaking of Lady Carpenter brings me to the parish church. That's the Norman church you can see just behind me," she began as the camera panned to a shot of the church, "the focus of today's ceremony. Elsie Pigeon was a girl of seventeen when she was married there to Bernard Carpenter in 1942. A few months after their wedding the church was badly damaged by a stray bomb and it has been closed ever since. After Sir Bernard retired from the Treasury he devoted himself to his hobby, wartime history, and on the rare occasions when he was interviewed, he reminisced fondly about the time he spent in Crowmarsh Priors when he and his wife were young. After his death, two years ago, Lady Carpenter heard that plans were afoot to demolish the ruined church because of the cost of repairs, and she decided to rebuild it in his memory.

"The church and the village of Crowmarsh Priors have a long and interesting history. Both are closely linked to the de Balfort family. William the Conqueror rewarded his knight Giles de Balfort with a fiefdom near the Sussex coast. Giles built a monastery to pray for William and a fortress to defend him. The fortress and monastery crumbled long ago, but remarkably, the property has remained in the ownership of the de Balforts until now. The last living member of the family still lives near the village and we hope he'll speak to us today.

"Until it burned down in the last war, the de Balforts' ancestral home was Gracecourt Hall, dating from the reign of Elizabethan I. The money to build it came from the wool trade, from intermarriage with England's richest and most powerful families, and, some say, even from the smuggling that flourished on this coast for nearly three centuries. Lady Carpenter furnished us with these photographs taken in Gracecourt's heyday in the 1930s. I believe they're on the screen as we speak.

"Like most young aristocrats, the young de Balfort men made the Grand Tour of Europe as part of their education and brought home treasures from their travels. Over the centuries the house acquired a splendid collection of paintings, tapestries, and silver—you can see some of them in the photos. The house was also at the heart of a glittering social scene—think of pheasant shoots and hunters on a frosty morning reining in excited horses, tennis parties, picnics and balls, and grand dinners. There on the screen you can see the croquet lawn and a picnic in progress in the background...there are the tennis courts, a Chinese pavilion for tea parties built just before the war, and here is the water garden, laid out by a famous German landscape architect, which replaced the old-fashioned lake. The water gardens were art deco, very fashionable at the time, an elaborate design of interconnecting rectangular pools. Sadly the house and its treasures were destroyed in a fire before the end of the war."

"You're rambling! Get back to the Carpenters and the church," ordered Simon. "Interview Lady Carpenter."

The camera followed Katie as she walked toward the Mercedes, looking over her shoulder at the television audience. "But let's get back to the lovely and romantic story of Sir Bernard and Lady Carpenter and the parish church..."

Lady Carpenter was oblivious to the approaching TV camera. She was trying to chivvy someone out of the car's passenger seat. "For God's sake, Graham!" she snapped at a young man in a red-and-white-striped shirt, navy blazer, and flamboyant tie. The Cockney accent of her youth was no longer apparent.

Her thirty-year-old grandson, successful estate agent and party-going man-about-town, was horribly hungover from a friend's stag night the previous evening. He sat slumped, ashen, and carsick, wishing he had not agreed to drive down with his grandmother. His grandfather had boasted that he liked his motors and his women fast and had kept a garage full of expensive cars, although he didn't like driving: they were for Elsie, who adored them even though she drove like a maniac. She never tired of reminding her family that she had driven tractors during the war. Bernard had enjoyed riding in the passenger seat, puffing one of his special Cuban cigars, encouraging Elsie to put her foot down. The smell of expensive tobacco still permeated the car.

If you weren't Grandpa, Graham thought, driving with Granny was terrifying, especially when she was in a hurry. The motorway had been a blur of lorries, overtaken at reckless speed.

"Hurry up, Graham! Your grandfather never complained about my driving."

Only because lung cancer got him before you killed him in a pileup, thought Graham but knew better than to say it aloud.

Lady Carpenter moved aside to let him out, and her eyes narrowed to squint at a bent figure in an ancient Home Guard uniform shuffling along, leaning on a cane and the arm of a girl in a long, flowery skirt. She was clutching a large straw bag, rugs, and a folding deck chair. They stopped near the "Ladies" and "Gents." The girl unfolded the chair and lowered the old gentleman into it. She settled a battered Panama hat on his head and, despite the sun, covered his knees with a plaid rug.

"As I live and breathe, it's Albert Hawthorne," murmured Lady Carpenter. She watched the girl spread a second rug on the ground for herself and retrieve a paperback, a Thermos, and sunglasses from her basket.

"Are you ready for your tea, Granddad?" she asked very loudly, in the kind of voice people use to the hard of hearing. The old man nodded.

Graham's gaze followed his grandmother's. Then his mobile phone shrilled.

Lady Carpenter scowled. It was the opening bars of Beethoven's "Ode to Joy," and a particularly irritating ring.

"Sorry! I think we've finally got a punter for that old place we haven't been able to shift," he muttered to his grandmother, his hand over the phone's mouthpiece. "Graham here," he said smoothly.

Lady Carpenter took out her compact and checked her lipstick. One thing she'd say for Graham, he'd inherited Bernie's knack for wheeling and dealing. She listened.

"The Regents Park Property?" he asked smoothly. "Yes, Park Village West. Enchanting house, Nash. Yes, Crown Estate, very exclusive. Well, the queen sort of owns it, but...Indeed they will be impressed back home in Dallas, though you'll need to act quickly. Those properties are rare, snapped up the minute they come on the market on account of the big gardens at the back...Very unusual for London, yes. There was a canal behind all those houses once...No, no, not any longer, you needn't worry about the little one falling in. Canal was filled in during the war; they say water reflects light at night and the Germans used it to navigate during the Blitz. Monday at ten...Excellent. See you then. Cheerio!" He pushed the end-call button. "House needs a fortune spent on it and no one's interested except this American bloke, investment banker moving to London. His wife is keen, she insists on a house with a garden and a park nearby. Have to strike while the iron's hot. Since we're early I'll stretch my legs, see if there's any weekend cottages for sale. I never understand why people want them—who'd want to be in the country at the weekend? But they're selling like hotcakes."

"Keep an eye open for Auntie Agnes and Uncle Ted," Lady Carpenter murmured through her powder puff.

Graham turned on his heel, aghast. "Bloody hell, Gran! You didn't invite Ted the Red! You know what he's like, and Agnes is worse. They'll drink too much and fall on the food like it's their last meal, then Ted'll be buttonholing people and haranguing them about how the Labor Party betrayed the working class. Agnes will pester people to sign some harebrained petition, and they'll drive the caterers crazy asking are they unionized. I hope you told them no Socialist Workers leaflets or whatever it is they distribute for Class War. And fat cousin Trotsky will..."

"It's not Trotsky, it's Leon," murmured his grandmother, brushing a bug off her silk-covered shoulder. "I did tell them no leaflets, but you know your auntie Agnes...she's never got over things. Still, I couldn't very well leave them out today, could I? Blood's thicker than water. I owe it to Mum."

"I just hope they don't unfurl any damned banners in front of the TV people." Graham put on his sunglasses and skulked off.

Lady Carpenter snapped her compact shut. Something Graham had said on the telephone about that house in London was buzzing in her mind...what was it? A piece missing from the puzzle, even after all the research the private detective had done. She and Bernie had tried and tried to work out what it was. Then she said, "I wonder..." very loudly. She pushed away the microphone Katie thrust at her, got back in the car, rang her personal assistant in London, and asked her to find out more about the area around the house that Graham was trying to sell, the canal he mentioned.

Graham walked slowly past the girl who had come with Albert Hawthorne. She had slipped off one ballet pump and was lying on her stomach, reading, idly kicking one tan leg and a bare foot up and down.

Katie looked about frantically for someone else to interview.

A battered airport taxi pulled up behind the silver Mercedes. Lady Carpenter checked the time on her little diamond watch. It had been a last Christmas gift from Bernie. Just gone ten a.m. She hoped they'd all be here soon. They had a lot to talk about. She retrieved one last item, a leather dossier, from the backseat, as a stout woman enveloped in flowing black jersey, feet bulging out of laced sandals, was helped out of the taxi by the driver, who reached back for her walking stick. Her gray hair was coming loose from an untidy bun and she looked hot and uncomfortable. Two teenagers holding McDonald's cups got out behind her, a boy in a T-shirt and *kippah* and a dark-haired girl in jeans and sandals and a baseball cap, who bickered in Hebrew as the woman adjusted a large handbag on her arm and smoothed her clothes. Leaning heavily on her cane, she walked toward Lady Carpenter, followed by the teenagers. The girl in the baseball cap raised her head, and Lady Carpenter exclaimed in surprise when she saw the teenager's face. She looked exactly like Tanni had at that age, exactly.

"Is it like you remembered, Bubbie?"

Mrs. Zayman looked at Crowmarsh Priors. "That's new," she said to her grandchildren, pointing at the housing estate beyond the pub, "but otherwise it's the same. I think." Perspiration beaded her upper lip, and she looked round for the taxi, as if she were having second thoughts and might decide to get back into it and leave. "You know," she murmured half to herself, half to her grandchildren, "some things come back to me clearly. Evangeline in the garden and all the vegetables she grew, the sewing basket by my chair in the kitchen, Elsie and her poisons, Alice cycling past to school, Frances hating her Land Girl uniform. Then I can't remember other things. I can't remember leaving. But the war was…at the sanatorium they told me to rest and not to worry, that the mind forgets what it needs to, that amnesia is nature's way of protecting us. So there's surely a lot of things I can't tell you. Ah, well," she shrugged. "I suppose it doesn't matter now. Elsie!" she exclaimed as Lady Carpenter came up and reached out to take her hands, exclaiming, "Tanni!"

The taxi's arrival had taken Katie by surprise, but she quickly signalled the cameraman to catch the first minutes of the reunion, bound to be emotional! "Handkerchiefs at dawn," muttered the cameraman to the soundman, "here we go!"

The two women clutched hands, looked at each other for a moment, then bent stiffly and hugged.

"Oh, Tanni! It's been so long!"

"Elsie, my dear!" They rocked a little, back and forth in their embrace. The teenagers stood back uncertainly. The taxi driver unloaded a suitcase and two backpacks, then drove off.

"We've just been watching the second war bride arrive," Katie confided on camera. "That's Antoinette Zayman with two of her grandchildren, Shifra and Chaim, who have flown in from Israel. Just before the war, she married Bruno

Zayman, the distinguished historian, and came to England. Professor Zayman was unfortunately too ill to make the trip from Israel, so Mrs. Zayman is escorted by two of her—let's see—twelve grandchildren! We'll go over and speak to the ladies now!"

Albert Hawthorne tapped the girl on her shoulder. "What is it, Granddad?" she asked, looking up from her book. He was pointing a shaking finger across the green. "They was both slips of girls when they came—right when the war started, that was. All big eyes, scared to death. It was that Mrs. Fairfax brought them here. Always meddlin', that woman."

Just then, on the opposite side of the green, a wooden door opened. It was set in the mellow brick of an old garden wall that enclosed the Princess Elizabeth Convalescent Home, with its fire escapes and ugly double glazing that marred the Queen Anne façade. A slim figure in a red dress and hat slipped out, letting the door bang carelessly behind her.

Katie whirled round. "And that is the third war bride, Mrs. Evangeline Fairfax, an American who married a British naval officer she met in the States before the war, now making her way across from the convalescent home, which before the war was...was...the home of..." Katie checked her notes but couldn't find it. "Somebody in the village," she finished lamely, "now sheltered housing for ex-service personnel and their spouses..."

Mrs. Fairfax was wearing a large straw hat with a bunch of fake cherries pinned to the brim, which wobbled disconcertingly as she walked. Up close, the hat was somewhat battered, as were the leather clutch with a rhinestone clasp and the open-toed shoes.

Ignoring Katie and cameras bearing down on her she cried, "Elsie! As I live and breathe!" She threw her arms round Lady Carpenter, who said "Blimey!" as she was engulfed in a fog of cheap sherry and Chanel No. 5.

Mrs. Zayman, breathing heavily and leaning on her stick, moved forward and threw her arms open. "Evangeline!" She hugged and kissed Mrs. Fairfax, then wrinkled her nose. She stood back and prodded the two teenagers, who stepped forward and shook hands awkwardly.

"Chaim," said the boy. "Pleased to meet you."

"Hello, I'm Shifra," said the girl.

"You don't half resemble your grandmother," Lady Carpenter exclaimed to Shifra. "And I'm so glad you could come. Nice to have the younger generation here. My grandson Graham's there somewhere," she said, waving vaguely in the direction of the cottages.

Mrs. Fairfax's head swivelled back and forth on her wrinkled neck. She had had a mild stroke two years before, and the local doctor had warned her to stay off the drink unless she wanted to court another, massive one, but she hadn't paid any attention. Now she smiled broadly and said, "Well, what nice-lookin' grandchildren you've got, Tanni. Anna's two youngest, aren't they? Hmmm?" She hiccupped. "How's Bruno doing? I heard he wasn't well. And what's Johnny up to?"

"Bruno's about the same," said Mrs. Zayman. "The surgery went well, thank God, but he has to keep quiet. Johnny's the same as ever, working too hard like his father, happy with his family. Expects to be a grandfather himself in a few months." She frowned at the fluffy microphone that hovered over their heads. The soundman ducked back just in time as she raised her stick and aimed a swipe at it. Shifra and Chaim stared at their grandmother in amazement.

"Well, hasn't it been such a long time since we were together! Everbody got scattered, Elsie and Bernie livin' abroad so much of the time, Tanni and Bruno in Israel, and Alice in the States...but here we are together at last!" Mrs. Fairfax struggled to regain her train of thought. "My condolences about Bernie."

Lady Carpenter's face became a mask. Evidently she was trying not to cry.

"Read his obituary when the papers came. Lung cancer...terrible...those awful Woodbines he used to smoke, until the Americans came and he got all those cigarettes from the PX—made a fortune reselling them, remember? Never missed a trick, Bernie didn't. We'll sure miss him today, won't we, Elsie. I heard rebuilding the church and this whole VE Day was really his idea, y'all having got married here and everything. He was a man of surprises, wasn't he?"

The expression on Lady Carpenter's face told Mrs. Fairfax she hadn't said the right thing. She changed tack. "And look at your outfit!" She rushed on, like an express train going nowhere but unable to stop. "I declare, it's so pretty...and that hat...well, it's hard to believe it's been so long since we all lived here together. It's been, well, just ages!" she gushed. The cherries bobbed and jiggled.

"Evangeline, pay attention! The Women's Institute said they'd leave refreshments for us in the new parish hall at the church. Nobody else has been allowed in yet so we can be private. As soon as Alice gets here, with some things she looked up," Lady Carpenter muttered, "I have something to

441

show you, because we only have this one chance—oh bloody hell, that girl with the microphone is a nuisance!"

Lady Carpenter saw that the cameraman and the blonde woman babbling into a microphone were edging closer again. "Where do you suppose Alice is?" she interrupted, loudly enough for Katie to hear.

"That will be Alice Osbourne Lightfoot," said Katie, forced to turn to the camera, as the old ladies had their backs to her again, "who became a war bride when she married a US Air Force pilot in 1944..."

Just then a gray Ford Fiesta with a hire-company sticker crunched noisily to a stop on the gravel and parked. A moment later a tall woman with curly gray hair, wearing a well-cut beige trouser suit and clean white sports shoes got out and fished an expensive cream leather shoulder bag, a camera, and a raincoat from the passenger seat. She looked at the sky, then folded the raincoat neatly and put it back. She locked the car and headed for the three women by the marquee.

"This is Mrs. Lightfoot's first trip back to England since she left on a transport ship full of war brides bound for the USA in 1946," Katie warbled as the camera panned to a photo of a liner with women crowded at the rails, waving handkerchiefs. "And here are Colonel and Mrs. Lightfoot on their wedding day!" The camera rested on a black-and-white photo of a smiling young woman in a matching coat and skirt, her hair in a victory roll, holding a bouquet and the arm of a tall man in uniform grinning down at her, with a carnation in his buttonhole and his hat under his arm. They stood on the steps of a dark Edwardian church, framed by an arched doorway. In the right-hand corner there was what looked like the hem of a vicar's cassock, and his feet were visible.

Now another old man came wandering into the camera's field. He paused and tipped his hat to Katie, revealing a lopsided face disfigured by old scar tissue and partially obscured by a long shock of white hair. "Forgive me. Hugo de Balfort," he said. She knew immediately who he was: he had been badly injured trying to rescue his invalid father during the terrible fire that had destroyed Gracecourt Hall. Katie's note told her that Sir Leander's body had been retrieved in the melted wheelchair.

"Oh, Sir Hugo, just the man to speak to," Katie said gamely. "You spent the war in Crowmarsh Priors, didn't you? You were medically unfit for the services, but your wartime work was just as important, farming the family estate. I'm sure most of our viewers know that feeding the country was crucial to the war effort. You also served in the Home Guard with Mr. Hawthorne there. Can you tell our viewers about the Home Guard? Was it terribly dangerous?"

Sir Hugo paused, leaning on his stick. He shook his head deprecatingly. "All a long time ago, my dear."

"Tell us what the Home Guard did."

"We were supposed to drill, so we did for a bit—though with so few of us there didn't seem much point in marching up and down the green in formation. We started out drilling with broom handles. After a while we gave it up. Churchill ordered that we were to 'fight them on the beaches' when the Germans came. Not sure what with. They promised us Sten guns. Teapots with a barrel, we called them. Jolly useless. It all seemed pretty hopeless."

"Now I believe, Sir Hugo, that the Home Guard were also responsible for finding any German pilots who were shot down. Weren't there some camouflaged antiaircraft gun emplacements nearby on the downs?"

"Useless," muttered Sir Hugo. "There were, but they weren't usually manned. The gunners were needed on the coast, and we'd found in the Blitz the ack-ack guns weren't very effective, you know. Didn't seem possible we could hold out much longer. The invasion seemed a sure thing. Expected it every minute."

"And did your Home Guard unit ever capture any Germans?"

"Bombers sometimes got shot down or crashed on the downs, but the men in them were usually killed, I believe. We did find two chaps dead once; the vicar insisted we bury them at St. Gabriel's."

"You probably saw the program on television the other night, Sir Hugo, when they interviewed a retired air marshal who said that Military Intelligence were concerned about spies or Nazi sympathizers in southern England, that someone was believed to be sending weather reports to the Luftwaffe—their bombing raids coincided remarkably with clear weather on this side of the channel. Would that have been likely, do you think?"

"My housekeeper has the telly on at night so I did see a bit, but the air marshal's memory is probably not what it was, my dear. Would have been difficult to do anything like that secretly. Everyone lived so closely together in those days, you see, everyone mucking in, doing their bit. And there was a general paranoia about spies and German agents and so on."

"But the air marshal said...ah, do please excuse me, our war brides are disappearing into the church hall, and I must try and speak to them. Thank you for sharing your recollections, Sir Hugo."

Interviewing old people was exhausting, Katie thought.

She wound up the first segment of the show, telling the cameraman to get a shot of the war brides entering the church when the time came. "So there they are, today's special guests, the four war brides. Antoinette Joseph Zayman, a refugee. Former Land Girl Elsie Pigeon Carpenter, who married her childhood sweetheart. Evangeline Fontaine Fairfax, an American who was swept off her feet by a dashing English officer. And Alice Osbourne Lightfoot, a girl from this village who taught at the school while serving as an air raid warden. It was when she joined the Women's Volunteer Service in London that she met her husband and was whisked away eventually to live happily ever after in the USA. Though time and distance have separated them, the ladies have come here today to share their memories and celebrate their enduring friendship, one of the happier legacies of a terrible, terrible war. Above all, this is their day and those are their stories.

"For Albion Television's *Heart of England VE Day Special*, this is Katie Hamilton-Jones. Now we go back to the studio, because it's time for the lunchtime news."

Mrs. Zayman's teenage grandchildren were tossing a Frisbee back and forth and other teenagers edged closer to join the game. The pub opened and the publican had put a blackboard outside that announced beer would be sold today at wartime prices. Lady Carpenter's grandson wondered if the pretty girl by the old man in his Home Guard uniform would like a drink...

The girl with the microphone who had been yammering about war brides a few feet from his deck chair had finally stopped. Through half-closed eyes Albert watched the four women follow the vicar toward the churchyard, where the new parish hall stood next to the church. Someone was missing, but he was ninety-five and his memory came and went. A musty smell rose as the sun warmed his old wool uniform, and in the distance, he thought he heard the whistle of a train...

34.

Crowmarsh Priors, Midday, 8 May 1995

*I*n St. Gabriel's churchyard the new vicar gestured expansively at the shrouded tower. The old ladies shaded their eyes, looking up and nodding at what he said. Then he waved toward the overgrown churchyard. "It may not look it, but things are vastly improved since the work started, Lady Carpenter. It was a dreadful mess, hadn't been cleared since the bomb, took ages to clear the area in front of the tower. The contractors found the graveyard sinking in some places; they weren't sure how stable the ground was. The engineers decided it might be too dangerous to bring in heavy machinery at the back where the older graves are, so they had them trim it by hand as best they could in time for the service. But the old knight's tomb is still over there." He pointed toward the back of the church where a lichen-covered stone sarcophagus lay half-buried on its side.

The ladies could see the familiar helmeted figure. Its face was now entirely worn away except for the nose, but the crossed legs, a sword, and a shield with traces of the de Balfort coat of arms were still visible. The vicar racked his brains to remember some interesting tidbit from the newly printed church brochure, on sale for twenty pence. "It's one of the de Balforts of course. Bit of inscription still on the side. You see that his legs are crossed at the knee? That meant he went twice on the Crusades. Ankles crossed, once, thighs crossed three times. The tomb's position is rather interesting, off by itself like that. Normally you would have expected a knight from the most powerful local family to be buried inside the church under the floor."

Elsie turned to Alice and raised her eyebrows. "So interesting to see it again, I'd forgotten exactly where it was," murmured Alice, strolling toward it through the weeds and wildflowers, then leaning over as if to read the inscription.

"Do mind the nettles, Mrs. Lightfoot," called the vicar anxiously as one stung his hand.

"It's all right, I'm in the garden club," Alice told him inconsequentially. Out of sight, her age-spotted hand with the huge diamond engagement ring and a diamond-studded wedding band fumbled under the ivy. Where was it? She was sure it had been just about...there! She felt the knobby skull on the corner of the tomb, then pushed it as hard as she could to one side. Nothing happened. She pushed again, harder, remembering to twist. Frances had gotten it to work just after the bomb, but that was a long time ago. She tried once more. The ivy rustled, there was a scraping noise, and a small gap appeared as one side of the tomb shifted. She looked round to see if the vicar had heard, but he was talking animatedly and hadn't noticed. She pushed again. There was a louder, grinding noise this time, like stone on stone.

This time Evangeline heard. "Come look at this, Vicar. This is real sweet," she interrupted him and immediately pulled him away to the other side of the graveyard. The others joined her to look at a Victorian stone angel standing guard over three flat sunken gravestones. "It's holding a smaller angel by the hand."

"Are you sure, Mrs. Fairfax?" asked the vicar, batting at the creeper growing over the angel's wings to have a closer look.

"Bend down and you'll see it. There under the right wing," urged Evangeline. Sure enough a little angel was peeking out. "The workmen must have straightened it up again; after they bombed the church I remember it was face-down."

"Wot I say is, let's go in and freshen up," said Elsie. The last thing Tanni needed was for them to start talking about baby angels and wherever that might lead. "Then we'll let you get on with things, Vicar. You'll want to be outside waiting for the bishop."

"Oh, Lady Carpenter, I'm quite happy to stay and—"

"Don't let us keep you. We'd like to put our feet up for a bit, have a cup of coffee and a chat, it's been a long time since we've seen each other," said Elsie firmly.

"Oh, quite. Then I'll just pop in and make sure the coffee things are there." The others moved on, but Evangeline slipped behind the angel's outspread wings, took a half-bottle of vodka from her handbag, unscrewed the top, and had a big swallow.

"Let's get in out of the heat, it's quite comfortable in our nice new parish hall." The vicar ushered Elsie and Tanni inside, talking nonstop. "Lovely new kitchenette, thanks to you, Lady Carpenter. Here's the new kettle, just the ticket. No one's used it yet except the ladies who were decorating the church earlier—yes, good as their word, left us coffee, sugar, cups, spoons..." he rattled on. "And here's some of that long-life milk in the fridge and a plate of sandwiches! The note on top says 'Welcome back to the War Brides! From the Women's Institute.' Lovely!"

The vicar bustled about, rattling cups and asking about milk and sugar and putting the kettle on to boil. "Tickety boo!" he chirped as it began to hum.

"How nice," said Tanni faintly, lowering herself onto a chair. Elsie sat down too, still clutching her gloves, handbag, and dossier. Her feet were swelling over the tops of her mauve pumps and the vicar was driving her crazy.

Evangeline came in and, hat now lopsided, drifted over to the window that looked toward the downs. She pushed it open and leaned out. "Here comes Alice," she said.

"While this boils, I'd like to know more about the fellow who was vicar during the war—Hammet, his name was. You all knew him, I'm sure. Cambridge man, I understand. I want to mention him in today's sermon, but I'm not sure what to say about him. Haven't been able to find out much, really. The church records went missing in the confusion after the war. Was he married? Any family? I understand he died in 1947." He looked at Lady Carpenter for confirmation. "His heart, I believe? Strain of the war, no doubt." He handed round mugs of coffee.

Evangeline murmured something that sounded like, "You could say it was his heart, yes," as she took one. "You'd never know it to look at him, but his heart gave out, just like that, one day." She walked over to the window and pointed.

"My husband is buried over there, next to his mother," she told the vicar. "After the church was hit they extended the graveyard into that field at the back. See the fence round it? Richard and Penelope, Nell Hawthorne and the Barrowses and I can't remember who else is back there. I plan on being buried there myself. Next to Richard."

"Sandwiches, ladies?"

For a minute they all ate in silence. Alice looked at her surroundings in amazement, remembering how the old vestry had smelled of beeswax and mice. Now it smelled of new Formica.

The vicar had settled comfortably with coffee and his fourth sandwich and did not look like moving. "I'm going to spend a penny," said Elsie decisively. "Which way to the ladies?"

There was a flurry of agreement. "I might as well powder my nose," said Alice, clutching her handbag.

"Good idea," said Tanni, heaving herself to her feet.

"Excuse me, Vicar," murmured Evangeline, putting down her untouched coffee.

"Just down that corridor," said the vicar, leaping to his feet and pointing down a hallway that smelled of new carpet. "I suppose I'd better get on putting together a few words about this Hammet fellow. I'll just be in the little room at the other end of the corridor."

But the women's heads were together and they were no longer listening to him.

The ladies' had been done up with strawberry-patterned wallpaper, festoon blinds at the windows, and pale green woodwork that matched the pale green washbasins. There was a small sitting room, with armchairs and a sofa bench with quilted covers, designed as an anteroom for brides and their attendants.

"Got it to ourselves. Good," said Elsie and sank down on the sofa. "Now, the reason we're all here is to put our heads together and work out what happened to Frances." She opened her dossier and Alice reached into her shoulder bag for a sheaf of notes. "Alice and I've worked out bits, and maybe we can figure the rest out. We all wondered how Frances could have disappeared without a by-your-leave. Even her father never knew what happened to her. The police weren't interested either, but my Bernie wouldn't give up. He fancied her, most men did, but it was more than that. I think it was—Bernie was loyal and there was something he used to insist was a last request—said he couldn't explain until he knew for sure what had happened. He insisted his sixth sense told him something wasn't right, but mainly, we all owed it to her to find what happened. For a long time he believed she must have had an accident, one of those wartime things, you know, people killed by bombs and never identified, or even foul play, and he put the word out with his underworld mates, offered a reward, even, but no one knew anything, not a dickie-bird.

"Finally he had to drop it, but he never forgot Frances. Later, after he'd made all his money advisin' the Treasury how to make banknotes and passports and things counterfeit proof, he started looking for Frances again, only this time he could afford to hire detectives. They never turned up much besides her pictures in the paper when she was a debutante and got into a lot of trouble, and something about her being due to inherit a lot of money when she got married. Rebuilding the church was the best excuse he could find for excavating down the tunnel. He always wondered if she'd gone back another time after that night..."

"After what night?" asked Tanni. "I don't remember what happened to the church, it was months later before I learned a bomb hit it. Yet if there was a bomb in the village I must have known it at the time. The amnesia, the doctors say, it happens if you have a terrible shock. It must have been a shock, the bomb." Tanni's face was suddenly pasty and the sick feeling seized her again. "Why do I feel there was something else, I've always felt there was something that happened! And I don't know what it is. Oh why can't I remember!"

Alice exchanged a significant look with Elsie and Evangeline and all three shook their heads. Bruno had rung each of them to say Tanni was coming and to tell them that she had never recovered any memory of her dead baby, Rebecca, and the doctors were certain that she never would. As far as Bruno was concerned, she had had enough grief to bear after the war, when she learned that she had lost her parents in Auschwitz and her twin sisters at a DP camp in France. Being unable to remember Rebecca was a blessing in disguise, he said, they mustn't worry.

Alice and Elsie had put down the phone with a mixed sense of relief and guilt. If Tanni didn't remember anything about that time she clearly didn't recall their plan to rescue Lili and Klara, or that the girls were meant to be in the tunnel the night the bomb fell. That was a blessing too, more than Bruno realized. Since he had never known about their rescue operation there was no point telling him he was wrong about the girls having died in France. And now, any explanation was impossible.

Alice hoped Evangeline wouldn't let something slip. "Evangeline, you were the last one of us to see Frances," Alice said quickly before Evangeline could blunder on about Rebecca.

The cherries bobbed as Evangeline nodded. "It wasn't long after the fire at Gracecourt. She must have been catching the London train, because she wasn't in her Land Girl uniform. She waved as she went past the house. I remember it clear as day. I never told anybody this, but I had made her a promise, that if anything happened to her…but you knew Frances—you couldn't imagine anything happening to her, and I kept expecting her to reappear. I'll tell you in a minute what I promised. You go on, Elsie."

Elsie continued. "A few years ago, when Bernie was sick with the chemotherapy, he liked me to read him the papers. One day I spotted this in an article about wartime France." She reached into the dossier, took out a newspaper photograph, and spread it on the vanity unit. "Recognize anybody?" The caption said: "Unidentified Wartime Photo of French Resistance." The others crowded round to look.

"Who is it? I never saw any of those people before," said Evangeline after a moment.

"Can't say I have either," said Alice, peering through her bifocals.

But Tanni exclaimed, "Yes!" and pointed to a woman in a head scarf and rough shoes. She was talking to someone out of the frame, oblivious of the person with the camera.

There were gasps as the others peered more closely. "It looks sort of like Frances, I guess, but…"

"I'm sure it's her. Definitely."

"It's Frances. I'd recognize her anywhere," Tanni said positively, "but the thing is, she's pregnant. Look at her!"

They looked at each other. "What on earth was she doing in France? And who could the baby's father be?" asked Alice. "Some Frenchman?"

Evangeline shook her head, cherries bobbing wildly. "Noooo...that's part of what I'm going to tell you, actually I think it was..."

The vicar knocked on the door. "Ladies? Everything all right in there?"

"Fine! Thank you. We're putting our feet up for a minute longer," bellowed Elsie. She lowered her voice. "No idea who the father was. But first things first. Bernie hired another detective right away, first time he'd taken an interest in anything since they made him retire from the Treasury. Even went into remission for a bit. The detective learned that the photo was probably taken sometime late in 1944, probably near the eastern border with Germany."

"But how did she get there with a war on?"

"I know! Bernie and me asked ourselves that over and over. It kept us awake nights. Then Bernie has an idea. He invites an old Treasury mate, who'd been in Military Intelligence during the war, to dinner, poured enough expensive wine to drown an elephant down his throat and showed him the photo. The mate hemmed and hawed, pretended he had no idea, but that was because they weren't supposed to say anything about what they'd done in the war. We could tell he was startled, but Bernie always got what he wanted. He kept topping up the bloke's glass and finally he said she'd been recruited for something undercover, because he definitely remembered the girl in the picture from one of the training centers, an admiral's daughter, he said. Stunning girl, but clever too, very determined. One of the controllers, funny little man, was half in love with her. The woman in the newspaper photo looked plainer than he remembered her, but he said that was probably a disguise and he was dead certain it was the same girl. So Bernie asked 'Was Frances Falconleigh her name?' and the man said 'That was it!'

"A few days later the mate rang, said something'd occurred to him. All the Special Operations Executive agents dropped behind enemy lines were accounted for after the war, alive or dead, and he'd checked, but no Frances Falconleigh was among them. So she wasn't SOE, at least not in the beginning, but she might have been recruited for Churchill's secret British resistance thing, the Auxiliary Units. They went through the same training as the SOE and by the autumn of 1944 a lot of SOE agents in eastern France had been betrayed and arrested, tortured and executed, or sent to concentration camps. Someone like Frances, trained for an Auxillary Unit, might have been parachuted into eastern France to take a captured SOE agent's place. He seemed to remember Frances was keen to be posted to France, but she was young and they felt she might be a bit of a loose cannon."

Elsie sighed and shook her head. "And all that time we knew her, we thought she was on a Land Girl committee! The detective found records of the training camps for the Auxis and the SOE where they taught all kinds of things like surviving in the field, hand-to-hand combat, how to use explosives, dynamite, and dodgy ones called 'sticky bombs.' At one training center the Shanghai Police trained them in interrogation. And silent killing."

They digested this for a minute.

"Alice did some work too. Maybe that'll help fill in the gap. Tell us, Alice."

Alice opened her bag and took out a yellow legal pad of notes. "After she found the photo, Elsie wrote me asking what we ought to do next. Well. Joe's nephew was at the University of Georgia doing a PhD on something about wartime France, so I went to the university library in Athens and got him to help me. He was a little surprised that his auntie Alice wanted to know about resistance movements, but he was real sweet."

She picked up the pad and read, "'France was mostly liberated by the autumn of 1944, but there was a big eastern push by the Allies into Germany itself. On that border of France, however, collaborators were actively helping the Germans in order to save their own skins. The Allies wanted the French collaborators eliminated, but they didn't want it generally known that they were using specially trained agents to assassinate them. Officially the British War Office disapproved of such tactics.' Officially."

"You don't think Frances—"

Evangeline interrupted Tanni, drawling, "I don't know... but explosives? Maybe. After Alice left, remember the fire at Gracecourt that killed Leander and put Hugo in hospital? I was the only one of us still here, and some people in the village said they'd heard an explosion in the direction of Gracecourt and wondered if another bomb had exploded. Sometimes they didn't go off right away...anyhow, it was not long after that Frances disappeared."

"My wedding was on the thirtieth of August, 1944," said Alice. "I rang Evangeline to tell her I was getting married and asked her to tell Frances because I couldn't reach her. I guessed she'd gone up to London, but she had given me her pretty dressing case and I wanted to let her know I was taking it on my honeymoon."

"And none of us ever saw her again," said Elsie. "But our detective told us that by 1943 they were combing southern England for a spy network, with a center of operations near the Sussex coast, where they expected the invasion to take place. But it wasn't till Graham said something this morning about a house he's got for sale that a bell rang in my head, one of those missing pieces Bernie and I never could find. The house is near an old canal in London, and Graham's client was worried about her child falling in. Graham said not to worry, it was filled in during the war, because at night it reflected light and the Germans used it to navigate."

"But Elsie, what has that got to do with Frances?"

Elsie picked up another file with "de Balfort" on the cover and opened it. "This. Bernie let drop to the detective that Hugo de Balfort had wanted to marry Frances, so the detective might as well look into the de Balforts. He came back and said they must have wanted Frances's money, because by the time the war came the de Balforts were ruined and unless Hugo married a rich woman, like his father had done, they would lose Gracecourt. But he also said the de Balforts were probably under observation by the authorities. A lot of Germans and Austrians with Nazi connections had stayed at Gracecourt before the war, a lot of them friends Hugo had made on his travels."

"I remember Leander de Balfort spending a fortune on one crazy scheme after another, landscaping, pavilions, and deer parks and so on, to impress his friends and how

Lady Marchmont disapproved of it all," said Alice. "Aesthetes annoyed her. Hugo's mother had been an heiress, and Lady Marchmont could never understand why Leander had wasted all poor Venetia's fortune so irresponsibly. It was one continuous house party for years, a frightfully smart and glamorous set." She sighed. Fifty-five years later the humiliating memory of the shooting lunch to which Lady Marchmont had dragged her still made her cheeks burn. "The women were that rather brittle society sort, with marcelled hair and rouge, all flirting madly with each other's husbands."

"Lady Marchmont didn't know the half of it," Elsie told her. "The detective said he had a hunch he wanted to follow and asked if we'd pay for him to go investigating in Germany. Bernie agreed, and a month later the detective was back with a pile of letters from Leander he had unearthed in a German archive. Got them all copied, and guess where he got the money to do all that building Lady Marchmont disapproved of?"

"Where?"

"According to the letters, his German friends had persuaded him that a Nazi takeover in England would be good for toffs like the de Balforts, that it was the only way to save Gracecourt. They paid Leander a lot of money in the years before the war, laying the groundwork, like, for marching into England. But Leander spent it all. Those pools, that water-garden thing? They were designed by a famous German architect who was a big Nazi supporter. But the Germans didn't take over in England as fast as Leander'd hoped. So he was desperate for money and depended on Hugo to marry Frances for her fortune, like he'd got Venetia's."

"You mean Leander de Balfort was one of those traitors we were supposed to watch out for?" Alice was appalled. "To think that anyone in our midst..." She was overwhelmed.

Elsie snorted. "There's worse! Leander's Nazi friends knew he was desperate to carry on the de Balfort line. To string him along, they let him into a secret, that they were doing experiments—all that nonsense about breeding a master race people didn't hear about until after the war. He was promised the de Balforts would benefit from that. And...here's a copy of Leander's reply. He wrote them about how he had found 'a perfect specimen of Aryan woman-hood' for his son. He goes on about how as an 'artist' he wanted to design a master race of de Balforts by breeding his son and Frances, and if the Nazi doctors were right, they would have twins over and over again. He got quite excited about Frances having twenty or thirty de Balforts, who'd each go on to have twenty or thirty, and so on till England was crawling with the little buggers. Makes you sick, it does. And here's the copy of that letter."

They passed it round in silence. Then Alice noticed Tanni looked as if she might faint and forced her head between her knees.

The vicar knocked again. "Ladies? Everything tickety boo in there? It's nearly time for the service and the bishop's car has just pulled up."

Elsie glowered at the door and lowered her voice. "So Hugo was under a lot of pressure from his father to get Frances to say yes. I don't know whether Hugo knew what his father was doing. The letters don't say anything about bombing the church or the tunnel..."

"What tunnel? You said something about a tunnel before," said Tanni. No one knew what to say. "Let's get back," she went on. "Shifra and Chaim will be worried." She felt ill and breathless—another anxiety attack from the nameless thing that haunted her. The room began to close round her the way it always did. She did her deep breathing exercises as she had been taught, but her heart was pounding. She had to get out of there.

"Ladies!" bellowed the vicar, rapping sharply at the door. The bishop was a stickler for punctuality.

They stood and smoothed their clothes and picked up their handbags.

"We'll finish later," said Elsie. "Now we've got this ruddy service to get through."

Outside St. Gabriel's the procession was forming. Two acolytes holding crosses fidgeted while the bishop, the vicar, the churchwardens, and twenty elderly residents of the Princess Elizabeth Convalescent Home milled at the entrance. The men all wore their old uniforms, and some had medals. Several of the women were in service uniforms. Those who were not wore hats and gloves. They all stood as upright as they could manage. All had canes or walkers.

Inside everyone was standing, waiting for the procession and for the four war brides to walk down the aisle and be seated.

At the door of the church Elsie closed her eyes and remembered her wedding day, Bernie fidgeting at the altar, his look of relief as she came toward him in the splendid wedding dress, careful step-pause-step-pause, on Albert's arm. Watching Bernie's eyes widen at her appearance, then taking her hand from Albert and hanging on to it for dear life. Saying "I will" too loudly. She bit her tongue hard to stop the tears from spilling over. "Gran, come on now," whispered Graham, giving her arm a little tug.

Tanni took her place between her grandchildren and was followed by Evangeline and Alice, who had chosen to walk together.

"Thought they'd never make it," muttered Katie to the cameraman as the war brides and their escorts moved slowly down the aisle between the pews, which were draped in red, white, and blue bunting. "But what a great shot."

35.

Crowmarsh Priors, Evening, VE Day 1995

The service was over, the bishop had blessed the new buildings, there had been a lavish tea on trestle tables in the marquee on the green. Several elderly inhabitants of the Princess Elizabeth Convalescent Home sat together with a last cup of tea, walkers behind their chairs.

Out of the corner of her eye Katie saw Elsie and Alice walking across to Evangeline, who was heading for the parish hall. She turned and the three came over and spoke to Tanni, who took money from her handbag and gave it to Shifra and Chaim. "But not too much to drink," she ordered, in Hebrew. The teenagers grinned, then set off toward the pub where the young people had collected and were busily eyeing each other.

Katie moved in quickly to get her interview.

Elsie knew she had to get it over with, so she answered her questions and wished the girl would stop tossing her hair about. "Yes, my husband would have been pleased the church was rebuilt," said Elsie, not really concentrating, just agreeing to what Katie said so she would finish the interview and go away. So annoying when she was trying to concentrate on putting the last pieces together. Her big hat nodded steadily as she distractedly fielded Katie's questions. "Yes, he died two years ago. Yes, it was a great pity. Yes, good to hear the bell ring again. Yes, brings back memories. Romantic gesture, yes it was, my husband was very romantic. Oh, yes, rags to riches, you could say that. Yes, yes…the war feels like yesterday, just like yesterday. You put it so well, love."

Katie gushed her thanks and moved on to the large woman in black.

"My memories?" asked Tanni bleakly. "What do I remember?" She sounded astonished to be asked.

"Tell her about the wedding dress for Lady Carpenter, Bubbie," prompted Shifra.

"Ooh, yes!" gushed Katie, flashing a wide-eyed "oooh" look at the camera. "The ladies will want to hear about *that*!"

Tanni warmed to her subject, explaining where they had gotten it and a little more about clothes rationing, how they'd made new clothes out of old ones, and how she had sewed for the village.

After she finished, Alice and Evangeline looked up from their tea to see Katie and her microphone hovering. "Now I want to hear all about our last two war brides! Tell our viewers all about yourselves, how you met your husbands and what you did in the war!" Katie burbled. "What are your most lasting memories of the war years?"

Alice looked thoughtful, as if she had trouble remembering. "Um, well, rationing of course. Food and clothes were in short supply and most people were terribly patriotic and tried to make a little go a long way. Make do and mend, you know. Victory gardens. Andersen shelters in the gardens. Evacuees. Trying to keep morale up, not let the side down...quick weddings. Like mine."

Katie said, "Ooooh!"

"Not what you're thinking, dear. It was just that you had to make up your mind quickly with the war on. No dawdling."

"How long had you known Colonel Lightfoot before he popped the question?" asked Katie.

Alice smiled. "A weekend. We met on a Friday night and married a week on Monday at a church near my husband's air force base. I pulled strings and got leave. He pulled strings and found a chaplain."

"I remember the music," said Evangeline dreamily. Her handbag was open and Katie saw a bottle of vodka.

"Now there's something no one else has mentioned yet!" said Katie. "The music! Those jolly singsongs! 'Roll out the Barrel,' 'We'll Meet Again, Dame Vera Lynn,' 'Bluebirds Over/The White Cliffs of Dover...'"

"No, I hated singalongs. I'm talking about swing and jazz," said Evangeline, looking off into the distance. "The Lindy Hop. Jazz clubs in Soho. Glenn Miller."

"Oh, yes, Glenn Miller!" said Katie.

"Yes, I've got a big collection of records. I knew someone once...a musician in Paris...always wanted to play with Glenn Miller. He used to send me records...all the records he played on...my husband, Richard, just loved listening to them. After he was torpedoed at sea and...never very well after that, and the thing he liked best was those records. I had to play them for him every day...then the fellow I knew...Glen Miller asked him to join the band, they were going to France and they needed to replace one of the band members who was sick...he was on the fatal flight."

Simon prompted through her earpiece, and Katie turned to the cameras. "For those of you too young to remember, Glenn Miller was a famous American bandleader who used to travel to entertain the troops, just like Gracie Fields and Vera Lynn. Unfortunately his plane disappeared over the English Channel in..."

"December 1944," said Simon.

"In December 1944. Tragically many of his band were on the plane too," finished Katie.

Evangeline nodded.

"Excuse us," said Elsie, and the four women moved away.

The fete was in full swing. The caterers had finally cleared the marquee tables of the tea things, then replaced them with huge tubs of ice holding bottles of beer and white wine, corks drawn and replaced, or red wine left open along the serving tables, with an array of plastic glasses, and squash for the children. A huge barbeque had been lit. Trays of sausages and kebabs had been brought out from a refrigerated lorry, and there were mountains of rolls and pita bread and vast bowls of salads. Young mothers in summer dresses who had moved from London to the country for the children's sake sipped white wine and agreed on the impossibility of a school run all the way to Tunbridge Wells, while their husbands held plastic mugs of beer and asked each other if they had talked to the fellow in the tie who was big in property and thought prices in Crowmarsh Priors could only go up.

Albert Hawthorne's pretty great-granddaughter brought Albert a half pint of stout from the Gentlemen's

Arms. "Know wine doesn't agree with you, Granddad. The barman wouldn't let me or Graham pay for it when he heard it was for you," she said. "It's because you were in the Home Guard with his grandfather."

"You're good lass, Lizzie," murmured Albert, taking a long drink. He'd need the lav soon, and that young man in the navy blazer and fancy tie hanging around Lizzie like a fly around jam could help him get up. He settled back in his deck chair and wondered why stout didn't taste as it used to.

"Why are they going back to the church?" said Lizzie. "They must have forgotten something." The four war brides were walking away in a little group. The vicar didn't see them go, because he was talking animatedly into Katie Hamilton-Jones's microphone about the crisis of faith today.

Katie was looking desperately over his head, hoping for a glimpse of her mother's friend, the recuperation home's titled patroness, to interview next.

"That old man has joined them, the one with the scarred face, Sir Hugo de Balfort," said Lizzie to Graham. "I guess they must all be a bit emotional, like you said your gran was, walking into church. They probably want a quiet chat away from the cameras. You can't get a word in edgewise with that woman bouncing around, sticking her microphone in your face. They look a bit tired now; they've all got canes to lean on. I heard your gran asking some of those people from the home if they could borrow theirs for a bit. She thinks of everything, doesn't she?"

"Come keep us company and have a chat, Hugo," Elsie murmured to Sir Hugo as they gathered round him, "we're just going back to the church to pay our final respects in private. Get away from that bloody girl and her microphone."

"Delighted, ladies." He fell into step as they detached themselves from the crowd.

"You of all people must have noticed an omission in today's service," said Elsie, puffing a little.

"Frances Falconleigh," said Evangeline.

"Ah, who? Frances," said Sir Hugo. "What became of her? I think I was rather smitten by her at one point. Dashing girl."

"We want to show you something," said Alice.

"At your service, naturally, ladies." Sir Hugo bowed slightly.

They reached St. Gabriel's.

"Come with us," said Elsie. "It's round the back." Elsie leaned on her cane as she walked. Her feet were killing her and it had been a long day. "Come round the side here."

"Ah, the old knight's tomb," said Sir Hugo, "interesting story about that…"

"Frances first. She found out that you and your father were signalling to the Germans during the war," said Elsie flatly. "They always knew someone near the south coast was doing it. And that the signals were coming from near Gracecourt. It was you."

"Certainly not!" spluttered Hugo. "Preposterous! How would I—or father who was an invalid—signal to anybody!"

"Your father spent a lot just before the war, money he didn't have once he had run through your mother's fortune. The estate was in debt, on the verge of being sold. It would have been the end of the de Balforts at Gracecourt Hall. Bernie checked. But suddenly there were new tennis courts, new stables, and the water garden. And if anybody knew how to get money from crime it was Bernie, but even he, with all his contacts, couldn't trace how you'd managed it. But on your Grand Tour, you made friends with some Germans who later visited you at Gracecourt and offered your father a great deal of money in return for some favors."

"Ridiculous!"

"It wasn't till today I knew what you'd done. I worked it out from something my grandson said. Those long pools in the water garden. Your father built them to German plans so the Germans could navigate by them."

"Nonsense! How on earth could you navigate on a little bit of water?"

"A little bit is all that's needed. On a clear night water reflects light, especially moonlight. Those long, narrow pools pointed the way for the German planes. And you were the one sending weather reports so they'd know when the weather would be clear. It was you who helped guide them to London for the blitz. And you were ready to help them when they signalled the invasion."

Sir Hugo's eyes narrowed.

"Meanwhile Frances was bored with being a Land Girl, and her father's friends agreed she could train as an English resistance agent, but they decided to send her back to Crowmarsh Priors with instructions to watch you and your father."

Alice stepped closer and Sir Hugo fell back a pace. "The net was closing round you, wasn't it? Traitors and spies were shot. By then the German money was long gone and Frances wouldn't marry you. You thought the reason was that she was sweet on Oliver Hammet, so you started watching the church, to see how often she was there. But you needed something else to sell to the Germans, and watching the vicarage you discovered what we were doing, and you remembered the smugglers' tunnels, the ones I'd told you about the time I lunched at Gracecourt. It was before the war. Lady Marchmont dragged me along. I had too much sherry and started babbling like I always did because I never knew what to say to men. You were a terribly polite listener," said Alice, "and kept asking me questions. I told you all about it, reminding you that the de Balforts had had a hand in the smuggling, and that there was a tunnel to the coast that could be entered from the churchyard."

"Rubbish!"

"You knew that a secret way into the country would be invaluable information for the Germans, and you bided your time to sell it. And then your father was determined you should marry Frances, and made you feel inadequate because you couldn't persuade her. He taunted you that she preferred the vicar so before you sold them the location of the tunnel, you persuaded your German friends to jettison a bomb over the vicarage to eliminate your rival. But they bombed the church and churchyard instead, the same night we were waiting for a rescue party to arrive with two children smuggled from France. Tanni's sisters."

Alice suddenly realized what this information would do to Tanni and stopped. Elsie and Evangeline looked horrified. But Tanni, looking white and shocked, said in a shaking voice, "No...I have always known there was something about that night, something very terrible...I remember, we had a plan, we tried to save them. We tried to save Lili and Klara...but..."

"Tanni...

"We tried...there was no other way. We had to take the chance."

"Tanni..."

"It's better, I know, at last, I must see this through to the end," said Tanni. Her voice was strangely calm. "Frances tried to save them. She was determined not to let them down. She used her jewelry..."

"It was a long time ago." Sir Hugo's voice had sunk to a whisper.

Elsie took over. "Frances had been watching Gracecourt for some time. She went back to Gracecourt shortly before she disappeared, found your father alone, she thought, and forced the truth out of him, that Gracecourt was the center of a British Nazi network. He taunted her that the Nazis would come soon enough, that England would have to surrender. You were hiding and overheard, but Frances was armed and you could do nothing. We don't know what happened next or how the fire started, though people say there was an explosion and Frances had access to sticky bombs. They didn't expect you to live. But you did and when you recovered, Frances had disappeared. You had heard enough from Frances to suspect she was an agent. And you sent word to your Nazi friends the same way you sent them weather reports. Somehow you learned she had been sent to France."

"Information is never secret, even in wartime, and our supporters were at all levels of the government here." Hugo said contemptuously.

"When you got out of hospital you sent the Germans her description," Alice went on, "and told them she was working for Military Intelligence, was probably in France..."

Sir Hugo looked directly at her. "The little fool! She should have married me when I asked her," he hissed. "Father practically begged her. I offered her a chance. The de Balfort name would have reached new glory. The German scientists had nearly perfected their genetic experiments..." His eyes glittered. "A new age was coming, but now—" He made a terrible noise, half sob, half shout. "We must wait for another Hitler to rise from the ashes of the Aryan dream like a phoenix."

The four old ladies had backed him against the tomb. "I was convinced she would have been sent to eastern France. We knew that many of the SOE circuits had been broken up and their agents arrested there. The British sent replacements, and as I suspected, Frances was one of them. The Germans found her in 1945—February, near Ardennes. They sent me a message. She was discovered hiding in a maternity hospital, posing as a Frenchwoman who had just given birth. Normally they would have sent her to a prison camp and tortured information out of her. But with the Allies approaching they shot her instead. A clean German bullet. I imagine at the last she regretted everything."

The four old women surrounded Sir Hugo. Then Elsie raised her cane and hit Hugo as hard as she could. Tanni struck him from behind. Evangeline hit hard across his knees and Alice brought hers down on his head. There was a crack and he stumbled and fell to the ground. In fury they hit and prodded him with all their strength. The old man curled into a ball, trying to escape the sticks. He fought back until he hit his head on the tomb and lay stunned.

They looked down with loathing at him.

"Oh, Frances," said Alice, breathing hard, "to think of your being shot like a dog!"

"For Mum and Jem and Violet and all the others you helped to kill," panted Elsie, swinging her cane again.

"My parents, Frau Zayman, Lili and Klara, may they rest in peace," said Tanni, breathless and weeping, but wielding her cane. "And...the camps, all the innocent people, all the deaths...and...and...I remember now!" she cried. "I had a baby, and it died...that night! I always knew it was something horrible, but I could never remember what. Oh, God!"

"Richard's convoy," said Evangeline, swinging her cane like a woman possessed. "Richard! He suffered, for twenty years I watched him suffer!"

"Frances!" said Alice. "My poor mother! You helped kill them all, you evil fiend!"

Evangeline ordered, "Push him in the tunnel and leave him!"

"No, no no," he wailed feebly, covered in blood and cowering.

"Push him in! It's what he deserves!"

Alice tottered backward. She twisted the skull at the side of the tomb and the hinge swung open.

"Quick," said Elsie, puffing. They all bent to push and roll him into the entrance beneath the lopsided knight. There was just room in the dark, narrow space. The old man fought back, scrabbling at the ground, but he was no match for their combined strength and fury.

There was a cry from the huddled figure as it disappeared into the black hole. Then something thudded at the bottom of the narrow steps. Alice swung the door shut. After all the years they had waited, it had been almost too easy. The four old ladies bent over their canes, breathing hard.

Tanni was now sobbing and moaning incoherently. Evangeline put her arms round her. "Bruno tried to protect you, you know. He loves you very much."

"Bernie's lawyers said there was never a chance of putting him in jail," wheezed Elsie. "We agreed he should pay," she said, looking at the others for confirmation. "We agreed?" The others nodded and smoothed their clothes. "We'll go back now."

"I wonder," said Alice as they went, "what happened to Frances's baby?"

"You know, when I said we should look for the dad, Bernie got that ferrety look that always made me suspect something, but he said maybe Frances wanted that to be a secret," said Elsie, leading the way. "For an awful moment I thought to meself, 'surely it's not Bernie!' but he saw the look and said no, before I could even ask him. Then he said something else about how you had to keep promises, if that was the last thing you were asked. I don't know what he meant."

"I do," said Evangeline. "And I'll tell you. But I need to sit down before I do."

"Great shot," muttered Katie to the cameraman, spotting the four ladies walking slowly toward them from the church. Obviously tired, poor old things, especially Mrs. Zayman, and looking their age in the twilight. Dishevelled too, like the day had been too much for them. "Let's close with a shot of them and then the fireworks," she said as a loud bang filled the sky with sparkles.

She raised her microphone. "Do you ladies have any final words for the viewers?"

"No, dear, we were just talking about war crimes. A bit tired now, I think. Excuse us. We're just going to sit down and be quiet for a moment, away from everybody."

"Oh," said Katie, not sure whether to pursue them.

"Get ready to wind up," said Simon.

The microphone picked up the voice of the old man in the Home Guard uniform wailing loudly that he wanted another pint; he didn't want to go home yet. He was saying to no one in particular, "There's only four. One's missing."

"Who's missing, Granddad?"

"The one married the parson—Oliver...what was his name? I were a witness. Sudden, it was, in Tunbridge, church there. Bernie drove us. Oliver said something about a husband can't testify against his wife. Bernie laughed and said was Frances planning on becoming a safecracker then? Oliver told him sometimes you took things and people on faith, but he was lookin' at Frances when he said it. Bernie and me was sworn to secrecy, not to ever tell anyone, not Elsie or Nell or nobody. They looked happy as Larry when it were over. Then they carried on in the village like nothing had happened, Frances kept coming and going, then she was gone for good. Left a letter with me for Oliver, told me to look after him if she didn't come back. Nell saw her before she disappeared and said if she hadn't known Frances wasn't married she would have sworn she was in the family way. Said you could always tell. 'Course, bein' sworn to secrecy I couldn't say anything..."

"What a story Granddad! What happened to her?"

"Don't remember, except we never saw her again after the last time. I finally gave him the letter, but he never said what was in it. Died a few days later, funnily enough. Turned out he had a dickey heart, poor chap. Nobody knew, he looked right as rain. Died in 'forty-six or 'forty-seven. Nell said...well, it were a long time ago. Long time ago."

The barbeques had turned to ash. The sun was setting and the caterers were rattling empty bowls, trays, and bottles back into their vans. The flowers drooped and the overexcited children with ice cream on their faces were handed Union Jacks to wave in the background while Katie signed off and the credits rolled. The war brides posed with the vicar while the local paper snapped a picture. Fireworks exploded festively across the village.

"It's been a memorable day. And that's it from me, Katie Hamilton-Jones for Albion Television. As we end this special edition of *Heart of England*, we hope you've enjoyed being with us at this special and poignant memorial celebration. We've heard mostly from the older generation today—let's let the next generation have the last word."

The camera panned to a mob of children bobbing in the background behind her, clutching ice creams and Union Jacks. "Have you all had a lovely day?"

Behind her the children jumped up and down and waved their flags frantically and shouted, "Yes!"

The credits rolled.

EPILOGUE

London, 12 May 1995, Missing Persons' Helpline

"*M*issing Persons' Helpline, Lily speaking. Can I help you? Yes, let me get a form. There we go. Now I need some information from you. Name of the person missing? Sir Hugo de Balfort. Address? Thank you. Age? Eighty-five or so you think...No, that will do. And the last time you saw him? At breakfast in the bungalow...Where and when did he go missing? Never came back from a VE Day celebration near his home in—where was that? Spell Crowmarsh Priors for me. On the Saturday, was it? Yes, a lot of places celebrated over the weekend."

"And you are?...Miss Pomfret. Annie Pomfret. Housekeeper. Any family? No, right. Did he seem confused, Miss Pomfret? Does he need any medication that you know of? No, I appreciate you don't snoop in his medicine cabinet, but sometimes people are more observant than they realize. Would there be a photo of him you could send us? I do understand that you don't feel it's your place to make free with his possessions, but if we're to put out a bulletin, the public will need to know what Sir Hugo looks like. And your contact telephone? I *quite* understand your sister does not wish to be rung at all hours.

"Miss Pomfret, we do work closely with the police, but unless you've any reason to suspect foul play...yes, we'll put out a bulletin right away. Usually elderly people are simply confused and wander off, we find them safe and sound and only lost because they've forgotten where they're supposed to be...Yes, we'll do our best. Thank you, Miss Pomfret. Try not to worry. We'll be in touch as soon as possible, when we know something. Good-bye."

Lily hung up, put the completed form in her out tray and stretched. "That's the fourteenth elderly person who went missing last weekend," she said to her coworker. "Good thing the weather's been warm, and they've all been located. Did I tell you they finally found the old lady from Herne Hill sitting behind an old air raid shelter? There was a VE day flypast and it triggered old memories. She was convinced she was back in the Blitz and the siren had gone. She was waiting for the shelter to open."

"They've gone overboard with this VE thing," said her colleague. "I mean, my grandfather says he's been through it once and he's not keen to relive it. He was in Italy and then the Normandy landings. He and my gran took their holiday to get away from it all—went to Florida. Your family in the war, Lily?"

"On my dad's side they were Quakers and conscientious objectors, so my granddad was a medic. Don't know much about Mum's side in the war."

"Oh? Why?"

"Don't know that much about Mum's side at all, really. My grandmother's dead now so I can't ask her, but she and her twin sister were raised by a foster family in Manchester. We never knew where they came from or who their family were, but there was some mystery about them. They both spoke French and German, even the twin, who was brain-damaged or something. According to my mother, her mother remembered a big house with a pink bedroom where a girl who might have been her sister or their nanny read stories to them. She remembered being on a train with other children and a farm and some old people and then men talking in the dark, and my grandmother being terrified that what she called 'the bad men' were going to kill her and her sister.

"Years after the war was over, her foster mother finally told her that one night a serviceman with a big duffel bag came knocking on their door to ask if he was in a Jewish neighborhood. He thought it was, because he'd lived in Manchester before the war. They'd thought he was looking for lodging, and as they had an extra room they let him in. Instead he told them some story about being shot down in France and being rescued back to England. Then he put his duffel bag on the floor, opened it, and there were two little girls asleep inside. 'Jewish kiddies,' he said and disappeared before they could ask him more. Strange, isn't it.

"All the girls knew were their names. My grandmother said that she and her sister remembered hearing the couple argue in English, which they didn't understand. The woman made them put on black dresses and thick stockings and they were told not to say anything in the streets. They were used to keeping quiet so it didn't seem strange at the time, any more than the fact it was evidently one of those really religious Jewish neighborhoods, with kosher butchers and men in frock coats and side curls. I think so much had happened to them that they just accepted it. But as my mum says, who knows?"

"What a story!"

"I know. When my grandmother married, my great-aunt went to live with her but she died young, when Mum was about nine. My mum said she looked exactly like my grandmother and they were both really pretty, only my grandmother was clever and did a university degree after she married, then became a teacher like her husband. My mother remembers her great-aunt being very sweet and gentle and looking after her while my grandmother went to classes. She said my grandmother never got over her death. I'm called Lily after her."

"Amazing! I guess there must be a lot of stories about the war that you never hear. Someone ought to write about it. 'Scuse me, Lils, there goes the phone again. No, you're due for your tea break. I'll get this one. Hope your wandering old man turns up OK."

ACKNOWLEDGMENTS

*A*n author's manuscript is one thing; its transition to a finished book on the shelf is another. The devil is in the detail, and I am grateful to everyone who has contributed to the transformation of *War Brides* from the former into the latter. As an author, I am fortunate to have worked with them all.

First of all, thanks are due to Terry Goodman, Senior Editor at Amazon Publishing, who first approached me via an irresistibly charming email to say that Amazon would like to publish my book, who has been available ever since as a point of contact to deal with any queries, and who has kept everything on track, making sure that everything that was supposed to happen to get the book out on schedule happened smoothly.

It has been a pleasure to work with the entire Amazon team. I especially want to thank the copyeditor Renee Johnson for her painstaking and thorough editing that transformed the earlier manuscript into a polished book. She is the kind of copyeditor every author wants—her eagle eye misses nothing.

Also at Amazon, Nikki Sprinkle the marketing manager and Jessica Poore who deals with author relations deserve thanks for all their input.

I want to acknowledge the invaluable help of my agents at Dystel & Goderich Literary Management. Jane Dystel and Miriam Goderich have been consistently supportive and quick to respond to questions. I am grateful for the benefit of their experience, professionalism, and advice.

Finally, I very fortunate in having the support of my family, especially that of my dear husband who is not only understanding about the connection between household disruption and a writing woman, but who generously says that in the long run, the writing matters more.

ABOUT THE AUTHOR

*H*elen Bryan was born in Virginia, grew up in Tennessee, and is a longtime resident of London. A former barrister, she is the author of an award-winning biography of Martha Washington. She was inspired to write *War Brides* "by the true wartime stories of family and friends in the United States and England, and by the little known stories of the brave young women who joined Churchill's Special Operations Executive." This is her first novel.